D1234692

THE BEST OF ASTOUNDING

THE BEST OF ASTOUNDING

Classic Short Novels from the Golden Age of Science Fiction

Edited by James Gunn
With an introduction by Poul Anderson

Carroll & Graf Publishers, Inc.
New York

Grateful acknowledgment is made to the following for their permission to reprint their copyrighted material: SUCKER BAIT by Isaac Asimov, copyright © 1954 by Street & Smith Publications, Inc., reprinted by permission of the author; THE STOLEN DORMOUSE by L. Sprague de Camp, copyright © 1941 by L. Sprague de Camp, reprinted by permission of the author; THE FIFTH-DIMENSION TUBE by Murray Leinster, copyright © 1932 by Street & Smith Publications, Inc., reprinted by permission of Scott Meredith Literary Agency, Inc.; THE SHADOW OUT OF TIME by H.P. Lovecraft, copyright © 1936 by H.P. Lovecraft, reprinted by permission of Scott Meredith Literary Agency, Inc.; BINDLESTIFF by James Blish, copyright © 1950 by James Blish, reprinted by permission of Judith Blish; WE HAVE FED OUR SEA by Poul Anderson, copyright © 1958 by Street & Smith Publications, Inc., reprinted by permission of the author.

Abridged from a three-volume series published by The Easton Press in arrangement with Davis Publications, Inc.

First Carroll & Graf edition 1992

Carroll & Graf Publishers, Inc.
260 Fifth Avenue
New York, NY 10001

Library of Congress Cataloging-in-Publication Data is available.

ISBN: 0-88184-808-5

Manufactured in the United States of America

Contents

Introduction

By Poul Anderson

ENOUGH people have written enough about the Golden Age, those high and far-off days when John W. Campbell took over the editorship of *Astounding* and captained the creation of modern science fiction, that I need say no more than may be necessary to give perspective. A mere naming of writers whose careers began at this time, wholly or largely under his aegis, evokes the achievement—Isaac Asimov, Cleve Cartmill, Hal Clement, L. Sprague de Camp, Lester del Rey, Robert A. Heinlein, Malcolm Jameson, Fritz Leiber, "Lewis Padgett," Eric Frank Russell, Theodore Sturgeon, A. E. van Vogt—as well as those already established who joined them—Fredric Brown, Raymond Z. Gallun, L. Ron Hubbard, Raymond F. Jones, Murray Leinster, C. L. Moore (who, with her husband Henry Kuttner, was also Lewis Padgett), Clifford D. Simak, E. E. Smith, Jack Williamson. The list, though incomplete, includes some virtually forgotten who then loomed large. Were their stories revived, they would stand comparison with anything contemporary.

After all, Campbell's writers won their reputations not through self-advertisement or the favor of the literary establishment, but by what they actually did. They raised anew a standard of craftsmanship that, with rare exceptions such as Stanley Weinbaum and Campbell himself, had fallen far since H. G. Wells and Rudyard Kipling did science fiction. They pioneered motifs and techniques that became basic to the species. In many ways, it has been living ever since on the intellectual capital it gained in that period.

The brilliance faded at last. Several mostly dull years ensued. World War II and America's eventual embroilment are often blamed. Doubtless this judgment has considerable truth. Most of the giants found themselves with jobs more urgent than spinning yarns. Meanwhile, Campbell must fill his magazine every month as best he could. Nonetheless, excellence flared occasionally. Van Vogt continued productive, Asimov and Sturgeon found odd moments in which they could write a little, and so on. Newcomers made contributions too, perhaps most notably A. Bertram Chandler's "Giant Killer," which the author, like numerous colleagues, admitted owed much to Campbell's guidance.

War or no, I think a certain leveling off was always inevitable. You can only enter a new territory once. That sense of utter freshness, of release into green pastures, will never come again.

This does not mean that creativity must have an end. As an analogy, consider the Golden Age of Greece. In sculpture and architecture, at least, it amounted to a culmination of what had long been developing; and the Nike of Samothrace came well afterward. For that matter, sculptors of still later eras took inspiration from the Greeks and produced masterpieces; an offhand thought ranges from Michelangelo to Milles. In due course science fiction regained liveliness. If originality was not quite so overwhelming as erstwhile, it was abundant; concepts were carried further, in directions undreamed of before; the literary standard continued, on the whole, to rise. Some commentators call this the Silver Age.

No more was Campbell an unchallenged leader. Anthony Boucher and J. Francis McComas founded *The Magazine of Fantasy and Science Fiction* in 1949; H. L. Gold's *Galaxy Science Fiction* made its debut in 1950; *Amazing* and *Fantastic,* those ancients of days, got new editors with new ideas; several other magazines were launched or revived. Book publishing became significant, at first carried out by tiny specialty houses, later by the large companies. Movies were made, nearly all atrocious, of course. This was, in fact, a boom of sorts.

It ended in a mass extinction, followed by lean and literarily rather dismal years, followed by a slower but perhaps more solid renaissance; and thus we came gradually to our present state of general popularity and relative respectability. That later stage has witnessed the rise of Ben Bova and Stanley Schmidt, who were to be Campbell's successors at *Analog,* as the magazine was called by then. But let us backtrack from it. What concerns us here is the upsurge in the late 1940's and the '50's, to which the volume on hand is a monument. Specifically, we are looking at the role of *Astounding.*

As said, Campbell no longer reigned alone. His fellow editors had their own styles, emphases, goals, each different from the rest. They attracted writers, sometimes new, sometimes out of Campbell's stable. This was a generally amicable rivalry, the more so when there was little direct competition. However, certain critics made a *Götterdämmerung* of it, in the usual manner of critics. They declared Campbell a has-been, an embarrassment and an obstruction to the movement he once led.

They pointed to his human share of weaknesses and follies —for example, the dianetics episode, which caused Willy Ley to cease writing science fact articles for him, and similar things. They did not mention continued reporting by the likes of the astronomer R. S. Richardson and the engineering physicist John R. Pierce ("J. J. Coupling"). They decried hackwork about psionics, Machiavellian do-gooders, and other clichés, ignoring the repetition of equally dreary themes everywhere else and, more important by far, the grand stuff that was being produced all along.

Let me in passing mention the artwork. After Hubert Rogers left for more lucrative fields, *Astounding* gained Chesley Bonestell and Kelly Freas, fully comparable in their special ways. Campbell did not merely commission paintings. I know from several artists and from personal observation how often he, although it was not officially his department, had a decisive voice in what they did, and that this was normally for the better.

As for the fiction, many leading lights had returned, if not always exclusively, to the magazine. In addition, many new talents came forth, either getting started with him or sending him much of their best. Again a partial list must serve—James Blish, John Brunner, A. J. Budrys, "Lee Correy," Gordon R. Dickson, Harry Harrison, Frank Herbert, Dean Ing, Donald Kingsbury, C. M. Kornbluth, Dean McLaughlin, Judith Merril, Walter Miller, Jr., Chad Oliver, H. Beam Piper, Mack Reynolds, James H. Schmitz, Robert Silverberg, "William Tenn," Jack Vance, and, to be sure, yours truly.

The stories you are about to read represent an effort to convey some idea of what we were up to in those days. The sample is, unavoidably, minuscule, but I think it will give a valid impression. The selection is well made (not by me) to show that, far from having become hidebound, *Astounding* remained vigorously innovative and varied.

Sucker Bait

By Isaac Asimov

THE ship *Triple G* flashed silently out of the nothingness of hyperspace and into the all-ness of space-time. It emerged into the glitter of the great star-cluster of Hercules.

It poised gingerly in space, surrounded by suns and suns and suns, each centering a gravitational field that wrenched at the little bubble of metal. But the ship's computers had done well and it had pin-pricked squarely into position. It was within a day's journey—ordinary spacedrive journey—of the Lagrange System.

This fact had varying significance to the different men aboard ship. To the crew it was another day's work and another day's flight pay and then shore rest. The planet for which they were aiming was uninhabited but shore rest could be a pleasant interlude even on an asteroid. They did not trouble themselves concerning a possible difference of opinion among the passengers.

The crew, in fact, were rather contemptuous of the passengers, and avoided them.

Eggheads!

And so they were, every one of them but one. Scientists, in

politer terms—and a heterogeneous lot. Their nearest approach to a common emotion at that moment was a final anxiety for their instruments, a vague desire for a last check.

And perhaps just a small increase of tension and anxiety. It *was* an uninhabited planet. Each had expressed himself as firmly of that belief a number of times. Still, each man's thoughts are his own.

As for the one unusual man on board ship—not a crewman and not really a scientist—his strongest feeling was one of bone-weariness. He stirred to his feet weakly and fought off the last dregs of spacesickness. He was Mark Annuncio, and he had been in bed now for four days, feeding on almost nothing, while the ship wove in and out of the Universe, jumping its light-years of space.

But now he felt less certain of imminent death and he had to answer the summons of the captain. In his inarticulate way, Mark resented that summons. He was used to having his own way, seeing what he felt like seeing. Who was the captain to—

The impulse kept returning to tell Dr. Sheffield about this and let it rest there.

But Mark was curious, so he knew he would have to go.

It was his one great vice. Curiosity!

It also happened to be his profession, and his mission in life.

CAPTAIN Follenbee of the *Triple G* was a hard-headed man. It was how he habitually thought of himself. He had made government-sponsored runs before. For one thing, they were profitable. The Confederacy didn't haggle. It meant a complete overhaul of his ship each time, replacement of defective parts, liberal terms for the crew. It was good business. Damned good business.

This run, of course, was a little different.

It wasn't so much the particular gang of passengers he had taken aboard. (He had expected temperament, tantrums and unbearable foolishness but it turned out that eggheads were much like normal people.) It wasn't that half his ship had been torn down and rebuilt into what the contract called a "universal central-access laboratory."

Actually, and he hated the thought, it was "Junior"—the planet that lay ahead of them.

The crew didn't know, of course, but he, himself, hard-head and all, was beginning to find the matter unpleasant.

But only beginning—

At the moment, he told himself, it was this Mark Annuncio, if that was the name, who was annoying him. He slapped the back of one hand against the palm of the other and thought angrily about it. His large, round face was ruddy with annoyance.

Insolence!

A boy of not more than twenty, with no position that he knew of among the passengers, to make a request like that.

What was behind it? *That* at least ought to be straightened out.

In his present mood, he would like to straighten it out by means of a jacket collar twisted in a fist and a rattle of teeth, but better not—

After all, this was a curious kind of flight for the Confederacy of Worlds to sponsor, and a twenty-year-old, over-curious rubberneck might be an integral part of the strangeness. What was he on board *for?* There was this Dr. Sheffield, for instance, who seemed to have no job but to play nursemaid for the boy. Now why was that? Who *was* this Annuncio?

He had been spacesick for the entire trick, or was that just a device to keep to his cabin—

There was a light burning as the door-signal sounded.

It would be the boy.

Easy now, thought the captain. *Easy now.*

MARK Annuncio entered the captain's cabin and licked his lips in a futile attempt to get rid of the bitter taste in his mouth. He felt lightheaded and heavyhearted.

At the moment he would have given up his Service status to be back on Earth.

He thought wishfully of his own familiar quarters; small but private; alone with his own kind. It was just a bed, desk, chair, and closet, but he had all of Central Library on free call. Here there was nothing. He had thought there would be a lot to learn on board ship. He had never been on board ship before. But he hadn't expected days and days of spacesickness.

He was so homesick he could cry, and he hated himself

because he knew that his eyes were red and moist and that the captain would see it. He hated himself because he wasn't large and wide; because he looked like a mouse.

In a word, that was it. He had mouse-brown hair with nothing but silken straightness to it; a narrow, receding chin, a small mouth and a pointed nose. All he needed were five or six delicate vibrissae on each side of the nose to make the illusion complete. And he was below average in height.

And then he saw the star-field in the captain's observation port and the breath went out of him.

Stars!

Stars as he had never seen them.

Mark had never left the planet Earth before. (Dr. Sheffield told him that was why he was spacesick. Mark didn't believe him. He had read in fifty different books that spacesickness was psychogenic. Even Dr. Sheffield tried to fool him sometimes.)

He had never left Earth before, and he was used to Earth's sky. He was accustomed to viewing two thousand stars spread over half a celestial sphere with only ten of the first magnitude.

But here they crowded madly. There were ten times the number in Earth's sky in that small square alone. And *bright!*

He fixed the star-pattern greedily in his mind. It overwhelmed him. He knew the figures on the Hercules cluster, of course. It contained between one million and ten million stars —no exact census had been taken as yet—but figures are one thing and stars are another.

He wanted to count them. It was a sudden overwhelming desire. He was curious about the number. He wondered if they all had names; if there were astronomic data on all of them. Let's see—

He counted them in groups of hundreds. Two—three—He might have used the mental pattern alone, but he liked to watch the actual physical objects when they were so startlingly beautiful. Six—seven—

The captain's hearty voice splattered over him and brought him back to ship's interior.

"Mr. Annuncio. Glad to meet you."

Mark looked up, startled, resentful. Why was his count being interrupted?

He said, irritably, "The stars!" and pointed.

The captain turned to stare. "What about them? What's wrong?"

Mark looked at the captain's wide back and his overdeveloped posterior. He looked at the gray stubble that covered the captain's head, at the two large hands with thick fingers that clasped one another in the small of the captain's back and flapped rhythmically against the shiny plastex of his jacket.

Mark thought: *What does* he *care about the stars? Does* he *care about their size and brightness and spectral classes?*

His lower lip trembled. The captain was just one of the noncompos. Everyone on ship was a noncompos. That's what they called them back in the Service. Noncompos. All of them. Couldn't cube fifteen without a computer.

Mark felt very lonely.

He let it go—no use trying to explain—and said, "The stars get so thick here. Like pea soup."

"All appearance, Mr. Annuncio." (The captain pronounced the "c" in Mark's name like an "s" rather than a "ts" and the sound grated on Mark's ear.) "Average distance between stars in the thickest cluster is over a light-year. Plenty of room, eh? Looks thick, though. Grant you that. If the lights were out, they'd shine like a trillion Chisholm points in an oscillating force-field."

But he didn't offer to put the lights out and Mark wasn't going to ask him to.

THE captain said, "Sit down, Mr. Annuncio. No use standing, eh? You smoke? Mind if I do? Sorry you couldn't be here this morning. Had an excellent view of Lagrange I and II at six space-hours. Red and green. Like traffic lights, eh? Missed you all trip. Space-legs need strengthening, eh?"

He barked out his "eh's" in a high-pitched voice that Mark found devilishly irritating.

Mark said in a low voice, "I'm all right now."

The captain seemed to find that unsatisfactory. He puffed at his cigar and stared down at Mark with eyebrows hunched down over his eyes. He said, slowly, "Glad to see you now, anyway. Get acquainted a little. Shake hands. The *Triple G*'s been on a good many government-chartered cruises. No trouble. Never had trouble. Wouldn't want trouble. You understand."

Mark didn't. He was tired of trying to. His eyes drifted back hungrily to the stars. The pattern had changed a little.

The captain caught his eyes for a moment. He was frowning and his shoulders seemed to tremble at the edge of a shrug. He walked to the control panel, and like a gigantic eyelid, metal slithered across the studded observation port.

Mark jumped up in a fury, shrieking, "What's the idea? I'm counting them, you fool."

"Counting—" The captain flushed, but maintained a quality of politeness in his voice. He said, "Sorry! Little matter of business we must discuss."

He stressed the word "business" lightly.

Mark knew what he meant. "There's nothing to discuss. I want to see the ship's log. I called you hours ago to tell you that. You're delaying me."

The captain said, "Suppose you tell me why you want to see it, eh? Never been asked before. Where's your authority?"

Mark felt astonished. "I can look at anything I want to. I'm in Mnemonic Service."

The captain puffed strongly at his cigar. (It was a special grade manufactured for use in space and on enclosed space-objects. It had an oxidant included so that atmospheric oxygen was not consumed.)

He said, cautiously, "That so? Never heard of it. What is it?"

Mark said indignantly, "It's the Mnemonic Service, that's all. It's my job to look at anything I want to and to ask anything I want to. And I've got the right to do it."

"Can't look at the log if I don't want you to."

"You've got no say in it, you . . . you *noncompos."*

The captain's coolness evaporated. He threw his cigar down violently and stamped at it, then picked it up and poked it carefully into the ash vent.

"What the Galactic Drift is this?" he demanded. "Who are you, anyway? Security agent? What's up? Let's have it straight. Right now."

"I've told you all I have to."

"Nothing to hide," said the captain, "but I've got rights."

"Nothing to hide?" squeaked Mark. "Then why is this ship called the *Triple G*?"

"That's its name."

"Go on. No such ship with an Earth registry. I knew that before I got on. I've been waiting to ask you."

The captain blinked. He said, "Official name is *George G. Grundy*. *Triple G* is what everyone calls it."

Mark laughed. "All right, then. And after I see the log book, I want to talk to the crew. I have the right. You ask Dr. Sheffield."

"The crew too, eh?" the captain seethed. "Let's talk to Dr. Sheffield, and then let's keep you in quarters till we land. Sprout!"

He snatched at the intercom box.

THE scientific complement of the *Triple G* were few in number for the job they had to do, and, as individuals, young. Not as young as Mark Annuncio, perhaps, who was in a class by himself, but even the oldest of them, Emmanuel George Cimon—astrophysicist—was not quite thirty-nine. And with his dark, unthinned hair and large, brilliant eyes, he looked still younger. To be sure, the optic brilliance was partly due to the wearing of contact lenses.

Cimon, who was perhaps overconscious of his relative age, and of the fact that he was the titular head of the expedition—a fact most of the others were inclined to ignore—usually affected an undramatic view of the mission. He ran the dotted tape through his fingers, then let it snake silently back into its spool.

"Run of the mill," he sighed, seating himself in the softest chair in the small passenger's lounge. "Nothing."

He looked at the latest color photographs of the Lagrange binary and was impervious to their beauty. Lagrange I, smaller and hotter than Earth's own sun, was a brilliant green-blue, with a pearly green-yellow corona surrounding it like the gold setting of an emerald. It appeared to be the size of a lentil or of a ball bearing out of a Lenser-ratchet. A short distance away—as distances go on a photograph—was Lagrange II. It appeared twice the size of Lagrange I, due to its position in space. (Actually, it was only four-fifths the diameter of Lagrange I, half its volume and two-thirds its mass.) Its orange-red, toward which the film was less sensitive, comparatively, than was the human retina, seemed dimmer than ever against the glory of its sister sun.

Surrounding both, undrowned by the near-by suns, as the result of the differentially-polarized lens specifically used for the purpose, was the unbelievable brilliance of the Hercules cluster. It was diamond dust, scattered thickly, yellow, white, blue, and red.

"Nothing," said Cimon.

"Looks good to me," said the other man in the lounge. He was Groot Knoevenaagle—physician—short, plump, and known to man by no name other than Novee.

He went on to ask, "Where's Junior?" then bent over Cimon's shoulder, peering out of slightly myopic eyes.

Cimon looked up and shuddered, "It's name is not Junior. You can't see the planet, Troas, if *that's* what you mean, in this wilderness of stars. This picture is *Scientific Earthman* material. It isn't particularly useful."

"Oh, Space and back!" Novee was disappointed.

"What difference is it to you, anyway?" demanded Cimon. "Suppose I said one of those dots was Troas—any one of them. You wouldn't know the difference and what good would it do you?"

"Now wait, Cimon. Don't be so superior. It's legitimate sentiment. We'll be living on Junior for a while. For all we know, we'll be dying on it."

"There's no audience, Novee, no orchestra, no mikes, no trumpets, so why be dramatic. We won't be dying on it. If we do, it'll be our own fault, and probably as a result of overeating." He said it with the peculiar emphasis men of small appetite use when speaking to men of hearty appetite, as though a poor digestion was something that came only of rigid virtue and superior intellect.

"A thousand people did die," said Novee, softly.

"Sure. About a billion men a day die all over the galaxy."

"Not this way."

"Not what way?"

With an effort, Novee kept to his usual drawl. "No discussions except at official meetings. That was the decision."

"I'll have nothing to discuss," said Cimon, gloomily. "They're just two ordinary stars. Damned if I know why I volunteered. I suppose it was just the chance of seeing an abnormally large Trojan system from close up. It was the thought of looking at a habitable planet with a double sun. I don't know why I should have thought there'd be anything amazing about it."

"Because you thought of a thousand dead men and women," said Novee, then went on hastily. "Listen, tell me something, will you? What's a Trojan planet, anyway?"

The physician bore the other's look of contempt for a moment, then said, "All right. All right. So I don't know. You don't know everything either. What do you know about ultrasonic incisions?"

Cimon said, "Nothing, and I think that's fine. It's my opinion that information outside a professional man's specialty is useless and a waste of psycho-potential. Sheffield's point of view leaves me cold."

"I still want to know. That is, if you can explain it."

"I can explain it. As a matter of fact, it was mentioned in the original briefing, if you were listening. Most multiple stars, and that means one third of all stars, have planets of a sort. The trouble is that the planets are never habitable. If they're far enough away from the center of gravity of the stellar system to have a fairly circular orbit, they're cold enough to have helium oceans. If they're close enough to get heat, their orbit is so erratic that at least once in each revolution, they get close enough to one or another of the stars to melt iron.

"Here in the Lagrange System, however, we have an unusual case. The two stars, Lagrange I and Lagrange II, and the planet, Troas—along with its satellite, Ilium—are at the corners of an imaginary equilateral triangle. Got that? Such an arrangement happens to be a stable one, and for the sake of anything you like, don't ask me to tell you why. Just take it as my professional opinion."

Novee muttered under his breath, "I wouldn't dream of doubting it."

Cimon looked displeased and continued, "The system revolves as a unit. Troas is always a hundred million miles from each sun, and the suns are always a hundred million miles from one another."

Novee rubbed his ear and looked dissatisfied. "I know all that. I *was* listening at the briefing. But why is it a *Trojan* planet? Why *Trojan?*"

Cimon's thin lips compressed for a moment as though holding back a nasty word by force. He said, "We have an arrangement like that in the Solar System. The sun, Jupiter and a group of small asteroids form a stable equilateral triangle. It so happens that the asteroids had been given such names as Hector, Achilles, Ajax and other heroes of the Trojan war, hence—or do I have to finish?"

"Is that all?" said Novee.

"Yes. Are you through bothering me?"

"Oh, boil your head."

NOVEE rose to leave the indignant astrophysicist but the door slid open a moment before his hand touched the activator and Boris Vernadsky—geochemist; dark eyebrows, wide mouth, broad face and with an inveterate tendency to polka-dot shirts and magnetic clip-ons in red plastic—stepped in.

He was oblivious to Novee's flushed face and Cimon's frozen expression of distaste.

He said, lightly, "Fellow scientists, if you listen very carefully you will probably hear an explosion to beat the Milky Way from up yonder in captain's quarters."

"What happened?" asked Novee.

"The captain got hold of Annuncio, Sheffield's little pet wizard, and Sheffield went charging up-deck, bleeding heavily at each eyeball."

Cimon, having listened so far, turned away, snorting.

Novee said, "Sheffield! The man can't get angry. I've never even heard him raise his voice."

"He did this time. When he found out the kid had left his cabin without telling him and that the captain was bullyragging him—Wow! Did you know he was up and about, Novee?"

"No, but I'm not surprised. Spacesickness is one of those things. When you have it, you think you're dying. In fact, you can hardly wait. Then, in two minutes it's gone and you feel all right. Weak, but all right. I told Mark this morning we'd be landing next day and I suppose it pulled him through. The thought of a planetary surface in clear prospect does wonders for spacesickness. We *are* landing soon, aren't we, Cimon?"

The astrophysicist made a peculiar sound that could have been interpreted as a grunt of assent. At least, Novee so interpreted it.

"Anyway," said Novee, "what happened?"

Vernadsky said, "Well, Sheffield's been bunking with me since the kid twirled on his toes and went over backward with spacesickness and he's sitting there at the desk with his charts and his Fist computer chug-chugging away, when the room-phone signals and it's the captain. Well, it turns out he's got the boy with him and he wants to know what the blankety-blank and assorted dot-and-dash the government means by planting a spy on him. So Sheffield yells back at him that he'll stab him with a Collamore macro-leveling-tube if he's been fooling with the kid and off he goes leaving the phone activated and the captain frothing."

"You're making this up," said Novee. "Sheffield wouldn't say anything like that."

"Words to that effect."

Novee turned to Cimon. "You're heading our group. Why don't you do something about this?"

Cimon snarled, "In cases like this, I'm heading the group. My responsibilities always come on suddenly. Let them fight it out. Sheffield talks an excellent fight and the captain never takes his hands out of the small of his back. Vernadsky's jitterbugging description doesn't mean there'll be physical violence."

"All right, but there's no point in having feuds of any kind in an expedition like ours."

"You mean our mission!" Vernadsky raised both hands in mock-awe and rolled his eyes upward. "How I dread the time when we must find ourselves among the rags and bones of the first expedition."

And as though the picture brought to mind by that was not one that bore levity well after all, there was suddenly nothing to say. Even the back of Cimon's head which was all that showed over the back of the easy-chair seemed a bit the stiffer for the thought.

OSWALD Mayer Sheffield—psychologist, thin as a string and as tall as a good length of it, and with a voice that could be used either for singing an operatic selection with surprising virtuosity or for making a point of argument softly but with stinging accuracy—did not show the anger one would have expected from Vernadsky's account.

He was even smiling when he entered the captain's cabin.

The captain broke out mauvely, as soon as he entered. "Look here, Sheffield—"

"One minute, Captain Follenbee," said Sheffield. "How are you, Mark?"

Mark's eyes fell and his words were muffled. "All right, Dr. Sheffield."

"I wasn't aware you'd gotten out of bed."

There wasn't the shade of reproach in his voice, but Mark grew apologetic. "I was feeling better, Dr. Sheffield, and I feel bad about not working. I haven't done anything in all the time I've been on the ship. So I put in a call to the captain to ask to see the log book and he had me come up here."

"All right. I'm sure he won't mind if you go back to your room now."

"Oh, won't I?" began the captain.

Sheffield's mild eyes rose to meet the captain. "I'm responsible for him, sir."

And somehow the captain could think of nothing further to say.

Mark turned obediently and Sheffield watched him leave and waited till the door was well-closed behind him.

Then he turned again to the captain. "What's the bloody idea, captain?"

The captain's knees bent a little, then straightened and bent again with a sort of threatening rhythm. The invisible slap of his hands, clasped behind his back, could be heard distinctly. "That's my question. I'm captain here, Sheffield."

"I know that."

"Know what it means, eh? This ship, in Space, is a legally recognized planet. I'm absolute ruler. In Space, what I say goes. Central Committee of the Confederacy can't say otherwise. I've got to maintain discipline and no spy—"

"All right, and now let me tell *you* something, captain. You're charted by the Bureau of Outer Provinces to carry a government-sponsored research expedition to the Lagrange System, to maintain it there as long as research necessity requires and the safety of the crew and vessel permits, and then to bring us home. You've signed that contract and you've assumed certain obligations, captain or not. For instance, you can't tamper with our instruments and destroy their research usefulness."

"Who in Space is doing that?" The captain's voice was a blast of indignation.

Sheffield replied calmly, "You are. Hands off Mark Annuncio, captain. Just as you've got to keep your hands off Cimon's monochrome and Vailleux's microptics, you've got to keep your hands off my Annuncio. And that means each one of your ten four-striped fingers. Got it?"

The captain's uniformed chest expanded. "I take no order on board my own ship. Your language is a breach of discipline, *Mister* Sheffield. Any more like that and it's cabin arrest—you *and* your Annuncio. Don't like it, then speak to Board of Review back on Earth. Till then, it's tongue behind teeth."

"Look, captain, let me explain something. Mark is in the Mnemonic Service—"

"Sure, he said so. Nummonic Service. Nummonic Service. It's plain secret police as far as I'm concerned. Well, not on board *my* ship, eh?"

"Mnemonic Service," said Sheffield, patiently. "Emm-enn-eee-emm-oh-enn-eye-see Service. You don't pronounce the first emm. It's from a Greek word meaning memory."

The captain's eyes narrowed. "He remembers things?"

"Correct, captain. Look, in a way this is my fault. I should have briefed you on this. I would have, too, if the boy hadn't gotten so sick right after the take-off. It drove most other matters out of my mind. Besides, it didn't occur to me that he might be interested in the workings of the ship itself. Space knows why not. He should be interested in everything."

"He should, eh?" The captain looked at the timepiece on the wall. "Brief me now, eh? But no fancy words. Not many of any other kind, either. Time limited."

"It won't take long, I assure you. Now you're a space-going man, captain. How many inhabited worlds would you say there were in the Confederation?"

"Eighty thousand," said the captain, promptly.

"Eighty-three thousand two hundred," said Sheffield. "What do you suppose it takes to run a political organization that size?"

Again the captain did not hesitate. "Computers," he said.

"All right. There's Earth, where half the population works for the government and does nothing but compute and there are computing subcenters on every other world. And even so data gets lost. Every world knows something no other world knows—almost every man. Look at our little group. Vernadsky doesn't know any biology and I don't know enough chemistry to stay alive. There's not one of us can pilot the simplest space-cruiser, except for Fawkes. So we work together, each one supplying the knowledge the others lack.

"Only there's a catch. Not one of us knows exactly which of our own data is meaningful to the other under a given set of circumstances. We can't sit and spout everything we know. So we guess, and sometimes we don't guess right. Two facts, A and B, can go together beautifully sometimes. So Person A, who knows Fact A, says to Person B, who knows Fact B, 'Why didn't you tell me this ten years ago?' and Person B answers, 'I didn't think it was important,' or 'I thought everyone knew that.' "

The captain said, "That's what computers are for."

Sheffield said, "Computers are limited, captain. They have to be asked questions. What's more the questions have to be the kind that can be put into a limited number of symbols. What's more computers are very literal minded. They answer exactly what you ask and not what you have in mind. Sometimes it never occurs to anyone to ask just the right question or feed the computer just the right symbols, and when that happens the computer doesn't volunteer information.

"What we need . . . what all mankind needs . . . is a computer that is nonmechanical; a computer with imagination. There's one like that, captain." The psychologist tapped his temple. "In everyone, captain."

"Maybe," grunted the captain, "but I'll stick to the usual, eh? Kind you punch a button."

"Are you sure? Machines don't have hunches. Did *you* ever have a hunch?"

"Is this on the point?" The captain looked at the timepiece again.

Sheffield said, "Somewhere inside the human brain is a record of every datum that has impinged upon it. Very little of it is consciously remembered, but all of it is there, and a small association can bring an individual datum back without a person's knowing where it comes from. So you get a 'hunch' or a 'feeling.' Some people are better at it than others. And some can be trained. Some are almost perfect, like Mark Annuncio and a hundred like him. Some day, I hope, there'll be a billion like him, and we'll *really* have a Mnemonic Service.

"All their lives," Sheffield went on, "they do nothing but read, look, and listen. And train to do that better and more efficiently. It doesn't matter what data they collect. It doesn't have to have obvious sense or obvious significance. It doesn't matter if any man in the Service wants to spend a week going over the records of the space-polo teams of the Canopus Sector for the last century. *Any* datum may be useful some day. That's the fundamental axiom.

"Every once in a while, one of the Service may correlate across a gap no machine could possibly manage. The machine would fail because no one machine is likely to possess those two pieces of thoroughly unconnected information; or else, if the machine does have it, no man would be insane enough to ask the right question. One good correlation out of the Service can pay for all the money appropriated for it in ten years or more."

The captain raised his broad hand. He looked troubled. He said, "Wait a minute. He said no ship named *Triple G* was under Earth registry. You mean he knows all registered ships by heart?"

"Probably," said Sheffield. "He may have read through the Merchantship Register. If he did, he knows all the names, tonnages, years of construction, ports of call, numbers of crew and anything else the Register would contain."

"And he was counting stars."

"Why not? It's a datum."

"I'm damned."

"Perhaps, captain. But the point is that a man like Mark is different from other men. He's got a queer, distorted upbringing and a queer, distorted view on life. This is the first time he's been away from Service grounds, since he entered them at the age of five. He's easily upset—and he can be ruined. That mustn't happen, and I'm in charge to see it doesn't. He's my instrument; a more valuable instrument than everything else on this entire ship baled into a neat little ball of plutonium wire. There are only a hundred like him in all the Milky Way."

Captain Follenbee assumed an air of wounded dignity. "All right, then. Log book. Strictly confidential, eh?"

"Strictly. He talks only to me, and I talk to no one unless a correlation has been made."

The captain did not look as though that fell under his classification of the word, strictly, but he said, "But no crew." He paused significantly. "You know what I mean."

Sheffield stepped to the door. "Mark knows about that. The crew won't hear about it from him, believe me."

And as he was about to leave, the captain called out, "Sheffield!"

"Yes?"

"What in Space is a 'noncompos'?"

Sheffield suppressed a smile. "Did he call you that?"

"What is it?"

"Just short for *non compos mentis.* Everyone in the Service uses it for everyone not in the Service. You're one. I'm one. It's Latin for 'not of sound mind.' And you know, captain—I think they're quite right."

He stepped out the door quickly.

MARK Annuncio went through the ship's log in some fifteen seconds. He found it incomprehensible, but then most of the material he put into his mind was that. That was no trouble. Nor was the fact that it was dull. The disappointment was that it did not satisfy his curiosity, so he left it with a mixture of relief and displeasure.

He had then gone into the ship's library and worked his way through three dozen books as quickly as he could work the scanner. He had spent three years of his early teens learning how to read by total gestalt and he still recalled proudly that he had set a school record at the final examinations.

Finally, he wandered into the laboratory sections of the ship and watched a bit here and a bit there. He asked no questions and he moved on when any of the men cast more than a casual glance at him.

He hated the insufferable way they looked at him as though he were some sort of queer animal. He hated their air of knowledge, as though there were something of value in spending an entire brain on one tiny subject and remembering only a little of that.

Eventually, of course, he would *have* to ask them questions. It was his job, and even if it weren't, curiosity would drive him. He hoped, though, he could hold off till they had made planetary surface.

He found it pleasant that they were inside a stellar system. Soon he would see a new world with new suns—two of them—and a new moon. Four objects with brand-new information in each; immense storehouses of facts to be collected lovingly and sorted out.

It thrilled him just to think of the amorphous mountain of data waiting for him. He thought of his mind as a tremendous filing system with index, cross-index, cross-cross-index. He thought of it as stretching indefinitely in all directions. Neat. Smooth. Well oiled. Perfect precision.

He thought of the dusty attic that the noncompos called minds and almost laughed. He could see it even talking to Dr. Sheffield, who was a nice fellow for a noncompos. He tried hard and sometimes he almost *understood.* The others, the men on board ship—their minds were lumberyards. Dusty lumberyards with splintery slats of wood tumbled every which way; and only whatever happened to be on top could be reached.

The poor fools! He could be sorry for them, if they weren't so sloppy-nasty. If only they *knew* what they were like. If only they *realized.*

WHENEVER he could, Mark haunted the observation posts and watched the new worlds come closer.

They passed quite close to the satellite, "Ilium." (Cimon, the astrophysicist, was very meticulous about calling their planetary destination "Troas" and the satellite "Ilium," but everyone else aboard ship called them "Junior" and "Sister," respectively.) On the other side of the two suns, in the opposite Trojan position, were a group of asteroids. Cimon called them "Lagrange Epsilon" but everyone else called them "The Puppies."

Mark thought of all this with vague simultaneity at the moment the thought "Ilium" occurred to him. He was scarcely conscious of it, and let it pass as material of no immediate interest. Still more vague, and still further below his skin of mental consciousness were the dim stirrings of five hundred such homely misnomers of astronomical dignities of nomenclature. He had read about some, picked up others on subetheric programs, heard about still others in ordinary conversation, come across a few in news reports. The material might have been told him directly, or it might have been a carelessly overheard word. Even the substitution of *Triple G* for *George G. Grundy* had its place in the shadowy file.

Sheffield had often questioned him about what went on in his mind—very gently, very cautiously.

"We want many more like you, Mark, for the Mnemonic Service. We need millions. Billions, eventually, if the race fills up the entire galaxy, as it will some day. But where do we get them. Relying on inborn talent won't do. We all have that more or less. It's the training that counts and unless we find out a little about what goes on, we won't know how to train."

And urged by Sheffield, Mark had watched himself, listened to himself, turned his eyes inward and tried to become *aware.* He learned of the filing cases in his head. He watched them marshal past. He observed individual items pop up on call, always tremblingly ready. It was hard to explain, but he did his best.

His own confidence grew with it. The anxieties of his childhood, those first years in Service, grew less. He stopped waking in the middle of the night, perspiration dripping, screaming with fear that he would forget. And his headaches stopped.

HE watched Ilium as it appeared in the viewport at closest approach. It was brighter than he could imagine a moon to be. (Figures for albedoes of three hundred inhabited planets marched through his mind, neatly arrayed in decreasing order. It scarcely stirred the skin of his mind. He ignored them.)

The brightness he blinked at was concentrated in the vast, irregular patches that Cimon said—he overheard him, in weary response to another's question—had once been sea bottom. A fact popped into Mark's mind. The original report of Hidosheki Makoyama had given the composition of those bright salts as 78.6% sodium chloride, 19.2% magnesium carbonate, 1.4% potassium sulf—The thought faded out. It wasn't necessary.

Ilium had an atmosphere. A total of about 100 mm. of mercury—a little over an eighth of Earth's, ten times Mars, 0.254 that of Coralemon, 0.1376 that of Aurora. Idly he let the decimals grow to more places. It was a form of exercise, but he grew bored. Instant arithmetic was fifth-grade stuff. Actually, he still had trouble with integrals and wondered if that was because he didn't know what an integral was. A half dozen definitions flashed by, but he had never had enough mathematics to understand the definitions, though he could quote them well enough.

At school, they had always said, "Don't ever get too interested in any one thing or group of things. As soon as you do that, you begin selecting your facts and you must never do that. *Everything, anything* is important. As long as you have the facts on file, it doesn't matter whether you understand them or not."

But the noncompos didn't think so. Arrogant minds with holes in them!

They were approaching Junior itself now. It was bright, too, but in a different way. It had ice caps north and south. (Textbooks of Earth's paleoclimatology drifted past and Mark made no move to stop them.) The ice caps were retreating. In a million years, Junior would have Earth's present climate. It was just about Earth's size and mass and it rotated in a period of thirty-six hours.

It might have been Earth's twin. What differences there were, according to Makoyama's reports, were to Junior's advantage. There was nothing on Junior to threaten mankind as far as was known. Nor would anyone imagine there possibly might be were it not for the fact that humanity's first colony on the planet had been wiped out to the last soul.

What was worse, the destruction had occurred in such a way that a study of all surviving information gave no reasonable clue whatever as to what had happened.

SHEFFIELD entered Mark's cabin and joined the boy two hours before landing. He and Mark had originally been assigned a room together. That had been an experiment. Mnemonics didn't like the company of noncompos, even the best of them. In any case, the experiment had failed. Almost immediately after take-off, Mark's sweating face and pleading eyes made privacy absolutely essential for him.

Sheffield felt responsible. He felt responsible for everything about Mark whether it was actually his fault or not. He and men like himself had taken Mark and children like him and trained them into personal ruin. They had been force-grown. They had been bent and molded. They had been allowed no normal contact with normal children lest they develop normal mental habits. No Mnemonic had contracted a normal marriage, even within the group.

It made for a terrible guilt-feeling on Sheffield's part.

Twenty years ago there had been a dozen lads trained at one school under the leadership of U Karaganda, as mad an Asiatic as had ever roused the snickers of a group of interviewing newsmen. Karaganda had committed suicide eventually, under some vague motivation, but other psychologists, Sheffield for one, of greater respectability and undoubtedly of lesser brilliance, had had time to join him and learn of him.

The school continued and others were established. One was even founded on Mars. It had an enrollment of five at the moment. At latest count, there were one hundred and three living graduates with full honors—naturally, only a minority of those enrolled actually absorbed the entire course. Five years ago, the Terrestrial planetary government—not to be confused with the Central Galactic Committee, based on Earth, and ruling the Galactic Confederation—allowed the establishment of the Mnemonic Service as a branch of the Department of the Interior.

It had already paid for itself many times over, but few people knew that. Nor did the Terrestrial government advertise the fact, or any other fact about the Mnemonics. It was a tender subject with them. It was an "experiment." They feared that failure might be politically expensive. The opposition—with difficulty prevented from making a campaign issue out of it as it was—spoke at the planetary conferences of "crackpotism" and "waste of the taxpayers' money." And the latter despite the existence of documentary proof of the precise opposite.

In the machine-centered civilization that filled the galaxy, it was difficult to learn to appreciate the achievements of naked mind without a long apprenticeship.

Sheffield wondered how long.

But there was no use being depressed in Mark's company. Too much danger of contagion. He said, instead, "You're looking fine, sport."

Mark seemed glad to see him. He said, thoughtfully, "When we get back to Earth, Dr. Sheffield—"

He stopped, flushed slightly, and said, "I mean, supposing we get back, I intend to get as many books and films as I can on folkways. I've hardly read anything on that subject. I was down in the ship's library and they had nothing—absolutely nothing."

"Why the interest?"

"It's the captain. Didn't you say he told you that the crew were not to know we were visiting a world on which the first expedition had died?"

"Yes, of course. Well?"

"Because spacemen consider it bad luck to touch on a world like that, especially one that looks harmless. 'Sucker bait,' they call it."

"That's right."

"So the captain *says*. It's just that I don't see how that can be true. I can think of seventeen habitable planets from which the first expedition never returned and never established residence. And each one was later colonized and now is a member of the Federation. Sarmatia is one of them, and it's a pretty big world now."

"There are planets of continuous disaster, too." Sheffield deliberately put that as a declarative statement.

(Never ask informational questions. That was one of the Rules of Karaganda. Mnemonic correlations weren't a matter of the conscious intelligence; they weren't volitional. As soon as a direct question was asked, the resultant correlations were plentiful but only such as any reasonably informed man might make. It was the unconscious mind that bridged the wide, unlikely gaps.)

MARK, as any Mnemonic would, fell into the trap. He said, energetically, "No, I've never heard of one. Not where the planet was at all habitable. If the planet is solid ice, or complete desert, that's different. Junior isn't like that."

"No it isn't," agreed Sheffield.

"Then why should the crew be afraid of it? I kept thinking about that all the time I was in bed. That's when I thought of looking at the log. I'd never actually seen one, so it would be a valuable thing to do in any case. And certainly, I thought, I would find the truth there."

"Uh huh," said Sheffield.

"And, well—I may have been wrong. In the whole log the purpose of the expedition was never mentioned. Now that wouldn't be so unless the purpose were secret. It was as if he were even keeping it from the other ship officers. And the name of the ship *is* given as the *George G. Grundy.*"

"It would be, of course," said Sheffield.

"I don't know; I suspected that business about *Triple G,*" said Mark, darkly.

Sheffield said, "You seem disappointed that the captain wasn't lying."

"Not disappointed. Relieved, I think. I thought . . . I thought—" He stopped and looked acutely embarrassed, but Sheffield made no effort to rescue him. He was forced to continue, "I thought everyone might be lying to me, not just the captain. Even *you* might, Dr. Sheffield. I thought you just didn't want me to talk to the crew for some reason."

Sheffield tried to smile and managed to succeed. The occupational disease of the Mnemonic Service was suspicion. They were isolated, these Mnemonics, and they were different. Cause and effect were obvious.

Sheffield said lightly, "I think you'll find in your reading on folkways that these superstitions are not necessarily based on logical analysis. A planet which has become notorious has evil expected of it. The good which happens is disregarded; the bad is cried up, advertised, and exaggerated. The thing snowballs."

He moved away from Mark. He busied himself with an inspection of the hydraulic chairs. They would be landing soon. He felt unnecessarily along the length of the broad webbing of the straps, keeping his back to the youngster. So protected, he said, almost in a whisper, "And, of course, what makes it worse is that Junior is so different."

(Easy now, easy. Don't push. He had tried that trick before this and—)

Mark was saying, "No, it isn't. Not a bit. The expeditions that failed were different. That's true."

Sheffield kept his back turned. He waited.

Mark said, "The seventeen other expeditions that failed on planets that are now inhabited were all small exploring expeditions. In sixteen of the cases the cause of death was shipwreck of one sort or another and in the remaining case, Coma Minor that one was, the failure resulted from a surprise attack by indigenous life-forms, not intelligent, of course. I have the details on all of them—"

(Sheffield couldn't forebear holding his breath. Mark *could* give the details on all of them. All the details. It was as easy for him to quote all the records on each expedition, word for word, as it was to say yes or no. And he might well choose to. A Mnemonic had no selectivity. It was one of the things that made ordinary companionship between Mnemonics and ordinary people impossible. Mnemonics were dreadful bores by the nature of things. Even Sheffield, who was trained and inured to listen to it all, and who had no intention of stopping Mark if he were really off on a talk-jag, sighed softly.)

"But what's the use," Mark continued, and Sheffield felt rescued from a horror. "They're just not in the same class with the Junior expedition. That consisted of an actual settlement of seven hundred eighty-nine men, two hundred seven women and fifteen children under the age of thirteen. In the course of the next year, three hundred fifteen women, nine men and two children were added by immigration. The settlement survived almost two years and the cause of death isn't known, except that from their report, it might be disease.

"Now *that* part is different. But Junior itself has nothing unusual about it, except, of course—"

Mark paused as though the information were too unimportant to bother with and Sheffield almost yelled. He forced himself to say calmly, "*That* difference. Of course."

Mark said, "We all know about that. It has two suns and the others only have one."

The psychologist could have cried his disappointment. Nothing!

But what was the use. Better luck next time. If you don't have patience with a Mnemonic, you might as well not have a Mnemonic.

He sat down in the hydraulic chair and buckled himself in tightly. Mark did likewise. (Sheffield would have liked to help, but that would have been injudicious.) He looked at his watch. They must be spiraling down even now.

Under his disappointment, Sheffield felt a stronger disturbance. Mark Annuncio had acted wrongly in following up his own hunch that the captain and everybody else had been lying. Mnemonics had a tendency to believe that because their store of facts was great, it was complete. This, obviously, is a prime error. It is therefore necessary—thus spake Karaganda—for them to present their correlations to properly constituted authority and never to act upon it themselves.

Well, how significant was this error of Mark's? He was the first Mnemonic to be taken away from Service headquarters; the first to be separated from all of his kind; the first to be isolated among noncompos. What did that do to him? What would it continue to do to him? Would it be bad? If so, how to stop it?

To all of which questions, Dr. Oswald Mayer Sheffield knew no answer.

THE men at the controls were the lucky ones. They and, of course, Cimon who, as astrophysicist and director of the expedition, joined them by special dispensation. The others of the crew had their separate duties, while the remaining scientific personnel preferred the relative comfort of their hydraulic seats during the spiral around and down to Junior.

It was while Junior was still far enough away to be seen as a whole that the scene was at its grandest.

North and south, a third of the way to the equator, lay the ice caps, still at the start of their millennial retreat. Since the *Triple G* was spiraling on a north-south great circle—deliberately chosen for the sake of viewing the polar regions, as Cimon, at the cost of less than maximum safety, insisted—each cap in turn was laid out below them.

Each burnt equally with sunlight, the consequence of Junior's untilted axis. And each cap was in sectors, cut like a pie with a rainbowed knife.

The sunward third of each was illuminated by both suns simultaneously into a brilliant white that slowly yellowed westward, and as slowly greened eastward. To the east of the white sector lay another, half as wide, which was reached by the light of Lagrange I only, and the snow there blazed a response of sapphire beauty. To the west, another half-sector, exposed to Lagrange II alone, shone in the warm orange-red of an Earthly sunset. The three colors graded into one another band-wise, and the similarity to a rainbow was increased thereby.

The final third was dark in contrast, but if one looked carefully enough, it, too, was in parts—unequal parts. The smaller portion was black indeed, but the larger portion had a faint milkiness about it.

Cimon muttered to himself, "Moonlight. Of course." Then looked about hastily to see if he were overheard. He did not like people to observe the actual process by which conclusions were brought to fruition in his mind. Rather they were to be presented to his students and listeners, to all about him in short, in a polished perfection that showed neither birth nor growth.

But there were only spacemen about and they did not hear him. Despite all their space-hardening, they were fixing whatever concentration they could spare from their duties and instruments upon the wonder before them.

The spiral curved, veered way from north-south to northeast-southwest, finally to the east-west in which a safe landing was most feasible. The dull thunder of atmosphere carried into the pilot room, thin and shrill at first, but gathering body and volume as the minutes passed.

Until now, in the interests of scientific observation—and to the considerable uneasiness of the captain—the spiral had been tight, deceleration slight, and the planetary circumnavigations numerous. As they bit into Junior's air-covering, however, deceleration pitched high and the surface rose to meet them.

The ice caps vanished on either side and there began an equal alternation of land and water. A continent, mountainous on either seacoast and flat in between, like a soup plate with two ice-topped rims, flashed below at lengthening intervals. It spread halfway around Junior and the rest was water.

Most of the ocean at the moment was in the dark sector, and what was not lay in the red-orange light of Lagrange II. In the light of that sun, the waters were a dusky purple with a sprinkling of ruddy specks that thickened north and south. Icebergs!

The land was distributed at the moment between the red-orange half-sector and the full white light. Only the eastern seacoast was in the blue-green. The eastern mountain range was a startling sight, with its western slopes red and its eastern slopes green.

The ship was slowing rapidly now; the final trip over ocean was done.

Next—landing!

THE first steps were cautious enough. Slow enough, too. Cimon inspected his photochromes of Junior as taken from space with minute care. Under protest, he passed them among the others of the expedition and more than a few groaned inwardly at the thought of having placed comfort before a chance to see the original of *that.*

Boris Vernadsky bent over his gas-analyzer interminably, a symphony in loud clothes and soft grunts.

"We're about at sea level, I should judge," he said, "going by the value of *g*."

Then, because he was explaining himself to the rest of the group, he added negligently, "The gravitational constant, that is," which didn't help most of them.

He said, "The atmospheric pressure is just about eight hundred millimeters of mercury which is about five per cent higher than on Earth. And two hundred forty millimeters of that is oxygen as compared to only one hundred fifty on Earth. Not bad."

He seemed to be waiting for approval, but scientists found it best to comment as little as possible on data in another man's specialty.

He went on, "Nitrogen, of course. Dull, isn't it, the way Nature repeats itself like a three-year-old who knows three lessons, period. Takes the fun away when it turns out that a water world always has an oxygen-nitrogen atmosphere. Makes the whole thing yawn-worthy."

"What else in the atmosphere?" asked Cimon, irritably. "So far all we have is oxygen, nitrogen, and homely philosophy from kindly Uncle Boris."

Vernadsky hooked his arm over his seat and said, amiably enough, "What are you? Director or something?"

Cimon, to whom the directorship meant little more than the annoyance of preparing composite reports for the Bureau flushed and said, grimly, "What else in the atmosphere, Dr. Vernadsky?"

Vernadsky said, without looking at his notes, "Under one per cent and over a hundredth of one per cent: hydrogen, helium, and carbon dioxide in that order. Under a hundredth of one per cent and over a ten thousandth of one per cent: methane, argon, and neon in that order. Under a ten thousandth of one per cent and over a millionth of a per cent: radon, krypton, and xenon in that order.

"The figures aren't very informative. About all I can get out of them is that Junior is going to be a happy hunting ground for uranium, that it's low in potassium and that it's no wonder it's such a lovely little double ice cap of a world."

He did that deliberately, so that someone could ask him how he knew, and someone, with gratifying wonder, inevitably did.

Vernadsky smiled blandly and said: "Atmospheric radon is ten to a hundred times as high here as on Earth. So is helium. Both radon and helium are produced as by-products of the radioactive breakdown of uranium and thorium. Conclusion: Uranium and thorium minerals are ten to a hundred times as copious in Junior's crust as in Earth's.

"Argon, on the other hand, is over a hundred times as low as on Earth. Chances are Junior has none of the argon it originally started with. A planet of this type has only the argon which forms from the breakdown of K^{40}, one of the potassium isotopes. Low argon; low potassium. Simple, kids."

One of the assembled groups asked, "What about the ice caps?"

Cimon, who knew the answer to that, asked, before Vernadsky could answer the other, "What's the carbon dioxide content exactly?"

"Zero point zero one six emm emm," said Vernadsky.

Cimon nodded, and vouchsafed nothing more.

"Well?" asked the inquirer impatiently.

"Carbon dioxide is only about half what it is on Earth, and it's the carbon dioxide that gives the hothouse effect. It lets the short waves of sunlight pass through to the planet's surface, but doesn't allow the long waves of planetary heat to radiate off. When carbon dioxide concentration goes up as a result of volcanic action, the planet heats up a bit and you have a carboniferous age with oceans high and land surface at a minimum. When carbon dioxide goes down as a result of the vegetation refusing to let a good thing alone, fattening up on the good old see-oh-two and losing its head about it, temperature drops, ice forms, a vicious cycle of glaciation starts, and *voilà*—"

"Anything else in the atmosphere?" asked Cimon.

"Water vapor and dust. I suppose there are a few million airborne spores of various virulent diseases per cubic centimeter in addition to that." He said it lightly enough, but there was a stir in the room. More than one of the bystanders looked as though he were holding his breath.

Vernadsky shrugged and said, "Don't worry about it for now. My analyzer washes out dust and spores quite thoroughly. But then, that's not my angle. I suggest Rodriguez grow his cultures under glass right away. Good thick glass."

MARK Annuncio wandered everywhere. His eyes shone as he listened, and he pressed himself forward to hear better. The group suffered him to do so with various degrees of reluctance, in accordance with individual personalities and temperaments. None spoke to him.

Sheffield stayed close to Mark. He scarcely spoke, either. He bent all his effort on remaining in the background of Mark's consciousness. He wanted to refrain from giving Mark the feeling of being haunted by himself; give the boy the illusion of freedom, instead. He wanted to seem to be there, each time, by accident only.

It was a most unsuccessful pretense, he felt, but what could he do? He *had* to keep the kid from getting into trouble.

MIGUEL Antonio Lopez y Rodriguez—microbiologist; small, tawny, with intensely black hair which he wore rather long, and with a reputation which he did nothing to discourage, of being a Latin in the grand style as far as the ladies were concerned—cultured the dust from Vernadsky's gas-analyzer trap with a combination of precision and respectful delicacy.

"Nothing," he said, eventually. "What foolish growths I get look harmless."

It was suggested that Junior's bacteria need not necessarily look harmful; that toxins and metabolic processes could not be analyzed by eye, even by microscopic eye.

This was met with hot contempt, as almost an invasion of professional function. He said, with an eyebrow lifted, "One gets a feeling for these things. When one has seen as much of the microcosm as I have, one can sense danger—or lack of danger."

This was an outright lie, and Rodriguez proved it by carefully transferring samples of the various germ colonies into buffered, isotonic media and injecting hamsters with the concentrated result. They did not seem to mind.

Raw atmosphere was trapped in large jars and several specimens of minor animal life from Earth and other planets were allowed to disport themselves within. None of them seemed to mind, either.

NEVILE Fawkes—botanist; a man who appreciated his own handsomeness by modeling his hair style after that shown on the traditional busts of Alexander the Great, but from whose appearance the presence of a nose, far more aquiline than Alexander ever possessed, noticeably detracted—was gone for two days, by Junior chronology, in one of the *Triple G*'s atmospheric coasters. He could navigate one like a dream and was, in fact, the only man outside the crew who could navigate one at all, so he was the natural choice for the task. Fawkes did not seem noticeably overjoyed about that.

He returned, completely unharmed and unable to hide a grin of relief. He submitted to irradiation for the sake of sterilizing the exterior of his flexible air-suit—designed to protect men from the deleterious effect of the outer environment where no pressure differential existed; the strength and jointedness of a true spacesuit being obviously unnecessary within an atmosphere as thick as Junior's. The coaster was subjected to a more extended irradiation, and pinned down under a plastic cover-all.

Fawkes flaunted color photographs in great number. The central valley of the continent was fertile almost beyond Earthly dreams. The rivers were mighty, the mountains rugged and snow-covered—with the usual pyrotechnic solar effects. Under Lagrange II alone, the vegetation looked vaguely repellant, seeming rather dark, like dried blood. Under Lagrange I, however, or under the suns together, the brilliant, flourishing green and the glisten of the numerous lakes—particularly north and south along the dead rims of the departing glaciers—brought an ache of homesickness to the hearts of many.

Fawkes said, "Look at these."

He had skimmed low to take a photochrome of a field of huge flowers, dripping with scarlet. In the high-ultraviolet radiation of Lagrange I, exposure times were of necessity extremely short and despite the motion of the coaster, each blossom stood out as a sharp blotch of strident color.

"I swear," said Fawkes, "each one of those was six feet across."

They admired the flowers unrestrainedly.

Fawkes then said, "No intelligent life whatever, of course."

Sheffield looked up from the photographs, with instant sharpness. Life and intelligence, after all, were by way of being his province. "How do you know?"

"Look for yourself," said the botanist. "There are the photos. No highways, no cities, no artificial waterways, no signs of anything manmade."

"No machine civilization," said Sheffield. "That's all."

"Even ape-men would build shelters and use fire," said Fawkes, offended.

"The continent is ten times as large as Africa and you've been over it for two days. There's a lot you could miss."

"Not as much as you'd think," was the warm response. "I followed every sizable river up and down and looked over both seacoasts. Any settlements are bound to be there."

"In allowing seventy-two hours for two eight-thousand-mile seacoasts ten thousand miles apart, plus how many thousand miles of river, that had to be a pretty quick lookover."

Cimon interrupted, "What's this all about? *Homo sapiens* is the only intelligence ever discovered in the galaxy through a hundred thousand and more explored planets. The chances of Troas possessing intelligence is virtually nil."

"Yes?" said Sheffield. "You could use the same argument to prove there's no intelligence on Earth."

"Makoyama," said Cimon, "in his report mentioned no intelligent life."

"And how much time did he have? It was a case of another quick feel through the haystack with one finger and a report of no needle."

"What the eternal universe," said Rodriguez, waspishly. "We argue like madmen. Call the hypothesis of indigenous intelligence unproven and let it go. We are not through investigating yet, I hope."

COPIES of those first pictures of Junior's surface were added to what might be termed the open files. After a second trip, Fawkes returned in more somber mood and the meeting was correspondingly more subdued.

New photographs went from hand to hand and were then placed by Cimon himself in the special safe that nothing could open short of Cimon's own hands or an all-destroying nuclear blast.

Fawkes said, "The two largest rivers have a generally north-south course along the eastern edges of the western mountain range. The larger river comes down from the northern ice cap, the smaller up from the southern one. Tributaries come in westward from the eastern range, interlacing the entire central plain. Apparently, the central plain is tipped, the eastern edge being higher. It's what ought to be expected maybe. The eastern mountain range is the taller, broader and more continuous of the two. I wasn't able to make actual measurements, but I wouldn't be surprised if they beat the Himalayas. In fact, they're a lot like the Wu Ch'ao range on Hesperus. You have to hit the stratosphere to get over them, and rugged—Wow!

"Anyway," he brought himself back to the immediate subject at hand, with an effort, "the two main rivers join about a hundred miles south of the equator and pour through a gap in the western range. They make it to the ocean after that in just short of eighty miles.

"Where it hits the ocean is a natural spot for the planetary metropolis. The trade routes into the interior of the continent have to converge there so it would be the inevitable emporium for space-trade. Even as far as surface trade is concerned, the continental east coast has to move goods across the ocean. Jumping the eastern range isn't worth the effort. Then, too, there are the islands we saw when we were landing.

"So right there is where I would have looked for the settlement even if we didn't have a record of the latitude and longitude. And those settlers had an eye for the future. It's where they set up shop."

Novee said in a low voice, "They thought they had an eye for the future, anyway. There isn't much left of them, is there?"

Fawkes tried to be philosophic about it. "It's been over a century. What do you expect? There's a lot more left of them than I honestly thought there would be. Their buildings were mostly prefab. They've tumbled and vegetation has forced its way over and through them. The fact that the climate of Junior is glacial is what's preserved it. The trees—or the objects that rather look like trees—are small and obviously very slow-growing.

"Even so, the clearing is gone. From the air, the only way you could tell there had once been a settlement in that spot was that the new growth had a slightly different color and . . . and, well, *texture,* than the surrounding forests."

He pointed at a particular photograph. "This is just a slag heap. Maybe it was machinery once. I think those are burial mounds."

Novee said, "Any actual remains? Bones?"

Fawkes shook his head.

Novee said, "The last survivors didn't bury themselves, did they?"

Fawkes said, "Animals, I suppose." He walked away, his back to the group. "It was raining when I poked my way through. It went *splat, splat* on the flat leaves above me and the ground was soggy and spongy underneath. It was dark, gloomy—There was a cold wind. The pictures I took didn't get it across. I felt as though there were a thousand ghosts, waiting—"

The mood was contagious.

Cimon said, savagely, "Stop that!"

In the background, Mark Annuncio's pointed nose fairly quivered with the intensity of his curiosity. He turned to Sheffield, who was at his side, and whispered, "Ghosts? No authentic case of seeing—"

Sheffield touched Mark's thin shoulder lightly. "Only a way of speaking, Mark. But don't feel badly, that he doesn't mean it literally. You're watching the birth of a superstition, and that's something, isn't it?"

A semi-sullen Captain Follenbee sought out Cimon the evening after Fawkes' second return, and said in his harumphy way, "Never do, Dr. Cimon. My men are unsettled. Very unsettled."

The port-shields were open. Lagrange I was six hours gone, and Lagrange II's ruddy light, deepened to crimson in setting, flushed the captain's face and tinged his short gray hair with red.

Cimon, whose attitude toward the crew in general and the captain in particular was one of controlled impatience, said, "What is the trouble, captain?"

"Been here two weeks, Earth-time. Still no one leaves without suits. Always irradiate before you come back. Anything wrong with the air?"

"Not as far as we know."

"Why not breathe it then?"

"Captain, that's for me to decide."

The flush on the captain's face became a real one. He said, "My papers say I don't have to stay if ship's safety is endangered. A frightened and mutinous crew is something I don't want."

"Can't you handle your own men?"

"Within reason."

"Well, what really bothers them? This is a new planet and we're being cautious. Can't they understand that?"

"Two weeks and still cautious. They think we're hiding something. And we are. You know that. Besides, surface leave is necessary. Crew's got to have it. Even if it's just on a bare rock a mile across. Gets them out of the ship. Away from the routine. Can't deny them that."

"Give me till tomorrow," said Cimon, contemptuously.

THE scientists gathered in the observatory the next day. Cimon said, "Vernadsky tells me the data on air is still negative, and Rodriguez has discovered no airborne pathogenic organism of any type."

There was a general air of dubiety over the last statement. Novee said, "The settlement died of disease. I'll swear to that."

"Maybe so," said Rodriguez at once, "but can you explain how? It's impossible. I tell you that and I tell you. See here. Almost all Earth-type planets give birth to life and that life is always protein in nature and always either cellular or virus in organization. But that's all. There the resemblance ends.

"You laymen think it's all the same; Earth or any planet. Germs are germs and viruses are viruses. I tell you, you don't understand the infinite possibilities for variation in the protein molecule. Even on Earth, every species has its own diseases. Some may spread over several species but there isn't one single pathogenic life form of any type on Earth that can attack all other species.

"You think that a virus or a bacterium developing independently for a billion years on another planet with different amino-acids, different enzyme systems, a different scheme of metabolism altogether, is just going to happen to find *Homo sapiens* succulent like a lollipop. I tell you it is childishness."

Novee, his physician's soul badly pierced at having been lumped under the phrase, "you laymen," was not disposed to let it go that easily. *"Homo sapiens* brings its own germs with it wherever it goes, Rod. Who's to say the virus of the common cold didn't mutate under some planetary influence into something that was suddenly deadly. Or influenza. Things like that have happened even on Earth. The 2755 para-meas—"

"I know all about the 2755 para-measles epidemic," said Rodriguez, "and the 1918 influenza epidemic, and the Black Death, too. But when has it happened lately? Granted the settlement was a matter of a century and more ago; still that wasn't exactly pre-atomic times, either. They included doctors. They had supplies of antibiotics and they knew the techniques of antibody induction. They're simple enough. And there was the medical relief expedition, too."

Novee patted his round abdomen and said, stubbornly, "The symptoms were those of a respiratory infection; dyspnea—"

"I know the list; but I tell you it wasn't a germ disease that got them. It couldn't be."

"What was it, then?"

"That's outside my professional competence. Talking from inside, I tell you it wasn't infection. Even mutant infection. It couldn't be. It *mathematically* couldn't be." He leaned heavily on the adverb.

There was a stir among the listeners as Mark Annuncio shoved his thin body forward into the space immediately before Rodriguez.

For the first time, he spoke at one of these gatherings.

"Mathematically?" he asked, eagerly.

Sheffield followed after, his long body all elbows and knees as he made a path. He murmured "Sorry" half a dozen times.

Rodriguez, in an advanced stage of exasperation thrust out his lower lip and said, "What do *you* want?"

Mark flinched. Less eagerly, he said, "You said you knew it wasn't infection mathematically. I was wondering how . . . mathematics—" He ran down.

Rodriguez said, "I have stated my professional opinion."

He said it formally, stiltedly, then turned away. No man questioned another's professional opinion unless he was of the same specialty. Otherwise the implication, clearly enough, was that the specialist's experience and knowledge was sufficiently dubious to be brought into question by an outsider.

Mark knew this, but then he was of the Mnemonic Service. He tapped Rodriguez's shoulder, while the others standing about listened in stunned fascination, and said, "I know it's your professional opinion, but still I'd like to have it explained."

He didn't mean to sound peremptory. He was just stating a fact.

Rodriguez whirled. "You'd like to have it explained? Who the eternal Universe are *you* to ask me questions?"

Mark was startled at the other's vehemence, but Sheffield had reached him now, and he gained courage and with it, anger. He disregarded Sheffield's quick whisper and said shrilly, "I'm Mark Annuncio of Mnemonic Service and I've asked you a question. I want your statement explained."

"It won't be explained. Sheffield, take this young nut out of here and tuck him into bed, will you? And keep him away from me after this. Young jackass." The last was a clearly-heard aside.

Sheffield took Mark's wrist but it was wrenched out of his grasp. The young Mnemonic screamed, "You stupid noncompos. You . . . you moron. You forgettery on two feet. Sievemind. Let me *go,* Dr. Sheffield—You're no expert. You don't remember anything you've learned, and you haven't learned much in the first place. You're not a specialist; none of you—"

"For space's sake," cried Cimon, "take the young idiot out of here, Sheffield."

Sheffield, his long cheeks burning, stooped and lifted Mark bodily into the air. Holding him close, he made his way out of the room.

Tears squeezed out of Mark's eyes and just outside the door, he managed to speak with difficulty. "Let me down, I want to hear—I want to hear what they say."

Sheffield said, "Don't go back in. Please, Mark."

"I won't. Don't worry. But—"

He didn't finish the but.

INSIDE the observatory room, Cimon, looking haggard, said, "All right. All right. Let's get back to the point. Come on, now. Quiet! I'm accepting Rodriguez's viewpoint. It's good enough for me and I don't suppose there's anyone else here who questions Rodriguez's professional opinion."

("Better not," muttered Rodriguez, his dark eyes hot with sustained fury.)

Cimon went on. "And since there's nothing to fear as far as infection is concerned, I'm telling Captain Follenbee that the crew may take surface leave without special protection against the atmosphere. Apparently the lack of surface leave is bad for morale. Are there any objections?"

There weren't any.

Cimon said, "I see no reason also why we can't pass on to the next stage of the investigation. I propose that we set up camp at the site of the original settlement. I appoint a committee of five to trek out there. Fawkes, since he can handle the coaster; Novee and Rodriguez to handle the biological data; Vernadsky and myself to take care of the chemistry and physics.

"The rest of you will, naturally, be apprised of all pertinent data in your own specialties, and will be expected to help in suggesting lines of attack, et cetera. Eventually, we may all be out there, but for the while only this small group. And until further notice, communication between ourselves and the main group on ship will be by radio only, since if the trouble, whatever it is, turns out to be localized at settlement site, five men are enough to lose."

Novee said, "The settlement lived on Junior several years before dying out—over a year, anyway. It could be a long time before we are certain we're safe."

"We," said Cimon, "are not a settlement. We are a group of specialists who are looking for trouble. We'll find it if it's there to find, and when we do find it, we'll beat it. And it won't take us a couple of years either. Now, are there any objections?"

There were none, and the meeting broke up.

MARK Annuncio sat on his bunk, hands clasped about his knee, chin sunken and touching his chest. He was dry-eyed now, but his voice was heady with frustration.

"They're not taking me," he said. "They won't let me go with them."

Sheffield was in the chair opposite the boy, bathed in an agony of perplexity. He said, "They may take you later on."

"No," said Mark, fiercely, "they won't. They hate me. Besides, I want to go now. I've never been on another planet before. There's so much to see and find out. They've got no right to hold me back if I want to go."

Sheffield shook his head. Mnemonics were so firmly trained into this belief that they *must* collect facts, and that no one or nothing could or ought to stop them. Perhaps when they returned, he might recommend a certain degree of counter-indoctrination. After all, Mnemonics had to live in the real world, occasionally. More and more with each generation, perhaps, as they grew to play an increasing role in the galaxy.

He tried an experiment. He said, "It may be dangerous, you know."

"I don't care. I've got to know. I've *got* to find out about this planet. Dr. Sheffield, you go to Dr. Cimon and tell him I'm going along."

"Now, Mark."

"If you don't, I will." He raised his small body from the bed in earnest of leaving that moment.

"Look, you're excited."

Mark's fists clenched. "It's not fair, Dr. Sheffield. I found this planet. It's *my* planet."

Sheffield's conscience hit him badly. What Mark said was true in a way. No one, except Mark, knew that better than Sheffield. And no one, again except Mark, knew the history of Junior better than Sheffield.

It was only in the last twenty years that, faced with the rising tide of population pressure in the older planets and the recession of the Galactic frontier from those same older planets, that the Confederation of Worlds began exploring the galaxy systematically. Before that, human expansion went on hit or miss. Men and women in search of new land and a better life followed rumor as to the existence of habitable planets or sent out amateur groups to find something promising.

A hundred ten years before, one such group found Junior. They didn't report their find officially because they didn't want a crowd of land speculators, promotion men, exploiters and general riffraff following. In the next months, some of the unattached men arranged to have women brought in, so the settlement must have flourished for a while.

It was a year later when some had died and most or all the rest were sick and dying that they beamed a cry of help to Pretoria, the nearest inhabited planet. The Pretorian government was in some sort of crisis at the time and relayed the message to the Sector Government at Altmark. Pretoria then felt justified in forgetting the matter.

The Altmark government, acting in reflex fashion, sent out a medical ship to Junior. It dropped anti-sera and various other supplies. The ship did not land because the medical officer diagnosed the matter, from a distance, as influenza, and minimized the danger. The medical supplies, his report said, would handle the matter perfectly. It was quite possible that the crew of the ship, fearing contagion, had prevented a landing, but nothing in the official report indicated that.

There was a final report from Junior three months later to the effect that only ten people were left alive and that they were dying. They begged for help. This report was forwarded to Earth itself along with the previous medical report. The Central Government, however, was a maze in which reports regularly were forgotten unless someone had sufficient personal interest, and influence, to keep them alive. No one had much interest in a far-off, unknown planet with ten dying men and women on it.

Filed and forgotten—and for a century, no human foot was felt on Junior.

Then, with the new furore over Galactic exploration, hundreds of ships began darting through the empty vastness, probing here and there. Reports trickled in, then flooded in.

Some came from Hidosheki Mikoyama, who passed through the Hercules Cluster twice—dying in a crash landing the second time, with his tight and despairing voice coming over the subether in a final message: "Surface coming up fast now; ship-walls frictioning into red he—" and no more.

Last year, the accumulation of reports, grown past any reasonable human handling, was fed into the over-worked Washington computer on a priority so high that there was only a five-month wait. The operators checked out the data for planetary habitability and lo, Abou ben Junior led all the rest.

SHEFFIELD remembered the wild hurrah over it. The stellar system was enthusiastically proclaimed to the galaxy and the name, Junior, was thought up by a bright young man in the Bureau of Outer Provinces who felt the need for personal friendliness between man and world. Junior's virtues were magnified. Its fertility, its climate—"a New England perpetual spring"—and most of all, its vast future, were put across without any feeling of need for discretion. For the next million years, propagandists declared, Junior will grow richer. While other planets age, Junior will grow younger as the ice recedes and fresh soil is exposed. Always a new frontier; always untapped resources.

For a million years!

It was the Bureau's masterpiece. It was to be the tremendously successful start of a program of government-sponsored colonization. It was to be the beginning, at long last, of the scientific exploitation of the galaxy for the good of humanity.

And then came Mark Annuncio, who heard much of all this and was as thrilled at the prospect as any Joe Earthman, but who one day thought of something he had seen while sniffing idly through the "dead-matter" files of the Bureau of Outer Provinces. He had seen a medical report about a colony on a planet of a system whose description and position in space tallied with that of the Lagrange group.

Sheffield remembered the day Mark came to him with that news.

He also remembered the face of the Secretary for the Outer Provinces when the news was passed on to *him*. He saw the secretary's square jaw slowly go slack and a look of infinite trouble come into his eyes.

The government was committed! It was going to ship millions of people to Junior. It was going to grant farmland and subsidize the first seed supplies, farm machinery, factories. Junior was going to be a paradise for numerous voters and a promise of more paradise for a myriad others.

If Junior turned out to be a killer planet for some reason or other, it would mean political suicide for all government figures concerned in the project. That meant some pretty big men, not least the Secretary for the Outer Provinces.

After days of checking and indecision, the secretary had said to Sheffield, "It looks as though we've got to find out what happened, and weave it into the propaganda somehow. Don't you think we could neutralize it that way?"

"If what happened isn't too horrible to neutralize."

"But it can't be, can it? I mean, what can it be?" The man was miserably unhappy.

Sheffield shrugged.

The secretary said, "See here. We can send a ship of specialists to the planet. Volunteers only and good reliable men, of course. We can give it the highest priority rating we can move, and Project Junior carries considerable weight, you know. We'll slow things up here, and hold on till they get back. That might work, don't you think?"

Sheffield wasn't sure, but he got the sudden dream of going on that expedition, of taking Mark with him. He could study a Mnemonic in an off-trail environment, and if Mark *should* be the means of working out the mystery—

From the beginning, a mystery was assumed. After all, people don't die of influenza. And the medical ship hadn't landed; they hadn't *really* observed what was going on. It was fortunate, indeed, that that medical man was now dead thirty-seven years, or he would be slated for court-martial now.

If Mark *should* help solve the matter, the Mnemonic Service would be enormously strengthened. The government had to be grateful.

But now—

Sheffield wondered if Cimon knew the story of how the matter of the first settlement had been brought to light. He was fairly certain that the rest of the crew did not. It was not something the Bureau would willingly speak about.

Nor would it be polite to use the story as a lever to pry concessions out of Cimon. If Mark's correction of Bureau "stupidity"—that would undoubtedly be the opposition's phrasing—were overpublicized, the Bureau would look bad. If they could be grateful, they could be vengeful, too. Retaliation against the Mnemonic Service would not be too petty a thing to expect.

Still—

Sheffield stood up with quick decision. "All right, Mark. I'll get you out to the settlement site. I'll get us both out there. Now you sit down and wait for me. Promise you'll try nothing on your own."

"All right," said Mark. He sat down on his bunk again.

"WELL, now, Dr. Sheffield, what is it?" said Cimon. The astrophysicist sat at his desk, on which papers and film formed rigidly arranged heaps about a small Macfreed integrator and watched Sheffield step over the threshold.

Sheffield sat carelessly down upon the tautly yanked top-sheet of Cimon's bunk. He was aware of Cimon's annoyed glance in that direction and it did not worry him. In fact, he rather enjoyed it.

He said, "I have a quarrel with your choice of men to go to the expedition site. It looks as though you've picked two men for the physical sciences, and three for the biological sciences. Right?"

"Yes."

"I suppose you think you've covered the ground like a Danielski ovospore at perihelion."

"Oh, space! Have you anything to suggest?"

"I would like to come along myself."

"Why?"

"You have no one to take care of the mental sciences."

"The *mental* sciences! Good galaxy! Dr. Sheffield, five men are quite enough to risk. As a matter of fact, doctor, you and your . . . uh . . . ward were assigned to the scientific personnel of this ship by order of the Bureau of Outer Provinces without any prior consultation of myself. I'll be frank—if I had been consulted, I would have advised against you. I don't see the function of mental science in an investigation such as this, which, after all, is purely physical. It is too bad that the Bureau wishes to experiment with Mnemonics on an occasion such as this. We can't afford scenes like that one with Rodriguez."

Sheffield decided that Cimon did not know of Mark's connection with the original decision to send out the expedition.

He sat upright, hands on knees, elbows cocked outward and let a freezing formality settle over him. "So you wonder about the function of mental science in an investigation such as this, Dr. Cimon. Suppose I told you that the end of the first settlement might possibly be explained on a simple, psychological basis."

"It wouldn't impress me. A psychologist is a man who can explain anything and prove nothing." Cimon smirked like a man who had made an epigram and was proud of it.

Sheffield ignored it. He said, "Let me go into a little detail. In what way is Junior different from every one of the eighty-three thousand inhabited worlds?"

"Our information is as yet incomplete. I cannot say."

"Oh, cobber-vitals. You had the necessary information before you ever came here. Junior has two suns."

"Well, of course." But the astrophysicist allowed a trace of discomfiture to enter his expression.

"Colored suns, mind you. Colored suns. Do you know what that means? It means that a human being, yourself or myself, standing in the full glare of the two suns, would cast two shadows. One blue-green, one red-orange. The length of each would naturally vary with the time of day. Have you taken the trouble to verify the color distribution in those shadows? The what-do-you-call-em—reflection spectrum?"

"I presume," said Cimon, loftily, "they'd be about the same as the radiation spectra of the suns. What are you getting at?"

"You should check. Wouldn't the air absorb some wavelengths? And the vegetation? What's left? And take Junior's moon, Sister. I've been watching it in the last few nights. It's in colors, too, and the colors change position."

"Well, of course. It runs through its phases independently with each sun."

"You haven't checked its reflection spectrum, either, have you?"

"We have that somewhere. There are no points of interest about it. Of what interest is it to you, anyway?"

"My dear Dr. Cimon. It is a well established psychological fact that combinations of red and green colors exert a deleterious effect on mental stability. We have a case here where the red-green chromopsychic picture—to use a technical term—is inescapable and is presented under circumstances which seem most unnatural to the human mind. It is quite possible that chromopsychosis could reach the fatal level by inducing hypertrophy of the trinitarian follicles with consequent cerebric catatonia."

Cimon looked floored. He said, "I never heard of such a thing."

"Naturally not," said Sheffield—it was his turn to be lofty. "You are not a psychologist. Surely you are not questioning my professional opinion."

"No, of course not. But it's quite plain from the last reports of the expedition that they were dying of something that sounded like a respiratory disease."

"Correct, but Rodriguez denies that and you accepted his professional opinion."

"I didn't say it was a respiratory disease. I said it sounded like one. Where does your red-green cromothingumbob come in?"

Sheffield shook his head. "You laymen have your misconceptions. Granted that there is a physical effect, it still does not imply that there may not be a mental cause. The most convincing point about my theory is that red-green chromopsychosis has been recorded to exhibit itself first as a psychogenic respiratory infection. I take it you are not acquainted with psychogenics."

"No. It's out of my field."

"Well, yes. I should say so. Now my own calculations show me that under the heightened oxygen tension of this world the psychogenic respiratory infection is both inevitable and particularly severe. For instance, you've observed the moon—Sister, I mean—in the last few nights."

"Yes, I have observed Ilium." Cimon did not forget Sister's official name, even now.

"You watched it closely and over lengthy periods? Under magnification?"

"Yes." Cimon was growing uneasy.

"Ah," said Sheffield, "now the moon colors in the last few nights have been particularly virulent. Surely you must be noticing just a small inflammation of the mucous membrane of the nose, a slight itching in the throat. Nothing painful yet, I imagine. Have you been coughing or sneezing? Is it a little hard to swallow?"

"I believe I—" Cimon swallowed, then drew in his breath sharply. He was testing.

Then he sprang to his feet, fists clenched and mouth working. "Great galaxy, Sheffield, you had no right to keep quiet about this. I can feel it now. What do I do, Sheffield? It's not incurable, is it? Damn it, Sheffield"—his voice went shrill—"why didn't you tell us this before?"

"Because," said Sheffield, calmly, "there's not a word of truth in anything I've said. Not one word. There's no harm in colors. Sit down, Dr. Cimon. You're beginning to look rather foolish to say the least."

"You said," said Cimon, thoroughly confused, and in a voice that was beginning to strangle, "that it was your professional opinion that—"

"My professional opinion! Space and little comets, Cimon, what's so magic about a professional opinion? A man can be lying or he can just plain be ignorant, even about the final details of his own specialty. A professional can be wrong because he's ignorant of a neighboring specialty. He may be certain he's right and still be wrong.

"Look at you. You know all about what makes the universe tick and I'm lost completely except that I know that a star is something that twinkles and a light-year is something that's long. And yet you'll swallow gibberish-psychology that a freshman student of mentics would laugh his head off at. Don't you think, Cimon, it's time we worried less about professional opinion and more about over-all co-ordination?"

THE color washed slowly out of Cimon's face. It turned waxy-pale. His lips trembled. He whispered, "You used professional status as a cloak to make a fool of me."

"That's about it," said Sheffield.

"I have never, *never—"* Cimon gasped and tried a new start. "I have never witnessed anything as cowardly and unethical."

"I was trying to make a point."

"Oh, you made it. You made it." Cimon was slowly recovering; his voice approaching normality. "You want me to take that boy of yours with us."

"That's right."

"No. No. Definitely no. It was no before you came in here and it's no a million times over now."

"What's your reason? I mean, before I came in."

"He's psychotic. He can't be trusted with normal people."

Sheffield said, grimly, "I'll thank you not to use the word, 'psychotic.' You are not competent to use it. If you're so precise in your feeling for professional ethics, remember to stay out of my specialty in my presence. Mark Annuncio is perfectly normal."

"After that scene with Rodriguez? Yes. Oh, yes."

"Mark had the right to ask his question. It was his job to do so and his duty. Rodriguez had no right to be boorish about it."

"I'll have to consider Rodriguez first, if you don't mind."

"Why? Mark Annuncio knows more than Rodriguez. For that matter, he knows more than you or I. Are you trying to bring back an intelligent report or to satisfy a petty vanity?"

"Your statements about what your boy knows do not impress me. I am quite aware he is an efficient parrot. He understands nothing, however. It is my duty to see to it that data are made available to him, because the Bureau has ordered that. They did not consult me, but very well. I will co-operate that far. He will receive his data here in the ship."

Sheffield said, "Not adequate, Cimon. He should be on the spot. He may see things our precious specialists will not."

Cimon said, freezingly, "Very likely. The answer, Sheffield, is no. There is no argument that can possibly persuade me." The astrophysicist's nose was pinched and white.

"Because I made a fool of you?"

"Because you violated the most fundamental obligation of a

professional man. No respectable professional would ever use his specialty to prey on the innocence of a non-associate professional."

"So I made a fool of you."

Cimon turned away. "Please leave. There will be no further communication between us, outside the most necessary business, for the duration of the trip."

"If I go," said Sheffield, "the rest of the boys may get to hear about this."

Cimon started. "You're going to repeat our little affair?" A cold smile rested on his lips, then went its transient and contemptuous way. "You'll broadcast the dastard you were."

"Oh, I doubt they'll take it seriously. Everyone knows psychologists will have their little jokes. Besides, they'll be so busy laughing at you. You know—the very impressive Dr. Cimon scared into a sore throat and howling for mercy after a few mystic words of gibberish."

"Who'd believe you?" cried Cimon.

Sheffield lifted his right hand. Between thumb and forefinger was a small rectangular object, studded with a line of control toggles.

"Pocket recorder," he said. He touched one of the toggles and Cimon's voice was suddenly saying, "Well, now, Dr. Sheffield, what is it?"

It sounded pompous, peremptory, and even a little smug.

"Give me that!" Cimon hurled himself at the lanky psychologist.

Sheffield held him off. "Don't try force, Cimon. I was in amateur wrestling not too long ago. Look, I'll make a deal with you."

Cimon was still writhing toward him, dignity forgotten, panting his fury. Sheffield kept him at arm's length, backing slowly.

Sheffield said, "Let Mark and myself come along and no one will ever see or hear this."

Slowly, Cimon simmered down. He gasped, "Will you let me have it, then?"

"After Mark and I are out at the settlement site."

"I'm to trust *you.*" He seemed to take pains to make that as offensive as possible.

"Why not? You can certainly trust me to broadcast this if you *don't* agree. I'll play it off for Vernadsky first. He'll love it. You know his corny sense of humor."

Cimon said in a voice so low it could hardly be heard, "You and the boy can come along." Then, vigorously, "But remember this, Sheffield. When we get back to Earth, I'll have you before the Central Committee of the G.A.A.S. That's a promise. You'll be de-professionalized."

Sheffield said, "I'm not afraid of the Galactic Association for the Advancement of Science." He let the syllables resound. "After all, what will you accuse me of? Are you going to play this recording before the Central Committee as evidence? Come, come, let's be friendly about this. You don't want to broadcast your own . . . uh . . . mistake before the primmest stuffed shirts in eighty-three thousand worlds."

Smiling gently, he backed out the door.

But when he closed the door between himself and Cimon, his smile vanished. He hadn't liked to do this. Now that he had done it, he wondered if it were worth the enemy he had made.

SEVEN tents had sprung up near the site of the original settlement on Junior. Nevile Fawkes could see them all from the low ridge on which he stood. They had been there seven days now.

He looked up at the sky. The clouds were thick overhead and pregnant with rain. That pleased him. With both suns behind those clouds, the diffused light was gray-white. It made things seem almost normal.

The wind was damp and a little raw, as though it were April in Vermont. Fawkes was a New Englander and he appreciated the resemblance. In four or five hours, Lagrange I would set and the clouds would turn ruddy while the landscape would become angrily dim. But Fawkes intended to be back in the tents by then.

So near the equator, yet so cool! Well, that would change with the millennia. As the glaciers retreated, the air would warm up and the soil would dry out. Jungles and deserts would make their appearance. The water level in the oceans would slowly creep higher, wiping out numberless islands. The two large rivers would become an inland sea, changing the configuration of Junior's one large continent; perhaps making several smaller ones out of it.

He wondered if the settlement site would be drowned. Probably, he decided. Maybe that would take the curse off it.

He could understand why the Confederation were so anxious to solve the mystery of that first settlement. Even if it were a simple matter of disease, there would have to be proof. Otherwise, who would settle the world? The "sucker bait" superstition held for more than merely spacemen.

He, himself—Well, his first visit to the settlement site hadn't been so bad, though he had been glad to leave the rain and the gloom. Returning was worse. It was difficult to sleep with the thought that a thousand mysterious deaths lay all about, separated from him only by that insubstantial thing, time.

With medical coolness, Novee had dug up the moldering graves of a dozen of the ancient settlers. (Fawkes could not and did not look at the remains.) There had been only crumbling bones, Novee had said, out of which nothing could be made.

"There seem to be abnormalities of bone deposition," he said.

Then on questioning, he admitted that the effects might be entirely owing to a hundred years' exposure to damp soil.

Fawkes had constructed a fantasy that followed him even into his waking hours. It concerned an elusive race of intelligent beings dwelling underground, never being seen but haunting that first settlement a century back with a deadly perseverance.

He pictured a silent bacteriological warfare. He could see them in laboratories beneath the tree roots, culturing their molds and spores, waiting for one that could live on human beings. Perhaps they captured children to experiment upon.

And when they found what they were looking for, spores drifted silently out over the settlement in venomous clouds—

Fawkes knew all this to be fantasy. He had made it up in the wakeful nights out of no evidence but that of his quivering stomach. Yet alone in the forest, he whirled more than once in a sudden horror-filled conviction that bright eyes were staring out of the duskiness of a tree's Lagrange I shadow.

Fawkes' botanist's eye did not miss the vegetation he

passed, absorbed as he was. He had deliberately struck out from camp in a new direction, but what he saw was what he had already seen. Junior's forests were neither thick nor tangled. They were scarcely a barrier to travel. The small trees—few were higher than ten feet, although their trunks were nearly as thick as the average Terrestrial tree—grew with considerable room between them.

Fawkes had constructed a rough scheme for arranging the plant-life of Junior into some sort of taxonomic order. He was not unaware of the fact that he might be arranging for his own immortality.

There was the scarlet "bayonet tree," for instance. Its huge, scarlet flowers attracted insectlike creatures that built small nests within it. Then—at what signal or what impulse Fawkes had not divined—all the flowers on some one given tree would grow a glistening white pistil over night. Each pistil stood two feet high, as though every bloom had been suddenly equipped with a bayonet.

By the next day, the flower had been fertilized, and the petals closed shut—about pistil, insects and all. The explorer, Makoyama, had named it the "bayonet tree," but Fawkes had made so bold as to rename it *Migrania Fawkesii.*

ONE thing the trees had in common. Their wood was incredibly tough. It would be the task of the biochemist to determine the physical state of the cellulose molecule and that of the biophysicist to determine how water could be transported through the wood's impervious texture. What Fawkes knew from experience was that blossoms would break if pulled, that stems would bend only with difficulty and break not at all. His pocketknife was blunted without as much as making a scratch.

The original settlers, in order to clear land, had obviously had to dig out the trees, root and all.

Compared to Earth, the woods were almost free of animal life. That might be due to the glacial slaughter. Fawkes didn't know.

The insectlike creatures were all two winged. And those wings were feathery little fronds that beat noiselessly. None, apparently, was a bloodsucker.

The only major experience with animals that they had had was the sudden appearance of a large flying creature over the camp. It took high-speed photography to reveal the actual shape of the beast, for the specimen they observed, apparently overcome with curiosity, swooped low over the tents, again and again, at speeds too great for comfortable, naked-eye observation.

It was four-winged, the forward wings terminating in powerful claws, being membranous and nearly naked, serving the office of gliding planes. The hind pair, covered with a hairlike fuzz, beat rapidly.

Rodriguez suggested the name *Tetrapierus.*

Fawkes paused in his reminiscence to look at a variety of grass he had not seen before. It grew in a dense patch and each stem forked in three toward the top. He brought out his magnifying glass, and felt one of the stems gingerly with his finger. Like other grasses on Junior, it—

It was here that he heard the rustle behind him—unmistakable. He listened for a moment, his own heartbeat drowning the sound, then whirled. A small manlike object dodged behind a tree.

Fawkes' breathing nearly stopped. He fumbled for the blaster he wore and his hand seemed to be moving through molasses.

Was his fantasy no fantasy at all? Was Junior inhabited after all?

Numbly, Fawkes found himself behind another tree. He couldn't leave it at this. He knew that. He could not report to the rest: I saw something alive. It might have been the answer to everything. But I was afraid and let it get away.

He would have to make some attempt.

There was a "chalice tree" just behind the tree that hid the creature. It was in bloom, the white and cream flowers lifted turgidly upward, waiting to catch the rain that would soon fall. There was the sharp tinkle of a breaking flower and cream slivers twisted and turned downward.

It wasn't imagination. Something *was* behind the tree.

Fawkes took a deep breath and dashed out, holding his blaster before him, nerving himself to shoot at the slightest sign of danger.

But a voice called out, "Don't. It's only I." A frightened, but definitely human face looked out from behind the tree.

It was Mark Annuncio.

Fawkes stopped in mid-stride and stared. Finally, he managed to croak, "What are you doing here?"

Mark said, staring at the blaster in the other's hand, "I was following you."

"Why?"

"To see what you would do. I was interested in what you might find. I thought if you saw me, you would send me away."

Fawkes became conscious of the weapon he was still holding and put it away. It took three tries to get it into the holster.

The first fat drops of rain began to fall. Fawkes said, harshly, "Don't say anything about this to the others."

He glared hostilely at the youngster and they walked back to camp separately and in silence.

A central hall of pre-fab had been added to the seven tents now, and the group was together within it, sitting about the long table.

It was a great moment, but a rather subdued one. Vernadsky, who had cooked for himself in his college days, was in charge. He lifted the steaming stew off the short-wave heater and said, "Calories, anyone?"

He ladled the stuff lavishly.

"It smells very good," said Novee, doubtfully.

He lifted a piece of meat with his fork. It was purplish and still felt tough despite internal heating. The shredded herbs that surrounded it seemed softer, but looked less edible.

"Well," said Vernadsky, "eat it. Put it in your mouth. I've tasted it and it's good."

He crammed his mouth and chewed. He kept on chewing. "Tough, but good."

Fawkes said, gloomily, "It'll probably kill us."

"Nuts," said Vernadsky. "The rats have been living on it for two weeks."

"Two weeks isn't much," said Novee.

Rodriguez said, "Well, one bite won't kill. Say, it *is* good."

And it was. They all agreed, eventually. So far, it seemed that whenever Junior's life could be eaten at all, it was good.

The grains were almost impossible to grind into flour, but that done, a protein-high cake could be baked. There was some on the table now; dark and heavy. It wasn't bad, either.

Fawkes had studied the herb life on Junior and come to the conclusion that an acre of Junior's surface, properly seeded and watered, could support ten times the number of grazing animals that an acre of Earthly alfalfa could.

Sheffield had been impressed; spoke of Junior as the granary of a hundred worlds, but Fawkes dismissed his own statements with a shrug.

He said, "Sucker bait."

About a week earlier, the party had been agitated by the sudden refusal of the hamsters and white rats to touch certain new herbs Fawkes had brought in. Mixing small quantities with regular rations had resulted in the death of those that fed on it.

Solution?

Not quite. Vernadsky came in a few hours later and said, calmly, "Copper, lead, and mercury."

"What?" said Cimon.

"Those plants. They're high in heavy metals. Probably an evolutionary development to keep from being eaten."

"The first settlers—" began Cimon.

"No. That's impossible. Most of the plants are perfectly all right. Just these, and no one would eat them."

"How do you know?"

"The rats didn't."

"They're just rats."

It was what Vernadsky was waiting for. He said, dramatically, "You may hail a modest martyr to science. I tasted the stuff."

"What?" yelled Novee.

"Just a lick. Don't worry. I'm the careful-type martyr. Anyway, the stuff is as bitter as strychnine. What do you expect? If a plant is going to fill itself with lead just to keep the animals off, what good does it do the plant to have the animal find out by dying after he's eaten it? A little bitter stuff in addition acts as a warning. The combination warning and punishment does the trick."

"Besides," said Novee, "it wasn't heavy metal poisoning that killed the settlers. The symptoms aren't right for it."

The rest knew the symptoms well enough. Some in lay terms and some in more technical language. Difficult and painful breathing that grew steadily worse. That's what it amounted to.

Fawkes put down his fork. "Look here, suppose this stuff contains some alkaloid that paralyzes the nerves that control the lung muscles."

"Rats have lung muscles," said Vernadsky. "It doesn't kill them."

"Maybe it's a cumulative thing."

"All right. All right. Any time your breathing gets painful, go back to ship rations and see if you improve. But no fair counting psychosomatics."

Sheffield grunted, "That's my job. Don't worry about it."

Fawkes drew a deep breath, then another. Glumly, he put another piece of meat into his mouth.

At one corner of the table, Mark Annuncio, eating more slowly than the rest, thought of Norris Vinograd's monograph on "Taste and Smell." Vinograd had made a taste-smell classification based on enzyme inhibition patterns within the taste buds. Annuncio did not know what that meant exactly but he remembered the symbols, their values, and the descriptive definitions.

While he placed the taste of the stew to three subclassifications, he finished his helping. His jaws ached faintly because of the difficult chewing.

EVENING was approaching and Lagrange I was low in the sky. It had been a bright day, reasonably warm, and Boris Vernadsky felt pleased. He had made interesting measurements and his brilliantly colored sweater had showed fascinating changes from hour to hour as the suns' positions shifted.

Right now, his shadow was a long red thing, with the lowest third of it gray, where the Lagrange II shadow coincided. He held out one arm and it cast two shadows. There was a smeared orange one some fifteen feet away and a denser blue one in the same direction but only five feet away. If he had time, he could work out a beautiful set of shadowgrams.

He was so pleased with the thought that he felt no resentment at seeing Mark Annuncio skirting his trail in the distance.

He put down his nucleometer and waved his hand. "Come here!"

The youngster approached diffidently. "Hello."

"Want something?"

"Just . . . just watching."

"Oh? Well, go ahead and watch. Do you know what I'm doing?"

Mark shook his head.

"This is a nucleometer," said Vernadsky. "You jab it into the ground like this. It's got a force-field generator at the top so it will penetrate any rock." He leaned on the nucleometer as he spoke, and it went two feet into the stony outcropping. "See?"

Mark's eyes shone, and Vernadsky felt pleased. The chemist said, "Along the sides of the uniped are microscopic atomic furnaces, each of which vaporizes about a million molecules or so in the surrounding rock and decomposes them into atoms. The atoms are then differentiated in terms of nuclear mass and charge and the results may be read off directly on the dials above. Do you follow all that?"

"I'm not sure. But it's a good thing to know."

Vernadsky smiled, and said, "We end up with figures on the different elements in the crust. It's pretty much the same on all oxygen/water planets."

Mark said, seriously, "The planet with the most silicon I know of is Lepta with 32.765 per cent. Earth is only 24.862. That's by weight."

Vernadsky's smile faded. He said, dryly, "You have the figures on all the planets, pal?"

"Oh, no. I couldn't. I don't think they've all been surveyed. Bischoon and Spenglow's 'Handbook of Planetary Crusts' only lists figures for twenty-one thousand eight hundred and fifty-four planets. I know all those, of course."

Vernadsky, with a definite feeling of deflation, said, "Now Junior has a more even distribution of elements than is usually met up with. Oxygen is low. So far my average is a lousy

42.113. So is silicon, with 22.722. The heavy metals are ten to a hundred times as concentrated as on Earth. That's not just a local phenomenon, either, since Junior's over-all density is five per cent higher than Earth's."

Vernadsky wasn't sure why he was telling the kid all this. Partly, he felt, because it was good to find someone who would listen. A man gets lonely and frustrated when there is no one of his own field to talk to.

He went on, beginning to relish the lecture. "On the other hand, the lighter elements are also better distributed. The ocean solids aren't predominantly sodium chloride as on Earth. Junior's oceans contain a respectable helping of magnesium salts. And take what they call the 'rare lights.' Those are the elements lithium, beryllium, and boron. They're lighter than carbon, all of them, but they are of very rare occurrence on Earth, and in fact, on all planets. Junior, on the other hand, is quite rich in them. The three of them total almost four-tenths of a per cent of the crust as compared to about four-thousandths on Earth."

Mark plucked at the other's sleeve. "Do you have a list of figures on all the elements? May I see?"

"I suppose so." He took a folded piece of paper out of his hip-pocket.

He grinned as Mark took the sheet and said, "Don't publish those figures before I do."

Mark glanced at them once and returned the paper.

"Are you through?" asked Vernadsky in surprise.

"Oh, yes," said Mark, thoughtfully, "I have it all." He turned on his heel and walked away with no word of parting.

The last glimmer of Lagrange I faded below the horizon.

Vernadsky gazed after Mark and shrugged. He plucked his nucleometer out of the ground, and followed after, walking back toward the tents.

SHEFFIELD was moderately pleased. Mark had been doing better than expected. To be sure, he scarcely talked but that was not very serious. At least, he showed interest and didn't sulk. And he threw no tantrums.

Vernadsky was even telling Sheffield that last evening Mark had spoken to him quite normally, without raised voices on either side, about planetary crust analyses. Vernadsky had laughed a bit about it, saying that Mark knew the crust analyses of twenty thousand planets and some day he'd have the boy repeat them all just to see how long it would take.

Mark, himself, had made no mention of the matter. In fact, he had spent the morning sitting in his tent. Sheffield had looked in, seen him on his cot, staring at his feet, and had left him to himself.

What he really needed at the moment, Sheffield felt, was a bright idea for himself—a really bright one.

So far, everything had come to nothing—a whole month of everything. Rodriguez held fast against any infection. Vernadsky absolutely barred food poisoning. Novee shook his head with vehement negativeness at suggestions of disturbed metabolism. "Where's the evidence?" he kept saying.

What it amounted to was that every physical cause of death was eliminated on the strength of expert opinion. But men, women, and children had died. There must be a reason. Could it be psychological?

He had satirized the matter to Cimon for a purpose before they had come out here, but it was now time and more than time to be serious about it. Could the settlers have been driven to suicide? Why? Humanity had colonized tens of thousands of planets without its having seriously affected mental stability. In fact, the suicide rate, as well as the incidence of psychoses, were higher on Earth than anywhere else in the galaxy.

Besides, the settlement had called frantically for medical help. They didn't want to die.

Personality disorders? Something peculiar to that one group? Enough to affect over a thousand people to the death? Unlikely. Besides, how could any evidence be uncovered? The settlement site had been ransacked for any films or records, even the most frivolous. Nothing. A century of dampness left nothing so fragile as purposeful records.

So he was working in a vacuum. He felt helpless. The others, at least, had data; something to chew on. He had nothing.

He found himself at Mark's tent again and looked inside automatically. It was empty. He looked about and spied Mark walking out of the camp and into the woods.

Sheffield cried out after him, "Mark! Wait for me!"

Mark stopped, made as though to go on, thought better of it, and let Sheffield's long legs consume the distance between them.

Sheffield said, "Where are you off to?" (Even after running, it was unnecessary to pant in Junior's rich atmosphere.)

Mark's eyes were sullen. "To the air-coaster."

"Oh?"

"I haven't had a chance to look at it."

"Why, of course you've had a chance," said Sheffield. "You were watching Fawkes like a hawk on the trip over."

Mark scowled. "Everyone was around. I want to see it for myself."

Sheffield felt disturbed. The kid was angry. He'd better tag along and try to find out what was wrong. He said, "Come to think of it, I'd like to see the coaster myself. You don't mind having me along, do you?"

Mark hesitated. Then he said, "We-ell. If you want to." It wasn't exactly a gracious invitation.

Sheffield said, "What are you carrying, Mark?"

"Tree branch. I cut it off with the buzz-field gun. I'm taking it with me just in case anyone wants to stop me." He swung it so that it whistled through the thick air.

"Why should anyone want to stop you, Mark? I'd throw it away. It's hard and heavy. You could hurt someone."

Mark was striding on. "I'm not throwing it away."

Sheffield pondered briefly, then decided against a quarrel at the moment. It would be better to get to the basic reason for this hostility first. "All right," he said.

The air-coaster lay in a clearing, its clear metal surface throwing back green highlights. (Lagrange II had not yet risen.)

Mark looked carefully about.

"There's no one in sight, Mark," said Sheffield.

They climbed aboard. It was a large coaster. It had carried seven men and the necessary supplies in only three trips.

Sheffield looked at its control panel with something quite close to awe. He said, "Imagine a botanist like Fawkes learning to run one of these things. It's so far outside his specialty."

"I can run one," said Mark, suddenly.

Sheffield stared at him in surprise. "You can?"

"I watched Dr. Fawkes when we came. I know everything he did. And he has a repair manual for the coaster. I sneaked that out once and read it."

Sheffield said lightly, "Well, that's very nice. We have a spare navigator for an emergency, then."

He turned away from Mark then, so he never saw the tree limb as it came down on his head. He didn't hear Mark's troubled voice saying, "I'm sorry, Dr. Sheffield." He didn't even, properly speaking, feel the concussion that knocked him out.

IT was the jar of the coaster's landing, Sheffield later thought, that first brought consciousness back. It was a dim aching sort of thing that had no understanding in it at first.

The sound of Mark's voice was floating up to him. That was his first sensation. Then as he tried to roll over and get a knee beneath him, he could feel his head throbbing.

For a while, Mark's voice was only a collection of sounds that meant nothing to him. Then they began to coalesce into words. Finally, when his eyes fluttered open and light entered stabbingly so that he had to close them again, he could make out sentences. He remained where he was, head hanging, one quivering knee holding him up.

Mark was saying in a breathless, high-pitched voice, ". . . A thousand people all dead. Just graves. And nobody knows why."

There was a rumble Sheffield couldn't make out. A hoarse deep voice.

Then Mark again, "It's true. Why do you suppose all the scientists are aboard?"

Sheffield lifted achingly to his feet and rested against one wall. He put his hand to his head and it came away bloody. His hair was caked and matted with it. Groaning, he staggered toward the coaster's cabin door. He fumbled for the hook and yanked it inward.

The landing ramp had been lowered. For a moment, he stood there, swaying, afraid to trust his legs.

He had to take in everything by installments. Both suns were high in the sky and a thousand feet away, the giant steel cylinder of the *Triple G* reared its nose high above the runty trees that ringed it.

Mark was at the foot of the ramp, semicircled by members of the crew. The crewmen were stripped to the waist and browned nearly black in the ultraviolet of Lagrange I. (Thanks only to the thick atmosphere and the heavy ozone coating in the upper reaches for keeping UV down to a livable range.)

The crewman directly before Mark was leaning on a baseball bat. Another tossed a ball in the air and caught it. Many of the rest were wearing gloves.

"Funny," thought Sheffield, erratically, "Mark landed right in the middle of a ball park."

Mark looked up and saw him. He screamed, excitedly, "All right, ask him. Go ahead, ask him. Dr. Sheffield, wasn't there an expedition to this planet once and they all died mysteriously?"

Sheffield tried to say: Mark, what are you doing? He couldn't. When he opened his mouth only a moan came out.

The crewman with the bat said, "Is this little gumboil telling the truth, mister?"

Sheffield held on to the railing with two perspiring hands. The crewman's face seemed to waver. The face had thick lips on it and small eyes buried under bristly eyebrows. It wavered very badly.

Then the ramp came up and whirled about his head. There was ground gripped in his hands suddenly and a cold ache on his cheekbone. He gave up the fight and let go of consciousness again.

HE came awake less painfully the second time. He was in bed now and two misty faces leaned over him. A long, thin object passed across his line of vision and a voice, just heard above the humming in his ears, said, "He'll come to now, Cimon."

Sheffield closed his eyes. Somehow he seemed to be aware of the fact that his skull was thoroughly bandaged.

He lay quietly for a minute, breathing deeply. When he opened his eyes again, the faces above him were clear. There was Novee's round face, a small, professionally-serious line between his eyes that cleared away when Sheffield said, "Hello, Novee."

The other man was Cimon, jaws set and angry, yet with a look of something like satisfaction in his eyes.

Sheffield said, "Where are we?"

Cimon said, coldly, "In space, Dr. Sheffield. Two days out in space."

"Two days, out—" Sheffield's eyes widened and he tried to rise.

Novee interposed. "You've had a bad concussion, nearly a fracture, Sheffield. Take it easy."

"Well, what hap—Where's Mark? *Where's Mark?*"

"Easy. Easy now." Novee put a hand on each of Sheffield's shoulders and pressed him down.

Cimon said, "Your boy is in the brig. In case you want to know why, he deliberately caused mutiny on board ship, thus endangering the safety of five men. We were almost marooned at our temporary camp, because the crew wanted to leave immediately. He persuaded them, the captain did, to pick us up."

Sheffield remembered now, very vaguely. There was just that fuzzy memory of Mark and a man with a bat. Mark saying ". . . A thousand people all dead—"

The psychologist hitched himself up on one elbow with a tremendous effort. "Listen, Cimon, I don't know why Mark did it, but let me talk to him. I'll find out."

Cimon said, "No need of that. It will all come out at the trial."

Sheffield tried to brush Novee's restraining arm to one side. "But why make it formal? Why involve the Bureau? We can settle this among ourselves."

"That's exactly what we intend to do. The captain is empowered by the laws of space to preside over trials involving crimes and misdemeanors in deep space."

"The captain. A trial here? On board ship? Cimon, don't let him do it. It will be murder."

"Not at all. It will be a fair and proper trial. I'm in full agreement with the captain. Discipline demands a trial."

Novee said, uneasily, "Look, Cimon, I wish you wouldn't. He's in no shape to take this."

"Too bad," said Cimon.

Sheffield said, "But you don't understand. I'm responsible for the boy."

"On the contrary, I do understand," said Cimon. "It's why we've been waiting for you to regain consciousness. You're standing trial with him."

"What!"

"You are generally responsible for his actions. Specifically, you were with him when he stole the air-coaster. The crew saw you at the coaster's cabin door while Mark was inciting mutiny."

"But he cracked my skull in order to take the coaster. Can't you see that's the act of a seriously disturbed mind? He can't be held responsible."

"We'll let the captain decide, Sheffield. You stay with him, Novee." He turned to go.

Sheffield called on what strength he could muster. "Cimon," he shouted, "you're doing this to get back at me for the lesson in psychology I taught you. You're a narrow . . . petty—"

He fell back on his pillow, breathless.

Cimon, from the door, said, "And by the way, Sheffield, the penalty for inciting mutiny on board ship is death!"

WELL, it was a *kind* of trial, Sheffield thought grimly. Nobody was following accurate legal procedure, but then, the psychologist felt certain, no one knew the accurate legal procedure, least of all the captain.

They were using the large assembly room where, on ordinary cruises, the crew got together to watch subetheric broadcasts. At this time, the crew was rigidly excluded, though all the scientific personnel were present.

Captain Follenbee sat behind a desk just underneath the subetheric reception cube. Sheffield and Mark Annuncio sat by themselves at his left, faces toward him.

The captain was not at ease. He alternated between informal exchanges with the various "witnesses" and sudden super-judicial blasts against whispering among the spectators.

Sheffield and Mark, having met one another in the "courtroom" for the first time since the flight of the air-coaster, shook hands solemnly on the former's initiative. Mark had hung back at first, looking up briefly at the crisscross of tape still present on the shaven patch on Sheffield's skull.

"I'm sorry, Dr. Sheffield. I'm very sorry."

"It's all right, Mark. How have they been treating you?"

"All right, I guess."

The captain's voice boomed out, "No talking among the accused."

Sheffield retorted in a conversational tone, "Listen, captain, we haven't had lawyers. We haven't had time to prepare a case."

"No lawyers necessary," said the captain. "This isn't a court trial on Earth. Captain's investigation. Different thing. Just interested in facts, not legal fireworks. Proceedings can be reviewed back on Earth."

"And we can be dead by then," said Sheffield, hotly.

"Let's get on with it," said the captain, banging his desk with an aluminum T-wedge.

Cimon sat in the front row of the audience, smiling thinly. It was he that Sheffield watched most uneasily.

The smile never varied as witnesses were called upon to state that they had been informed that the crew was on no account to be told of the true nature of the trip; that Sheffield and Mark had been present when told. A mycologist testified to a conversation he had had with Sheffield which indicated the latter to be well aware of the prohibition.

It was brought out that Mark had been sick for most of the trip out to Junior, that he had behaved erratically after they had landed on Junior.

"How do you explain all that?" asked the captain.

From the audience, Cimon's calm voice suddenly sounded. "He was frightened. He was willing to do anything that would get him off the planet."

Sheffield sprang to his feet. "His remarks are out of order. He's not a witness."

The captain banged his T-wedge and said, "Sit down!"

The trial went on. A crew member was called in to testify that Mark had informed him of the first expedition and that Sheffield had stood by while that was done.

Sheffield cried, "I want to cross-examine!"

The captain said, "You'll get your chance later."

The crewman was shooed out.

SHEFFIELD studied the audience. It seemed obvious that their sympathy was not entirely with the captain. He was psychologist enough to be able to wonder, even at this point, how many of them were secretly relieved at having left Junior, and actually grateful to Mark for having precipitated the matter as he did. Then, too, the obvious kangaroo nature of the court didn't sit well with them. Vernadsky was frowning darkly, while Novee stared at Cimon with obvious distaste.

It was Cimon who worried Sheffield. He, the psychologist felt, must have argued the captain into this and it was he who might insist on the extreme penalty. Sheffield was bitterly regretful of having punctured the man's pathological vanity.

But what really puzzled Sheffield above all was Mark's attitude. He was showing no signs of spacesickness or of unease of any kind. He listened to everything closely but seemed moved by nothing. He acted as though nothing mundane concerned him at the moment; as though certain information he himself held made everything else of no account.

The captain banged his T-wedge and said, "I guess we have it all. Facts all clear. No argument. We can finish this."

Sheffield jumped up again. "Hold on. Aren't we getting our turn?"

"Quiet," ordered the captain.

"*You* keep quiet." Sheffield turned to the audience. "Listen, we haven't had a chance to defend ourselves. We haven't even had the right to cross-examine. Is that just?"

There was a murmur that buzzed up above the sound of the T-wedge.

Cimon said, coldly, "What's there to defend?"

"Maybe nothing," shouted back Sheffield, "in which case what have you to lose by hearing us? Or are you afraid we have considerable to defend?"

Individual calls from the audience were sounding now. "Let him talk!"

Cimon shrugged. "Go ahead."

The captain said, sullenly, "What do you want to do?"

Sheffield said, "Act as my own lawyer and call Mark Annuncio as my principal witness."

Mark stood up, calmly enough. Sheffield turned his chair to face the audience and motioned him down again.

Sheffield decided there was no use in trying to imitate the courtroom dramas he had watched on the subether. Pompous questions on name and condition of past life would get nowhere. Better to be direct.

So he said, "Mark, did you know what would happen when you told the crew about the first expedition?"

"Yes, Dr. Sheffield."

"Why did you do it then?"

"Because it was important that we all get away from Junior without losing a minute. Telling the crew the truth was the fastest way of getting us off the planet."

Sheffield could feel the bad impression that answer made on the audience, but he could only follow his instinct. That, and his psychologist's decision that only special knowledge could make Mark or any Mnemonic so calm in the face of adversity. After all, special knowledge was their business.

He said, "Why was it important to leave Junior, Mark?"

Mark didn't flinch. He looked straight at the watching scientists. "Because I know what killed the first expedition, and it was only a question of time before it killed us. In fact, it may be too late already. We may be dying now. We may, every one of us, be dead men."

Sheffield let the murmur from the audience well up and subside. Even the captain seemed shocked into T-wedge immobility while Cimon's smile grew quite faint.

For the moment, Sheffield was less concerned with Mark's "knowledge," whatever it was, than that he had acted independently on the basis of it. It had happened before. Mark had searched the ship's log on the basis of a theory of his own. Sheffield felt pure chagrin at not having probed that tendency to the uttermost then and there.

So his next question, asked in a grim enough voice, was, "Why didn't you consult me about this, Mark?"

Mark faltered a trifle. "You wouldn't have believed me. It's why I had to hit you to keep you from stopping me. None of them would have believed me. They all hated me."

"What makes you think they hated you?"

"Well, you remember about Dr. Rodriguez."

"That was quite a while ago. The others had no arguments with you."

"I could tell the way Dr. Cimon looked at me. And Dr. Fawkes wanted to shoot me with a blaster."

"What?" Sheffield whirled, forgetting in his own turn any formality due the trial. "Say, Fawkes, did you try to shoot him?"

Fawkes stood up, face crimson, as all turned to look at him. He said, "I was out in the woods and he came sneaking up on me. I thought it was an animal and took precautions. When I saw it was he, I put the blaster away."

Sheffield turned back to Mark. "Is that right?"

Mark turned sullen again. "Well—I asked Dr. Vernadsky to see some data he had collected and he told me not to publish it before he did. He tried to make out that I was dishonest."

"For the love of Earth, I was only joking," came a yell from the audience.

Sheffield said, hurriedly, "Very well, Mark, you didn't trust us and you felt you had to take action on your own. Now, Mark, let's get to the point. What did you think killed the first settlers?"

Mark said, "It might have killed the explorer Makoyama, too, for all I know except that he died in a crash two months and three days after reporting on Junior, so we'll never know."

"All right, but what is it you're talking about?"

A hush fell over everyone.

Mark looked about and said, "The dust."

Sheffield said, "What do you mean?"

"The dust! The dust in the air. It has beryllium in it. Ask Dr. Vernadsky."

Vernadsky stood up and pushed his way forward. "What's this?"

"Sure," said Mark. "It was in the data you showed me. Beryllium was very high in the crust, so it must be in the dust in the air as well."

Sheffield said, "What if beryllium is there? Let me ask the questions, Vernadsky. Please."

"Beryllium poisoning, that's what. If you breathe beryllium

dust, non-healing granulomata, whatever they are, form in the lungs. Anyway, it gets hard to breathe and then you die."

A new voice, quite agitated, joined the melee. "What are you talking about? You're no physician."

"I know that," said Mark, earnestly, "but I once read a very old book about poisons. It was so old, it was printed on actual sheets of paper. The library had some and I went through them, because it was such a novelty, you know."

"All right," said Novee, "what did you read? Can you tell me?"

Mark's chin lifted, "I can quote it. Word for word. 'A surprising variety of enzymatic reactions in the body are activated by any of a number of divalent metallic ions of similar ionic radius. Among these activators are magnesium, manganous zinc, ferrous, cobaltous, and nickelous ions, as well as others. Against all of these, the beryllium ion, which has a similar charge and size, acts as an inhibitor. Beryllium, therefore, serves to derange a number of enzyme-catalyzed reactions. Since the lungs have, apparently, no way of excreting beryllium, diverse metabolic derangements causing serious illness and death can result from inhaling dust containing certain beryllium salts. Cases exist in which one known exposure has resulted in death. The onset of symptoms is insidious, being delayed sometimes for as long as three years after exposure. Prognosis is not good.' "

The captain leaned forward in agitation. "Novee, is he making sense?"

Novee said, "I don't know if he's right or not, but there's nothing absurd in what he's saying."

Sheffield said sharply, "You mean you don't know if beryllium is poisonous or not."

"No, I don't," said Novee.

"Isn't beryllium used for anything?" Sheffield turned to Vernadsky. "Is it?"

Vernadsky said in vast surprise, "No, it isn't. Damn it, I can't think of a single use. I tell you what, though. In the early days of atomic power, it was used in the primitive uranium piles as a neutron decelerator, along with other things like paraffin and graphite. I'm almost sure of that."

"It isn't used now, though?" asked Sheffield.

"No."

An electronics man said, quite suddenly, "I think beryllium-zinc coatings were used in the first fluorescent lights."

"No more, though?" asked Sheffield.

"No."

Sheffield said, "Well, then, listen, all of you. In the first place, anything Mark quotes is accurate. That's what the book said, if he says so. It's my opinion that beryllium *is* poisonous. In ordinary life it doesn't matter because the beryllium content of the soil is so low. When man concentrates beryllium to use in nuclear piles or in fluorescent lights or even in alloys, he comes across the toxicity and looks for substitutes.

"He finds substitutes, forgets about beryllium, and eventually forgets about its toxicity. And then we come across an unusual beryllium-rich planet like Junior and we can't figure out what hits us. It takes a Mnemonic to remember the old, forgotten data."

Cimon didn't seem to be listening. He said, in a low voice, "What does that mean, 'prognosis is not good'?"

Novee said, abstractedly, "It means that if you've got beryllium poisoning, you won't recover."

Cimon fell back in his chair, chewing his lip.

Novee said to Mark, "I suppose the symptoms of beryllium poisoning—"

Mark said at once, "I can give you the full list. I don't understand the words but—"

"Was one of them 'dyspnea'?"

"Yes."

Novee sighed and said, "I say that we get back to Earth as quickly as possible and get under medical investigation."

Cimon said, weakly, "But if we won't recover, what use is it?"

Novee said, "Medical science has advanced since the days of books printed on paper. Besides, we may not have received the toxic dose. The first settlers survived for over a year of continuous exposure. We've had only a month, thanks to Mark Annuncio's quick and drastic action."

Fawkes, miserably unhappy, yelled, "Captain, get us back to Earth."

It amounted to the end of the trial. Sheffield and Mark walked out among the first.

Cimon was the last, with the gait of a man already dead in all but fact.

THE Lagrange system was only a star lost in the receding cluster. Sheffield looked at that large patch of light and said, "So beautiful a planet." He sighed. "Well, let's hope we live. In any case, the government will watch out for beryllium-high planets in the future. There'll be no catching mankind with that particular variety of sucker bait any more."

Mark did not respond to that idealism. The trial was over; the excitement was gone. There were tears in his eyes. He could only think that he might die; and that if he did, there were so many things, so many, many things in the universe that he would never learn.

The Stolen Dormouse

By L. Sprague de Camp

THE riot started during the Los Angeles Radio Exposition, in the third week of February, 2236. The foresighted managers of the Exposition had put the Crosley and Stromberg exhibits as far apart as possible. But they could not prevent the members of these companies from meeting occasionally.

Thus, on the day in question, His Integrity, Billiam Bickham-Smith, chairman of Stromberg, had passed into the recesses of the Stromberg booth, leaving a froth of lesser nobility and whitecollars in his wake, when a couple of Crosley whitecollars dropped an injudicious remark within hearing.

A Stromberg whitecollar said to one of these stiffly: "Did I hear you say our prefab houses leaked, sir?"

"You did, sir," replied one of the Crosleys evenly.

"Are you picking a fight with me, sir?" The Stromberg fingered his duelling stick.

"I am not. I am merely stating a fact, sir."

"Slandering our product is the same as picking a fight, sir."

"When I state a fact I state a fact, sir. Good day." The Crosley turned his back.

The Stromberg's stick hissed through the air and whacked the Crosley's skull. The Crosley's skull gave forth a muffled clang, whereupon the Stromberg knew that his enemy wore a steel cap disguised by a wig.

Now, no member of the nobility would have hit an enemy from behind. But the Stromberg was a mere low-born whitecollar, which somewhat excused his action in the eyes of his contemporaries.

The Crosley who had been hit, shrieked "Foul!" and broke his assailant's nose with a neat backhand. Strombergs boiled out of the exhibit, pulling on padded gloves and duelling goggles.

At that instant, Horace Crosley Juniper-Hallett passed on his way to the Crosley booth to take up his outhanding for the day. His job was to pass out catalogues, printed in bright colors on slick paper, describing the Crosley exhibits, and also the many commodities other than radios, such as automobiles and microscopes, manufactured by this "radio" company. Exhibit-goers, unable to resist the lure of something for nothing, would collect up to twenty pounds of these brochures in the course of their visit, and like as not, drop them in a heap beside the gate on their way out. Horace Juniper-Hallett himself was of medium height and slim—skinny, if you want the brutal truth. His complexion was fair and his hair pale blond. He had twice given up trying to grow a mustache; after a month of trying, nobody could see the results of his cultivation except himself. Take a good look at him, for this ineffectual-looking youth is our hero.

As he was barely twenty-two, and not too mature for his age, his behavior patterns had not yet hardened in the mold of experience. Just now, of the several conflicting impulses that seized him, that of playing peacemaker was uppermost. He ran up and pulled the nearest of the embattled partisans back. His eye caught that of Justin Lane-Walsh, heir to the Stromberg vice-presidential chair. He shouted: "Here, you, help me separate 'em!"

"Bah!" roared the heir to the vice presidency. "I hate all Crosleys, 'specially you. Defend yourself!" And he advanced, whirling his duelling stick around his head. He and Juniper-Hallett were whacking away merrily, as were all the other members of the feuding companies in sight, when the police arrived.

A DUELLING stick, whose weight is regulated by the conventions, is no match for a three-foot nightstick. When the clatter had died down, and the physicians were doing emergency repairs on assorted skulls, collar bones, and so forth, the chief of police summoned the chairmen of the rival houses.

Billiam Bickham-Smith of Stromberg and Archwin Taylor-Thing of Crosley appeared, glaring.

"Aw right," said the chief. "I warned you 'bout this here feudin'. I said, the next time they's a scrap in a public place, I'd close up your show. I wouldn't say a word if you'd fight your duels out in the hills somewhere. But I got to proteck the innocent bystanders."

The chief of police was a small, sallow man. He wore the blue tunic of officialdom, with a shield bearing the motto of the Corporate State: *Alle was nicht Pflicht ist, ist verboten*—"All that is not compulsory is forbidden." His trouser legs were gayly colored, in different patterns: one that of the American Empire, the other that of Los Angeles, the capital.

Archwin of Crosley looked through the head of the rival house as though Billiam of Stromberg were not there. He said to the chief: "You can't expect my men to submit to unprovoked assault. Unprovoked assault."

"Unprovoked!" snorted Billiam of Stromberg. "My lord chief, I've got all the witnesses you want that egghead's men struck first."

"What?" yelled Archwin of Crosley. "Where's my stick?"

Whereas, Billiam of Stromberg had a beautiful head of silky white hair, Archwin of Crosley had no hair at all. He was sensitive to references to this fact.

"Won't do you no good to start a fight here," said the chief. "I'm going to close you up. I represent the plain citizens of Los Angeles, and we don't want no feudin' in the city limits. The Imperial Board of Control will back me up, too."

"Vulgar rabble," muttered Billiam of Stromberg.

"Have to travel all day to get out of the limits of *this* city," growled Archwin of Crosley.

The chairmen subsided, looking unhappy. They did not want the Exposition closed; neither, really, did the chief of police. Aside from the dangers of antagonizing two of the noblest clans of the American Empire, there was the loss of business.

He let them think for half a minute, then said: "Course, if you'd agree to discipline your men hard enough next time there's a fight, maybe we could let the show go on."

"I'll go as far as *that* old goat will," said Archwin of Crosley.

"What's your plan?" asked Billiam of Stromberg, controlling himself with visible effort.

"This," said the chief. "Any man who gets in a scrap gets degraded, if he belongs to one of the orders, and read out of his company."

The chairmen looked startled. This was drastic. Billiam Bickham-Smith asked: "Even if he's of the rank of executive?"

"Even if he's of the rank of entrepreneur."

"Whew!" That was little short of sacrilege.

Archwin of Crosley asked: "Even if he's the innocent party?"

"Even if he's the innocent party. 'Count of both of 'em would claim they was innocent, and the only thing we could do would be give 'em a trial by liedetector, and everybody knows how to beat the liedetector nowadays. Do you agree on your honor as an entrepreneur, Lord Archwin?"

"I agree."

"You, Your Integrity of Stromberg?"

"Uh-huh."

BACK at the Crosley exhibit, Archwin Taylor-Thing searched out Horace Juniper-Hallett. His Integrity's eye had the sparkle of one who bears devastatingly good news.

He said: "Horace, that was a fine piece of work you did this morning. A fine piece of work. That was just the right course to follow; just the right course. Try to prevent trouble, but if your honor's attacked, give back better than you get. I've had my eye on you for some time. But, until today, you minded your own affairs and didn't do anything to businessman you for." The chairman raised his voice: "Come gather round, all you loyal Crosleys. Gimme a stick, somebody. Thanks. Kneel, Whitecollar Juniper-Hallett." He tapped Juniper-Hallett on the shoulder and said: "Rise, Horace Juniper-Hallett, Esquire. You are now of the rank of businessman, with all the privileges and responsibilities of that honorable rank. I hereby present to you the gold-inlaid fountain pen and the brief case that are the insignia of your new status. Guard them with your life."

It was over. The Crosleys crowded around, slapping Juniper-Hallett's back and wringing his hand. Dimly, he heard Lord Archwin's voice telling him he could have the rest of the day off.

Then he was instructing a still younger whitecollar, Wilmot Dunn-Terry, in the duties of the outhander. "You encourage 'em to take one of each of the catalogues," he said, "but not more than one. Some of these birds'll try to walk off with half a dozen of each, just because they're free." He lowered his voice. "Along around fifteen o'clock, your feet will begin to hurt. If there's a lull in the business, look around carefully to see that none of the nobles is in sight, and sit down. But don't stay sat long, and don't get to reading or talking. Keep your eyes open for visitors and nobles, especially nobles. Got it?"

Dunn-Terry grinned at him. "Thanks, Horace. Can I still call you Horace, now that you're a businessman and all? Say, what's this about the theft of a dormouse from Sleepers' Crypt?"

"Huh? I haven't heard. Haven't seen a paper this morning."

"One of 'em's disappeared," said Dunn-Terry. "I overheard some of the nobility talking about it. They sounded all worked up. There was some talk about the Hawaiians, too."

Juniper-Hallett shrugged. His head was too full of his recent good fortune to pay much attention. The clock hands reached ten; the gates opened; the visitors started to trickle in. A still slightly dazed Horace Juniper-Hallett wandered off.

His hand still tingled from the squeezing it had received. He wondered what on earth he had done to deserve his elevation to businessmanhood. He was young for the rank, he knew. True, he was of noble blood on his mother's side, but Archwin of Crosley had the reputation of leaning over backward to avoid favoring members of the ruling class in dealing out businessmanhoods; he had even been known to elevate proletarians.

What Juniper-Hallett did not know was that the chairman was trying to build him up as a possible heir to the presidency. His Acumen, the president of Crosley, was getting on; he had two sons, one a moron and the other a young hellion. Next in line, by relationship, was Juniper-Hallett himself. Though, as the relationship was remote, and Juniper-Hallett was of noble blood on his mother's side only, he had not given the prospect any thought. His Acumen, the president, father of the precious pair of misfits, did not know the chairman's plans, either.

JUNIPER-HALLETT, in his happy daze, noted casually the scowls of the Stromberg whitecollars. But the brief case and the fancy fountain pen in his breast pocket gave him the feeling that the hostility of such rabble could no longer affect him.

Then he saw a girl. The daze cleared instantly, to be replaced by one of pinkish hue. She was a stunning brunette, and she wore the Stromberg colors of green, brown, and yellow. She was leaning against part of one of the Stromberg booths. Juniper-Hallett had seen her picture, and knew she was the daughter of His Integrity Billiam Bickham-Smith, chairman of Stromberg. Her name was Janet Bickham-Coates, "Coates" being her mother's father's family name.

Juniper-Hallett stood very still, listening to the blood pounding in his ears, and looking, not at the girl, but at a point three meters to the left of her. He ran over what he knew of her —she was just about his age; went in for sports—

He was determined to do something about her. At the moment, he could not think what. If the Strombergs had been friendly, it would have been simple; some of them undoubtedly knew her to speak to. But as things were, she'd probably be no more ingratiated by the sight of the Crosley colors—a blue-and-yellow-striped coat and red pants—than the rest of them.

Nor would it be simple to get a suit of Stromberg colors. First, the obligations of businessmanhood forbade it. Second, the salesman in the clothing department of the drugstore would make you identify yourself. He'd want no trouble with the genuine Strombergs for having sold a suit of their colors to an outsider.

And the Strombergs were throwing a big dinner that night.

Justin Lane-Walsh appeared. He put his hat on his head of copper-wire curls and walked past Juniper-Hallett. He slowed down as he passed, growling: "If it weren't for the old man's orders, you dirty Crosley, I'd finish what we started, sir."

Juniper-Hallett fell into step beside him. "I'm sorry I can't oblige you, you dirty Stromberg. I'd like nothing better, sir."

"I'm sorry, too. Don't know what we can do about it."

Juniper-Hallett felt an idea coming. He said: "Let's grab some lunch, and then go somewhere and drink to our mutual sorrow."

"By the great god Service, that's an idea!" Lane-Walsh looked down at his enemy with an almost friendly expression. "Come along, sister."

"Coming, you big louse." They went.

"SIR," said Lane-Walsh over his third drink, "I can just imagine my stick crunching through that baby face of yours. Swell thought, huh?"

"I don't know," said Juniper-Hallett. He winced every time Lane-Walsh made a crack like that about his looks. But he was learning, somewhat late in life, not to let such taunts drive him into a fury. "I find the idea of knocking those big ears loose a lot nicer. Why do all Strombergs have ears that stick out?"

Lane-Walsh shrugged. "Why are all Crosleys baby-faced shrimps?"

"I wouldn't call Lord Archwin baby-faced," said Juniper-Hallett judiciously. "Any baby with a face like his would probably scare its parents to death."

"That's so. Maybe I judge the rest of 'em by you. Well," he held up his glass, "here's to an early and bloody settlement of our differences."

"Right," said Juniper-Hallett. "May the worst man get all his teeth knocked out. Look, Justin old scum, what have you heard about the stealing of a dormouse from the Crypt?"

Lane-Walsh's face went elaborately blank. "Not a thing, sister, not a thing."

"I heard the Hawaiians might be mixed up in it."

"Might be," said Lane-Walsh. "The dormouse that was stolen, a guy named Arnold Ryan, was half Hawaiian, they say."

"He must date back to the days of single surnames. Wasn't he the original inventor of hibernine?"

"He—" Lane-Walsh's face went through a perfect double-take, as he realized that he had fallen over his own mental feet. He covered his confusion with a big gulp of rye-and-soda. Then he said: "You never know what those devilish Hawaiians are up to. Loafers, pirates, blasphemers against the good god Service. They've stopped another shipment of tungsten from New Caledonia."

"Sure," said Juniper-Hallett. "But about this dormouse Ryan, whom you just said you didn't know anything about—"

"I said I didn't *know,"* said Lane-Walsh angrily. "I may have *heard* a few things. Now, I say these Hawaiians ought to be wiped out. What's the matter with our admirals? Scared of a few flying torpedoes? I—"

"Pipe down," said Juniper-Hallett.

Lane-Walsh saw that he was attracting attention, and lowered his brassy voice. "Right. Say, I'll be getting drunk at this rate. And I've got to be at the speakers' table tonight."

Juniper-Hallett smiled. "I'm an A. C. member. How about dropping in there for a steam bath and a rubdown?"

"Swell. You really take exercise and everything? You'll be a man before your mother, sir."

"Yep. One of these days I'll pull your neck out by the roots and tie it in knots, Your Loyalty."

"O. K., if you can do it. Makes me almost wish you were a human being instead of a stinking Crosley. Let's go."

JUNIPER-HALLETT took a steam bath with his enemy, wishing that he, too, had a set of muscles like the tires of a transcontinental bus. Years of conscientious weight-lifting and other, equally dull, exercise had hardened Juniper-Hallett's stringy muscles until he was much stronger than he looked. But still he was not satisfied. Every bathing suit advertisement roused his inferiority complex.

He said to Justin Lane-Walsh: "About that dormouse—"

"Oh, forget the dormouse," said Lane-Walsh. "You know as

much about him as I do. As I understand it, he's not due to wake up for another fifty years, so whoever's stolen him is welcome to him."

"But suppose somebody's found a way of rousing a man from a hibernine trance—"

"Bunk. They've tried over and over again, and all they accomplished was killing a few dormice. Shut up, sister, and let me enjoy the steam."

Juniper-Hallett was too angry to say anything. But the heat soon sweated his sulks out of him, and he put his mind on the problem of the stunning brunette. When he spoke to Lane-Walsh again, it was to extol the abilities of a masseur named Gustav. Lane-Walsh bit.

While Gustav was sinking his thumbs up to the second joint in Lane-Walsh's tortured muscles, Horace Juniper-Hallett calmly dressed, put Lane-Walsh's coat and pants in his new brief case, and walked out.

Three hours later, he showed up at the ballroom of the American Empire Hotel. He was wearing Lane-Walsh's suit, with the Stromberg colors of green for the coat and brown, with yellow stars, for the pants. His landlady, Service bless her, had taken a few reefs in it, so that it did not fit quite as badly as when he had first tried it on. He had further disguised himself by screwing Lane-Walsh's monocle, which had been attached by a thread to the coat lapel, into his right eye. It made him see double, but that was a detail.

Horace Juniper-Hallett was young; he was thin-skinned; he was afraid of doormen, headwaiters, and policemen; he had an inferiority complex a yard wide. But such is the magic of sex—well, love, if you want a nicer word for it—that he now marched up to the doorman of this ballroom as if he had had the courage of six lions poured into him. He had always considered himself a poor actor. But now he beamed confidence as he put his hand in his pocket. When the hand of course found no admission card, his expression of shocked dismay would have melted an even harder heart than that of this doorman—who had been specially picked for hardness of heart.

"Must have left it in my other suit!" he bleated.

"That's all right, sir," said the doorman, eyeing the green

coat, the star-spangled pants, and the businessman's fountain pen. "Just give me your name."

Juniper-Hallett gave an alias, and described himself as a Stromberg salesologist from Miami. He checked his hat and duelling stick, and went in.

II.

THE ballroom was full of Strombergs and their women. Juniper-Hallett thought that the Stromberg colors en masse were pretty depressing. Now, at a Crosley ball—

A couple of Strombergs near him were talking; executives by their heavy watch chains, nobles by their self-assured bearing. One said: "When the uranium gave out, we went back to petroleum, and when that gave out, we went back to coal. If the antarctic coal gives out—"

"How about alcohol?" asked the other.

"All you'd have to do would be to cut the earth's population by three quarters. You can't grow alcohol grains in little tin trays, you know."

"The Hawaiians—" The speaker realized that his voice was carrying to Juniper-Hallett; he lowered it and pulled his companion farther away.

Juniper-Hallett was not listening. He had located Janet Bickham-Coates. She was standing on the edge of a crowd of portly Stromberg lesser nobility surrounding His Integrity, the chairman.

Juniper-Hallett strolled up and tapped his forehead in greeting. "Care to dance, my lady?" he asked casually. "Oh, I'm sorry, I'm afraid you don't remember me. Horace Stromberg Esker-Vanguard, Esquire. I met you at the last convention. You don't mind?"

She touched her forehead too, then, and melted into his arms. She murmured: "I'm glad you had the nerve to ask me. The young whitecollars are all afraid to go near father. So I've been dancing with fat His Acumen this and His Efficiency that for an hour."

"How was the dinner?" he asked.

"Frightful. The speeches, I mean; the food was all right."

"Was His Loyalty, Justin Lane-Walsh, there?"

"No, now that I think, he wasn't." Then she asked: "What's your *real* name?"

"Didn't I tell you?"

"No, you didn't." She laughed up at him. It buoyed his ego to find that this girl laughed *up* at him, even if he was a shrimp compared to Lane-Walsh. She said: "You see, I never attended the last convention."

"The music's good, isn't it?"

"Now, my young friend, you can't get away with—"

"Janet!" said a hearty female voice. Juniper-Hallett saw a tall, beaky, gray-haired woman. "I don't think I know this one."

"Mother," said Janet, "this is . . . uh . . . Businessman—"

"Horace Esker-Vanguard," put in Juniper-Hallett pleasantly.

"Not a bad-looking young fellow," said the grand dame critically, "in spite of the silly eyeglass. I don't know why they wear them. What did you catch him with, Janet? Salt?"

"Mother!"

"Ha-ha, now she's embarrassed, Businessman Horace. Does the young good to be embarrassed occasionally. Keeps 'em from taking themselves too seriously. She's quite a pretty girl when she blushes, don't you think? Well, run along, children, and try not to be bored. These conventions are stupid, don't you think? Poor Janet's been dancing all evening with dodos of *my* generation." She and Juniper-Hallett touched their foreheads.

"And now," said the girl, "how about telling me who you really are?"

"Must we come back to that subject? They're starting a trepak."

"I'm afraid we must."

"You wouldn't want to see me scattered all over the ballroom, would you? A head here, a leg there?"

"I'd hate to see you scattered all over anything. But there'll be some investigating unless you talk."

So Juniper-Hallett, his heart pounding with apprehension, told her who he was. Instead of being angry, she took it as a joke. Then she insisted on being told how he had come by the suit of Stromberg colors. She took this for an even better joke.

"It served Justin right," she said. "I don't like his type—loud-mouthed ruffian, always bragging of his success with women. I suppose I shouldn't talk that way about my own cousin, especially in the presence of the enemy. But now, why did you go to all that trouble to crash our gate?"

"To meet you."

"Do I come up to your expectations?"

"I could judge that better," he said thoughtfully, "on neutral ground. You remember what your mother said about conventions."

"My mother," she replied, "has remarkably good sense at times."

ON the way out, Juniper-Hallett's ear caught a phrase ending with "—do with the dormouse."

Hell's bones, he thought, why did that subject have to come up to distract him from his present business? The Strombergs were up to something; he was sure he hadn't been taken in by Lane-Walsh's elaborate protestations of ignorance. And then there was the Stromberg who had spoken of exhaustion of antarctic coal. It never rained but it poured. You droned along with an uneventful existence. Then all at once you met the most wonderful girl in the world; you were elevated to businessmanhood, with the prospect of eventually becoming an executive or even an entrepreneur and being allowed to carry a personal two-way radiophone; a couple of first-class mysteries were thrust under your nose. You couldn't do all these subjects justice at the same time. The good god Service ought to arrange his timing better.

He was sure Janet was the most wonderful girl in the world, on the quite inadequate grounds that her presence made him feel tall, brave, debonair, resourceful, cool-headed, and all the other things he'd wanted to be. He felt, in fact, as though he wouldn't mind taking on a dozen Justin Lane-Walshes with duelling sticks at the same time.

He was lucky enough to get a couple of good seats to a show. He and Janet whispered for the first twenty minutes, until people shushed them.

But Juniper-Hallett still had too much to think about to pay attention to the mesh—the three-dimensional woven structure on which the images were projected. He did remember later that the show was a violent melodrama laid in the Century of Revolutions, and that at one point the heroine said: "I am going to die, Boris! Do you hear me? I am going to die!" Whereat, Boris had ungallantly replied, "Well, stop talking about it and *do* it!"

The Hawaiians—Justin Lane-Walsh had mentioned them; so had the Stromberg executive at the ball. Horace Juniper-Hallett had been brought up to scorn and suspect them. They did not acknowledge the sovereignty of any of the big, orderly empires that divided the globe between them. They did not worship the great god Service. Instead of trying with all their might to increase production and consumption, as civilized people did, the wicked, immoral Hawaiians made their goods as durable as possible, worked no more than they had to, and sat around in the sun, loafing the rest of the time.

To add injury to insult, they raided the shipping lanes now and then with their privateering submarines, robbing the ships of raw materials. And nothing, it seemed, could be done about it. An attempt by the combined American and Mongolian navies to do something about it, some years before, had ended in disaster for the attackers—

"The show's over," said Janet in his ear.

"Oh, is it?" he replied blankly. "Let's go somewhere where we can talk."

NEXT morning, Horace Juniper-Hallett showed up at the Exposition, walking warily and frowning. He was wondering what he ought to do, being a young man much given to wondering what he ought to do. If he showed his face around there too much, Justin Lane-Walsh would appear thirsting for his blood. He was not afraid of Lane-Walsh, having exchanged a few stick slashes with him the day before and found him nothing extraordinary. But if he got in a fight, it would lead to all sorts of complications; perhaps his own degradation. And with his private affairs in such a delicate stage, he did not want complications. On the other hand he didn't want people to think he was afraid—On the other hand—

He ascertained that Lord Archwin of Crosley was in his semi-office in back of the Crosley exhibit. A conference with His Integrity would solve the problem for the present.

"Well, my boy," said the bald, billikenlike chairman, "how does it feel to be a businessman?"

"Fine. But, Your Integrity, I thought you'd be interested in a couple of clues to the whereabouts of the stolen dormouse."

Archwin's eyebrows, what little there was of them, went up. "Yes, Horace, I would be. Yes, I would be. What do you know about it?"

Juniper-Hallett told him of Lane-Walsh's reaction, and of the mention of the dormouse at the Stromberg ball.

"That's interesting, if hardly conclusive," said Archwin. "What interests me more is how *you* got into that ball."

Juniper-Hallett gulped. He thought he'd been keeping out of trouble! But a businessman could not tell a lie, except in advertising his product. At least, so Juniper-Hallett had been taught to believe. He was in for disgrace and disaster, no doubt, but—He blurted out the story of his embezzlement of Lane-Walsh's clothes, without mentioning his evening with Janet. Then he waited for the lightning to strike.

The chairman's forehead wrinkled; his nose twitched; his lips jerked; he burst into a roar of laughter. "That's the best thing since Billiam lost his pants in a duel with me back in '12! Congratulations, Horace."

"Then . . . then I'm not going to be degraded for wearing false colors?"

"Service bless you, no. If they'd caught you and made a protest, I might have had to go through some motion or other. But if they'd caught you, you probably wouldn't have survived to tell the story."

"Whew!" Juniper-Hallett gave a long sigh of relief. Mixed with the relief was a slight feeling of disillusionment. He'd always been taught that the rules of businessmanhood were adamantine. Now they seemed to have a few soft spots, after all. And His Integrity's integrity had acquired the faintest tarnish. Juniper-Hallett had taken his code so seriously, and worried so about its violation—

"Let me think it over," said Archwin. "I didn't know you were such a Sherlock. The last regular agent we sent around to the Stromberg building was beaten nearly to death with sticks. Maybe I'll have some more use for you. Maybe I shall."

The chairman agreed that it would be prudent to transfer Juniper-Hallett from the Exposition back to the main office in the Crosley building. Thither Juniper-Hallett went, almost getting run over twice. His mind was on his date with Janet the coming evening. Not until he reached the office, which was over the main showroom, which stretched along Wilshire Boulevard for six blocks, did he remember that he had meant to ask Lord Archwin about the state of the antarctic coal fields.

THEY met in the Los Angeles Nominatorium, one place they were unlikely to be disturbed. The long lines of columns stretched for blocks in all directions. Each line was sacred to one company or clan, and each pillar bore the names and dates of the members of one family of that company.

"Now up here," said the guide, "is somethin' interesting. You see that blank space on the Froman column? That's where they'd put John Generalmotors Froman-Epstein, only they didn't put him nowheres. And on the Packard colonnade, they's a blank space where they didn't put Theodora Packard Hughes-Halloran, who married him. A Generalmotors marryin' a Packard—hm-m-m." He saw that his visitors were clearly not listening, and gave up.

"Personally," said Janet, "I don't care whether they put me on a column or not."

"Neither do I," said Juniper-Hallett.

"Do we have to agree on *everything,* Horace?"

"It sure looks that way. Maybe you agree with me that this Crosley-Stromberg feud's gone on long enough."

"I certainly do. I asked father once what started it, and he said nobody in the company remembered any more, but I could probably find out if I wanted to dig back far enough into the records."

"It's a lot of bunk," said Juniper-Hallett. Taking his courage in both hands, he added: "I don't see why a person can't marry whom he pleases, companies or no companies."

She nodded gravely. "It's their affair, isn't it? Of course they ought to stay within their own *class.*"

"Right. It doesn't do to mix classes. But there's no logical reason why you and I shouldn't marry if we felt like it, for instance."

"No reason at all, if we felt like it. Why, you're much better suited to me than anyone in the Stromberg Co."

"Make it both ways. As a matter of fact, I think it would be about a perfect match."

"Just about, wouldn't it?"

"If we felt like it."

"Oh, of course."

Juniper-Hallett looked at his shoe buckles. "Matter of fact, I know an old geneticist who'd do it if I asked him to."

She turned to face him. "Horace, you mean you *do* feel like it?"

"Sure. Do you?"

"Of course! I was afraid you were just citing an imaginary case—"

"And I was afraid you were just being nice—"

"Ever since I met you last—"

"Ever since I saw you—"

The guide looked back over his shoulder. He said "Hm-m-m!" and shuffled off into the night.

"I'm afraid," said Juniper-Hallett.

"You afraid? You weren't afraid of Justin yesterday. And you weren't afraid to invade the ball last night."

"It's not that. I feel somehow that something's going to happen. Something to separate us."

"How frightful, Horace!"

"Yep, that's the word for it. For instance, do you know anything about the antarctic coal situation?"

"No, I don't suppose I do. Though I've heard father—"

"Go on."

"Nothing definite; just a few words now and then. I suppose I ought to be more interested in coal and such things. But if that's the case, I don't suppose we ought to wait—"

"Any longer than we have to—" said Juniper-Hallett.

"We could start right now—" said Janet.

"And see that geneticist of mine. I'll have to go back to my house, though, and get my pedigree. I suppose you will, too."

"No," she said brightly, "I brought mine along with me!"

THE geneticist was a benevolent old gent named Miles Carey-West.

He said hello to Juniper-Hallett, and implied with a look that he knew what his young friend had come for.

"Got your pedigrees?" he asked. He glanced over Juniper-Hallett's. Then he looked at Janet's. He whistled when he saw the name at the top.

"I *thought* I'd seen your face somewhere," he said, peering through thick glasses. "Won't this cause all kinds of trouble?"

The young pair shrugged. Juniper-Hallett said: "Yep. We're ready for it."

"Ah, well," said Carey-West. "No reasoning with the young and headstrong. Maybe it'll be a good thing; heal up this silly feud. Just like Romeo and Juliet."

"Who?" asked Juniper-Hallett.

"Romeo and Juliet. Couple of characters in a play by a pre-industrial English dramatist. Hope you make out better than they did, though."

"What happened to them? I'd like to read it."

"They died. And you'd have to read it in translation, unless you're a student of Old English. Raise your right hands, both of you."

OF course, thought Horace Juniper-Hallett, it was another dazzling piece of luck, getting the girl of one's dreams right off the bat. But he couldn't help a slight feeling of dissatisfaction; a feeling that by rushing things so impetuously he'd missed something. Maybe it meant nothing to have a big wedding and walk out of the Gyratory Club under an arch of duelling sticks held by his fellow businessmen. But it would have been nice to have had the experience.

It would not do to voice these fugitive thoughts.

"Well—" he said uncertainly. They were standing outside the geneticist's house, which was on a back street near Wilshire and Vermont. Now that Juniper-Hallett was no longer dazzled by the approaching headlights of matrimony, he could see the swarm of problems ahead of him clearly enough.

Janet was waxing her nose. She said: "I'll have to go back to the Stromberg building for a few days, anyway."

"What? But I always thought—I was led to believe—*gulp*—"

"That a bride went to live with her husband? Don't be silly, darling. I'll have to break the news gently to my parents. Or they'll make a frightful row. I can't go to live with a member of a rival company without my own company's consent, you know."

"Oh, very well." Juniper-Hallett had an uneasy feeling that his wife would always be about three jumps ahead of him in making decisions. "Every hour we're separated will be hell for me, sweetheart."

"Every minute will be for me, precious. But it can't be helped."

IT was too early to go to bed; besides which Horace Juniper-Hallett's mind was too full of a number of things. Instead of heading for his rooming house, he walked along Wilshire Boulevard toward Western Avenue. The Crosley building reared into the low clouds ahead of him. The sight always aroused Juniper-Hallett's pride in his company. Time had been when such tall buildings were forbidden because of earthquakes. Then they had excavated the San Andreas rift and filled it full of graphite. This, acting as a lubricant, allowed relative motion of the earth on the two sides to be smooth instead of jerks.

A light, cold drizzle began; one of those Los Angeles winter rains that may last for an hour or a week.

If he made good as a businessman, he'd soon be able to move into the Crosley building with the executives and full-blooded nobility. If—

"Hey!" Juniper-Hallett saw Justin-Walsh running toward him, making aggressive motions with his duelling stick. The Stromberg must have been hanging around the Crosley building just in case. He yelled: "You're the punk who stole my clothes!"

"Now, Your Loyalty," said Juniper-Hallett, "I'll explain—"

"To hell with your explanations! Defend yourself!"

"But the chief's order—"

Whack! Juniper-Hallett got his stick up just in time to parry a downright cut at his head. After that, his reflexes took hold. The sticks swished and clattered. Pedestrians formed a dense ring around them; a ring that would suddenly bulge outward when one of the fighters came close to its boundary.

Lane-Walsh was stronger, but Juniper-Hallett was faster. That, with sticks of the standard Convention weight, gave him an advantage. He feinted a flank-cut; followed it by a left-cheek-cut. He was a little high; the stick hit Lane-Walsh in the temple. The heir to the Stromberg vice presidency dropped his stick, and followed it to the pavement.

Juniper-Hallett saw a policeman coming up, drawn by the crowd and the clatter of sticks. Juniper-Hallett pushed out through the opposite side of the ring. The crowd knew what to do: they opened a lane for him, meanwhile getting as much as possible in the way of his pursuer. Juniper-Hallett ducked down the stairs of the Western Avenue station of the Wilshire Boulevard subway before the cop broke through the crowd. After all, the young man had furnished them with free entertainment.

But, though Juniper-Hallett got away, the police soon learned who had sent Justin Lane-Walsh to the hospital with a fractured skull. Everybody knew the colors of the Crosley Co., which appeared on the raincoat Juniper-Hallett had been wearing as well as on his suit. His brief case identified him as of the rank of businessman. And, of the members of that order, there was only one Crosley of Juniper-Hallett's physical properties in Los Angeles at that time.

They picked him up late that night, still riding the subway back and forth and wondering whether to give himself up to them, go home as if nothing had happened, or take an airplane for Mongolia.

III.

THEY led him into the Crosley Co.'s private courtroom, wherein cases between one member of the company and another were normally decided. The Old Man was there, and the chief of police, and all the Crosley higher-ups. Juniper-Hallett looked around the semicircle of stony faces. Whether they felt sorrow, or indignation, or hostility, they gave no sign.

Archwin Taylor-Thing, chairman of Crosley, cleared his throat. "Might as well get this over with. Get it over with," he muttered to nobody in particular. He stepped forward and raised his voice. "Horace Crosley Juniper-Hallett, Esquire, you have been found unworthy of the honors of businessmanhood. Hand over your brief case."

Juniper-Hallett handed it over. Archwin of Crosley took it and gave it to His Economy, the treasurer.

"Your fountain pen, sir."

Juniper-Hallett gulped at giving up the last emblem of his status. Archwin of Crosley broke the pen over his knee. He got ink down his trouser leg, but paid it no attention. He threw the pieces into the wastebasket.

He said: "Horace Crosley Juniper-Hallett, Esquire, no longer, you are hereby degraded to the rank of whitecollar. You shall never again aspire to the honorable status of businessmanhood, which you have so lightly abused.

"Furthermore, in accordance with the agreement of this honorable company with the city of Los Angeles, we are compelled to expel you from our membership. From this time forth, you are no longer a Crosley. You shall, therefore, cease using that honorable name. You are forever excluded from the Crosley section of the Imperial Nominatorium. Neither we nor any of our affiliated companies will have any further commerce, correspondence, or communication with you. We renounce you, cast you out, utterly dissociate ourselves from you.

"Go, Horace Juniper-Hallett, never to return."

Juniper-Hallett stumbled out.

He was halfway home, shuffling along with bowed head, when he put a hand in his coat pocket for a cigarette. He snatched out the note he found, which had gotten there he knew not how. It read:

> Meet me twenty-three o'clock basement Kergulen's Restaurant tomorrow night. Don't tell anybody. Anybody. A. T.-T.

Juniper-Hallett decided he could defer thoughts of suicide, at least until he saw what the Old Man had up his sleeve.

JUNIPER-HALLETT'S old friend, the geneticist, was surprised, a week later, to get a visit from Janet Juniper-Hallett, née Bickham-Coates. The girl looked a good deal thinner than when Carey-West had seen her last. She poured out a rush of explanation: "Father was wild—simply wild. This is the first time they've let me out of the Stromberg building—and they sent my maid along to make sure I wouldn't sneak off to Horace. Where is he? What's he doing?"

"He was in once after his expulsion," said the geneticist. "He looked like a wreck—unshaven, and he'd been drinking pretty hard. Told me he'd moved to a cheaper place."

"What'll we do? Isn't there any way to rehabilitate him?"

"I think so," said the old gentleman. "If he can get along for a year, and moves to some city other than the capital, I could arrange to have another radio company take him in. The Arsiays are looking for new blood, I hear."

Janet's eyes were round. "Do companies actually take in outcasts like that?"

The geneticist chuckled. "Of course they do! It's highly irregular, but it does happen, if you know how to finagle it. Our man won't have to stay proletarianized forever. These watertight compartments that our fine Corporate State is divided into, have a way of developing leaks. You're shocked, my dear?"

"N-no. But you sound almost as if you approved of the way they did things back in the Age of Promiscuity, when everyone married and worked for whomever he pleased."

"They got along. But let's decide about you and Horace."

She sighed. "I can't live with him, and I can't live without him. I'd almost rather become a dormouse than go on like this."

"Now don't look at me, my dear. I wouldn't sell you any hibernine if I thought you should take it. Don't want to spend my declining years in jail."

Janet looked puzzled. "You mean you might approve of it in some cases?"

"Might, though you needn't repeat that. In general, the laws against the use of hibernine are sound, but there are cases—"

The doorbell rang. Carey-West admitted Horace Juniper-Hallett, dressed as a proletarian, and whistling.

"Janet!" he yelled, and reached for her.

"Why, Horace!" she said a few minutes later. "I thought you were a wreck. Didn't you mind being expelled and degraded—and even being separated from me?"

He grinned a little bashfully. If he'd thought, he'd have put on a better act. "That was all a phony, darling. The general performance, that is. I really got drunk. But that was at the Old Man's orders, to make it more convincing."

"Horace! What on earth do you mean?"

"Oh, I'm technically an outcast, working as an ashman for the city of Los Angeles. But actually, I'm doing a secret investigation for the Crosleys. Lord Archwin saw me after the ceremony and told me that if I was successful, he'd have me reinstated and—oh, gee!" Juniper-Hallett's boyish face registered dismay. "I forgot I wasn't supposed to tell anybody, even you!"

"Huh," said Carey-West. "A fine Sherlock your chairman picked."

"But now that you've gone that far," said Janet thoughtfully, "you might as well tell us the rest."

"I really oughtn't—"

"Horace! You don't mistrust your wife, do you?"

"Oh, very well. I'm supposed to find out about this stolen dormouse. And I'm starting with the Strombergs."

"My company!"

"Yep. Remember, we're trying to stop the feud and bring about a merger between your company and mine. So it's mine as well as yours, really."

"But my own company—"

Juniper-Hallett did his best to look masterful. "That's enough, Janet old girl! You want me reinstated and everything, don't you? Well, then, you'll have to help me."

THE precise form of that help Janet learned the following evening.

She was sitting at her window in the Stromberg building, which towered up out of the clump of low and often fog-bound hills in the Inglewood district. She was watching the lights of Los Angeles and reading "How to Hold a Husband," by the thrice-divorced Vivienne Banks-Carmody. She was also scratching Dolores behind the ear. Dolores was purring.

Came a knock, and Dolores, who was shy about strangers, slunk under the bed. Janet opened the door. She squeaked: "Hor—"

"Sh!" said Juniper-Hallett, slipping in and closing the door

behind him. A fine rain of powdered ash sifted from his work clothes to the carpet.

"How on earth did you get in here?" she whispered.

"Simple." He grinned, a little nervously. "I stuck a wrench into the works of the ash hopper and jammed it. While the boys were clustering about it and wondering what to do, I slipped in through the kitchen door. I rode up the service elevator; nobody stopped me." He sat down, rustling and clanking a bit. His clothes bulged.

"How did you know how to get here? The place is like a maze."

"Oh, that." He took a huge fistful of papers from under his coat, leafed through them, and selected one. "They gave me a complete set of plans before I started out. I've got enough tools and things hung around me to burgle the National Treasury. I'm supposed to climb through your air conditioning system to the laboratory, to see if they've got the stolen dormouse there."

"But—"

He stopped her with a wave. "I can't start until early in the morning, when things'll be quiet."

"About when?"

"Between three and four, they told me. You've had your dinner, haven't you, darling?" He took out a sandwich and munched.

"But Horace, you can't stay here!"

"Why not?" He rose and entered the bathroom to get a glass of water.

"I have to get to bed some time, and I can't have a man—"

"You're my wife, aren't you?"

"Good Service, so I am! This is frightful!"

"What do you mean, frightful?" he said indignantly. "Matter of fact, I was considering—"

A knock interrupted him. Janet asked: "Who's there?"

"Me," said the voice of Janet's mother.

"Quick, Horace! *Just a minute, mother!* Hide under the bed! Dolores won't hurt you."

"Who's Dolores?"

"My cat. *I'll be right there, mother.* Quick, please, please!"

Juniper-Hallett, thinking that his bride might have shown a little more enthusiasm for his company, stuffed the rest of his sandwich into his mouth, put away the transparent sheet it had been wrapped in, and rolled under the bed. Janet opened the door.

"I thought I'd spend the night with you," said Janet's mother. "I've been having those nightmares again."

Janet gave a vaguely affirmative reply. But Horace Juniper-Hallett did not hear it. His hand was clutching his mouth, which was open in a silent yell. Every muscle in his body was at maximum tension.

Two feet from his head, a pair of green eyes, seemingly the size of dinner plates, were staring at him.

When the first horrifying shock wore off, Juniper-Hallett was able to reason that if Janet wanted to call a full-grown puma a "cat," she had every right to do so. But she might have warned him.

Dolores opened her fanged mouth and gave a faint snarl. When Juniper-Hallett simply lay where he was, Dolores relaxed.

Lady Bickham-Smith was talking: "—and even if your father is a bit rigid in his ideas, Janet, it was a crazy thing to do, don't you think? You don't really know anything about this man—"

"Mother! I thought we weren't going to argue about that—"

Dolores kept her green eyes open with a faint, lingering suspicion, but did not move as Juniper-Hallett touched her head. He stroked it. Dolores' eyelids drooped; Dolores purred. The sound was like an eggbeater churning up a bowlful of marbles, but still it was a purr.

Then Juniper-Hallett's mucous membrane went into action. He just stopped a sneeze by pressing a finger under his nose. His nasal passages filled with colorless liquid. His eyes itched and watered.

He was allergic to cats, and he'd been neglecting his injections lately. And cats evidently included lions, tigers, leopards, pumas, jaguars, ounces, servals, ocelots, jaguarundis, and all the other members of the tribe.

In an hour, when he was treated to the sight of the bare ankles of the two women, moving about preparatory to going to bed, he had the finest case of hay fever in the city of Los

Angeles, which stretched from San Diego to Santa Barbara. And there was nothing he could do about it.

But, he assured himself, no situation would ever seem grotesque to him again.

IV.

JUNIPER-HALLETT awoke after five or six hours' fitful slumber.

He tried to raise his head, bumped it on the bottom of the mattress, and realized where he was. It seemed incredible to him that he should have slept at all under those bizarre circumstances.

But there he was, with a gray wet dawn coming in through the windows, and Dolores' head resting peacefully on his stomach.

After several years, it seemed, of his lying and silently sniffling, the women got up and dressed. Janet said: "I didn't . . . *yawn* . . . sleep very well."

"Neither did I. It's that beast of yours. I wish you wouldn't keep her in here, Janet. She gives me the williejitters. She kept purring all night long, and it sounded just like a man snoring."

When Lady Bickham-Smith had departed, Juniper-Hallett rolled out from under the bed. When he got to his feet, he threw back his head, closed his eyes, opened his mouth, and gave vent to a sneeze that fluttered the pages of a magazine on the table. He looked vastly relieved, though his eyes were red and watery and his hair was mussed. "There," he said, "I've been wadtig to do that all dight!"

"Was that all you thought about last night?"

"Just ab—Do, of course dot!"

"Darling!"

"Sweetheart!"

She stepped back and looked at him. "Horace, did you snore last night?" Her tone suggested that she wished she'd known about this sooner.

"How should I dow? Have you got sobe ephedride id your bathroob?"

"No, but Pamela Starr-Gilligan down the hall, may have some. Why?"

Juniper-Hallett gestured toward the puma, who was standing with her forepaws on the window sill, looking at the rain. "I'b afraid that whed we have our owd hobe, dear, it'll have to be without her."

"Oh, but Horace, how frightful! I love Dolores—"

"Well, let's dot argue dow. Will you get be sobe ephedride, old girl, before I drowd in by owd hay fever?"

When she returned with the medicine, she found a thinner-looking Juniper-Hallett eating another sandwich and examining the air conditioning registers. On the floor lay a lot of engineering drawings, a coil of rope with a hook at one end, a flashlight, and a couple of burglarious-looking tools.

"Horace! What on earth—"

He blew his nose violently and explained: "I'm trying to figure out which system would get me to the lab quicker, the risers or the returns." He looked at the plans. "Let's see. The Stromberg building has a low-velocity air conditioning system designed to furnish six air changes an hour with a maximum temperature differential of thirty degrees centigrade and a trunk line velocity of three hundred meters per minute. Ducts are of the all asbestos Carey type. There are 1,406 outlet registers and 1,323 return registers, *mumble-mumble-mumble*— Looks like the distance is the same in either case; but if I take the warm air side I'll get toasted when I get down near the furnace. So it'll be the returns."

He took his ephedrine and addressed himself to the return register. The grate was locked in place, but the frame to which it was hinged was held to the wall by four ordinary screws. These he took out in a hurry. He stowed his elaborate apparatus about his person, kissed his bride, and pushed himself into the duct head first.

THE duct dropped straight for two feet, then turned horizontally.

The corner was square, and was full of little curved vanes to guide the air around. Juniper-Hallett fetched up against these while his legs were still in Janet's room.

He backed out, muttering, got out his wrecking bar, kissed Janet again, stuck his upper half into the duct, and attacked the vanes. They came loose and plunked to the bottom wall of the duct one by one. Then Juniper-Hallett wormed himself completely into the duct and around the bend. "Wormed" is no exaggeration. The duct was a mere twenty by forty centimeters, and, thin as Juniper-Hallett was, it took all his patience and persistence to get himself around that hellish corner. Too late he remembered that he had a third sandwich in an inside pocket; he probably had jam all over the inside of his clothes by now.

The duct soon enlarged where others joined it, so that Juniper-Hallett could proceed on hands and knees. Faint gleams of light came down the ducts from the registers. The breeze purred softly past his neck. The inside of the ducts was waxy to his touch. He came to another bend, and had to pry loose another set of vanes that blocked his path. He hoped he wasn't making too much noise. But the asbestos muffled even the sound of the wrecking bar.

Then he arrived at deeper blackness in the darkness around him; his right hand met nothing when he put it down. He jerked back in horror; in his hurry he'd almost tumbled down one of the main return stacks. It would have a straight drop of about a hundred meters.

His viscera crawling, he turned on his flashlight. He found he'd have to pry a couple of baffle plates out of the way to get into the stack.

That took a bit of straining, cramped as he was. When it was done, he stuck his head into the stack and flashed the light down against the stack wall below him. There ought to be a ladder of hand holds all the way from top to bottom.

But there were no hand holds below him; nor above him, either. With great difficulty, he got out the plans and read them by the flashlight. His underwear was now clammy with sweat. The plan showed the hand holds. The plan was wrong, or the hand holds had been removed since it was made. He could not think why the latter should be.

He took another look, and there were the hand holds—on the side of the stack opposite him.

The idea of jumping across the two-meter gap over the black hole below him, and catching the hand holds on the fly monkeywise, made his scalp crawl. He sat for a minute, listening to the faint, deep, organlike note of the air rushing down the stack. Then he knew what he must do. He unwound the rope from around his middle, and tossed the hook on its end across the gap until it caught on one of the hand holds. Then he took the rope in both hands and slid off the baffle plates. He fetched up sharply against the other side of the stack.

AN hour later, Juniper-Hallett arrived at the return-register, opening into the biology room of the Stromberg laboratories, well below ground. He was shaking from his hundred-meter climb down the stack. Without the plans, it would have taken him all day to find the right duct.

He stifled a grunt of disappointment. The register was high up on one wall, giving him a good view of the room. The duct, serving a room much larger than Janet's, was thrice the size of the one leading to hers, so Juniper-Hallett could move around easily.

But there was no sign of the body of a dormouse anywhere.

His watch told him it was eight-thirty. That was dangerously close to the hour when the scientists went to work. But if there was no dormouse, there would be no reason for invading—

A lock clicked and a man entered the room. He stared at a long, bare table, and bolted out, slamming the door. Soon he was back with several more. They all shouted at once. "Ryan's gone!" "Who was here last—" "I saw him on the table—" "—must have stolen—" "—the Crosleys—" "—shall we call the police—" "—the department'll catch hell from—" "Shut up, sir! Let me think!"

The last was from a man Juniper-Hallett recognized as Hosea Beverly-Heil, Stromberg's chief engineer. He was a tall, masterful-looking man. He pressed his fingertips against his temples and squeezed his eyes shut.

After a while he said: "It's either the Crosleys, or the Ayesmies, or the Hawaiians. The Crosleys, on general principles; if we steal something, that is to say, it obviously has value for us; wherefore it behooves them to steal it from us. The Ayesmies, because Arnold Ryan was a prominent member of the A. S. M. E. back in the days when it was a legal organization; that is to say, now that they are an illegal, secret group, I mean, clique or . . . uh . . . group, and have been driven almost out of existence by our good dictator's vigilant agents—" Here somebody snickered. Beverly-Heil frowned at him, as though everybody didn't know that the dictator was a mere powerless puppet in the hands of the turbulent aristocracy of the great companies. "—our . . . his vigilant agents, as I was saying, they may wish the help of one of their former leaders in saving them from extinction. The Hawaiians, because they may suspect that Ryan, who, as is well known, is part Hawaiian, may give us their power secret; that is to say—Well, of the three possibilities, I think the second and last are too far-fetched and melodramatic to be worth serious consideration; I mean to say, to merit further pursuit along that line. Therefore, by a simple process of elimination, we have to conclude that the Crosleys are the men—that is to say, the most likely suspects."

Juniper-Hallett, huddled behind the grill of the register, began to understand why Janet had called the Stromberg dinner "frightful." Undoubtedly, Hosea Beverly-Heil had made a speech.

THE chief engineer now turned on a squarely built, blond man with monocle stuck in a red face. "As for your suggestion, Duke-Holmquist, by which I mean your proposal that we call the police, I may say that I consider it about the silliest thing I ever heard, sir; that is, it's utterly absurd. I mean by that, that to do so, would involve the admission that we had stolen, I mean expropriated, the body of Arnold Ryan in the first place."

Horace Juniper-Hallett was leaning against the grill, straining his ears. He was sure that *his* company hadn't stolen the dormouse. Why should the Old Man send him out to hunt for the body at a time when he must have known of its whereabouts and of plans for its seizure?

And then the grill, which was not locked in place at all but was merely held upright by friction, came loose and fell out and down on its hinges with a loud clang. Juniper-Hallett caught the register frame just in time to keep himself from tumbling into the laboratory.

For a few seconds, Juniper-Hallett looked at the engineers, and the engineers looked at him. His face started to take on a friendly smile, until he noticed that the couple nearest him started moving toward him with grim looks. Men had been beaten to death with duelling sticks when caught in the enemy's—

Juniper-Hallett tumbled backward and raced down the duct on hands and knees. Behind him the technicians broke into angry shouts. The light was dimmed as the head and shoulders of one of them was thrust into the opening.

Juniper-Hallett thought of trying to lose his pursuer in the maze of ducts. But he'd undoubtedly lose himself much sooner; and then they'd post somebody at each of the fourteen hundred registers and wait for him to come out—

The man was gaining on him, from the sound. The laboratory was connected to the main air conditioning system; there were smaller special temperature rooms, with a little circulating system of their own. The duct that Juniper-Hallett was in turned up a little way on, to reach the basement level where it joined the main trunks from the air conditioner. He had come down the one-story drop by his rope. It was still there; he went up it hand over hand. Just as he reached the top, it went taut below him; the other man was coming up, too.

JUNIPER-HALLETT tried to pry the hook out, but it had worked itself firmly into the asbestos, and the weight of his pursuer kept it there.

He took out his flashlight and wrecking bar. A businessman could hit another businessman, or a whitecollar, with a duelling stick. A whitecollar could hit another whitecollar or a businessman with a duelling stick. A whitecollar could use his fists on another whitecollar, but for a businessman to either strike with or be struck by a fist was a violation of the convention. An engineer ranked above a white collar and below a businessman; he could not be promoted to a businessman, executive, or entrepreneur, however. He could be struck with —Juniper-Hallett had forgotten. But it was utterly certain that hitting a man with a wrecking bar was a horrible violation of the code. Maybe an entrepreneur could hit a proletarian with such an implement, but even that—

The man's head appeared over the edge of the bend. As Juniper-Hallett turned the flashlight on, the man's monocle gleamed balefully back at him. It was the thick-set fellow addressed as Duke-Holmquist.

Juniper-Hallett hit him over the head with the wrecking bar; gently, not wishing to do him serious damage.

"Ouch!" said Duke-Holmquist. He slipped back a little; then pulled himself up again.

Juniper-Hallett hit him again, a little harder.

"Uh," grunted the man. "Damn it, sir, stop that!" He reached a large red hand out for Juniper-Hallett.

Juniper-Hallett hit him again, quite a bit harder. The monocle popped out of the large red face, and the face itself disappeared. Juniper-Hallett heard him strike the bottom of the duct. He worked his hook loose and pulled the rope up.

He could walk almost erect along the main duct. He hiked along, referring to his plan now and then, until he found the stack down which he had come. He stumbled over the vanes he had knocked loose before.

He started to climb. By the time he had ascended ten meters, he had discarded the wrecking bar and the other implement, a thing like a large can opener. By the time he had gone twenty, he had stuffed his papers into his pants pocket and dropped his coat. He would have discarded the flashlight and the rope, except that he might need them yet.

At thirty meters, he was sure he had climbed a hundred, and was playing the flashlight up and down the shaft to make sure he hadn't already passed the takeoff with the bent baffle plate. The ephedrine made his heart pound even more than it would have, anyway.

By and by, he worked out a system of looping his rope into a kind of sling, slipping the hook over one of the hand holds, and resting between climbs. The climbs grew shorter and shorter. He'd *never* make it. Anyone but a thin, wiry young man in first-rate condition would have collapsed long before.

But he kept on; ten rungs; rest; ten rungs; rest.

The ten rungs became nine, eight, seven—Pretty soon he'd give up and crawl out the first duct he passed. It might land him almost anywhere—but how could he get into and through it, without his burglary tools?

He'd stop the next time he rested; just hang there in black space, until the Strombergs lowered a rope for him from above.

THERE was the bent baffle! Feeling ashamed of his own weakness, Juniper-Hallett hurried up to it. How to get across the two meters of empty space? He climbed ten extra rungs, hooked the hook over a hand hold, climbed back down, took the rope in his hands, and kicked out, swinging himself pendulumwise across the stack. He caught the baffle all right and wormed his way into the duct. He found he would have to leave his rope behind. He said to hell with it, and squirmed out through the duct leading to Janet's room.

She was there alone. She squeaked with concern as Juniper-Hallett poured himself out of the register and collapsed on the rug. He had sweated off five of his meager sixty kilos, and looked it. She said, "Oh, darling!" and gathered him up. Dolores, not yet altogether used to Juniper-Hallett, slid under the bed again.

With his little remaining strength, he tottered back to the register and began putting the frame of the grill back in place. A knock sounded. Juniper-Hallett looked up and mumbled: "S'pose I could go back and get my rope—don't know how—and hang out the window—"

"You'll do nothing of the sort!" Janet bowled him over and rolled him under the bed.

The visitor was a strapping young Stromberg guardsman. He explained: "Those fool engineers—begging my lady's pardon—took half an hour getting Duke-Holmquist out of the flues before they thought to tell us. But we'll catch the marauder; isolate the main stacks and clean them and their branches out one at a time—what's that?" He bent over and examined the register. "Somebody's been taking the screws out of this, and he didn't put them all the way back in. The man hasn't come out through your room, has he, my lady?"

"No," said Janet. "But, then, I was out until a few minutes ago."

"Hm-m-m." The guardsman removed the register frame and stuck his flashlight inside the duct. "The vanes have all been knocked out of this bend. Somebody's been through here all right. Mind if I search your room, my lady?"

"No. But please don't muss up my things any more than you have to."

The guardsman went through the closets and the bureau

drawers. Then he approached the bed. Janet's heart was in her mouth. Being a sensible girl, she knew that her husband in his present condition, had not the ghost of a chance of throttling or stunning the man before he could give the alarm. And there was nothing in sight to use as a club—

The guardsman bent over and pulled up the bedspread. Something hissed at him; he jumped back, dropping his flashlight. "Wow!" he said. "I'd forgotten about your lioness, my lady. I guess the fellow sneaked out through your room while you were out of it." He touched his forehead and departed.

Janet looked under the bed in her turn. "Horace," she said.

A snore answered her.

V.

JUNIPER-HALLETT awoke after dark. He felt almost human again, and very hungry. The cause of his awakening was the click of the door as Janet returned to her room after dinner.

"Here, sweetheart," she said, producing a couple of hard rolls.

"Wonderful woman!" he replied, sinking his teeth.

She said: "Mother's going to spend the night here again. It's her nightmares."

"Then I'll have to get out somehow. Right away."

"Oh, must you, Horace?"

"Yep. I don't fancy another night with Dolores."

The puma, hearing her name, came over to Juniper-Hallett and rubbed her head against his knee.

"She likes you," said Janet.

"That may be. But she gives me hay fever, and she has too much claws and teeth for my idea of a pet. How'll I get out, old girl?"

Janet got a raincoat, a hat, and a pair of shoes out of a closet. "If you put these on—"

"What? Good Service, no! If it ever got out that I'd been doing a female impersonation, I'd never live it down. The mere idea gives me the horrors."

"But that's the only thing I can think of—"

"Me run around in a girl's clothes? Yeeow!" He closed his eyes and shuddered. "If they caught me in what I'm wearing, the worst they could do would be to beat me to death. But that —*br-r-r-r!* No, a thousand times no!"

Half an hour later he had his pants legs rolled up under the raincoat, and was putting on the hat. His expression was that of a man about to have a boil lanced by a drunken friend with a rusty jackknife.

He stood up. Dolores rubbed against his legs; then suddenly reared up, embraced him with her muscular forelegs, and threw him. She sat down on him and licked his chin. She had a tongue like sandpaper of the coarsest grade.

"Hey!" said Juniper-Hallett.

"She wants you to stay and play with her," said Janet. "She loves to wrestle."

"But I don't," said Juniper-Hallett.

Dolores was persuaded to let Juniper-Hallett up, and was sent out for a walk with Janet's maid while Juniper-Hallett hid.

When Horace Juniper-Hallett got home late that night, he took off the hat and the shoes and flung them on the floor with a violence all out of proportion to the crime, if any, of these inoffensive garments.

JUNIPER-HALLETT'S next obvious step was to report to Lord Archwin of Crosley that he had arrived at the Stromberg laboratories just as the Strombergs learned that somebody else had made off with the precious dormouse.

He didn't relish the prospect. Lord Archwin might have regretted already sending an untrained young sprig out to gumshoe and be glad of an excuse to call the deal off and put a professional Sherlock on the job. So Juniper-Hallett was relieved next morning when he learned at the Crosley building that Archwin Taylor-Thing was down at the Exposition, which was closing that day.

Juniper-Hallett was starting out of the receptionist's vestibule when he noticed a man sitting with a brief case—not a businessman's fancy leather one, but a plain rubberoid bag—in his lap. The man had a large quantity of curly black hair, tinted spectacles, and beard. Juniper-Hallett did not know any men with beards, but still this one did not look unfamiliar to him.

"Waiting to see the Old Man, sir?" he asked pleasantly.

"*Da.* Yes."

"He won't be back until late this afternoon, sir."

"Saw? That is too bad. But I shall wait for him anyway."

"I'm going down to see him now. Can I take a message?"

"*Da.* Tell him that Professor Ivan Ivanovitch Chelyushkin waits to see him. He has wery important inwention to shaw him."

"How long have you worn those whiskers?" asked Juniper-Hallett.

"Years and years. Gaw, young man, and geev your master my message!" The professor rose and pointed imperiously to the door.

"I think," said Juniper-Hallett in a low voice, "that you're the lousiest actor I ever saw, Justin old slug."

The eyes behind the tinted glasses took on an alarmed, hunted look. "You damn dirty Crosley," whispered the bearded man fiercely. "If you say a word, I'll break your neck before they can—"

Juniper-Hallett laughed at him. "Now, now, I don't want Your Loyalty beaten to a jelly. That's what they'd do; beat you to a jelly." He repeated the word "jelly" with relish. "I'm not technically a Crosley any more, you know."

"That's right, so you aren't. And I'm nobody's Loyalty. But—"

"Let us gaw outside, my frand, where we can talk wizzout wulgar interruptions," said Juniper-Hallett.

JUSTIN LANE-WALSH explained, crestfallen: "After I got out of the hospital, they degraded and expelled me, just as they said they would. But our Old Man told me not to go off the deep end, because he might have some confidential work for me.

"So last night I get a call from him, and he tells me somebody's got our dormouse, the one we expropriated from the Crypt. You know all about that, don't you? So the Old Man says, you find where the dormouse has gone, and we'll see about giving you your rank back."

"Same thing happened to me, exactly," said Juniper-Hallett. He explained why he was sure the Crosleys had not stolen the dormouse. Lane-Walsh scratched his head, getting black hair dye on his fingertips, but he could not see a hole in Juniper-Hallett's reasoning.

Juniper-Hallett went on: "Matter of fact I had an idea, when I saw you, that we'd do better together than working against one another. Why not? We're both outcasts."

"Well," said Lane-Walsh hesitantly, "suppose we find the dormouse; which of us—or which of our two companies—gets him?"

"We could fight it out," said Juniper-Hallett. He was sure he could handle Lane-Walsh, despite the latter's size.

"Can't. The doc told me I couldn't fight any more duels for a year, on account of what you did to my skull last time. Are there any other honorable methods?"

"We'll have to flip a coin or something." Juniper-Hallett dismissed the disposal of the dormouse with an airy wave. Lane-Walsh, still doubtful, gave in.

Juniper-Hallett said: "I don't guess there's much point in prowling around our own companies' buildings any more. What we want is a lead to the Hawaiians or the Ayesmies."

"Do you know any Hawaiians?"

"No. Do you?" asked Juniper-Hallett.

"I've never even seen one. I understand they have brown skins and flat faces, sort of like Mongolians."

"Well, if we don't know any Hawaiians, how are we going to find their secret headquarters? If they've got a secret headquarters."

Lane-Walsh shrugged. "I suppose we'll have to go after the Ayesmies then. But I don't know any Ayesmies, either."

"We both know some engineers, though. And any engineer might be an Ayesmy."

Lane-Walsh opened his eyes as if this was a great revelation. "That's so! There's one engineer around our building I don't like. He ought to be an Ayesmy."

SO evening found the amateur Sherlocks lurking in the shrubbery—literally—in front of the Stromberg building.

"That's him," said Justin Lane-Walsh. A portly man had just come out of the front entrance. "He walks home every night at this time."

They rose and followed the engineer Lane-Walsh didn't like.

They followed him to the restaurant where he ate his dinner. Lane-Walsh whispered to Juniper-Hallett: "That's one of the things that made me suspect him. What's his idea of sneaking off to eat by himself? They serve good grub in the Engineers' Mess in our building."

Juniper-Hallett replied: "Let's order something; but not too much. We don't want to be in the middle of our meal when he finishes."

Juniper-Hallett had a tuna-fish sandwich and a glass of wine. Lane-Walsh had a glass of milk. The milk got in his beard, which was held on with a water-soluble adhesive. He had to hold the object in place with one hand. He muttered: "What's this about your getting married to the Old Man's daughter?"

Juniper-Hallett told him.

"I'll be damned," said Lane-Walsh. "That's another reason for knocking your head off, when we have our duel after I get well. Janet's a good kid, though. If I were sap enough to marry anybody, she'd do very nicely. Reminds me of a Spanish girl I met at a party last week. She was shaped like *this* and like *this.*" He gestured. "And when I woke up—"

Just then the stout engineer whom Lane-Walsh didn't like got up. His pursuers got up, too, and followed him out.

As they mounted the stairs to the sidewalk, the engineer was there waiting for them. He came right to the point. "What the devil are you two following me for?"

"We aren't," said Juniper-Hallett.

"We were just waiting for an airplane, sir," said Lane-Walsh.

"Bunk!" roared the engineer Lane-Walsh didn't like. "Get out of here. Right now, or I'll call a cop!"

They went.

VI.

SLEEPER'S Crypt, colloquially known as Dormous Crypt, occupied the southern corner of Griffith Park, at Western and Los Feliz. From this elevation the Crypt commanded a fine view of the capital city, which its permanent residents were in no condition to appreciate. The Crypt itself was a big mausoleumlike building, streamlined. "Streamlined," in the language of the time, meant, not shaped so as to pass through a fluid with the least resistance, but covered with useless ornamentation. The word got this meaning as a result of its misuse by twentieth-century manufacturers, who took to calling boilers, refrigerators, and other normally stationary objects "streamlined" when they merely meant that they had dressed their products up in sheetmetal housings and bright paint. Hence "streamlined" came to mean dressed up or ornamented, with no reference to aërodynamics.

At the entrance to the Crypt was a cluster of watchmen. At sixteen o'clock, the line of sightseers entering the Crypt contained Justin Lane-Walsh and Horace Juniper-Hallett, conspicuous in their sober proletarian off-hour costume among the gaudy colors of the great companies.

As they entered, Lane-Walsh remarked: "They've got about twice as many watchmen as usual here today."

"I guess they're not taking any more chances of having another dormouse stolen," said Juniper-Hallett. Just then they passed through a turnstile; one of a pair, one for incomers and the other for outgoers.

Like all visitors to the Crypt, they lowered their voices. It was that kind of place. There was hall after hall, each with its rows of glasstopped caskets. In each casket was a sleeper. There was a little light above the head of the sleeper, which a visitor could flash on by a button if he wished to examine the sleeper's face. At the foot of the casket was a plate with the sleeper's name and other pertinent information, including the estimated date of his awakening.

Lane-Walsh switched on one of these lights. The sleeper was a girl.

"Some babe," said Lane-Walsh. "If she was ready to wake up, now—"

"Wouldn't do you much good," said Juniper-Hallett, reading the plate. "She isn't due to wake for fifty years. And you won't be up to much then."

" 'Sall right, I'll be up to more at seventy-five than you are right now, shrimp. Say, I always wondered if they called 'em dormice because the top of the coffin comes up like a door when they wake up and pull the switch."

"Nope. Matter of fact they're named after some kind of

mouse they have in Europe. It goes into a very deep sleep when it hibernates. Oh-oh, here's a new one. I didn't know they were still taking them in."

"Sure," said Lane-Walsh with much worldly wisdom. "You can get hibernine easy if you got the right connections."

Another of Juniper-Hallett's youthful illusions popped. He concealed his feeling of shock, and led the way to the hall that had contained the torpid body of Arnold Ryan. There was quite a crowd around the empty Ryan casket. When Juniper-Hallett and Lane-Walsh wormed their way in close, they bent over and examined the object eagerly. This was what they had come for: having run out of all other ideas, they thought there might possibly be a clue in or around the Ryan casket.

But the casket was exactly the same as all the others in the Crypt, except that the padding and the electrical connections had been removed from the interior. There remained nothing but a big plastic box, without even a scratch to hint at the destination of the victim.

DISAPPOINTED, they strolled off, snapping casket lights on at random. Juniper-Hallett said: "All these folks, I understand, took a hibernine pill because they hoped they'd wake up in a better world than the one they were in. I wonder how many of 'em will really like it better."

Lane-Walsh laughed harshly. "Whaddya mean, better? We've got a properly organized set-up, haven't we, with a place for everybody and everybody in his place? What more could they want?"

"I was just wondering—"

"That's the trouble with you, shrimp. You'd almost be a man if you weren't always wondering and thinking. Hell, what does anybody want to think for? We hire the engineers to do that. Hey, what—"

Juniper-Hallett was bending over behind one of the caskets. He said softly: "They ought to polish this floor up better." He waved Lane-Walsh to silence as the latter opened his mouth to speak. Lane-Walsh, for all his bluster, took orders docilely enough in the presence of anything he did not understand.

"See," said Juniper-Hallett. There were a lot of parallel scratches running from the casket to the wall. "Somebody's been shoving this box back and forth. Now if we could stick around here after the guards chase the rest out at seventeen—Oh-oh!"

"What's up, sister?" asked Lane-Walsh.

"You wouldn't understand, lame brain. It occurs to me that there's a comptometer hitched to each of those turnstiles, so the guards can tell after they close the place whether as many people came out as went in. Got it?"

"Oh. I get it. What'll we do then?"

"If you'll shut up and let a man with a brain think, maybe I can figure a way." Juniper-Hallett fell silent. Then he gave his friendly enemy instructions.

They started out the front door, Lane-Walsh leading. Lane-Walsh passed through the outgoing turnstile and halted a couple of steps beyond it to light a cigarette. He remarked to the nearest guard: "So this is your wonderful Los Angeles climate, huh? I've been here just a week, and it's rained the whole time."

The guard grinned. "You oughta be here in summer, mister. Say, would you move out of the way a little? People want to get by you."

"People" in this case meant Horace Juniper-Hallett. He had gone through the turnstile behind Lane-Walsh. When Lane-Walsh had stopped, he had stopped, too. While concealed from the doormen by Lane-Walsh's broad shoulders, he reached back and gave the turnstile a couple of quick yanks.

They strolled off into the drizzle while Lane-Walsh finished his cigarette. Juniper-Hallett explained: "I turned the out turnstile a couple of extra quadrants, so it reads two visitors too many."

"So what? If the out stile reads two more than the in, they'll know something's wrong—"

"Dimwit! When we go back in we'll raise the reading on the in stile by two, so they'll balance after everybody but us has been cleared out."

"Oh," said Lane-Walsh. "I get it. We better hurry back, or they'll wonder why we're coming in just before closing time."

"Almost human intelligence," said Juniper-Hallett. "It'll be too bad to spoil what little wits you have by cracking your skull again, when we have our duel."

AT seventeen the guards blew their whistles and herded everybody out. Juniper-Hallett and Lane-Walsh, by a bit of adroit dodging, hid from the guards, and were left in the empty Crypt. Most of the lights went out. There was no sound but the occasional, very faint, honk of an automobile horn wafted in from outside.

Juniper-Hallett took out a sandwich and divided it with Lane-Walsh, who had not thought to bring one. Between bites Juniper-Hallett pointed to a bit of incomplete electrical wiring along the wall. He whispered: "I guess they're putting in a fancy burglar-alarm system. Good thing we got here before they finished it."

"Say," said Lane-Walsh, "wouldn't it be something if all the dormice woke up at once and came out of their coffins?"

"It would scare me silly," said Juniper-Hallett.

"Me, too," said Lane-Walsh.

They fell silent for a long time, huddling behind a pair of caskets and listening to their own breathing. Even the breathing stopped when a night watchman passed through the hall on his rounds, his keys jingling faintly.

An hour later, when the watchman was due to pass again, Juniper-Hallett took off his shoes. When the watchman passed, Juniper-Hallett followed him, flitting from casket to casket like an apprehensive ghost.

He came back in a few minutes. He explained: "I wanted to find what route he takes. The last station he keys into is in the next hall; after he works the dingus there he goes down to the basement and smokes his pipe."

"So what?" whispered Lane-Walsh. "If you make me sit on this floor all night just to watch the watchman make his rounds, I'll—"

"You suggested looking into this place!"

"Sure I did, but staying here all night was your—"

"Sh!"

TWO more hours passed, marked by the watchman's plod past.

Then the watchers heard another step; a quicker one. They did not have to see the man to know that he was not the watchman. He walked straight down the passage between the rows of caskets, and stopped at the casket that Juniper-Hallett thought had been moved.

The two outcasts peeked around the corners of their respective caskets. The stranger was pressing the button that lit up the inside of the casket, making a series of short and long flashes. When he had finished, the casket rumbled back toward the wall, exposing a hole in the floor. Light illuminated the stranger's face from below, giving him a satanic look. He climbed down into the hole, and the casket slid back into place.

Juniper-Hallett whispered: "That was Hogarth-Weems, one of the Arsiay engineers!"

"Does that mean the Arsiays are back of all this?"

"Don't know yet."

They started to crawl toward the movable casket; then snapped back into their original positions as more footsteps approached. Another man walked in, flashed the light as the first one had done, and descended out of sight. Then came another, and another. Lane-Walsh recognized this one as a Stromberg engineer; so was the next one. Then followed a couple that neither knew; then a Crosley engineer.

Juniper-Hallett speculated: "It must be an Ayesmy meeting."

"Because they have engineers from all the different companies?"

"Right."

"Boy!" breathed Lane-Walsh. "What wouldn't Bickham-Smith give to know where their hide-out is! He hates 'em like poison, and so do I. Even worse than the Crosleys."

"What's so terrible about them?" asked Juniper-Hallett, more to be contrary than because he wished to defend the secret brotherhood.

"They don't know their place, that's what. They've got a lot of wild revolutionary ideas about abolishing compulsory technician's contracts, and letting engineers decide for themselves which company they'd like to work for. If their ideas were put through, it would gum up the whole machinery of our Corporate State. They—"

"Sh!"

They waited a while longer, but no more men came in. Eleven had entered the hole in the floor. Juniper-Hallett and

Lane-Walsh crawled over to the movable casket. They put their heads down next to the floor and next to various parts of the casket. From one place it was possible to hear a faint murmur of voices, but no words could be distinguished.

Juniper-Hallett said: "The watchmen must be in on it."

Lane-Walsh nodded. They went back to their hiding places and waited for something to happen.

It did, in the form of another visit by the night watchman. Juniper-Hallett rose and followed him in stocking feet, beckoning to Lane-Walsh.

The watchman had just turned the key in the last signal station on his route, when Lane-Walsh's big hands shut off his windpipe. He struggled and tried to yell, but nothing came out but a faint gurgle. Presently he was unconscious. Lane-Walsh relieved him of his pistol.

Juniper-Hallett looked doubtful at this. "You know what the law and the Convention say about carrying a firearm," he said.

Lane-Walsh sneered silently. "Bunk! A lot of the upper execs and entrepreneurs carry 'em. I know."

Juniper-Hallett subsided, and helped to tie up and gag the watchman. For anybody other than an authorized person, such as a watchman or soldier, to have a firearm in his possession was a serious violation of the statutes, and was an even worse violation of the Convention than hitting an engineer over the head with a wrecking bar. Young company members were allowed to settle their differences with duelling sticks instead, whose use seldom resulted in fatal injuries.

Juniper-Hallett admitted that Lane-Walsh probably knew what he was talking about. On the other hand it irritated him that the man should be so violently in favor of the legal and social scheme under which he lived, and at the same time be so cynically tolerant of violations of its laws and mores, at least by members of his own group. Juniper-Hallett was one of those serious-minded persons who can never understand wide discrepancies between theory and practice in human affairs.

THEY went back to the hall containing the movable casket. Lane-Walsh wanted to flash the light in the movable casket and, when the casket moved, to jump down and hold up the whole meeting. Juniper-Hallett refused.

They waited three hours more. Then the casket rumbled back. The eleven men climbed out one by one, five minutes apart, and disappeared.

"Now," said Juniper-Hallett.

"But, you damn fool, they're all gone! There won't be anybody in the hole!"

"Somebody let the first bird in," said Juniper-Hallett. "And unless he's gone out another exit he's there yet." He put his shoes on, went over to the movable casket, and pressed the light switch in the sequence of flashes used by the engineers.

The casket rumbled back. Light flooded up out of the hole.

Lane-Walsh, pistol ready, tumbled down the steep steps. Juniper-Hallett followed.

They were in a room, four or five meters square, with a door leading into another room. Two men were in the room. One was emptying ashtrays into a wastebasket. The other was gathering up empty coffee cups.

They stared at the intruders and at the intruders' gun. They slowly raised their hands.

One of them was the square man with the monocle, Duke-Holmquist. A patch of his scalp was shaven and covered with adhesive tape, where the wrecking bar had landed. The other man Juniper-Hallett did not know; he was a dark-skinned man with stiff gray hair and a smooth-contoured, slightly Mongoloid face.

"That's him. The dormouse," said Lane-Walsh, referring evidently to the dark man.

"Arnold Ryan to you, mister," said the dark man. "I'm tired of having people talk as if I were a rodent."

"All right, Arnold Ryan," said Lane-Walsh, "what's this all about? What are you doing here?"

"Looking for four-leafed clovers, sir," said Arnold Ryan.

"Come on, come on, no funny stuff. You see this gun?"

"I say, is that a gun? I thought it was a grand piano."

Lane-Walsh got red in the face. "When I ask you something I want an answer!" he roared.

"You got one. Two, to be exact."

Lane-Walsh showed signs of imminent apoplexy. "I want to know what this meeting was! Ayesmies or what?"

"The meeting," said Ryan imperturbably, "was of the Los Angeles Three-dimensional Chess Club."

Lane-Walsh tore at his coppery hair with his free hand. "Liar! If it were a chess club, you'd have boards and pieces!"

"That's simple. We play it in our heads."

Juniper-Hallett touched Lane-Walsh's arm. "Better let me talk to him," he said. He asked a few questions of the two men, but got no more satisfaction than had Lane-Walsh.

They held a whispered consultation. "What'll we do with 'em?" said Lane-Walsh. "If we start a public row, we'll expose the Ayesmy, but they'll take the dormouse away from us."

Juniper-Hallett thought. "I think I know a place where we can hide 'em for a few days." He addressed Duke-Holmquist: "Mr. Duke-Holmquist, I don't know why you went to so much trouble to steal Mr. Ryan. But it's obvious that you wanted him pretty badly. So I won't threaten you; I'll just say that unless you come along peacefully, we'll shoot Mr. Ryan. We'll *try* not to shoot him fatally. All right, Justin old fathead, make 'em follow me."

He led the way out of the secret room. Behind him he could hear a whispered argument between the two engineers: "I told you we ought to have changed the meeting place." "But we couldn't on such short notice; you know why." "Bunk! Once a dormouse was involved, somebody was bound to stumble on us sooner or later—"

VII.

MILES CAREY-WEST, Juniper-Hallett's elderly geneticist friend, was astonished to find four men ringing his doorbell at half-past one.

When the prisoners had filed in, Juniper-Hallett took Carey-West aside and explained the situation.

"Horace!" protested Carey-West. "I can't—That's a terrible thing to do to me! Where would I keep them? What if it were found out—"

"You could blame it all on us," said Juniper-Hallett. "And we'll keep them in your basement. Please! Maybe I can use them to stop the Stromberg-Crosley feud. And Janet—"

"Oh, very well," grumbled the geneticist. "No arguing with you, I see."

Duke-Holmquist and the ex-dormouse were taken down to the basement and made more or less comfortable.

"What'll we do now?" asked Lane-Walsh. "Flip a coin to see who gets 'em?"

"I've got a better idea than that," said Juniper-Hallett. He explained his plan for using the dormouse as bait to persuade the heads of the Stromberg and Crosley companies to bury their feud and merge.

"What!" cried Lane-Walsh. "Us join up with a lot of lousy Crosleys? The worst manufacturing company in the business?"

"Yep. You'll find we're not so bad."

"Oh, *I* see why you want it—so they'll let you and Janet live together peacefully. Though why some people are so hot about married life I never could see."

"That does enter in."

"Huh! As if it weren't bad enough that a good Stromberg gal goes and marries a weak sister like you, you want to ruin the proudest and noblest house of 'em all by—"

"Wait a minute, wait a minute, Justin old louse. Think of all the credit we'll get for stopping the feud and bringing about the merger! Everybody's forgotten what started it in the first place, and I'm sure the execs would be glad to call it off if they could do so without losing face."

"Hm-m-m. Well. Now that you put it that way—but I'd have to think about it."

"That's easy enough. We'll have to get some sleep before we can start our campaign."

They agreed that Lane-Walsh should take the first watch. Juniper-Hallett, as he curled up, gave his partner a fleeting glance. In his mind were the first seeds of suspicion. If he were asleep, and Lane-Walsh had the gun, and Lane-Walsh decided to double-cross him and turn Ryan over to his company forthwith—

But so far Lane-Walsh had played the game fairly enough, even though he and Juniper-Hallett liked each other no better than when they started. A double cross like that, so easy, would be a violation of the code. And Horace Juniper-Hallett still had a good deal of faith in his code. What would be would be. He went to sleep.

LANE-WALSH awakened him at three, gave him the gun, and went to sleep in his turn.

Across the dimly lit basement the prisoners sprawled on their mattress. Duke-Holmquist was asleep, but Arnold Ryan was looking at him silently with bright black eyes.

"I wish you birds would tell me something about your activities," said Juniper-Hallett.

"I," said Ryan, "am a biological engineer, as you ought to know. I'm working on the development of a variety of pepper tree that doesn't shed little sticky red berries all over the sidewalk, to stick to the soles of your shoes. Those little berries are one of the major drawbacks to life in your charming capital, as I see it."

"No, seriously," said Juniper-Hallett, feeling very young and inadequate in the presence of this smooth jokester. "If I knew what you were up to, I'd have a better idea of whether I was doing the right thing. For instance, you're part Hawaiian, aren't you?"

"Everybody knows that," said Ryan. "My mother's name was Victoria Liliuokalani Hashimoto, which is as good an old Hawaiian name as you'll find. Each of the names carries the flavor of one of the three main ethnic strains we're descended from."

"Are you working for the Hawaiians?"

Ryan laughed. "You wouldn't expect me to admit it if I were?" he asked.

"All right. Can you tell me something about Hawaii? As far as I know, no American has been there for many years."

Ryan shrugged. "I can tell you what I knew from first-hand experience before I went into the hibernine sleep; or I can tell you what I've heard in the few days since my awakening. Not, you understand, that I've been in personal touch with Hawaiians."

"Mainly I'd like to know why they don't let themselves be civilized like other people, and won't let anybody on their islands."

"Oh, that," said Ryan. "You think they should organize themselves into a tightly compartmented Corporate State like the American Empire, with an arrogant and disorderly aristocracy at the head of it, and worship Service at the Gyratory and Tigers' Clubs every Sunday, and spend half their time running their legs off to produce as much as possible, and the other half running their legs off trying to consume what they have produced?"

"Well—I didn't say they should; I asked why they didn't."

"They don't like the idea, that's all. They'd rather just lie on the beach. They've got a stationary population, all the food they can eat, and all the houses they can live in. And in that climate nobody wears much of anything anyway. They do a good deal of scientific research, partly for fun and partly to devise new ways of keeping out people they don't want. But production—phooey!"

"They sound like a lazy lot."

"They are. And they value the right to be lazy so much that they've wiped out three fleets sent out from the American and Mongolian empires to change their way of living."

JUNIPER-HALLETT'S conscience bothered him a little for getting all this information while his partner was asleep. But, he thought, he could tell him the important parts later. He asked: "Are they hooked up with the Ayesmy somehow?"

Ryan grinned. "Sorry, my boy, but you ought to know that topic is *kapu.*"

"Well, what *do* they want? They're up to something, I'm sure."

"I am told," said Ryan carefully, "that they're tired of living in a perpetual state of siege. They'd like to travel and see the world now and then. So, I suppose, they'd be glad to back any change in conditions in the empires that would enable them to do so."

"How did they manage to defeat those fleets?"

"As I understand it, by three means: one, a new source of power—neither coal, nor petroleum, nor atomic power. Don't ask me what it is, because I wouldn't tell you even if I knew. You'll hear more about it when the Antarctic coal fields run out. Two: a system of multiplying terrestrial magnetism over a given area, so that any fast-moving metal object, like an airplane engine, gets red-hot from eddy currents when it passes through the field. And finally their aërial torpedoes, which are nothing very remarkable except for their system of remote control. Now you know almost as much about their defenses as the defense chief of the Empire."

"What's the Ayesmy?"

"The American Society of Mechanical Engineers."

"I know that," said Juniper-Hallett. "But *who* are they and what are they trying to do?"

"You're the most persistent young fellow. But I'm not telling you anything that the heads of your companies don't know already. When the professional societies were suppressed as a disrupting influence by the first dictator, who came to power following the short-lived Communist regime that ruled after we lost the War of 1968—as I was saying, the A. S. M. E. was the only one that survived; underground, of course. And when the dictatorship began to decay under the fourth and fifth dictators, with the actual power being taken by a Board of Control representing the companies, they revived, though the companies fought them almost as hard as the dictators had done.

"Nowadays, as I understand it, the Ayesmy consists of a lot of engineers who don't like the Corporate State generally and the compulsory contract system in particular. They claim it makes them just high-priced slaves."

Juniper-Hallett was silent for a few seconds while he tried to figure out how the term "high-priced slave" applied to the engineers, and, if it did, what was so objectionable about that status. He asked: "What do you think about the compulsory contract system?"

"I don't. I never have opinions on political questions." Ryan gave a slight, malicious grin that told Juniper-Hallett he wasn't to take these statements too seriously.

"Look here, what would you like us to do with you?"

"Let us go, and forget you'd ever seen us or the room under the Crypt."

"Why?"

"We'd just prefer it, that's all."

"We can't very well do that," said Juniper-Hallett. "Our reinstatement depends on giving you up."

"I was afraid that was the case. But you asked me what we'd like."

"Is there any particular reason why we should let you go?"

Ryan shrugged. "Just say we're allergic to having the affairs of the Los Angeles Three-dimensional Chess Club poked into."

"Oh, now, you don't expect me to believe—"

"I don't care what you believe, young man."

Juniper-Hallett, feeling a bit hurt, shut up. This man fascinated him; Juniper-Hallett was sure he had the solution of all the little mysteries and discrepancies that had been puzzling him. But the man was not, he thought, inclined to meet him halfway.

"YOU understand," Juniper-Hallett told Lane-Walsh when they had breakfasted, "you're to telephone first to Lord Archwin, and then to Lord Billiam. You tell each one you'll hand the dormouse over to the other unless they'll listen to our proposals. When you've softened 'em up, arrange a three-way connection so you can talk terms. And—if you get a chance to send Janet here without letting the other Strombergs know where our hide-out is, I wish you would. This being just married and not even being able to see your wife is driving me nuts. Got it?"

"I get it, shrimp."

Juniper-Hallett hesitated. "I . . . I don't want you to think I'm suspicious, Justin old scum, but will you give me your word as a businessman?"

"Sure. You've got it."

Juniper-Hallett gave a sigh of relief. The word of a businessman was a pretty serious thing. He took the pistol from Lane-Walsh, and watched his partner tramp up the basement steps and out.

Duke-Holmquist turned his monocle on Juniper-Hallett. "You're a pretty trusting young man," he said.

Juniper-Hallett shrugged. "He gave me his word. And if he ever wants to be reinstated, he won't dare break it."

Arnold Ryan grinned sardonically. "You have a lot to learn," he said.

They were all silent. Juniper-Hallett paced the floor nervously, keeping an eye on his captives. These did not seem much disturbed. Ryan was chewing gum and Duke-Holmquist smoking a malodorous pipe.

"Tell me," said Juniper-Hallett to Ryan, "how did they wake you up?"

Ryan shrugged. "Strontium bromide; an otherwise more or less useless salt. Some bright Stromberg engineer discovered that it counteracted hibernine. They kidnapped me from the Crypt so they could wake me up and ask foolish questions about the Hawaiians' power, without having to release the formula to the Board of Control and bid against the other companies for my custody. If any one company got the secret of the Hawaiians' power, it could practically extort control of the Board when the coal shortage arrives."

Juniper-Hallett continued pacing. For the first hour he was not much concerned. But as the second wore on, he felt more and more queasy. Lane-Walsh, in accordance with his instructions, should have finished his telephoning and reported back by now. Of course, the fact that he was to make his different calls from different drugstores, in case one of the chairmen should try to locate him, would complicate matters. Juniper-Hallett couldn't leave his prisoners to do some telephoning of his own.

Time passed, and suspicion and alarm grew in Juniper-Hallett's young brain. Lane-Walsh might have met with foul play, or he might be indulging in a little of the same himself—

And he was tied to his prisoners. He didn't dare use his host's phone for fear of being located. He could not walk the captives around the streets in broad daylight at the point of a gun. He regarded the weapon with distaste; he had never fired one, and had been brought up to consider the possession of one by a whitecollar or businessman a disgraceful thing.

He heard old Carey-West's doorbell ring. He listened, tensely, for Lane-Walsh's return.

But it was Janet.

"Darling!" they both cried at once. In the midst of the embrace that followed, Juniper-Hallett had the presence of mind to swing his beloved around so that her back was to the captives, whom he still menaced with the gun.

"Here," said Juniper-Hallett, pressing the gun into her hand. "Cover these men; don't let them get away until I get back."

"But, Horace—"

"Can't explain now. Going out to phone. I'll be back shortly." And he bounded up the steps. Good old Justin—the louse had stuck to his word after all.

OUTSIDE the drizzle had ceased. Pools of water lay on the sidewalk, reflecting the cold blue of the sky. Juniper-Hallett shivered and stuck his hands deep in his pockets. He wished he had his overcoat along.

The nearest drugstore was The Sun at the corner of Wilshire. Juniper-Hallett found his way through the hardware and furniture departments to the phone booths, tucked in one corner of the sporting goods department.

He called Archwin of Crosley. As Lord Archwin was ex officio of the rank of entrepreneur, he could be located at any time through his private portable radiotelephone set.

"Horace!" cried Lord Archwin. "Where are you, my boy? I've been worried about you. Very much worried."

"I'm all right, Your Integrity," said Juniper-Hallett. "And I've got the dormouse."

"You have? You have? Where? We'll come collect him, at once!"

"Just a minute, Your Integrity. You see, I didn't catch him all by myself." He gave a thumbnail account of his co-operation with Justin Lane-Walsh, and of his offer to give up the dormouse in return for the chairman's promise to initiate a merger.

Archwin of Crosley heard him through, then asked suspiciously: "Where's that Lane-Walsh? Is he with you?"

"No, sir, he went out to phone you and his own chairman, leaving me with the prisoners. But I haven't heard from him, and I'm afraid something happened to—"

"You idiot!" yelled Archwin into his transmitter. "Idiot! Idiot! Imbecile! Fool! Don't you know he's gone to get the Strombergs to take your men away from you? Don't you know that?"

"But he gave me his word as a businessman—"

"Idiot! What's a businessman's word worth? Nothing, when his company's interests are involved! Nothing! What's any Stromberg's word worth? Nothing, again! You tell us where to find the dormouse, quick, before the Strombergs get there, or—"

"Hey!" said Juniper-Hallett. "I won't do anything of the kind. And Justin Lane-Walsh did keep his word, at least as far as sending my wife to me. I've kept my word and he's—"

"You utter nitwit!" shrieked the chairman. "You young jackass! You can kiss your reinstatement good-by! We don't want traitors and sentimental pantywaists in the organization! You—"

Juniper-Hallett had heard Lord Archwin in a tantrum before, and knew that arguments were useless. He hung up and started sadly back to the geneticist's house. If the chairman said he wouldn't readmit him to the company, he wouldn't readmit him to the company. He wondered whether Lane-Walsh had gotten in touch with his own chairman—

And then an ominous thought struck him. He walked faster.

Janet was still there in the basement, covering the two engineers, who were being gallant.

Juniper-Hallett bounded down the steps. "Janet! Didn't Justin Lane-Walsh send you here?"

"Why no, Horace. I haven't heard from Justin since he was degraded. I came here because I thought Mr. Carey-West could tell me where you—"

"Oh my Service! Then Justin did double-cross me! Lord Archwin was right; I *am* an idiot. Now I'm in bad with the Crosleys, and Justin'll be here any minute with a gang of Strombergs!" He took the pistol from Janet and laid it on the table. He turned to Ryan and Duke-Holmquist. "I guess you birds can go; I don't see how I can do any good keeping you here."

The engineers grinned as if they had expected something of the sort all along. Duke-Holmquist said: "Why don't you throw in with us, young man? You can't expect anything from the companies, you know."

"I don't know . . . I don't know what you stand for—"

Duke-Holmquist opened his mouth to say something. Just then the door flew open, and four Strombergs with duelling sticks tumbled down the steps. In their lead was Justin Lane-Walsh.

LANE-WALSH pounced on the pistol. He turned to Juniper-Hallett, grinning nastily. "Hah, sister, so you're still here, huh? Very nice, ve-ery nice indeed. We'll take these smart engineers along. But first we'll teach you to marry a decent Stromberg girl."

Janet exploded. "You let him alone! He's my husband!"

"Exactly; that's just the point. But when we get through with him he won't be anybody's husband. Then maybe you can marry some decent Stromberg. Not me, of course," he added hastily.

Janet punched Justin Lane-Walsh in the nose.

Horace Juniper-Hallett kicked one of the Strombergs in the shin, violating Paragraph 9a, Section D, Rule 5 of the Convention. Then he wrenched the stick out of the man's hands, and hit him over the head with it.

The two engineers went into action likewise. Juniper-Hallett never could remember just what happened next. He did remember boosting Janet up the steps by main force, the engineers behind him, and slamming and locking the basement door just as the pistol roared and a bullet tore through the plastic.

"Mmglph," said a bundle of ropes on the floor. It was Miles Carey-West. They cut him loose. Another bullet crashed through the door; they all ducked.

"What do we do now?" asked Juniper-Hallett.

The two engineers had been whispering. Duke-Holmquist said: "Follow me."

They sprinted out of the house. Carey-West panted after them, crying: "Can I come, too? I'm sunk anyway once it comes out that you used my house."

Duke-Holmquist nodded curtly and walked swiftly to Wilshire Boulevard. There he hailed a cab and piled his whole party into it. "The Dormouse Crypt," he told the driver.

"Where are we going?" asked Juniper-Hallett.

"Hawaii," said Duke-Holmquist.

"What?" Juniper-Hallett turned his puzzled frown to Ryan.

Ryan, instead of explaining how one got to Hawaii via the Crypt, said: "He's convinced finally that his strike plan's fallen through. We'll have to skip. You'd better come along."

Duke-Holmquist nodded gloomily. "If I'd had a couple more years to prepare—"

They zipped up the steep hill at the north end of Western Avenue.

Janet said: "But I'm not sure I want to go to Hawaii—"

"Sh, sweetheart," said Juniper-Hallett. "We're in this up to our necks, and we might as well stick with them." He turned to Ryan. "I can't understand why Lane-Walsh, if he was going to double-cross me, didn't do it last night while I was asleep and he had the gun."

Ryan shrugged. "He probably didn't make up his mind to do so until after he left Carey-West's house. He's not terribly bright, from what I hear."

They stopped and got out. Duke-Holmquist told the driver to wait, and strode up to the front entrance of the Crypt. He whispered to the doorman.

The doorman stepped inside and shouted: "All visitors out, please! There's a time bomb in the Crypt, and it may go off any minute. All out, please! There's a time bomb, and these experts have come to take it away. All—"

He jumped aside as the first of the visitors to realize what he was saying went through the turnstile with his overcoat fluttering behind him. The others followed in record time. It did not take long, for it was still morning, and the Crypt was not yet full of visitors.

The engineers went straight to the movable casket, put their shoulders to it, and rolled it back. Juniper-Hallett and his bride followed them down into the underground room.

They did not take the time to pull the rope that slid the casket back over the hole. They went straight to a wall cupboard, opened it, and took out a simple electrical apparatus which Juniper-Hallett did not recognize.

A couple of wires led from the apparatus back into the cabinet. The apparatus had a brass arm with a circular pad on the end of it. Duke-Holmquist began depressing and releasing this arm, so that it went *tick-tick-tick, tick, tick-tick,* and so on. Juniper-Hallett was mystified. Then he remembered that one of the pioneers in electrical communication, centuries before, had invented a system of sending words over wires by having intermittent impulses represent the letters. The man's name had been—Morris? Marcy? No matter. Duke-Holmquist was sending a message of some kind. And now and then he paused while the machine ticked back at him.

One of the Crypt guards put his head down the hole. "Mr. Duke-Holmquist, sir!" he said. "They've come!"

"The Strombergs?"

"Yes, sir. Automobiles full of them."

VIII.

DUKE-HOLMQUIST finished his ticking and stood up. He asked: "Have any of you boys guns?"

"No, sir. Toomey-Johnson, the night watchman, is the only one of us allowed to have one, and his was taken off him the other night."

The burly engineer cursed softly. Then he bounded up the steep steps. The others followed.

About fifteen Strombergs stood around the entrance, hefting their sticks. Their way was barred by three guards with billies. Justin Lane-Walsh, among them, yelled in: "You might as well send 'em out, or we'll come in and get 'em!"

Juniper-Hallett asked Duke-Holmquist: "What are the cops doing?"

"We don't want to call in the police, and neither do they." The engineer turned to the guard who had called them: "How about the rear entrance?"

"They got some men there, too, sir; all around."

"Looks as though we were stuck," said Duke-Holmquist somberly.

Juniper-Hallett fingered the stick he had taken from the Stromberg. "Our cab's still out there."

"Yes, but we haven't got a chance of getting to it."

"I don't know," said Juniper-Hallett. "I can run pretty fast."

"You've got an idea, Juniper-Hallett?"

"Yep. I'll draw 'em off, and you make a run for the cab."

"Horace!" said Janet. "You must not take such a risk—"

"That's all right, darling." He kissed her and trotted off to the rear entrance.

Two guards inside it faced three Strombergs outside. Juniper-Hallett pushed between the guards and leaped at the nearest Stromberg. *Whack! Whack!* The Stromberg dropped his stick with a howl. The others closed in on Juniper-Hallett; one of them landed a blow on his shoulder. Then Juniper-Hallett wasn't there any more. He dodged past them and raced around the big building over the smooth lawn. He hit one of the front-door Strombergs and kept on running, pausing just long enough to thumb his nose at the rest as they turned startled faces toward him.

Yapping like a pack of hounds, they streamed away after him. He ran down the long hill, breathing easily. This was fun. He could outrun the whole lot—

He took another glance back, and ran into a fire hydrant. He went sprawling, fiery pain shooting through his right leg. The yells rose as they pounded down to seize him.

The cab squealed to a stop just beside him. He had barely the strength and presence of mind to reach a hand up; a hand from the cab caught it and pulled him in. That is, it pulled him part way in; a Stromberg got a hand on his ankle.

"Ow!" yelled Juniper-Hallett.

The tug-of-war was decided by the cab driver, who spun his rheostat. Off they went. The would-be captor was dragged a few steps, and then let go.

"I think my leg's broken," said Juniper-Hallett. Ryan felt the leg and decided it was just bruised.

Janet, looking out the rear window, said: "They're coming in their cars."

"Can't you go any faster?" Duke-Holmquist asked the driver.

"Governor's on," was the reply. "Can't do over sixty k's."

"Damn," said Duke-Holmquist.

"What's that?" asked Ryan. "Cars have governors nowadays?"

"Yes. They go on automatically when you enter a built-up area. But if we can't do over sixty, neither can they."

THEY purred sedately down Western Avenue at sixty kilometers per hour, and the Stromberg force purred after them. Now and then one party would gain when the other was held up by traffic. But on the whole they maintained the same interval.

Duke-Holmquist asked the driver: "When does it go off?"

"Slauson Avenue."

"When it does go off," said Juniper-Hallett, "they'll be able to catch us. They've got big, fast cars. Where are we headed for, anyway?"

"San Pedro," said Duke-Holmquist.

"Are we taking a seaplane?"

"No. The navy could catch us easily."

"Submarine?"

"No. There hasn't been time for the Hawaiians to send us one."

"What, then?"

"You'll see."

"But—" Just then they reached the southern limit of the governor zone, and Juniper-Hallett's question was choked off by the cab's spurt. The driver kept his hand on the horn button. They gained several blocks on the pursuers before the latter reached the edge of the zone and accelerated.

"They're gaining," said Janet.

"Oh, dear," said Carey-West. The little oldster was trembling.

They squealed around a corner and raced over to Main Street, then took another corner.

"They're still coming," said Janet.

A little while later she said: "They're gaining again."

Duke-Holmquist and Ryan looked at each other. "Maybe we could figure the point where they'll catch us by differentials," said the former.

"Maybe," said Ryan, "we could tell 'em we're not us, but a family on its way to a polo game."

Juniper-Hallett looked to the right of the car into the open cut in which the Pacific Electric's inter-urban line ran. "Hey!" he said, "look down there!"

Half a mile ahead of them they could see the tapering stern of a car pulling into the North Compton station.

"Change to a streetcar?" said Duke-Holmquist.

"Right. Hey, driver!"

They skidded into the station. They were scrambling aboard a few seconds later when the Stromberg cars pulled up.

The streetcar was a thirty-meter torpedo that ran on two rails, one below it and the other overhead. The motorman's compartment was a closed-off section in the nose. The four men and the girl marched up to the front of the car, threw open the door, and crowded into the compartment. The legitimate passengers looked at one another. They had never seen that happen before. But then these people had seemed to know what they were doing, so *they* didn't feel called upon to interfere. The car started, a bit jerkily. It accelerated up to its normal two hundred kilometers per hour. It kept on accelerating. The passengers began to mutter and look to their safety belts.

Inside the compartment, the motorman, who was being firmly sat upon by Duke-Holmquist and Ryan, protested: "You'll pass Gardena station! This is a local! You gotta stop at Gardena!"

"Hell with Gardena," said Juniper-Hallett over his shoulder. He was at the controls.

"How fast is she going?" asked Ryan.

"Three hundred and thirty-six k's."

"You'll burn out the fuel batteries!" wailed the motorman.

Juniper-Hallett said soothingly: "The P.E. can sue us, then. Say, maybe you'd better tell me how to stop this thing, motorman old sock!"

"What?" shrieked the motorman. "You don't even know?"

Somebody knocked on the door. The committee ignored the knock. Somebody tried the door, but they had locked it in advance.

The motorman told Juniper-Hallett how to stop the car. He also asked where they were.

"I'm not sure," said Juniper-Hallett, "everything goes by in such a blur. Matter of fact, I think we're near Anaheim Road."

"Then stop it! Stop it!" yelled the motorman. "Or we'll go right off the end of the track into the drink!"

"Oh, my!" said Carey-West.

JUNIPER-HALLETT applied the brake. The landscape continued to flash past; they had come out of the cut onto an embankment. Juniper-Hallett applied more brake. Wilmington rushed at them. The deceleration squashed them all against the front of the car. They were through Wilmington and screeching down the end of the line. The bumpers grew at them as the landscape finally slowed down. They hit the bumpers with a bang, and tumbled backward.

They raced out through a car full of jade-faced passengers. Duke-Holmquist led them a couple of blocks to the waterfront.

"Damaso!" yelled Duke-Holmquist.

A swarthy man stuck his face up over the edge of the nearest pier. "Hiya, boss!" he said.

"Everything ready?"

"Sure is, sir."

They tumbled breathlessly down steps and into an outboard boat. Before they had recovered their breath, Damaso had cast off and purred out to a dirty-white yawl anchored among a flock of motorboats, sailboats, and tuna clippers.

"Are we going in *that?*" gasped Juniper-Hallett.

"Uh-huh. Climb aboard."

"But you're crazy! They'll catch us in a police launch or something in ten minutes!"

"Do as you're told," snapped Duke-Holmquist.

Juniper-Hallett, half convinced that he was accompanying a party of lunatics, hopped aboard the yawl and helped Janet up. Damaso was already casting off from the buoy. The yawl had a little coke-gas auxiliary that sputtered into feeble life. Juniper-Hallett was sure the engineers were crazy; starting for Hawaii—with half the Stromberg Co., and the Los Angeles Harbor Police, not to mention the Imperial American Navy, likely to be after them any time—in a little cockleshell designed for taking people out for a day's fishing. The boat did stink of fish, at that, and the low afternoon sun glinted on a silvery scale here and there.

They vibrated out of the long channel with maddening slowness. Juniper-Hallett squeezed Janet's hand until she complained he was hurting her.

"Take it easy," said Ryan. "Duke-Holmquist knows what he's doing."

"I hope he does," said Carey-West. "Oh, dear, why did I get mixed up in this?"

"Don't worry about the police," said Duke-Holmquist, his monocle reflecting the sun as he stood at the wheel. "Lieutenant More-Love is one of our sympathizers. The P.E. will try to set them after us, but he'll see that they look every place except the right one."

"How about the Strombergs?" asked Juniper-Hallett.

"I think one of those young nobles owns a seaplane. If they come after us, there may be trouble. We'll worry about that when the time comes."

THEY were out of the channel. In the outer harbor sat part of the navy: a seaplane mother ship, three hundred meters long, with five of her birds around her; flying boats with a one-hundred and fifty-meter wing-spread, each of which carried launches and dinghies larger than the fishing yawl.

Juniper-Hallett looked at Duke-Holmquist, jerked his thumb toward the flying boats, and raised his eyebrows.

Duke-Holmquist said: "I think the Strombergs will do everything they can to catch us themselves first, before they call in the Board of Control. If they take us, it probably won't be alive."

"You're the head of the Ayesmy, aren't you, sir?"

Duke-Holmquist permitted himself a wry smile. "You're right, youngster. Or I was until I had to run away."

They were rising and falling in the Pacific swells now. Juniper-Hallett said: "I wish they'd come if they're going to. I don't like this waiting."

"The longer the wait, the better our chances," said Ryan imperturbably.

Juniper-Hallett asked: "What was the Ayesmy up to?"

Duke-Holmquist replied: "We were going to pull a strike of all engineers, to have the compulsory contract system abolished. We were going to force a lot of other reforms, too, to break down the compartmentation of the Corporate State and give everybody a hand in the government. But it was terribly slow work operating by means of an illegal organization. If we tried to take in all the technicians, there'd bound to be a leak. And if we didn't, we couldn't count on the nonmembers when the time came."

"The truth is," said Ryan, "that they'd never have gotten sufficient co-operation from the profession anyway. Your average engineer is too much enamored of respectability and dignity to go in for revolutionary conspiracy. For the privilege of rating salutes from the whitecollars, they'll put up with their state of gilded peonage indefinitely."

"That's not fair, Arnold," protested Duke-Holmquist. "You know those—"

"We've argued this before," said Ryan, "and we've never gotten anywhere. I say, isn't that our friends?" He pointed north at a silvery speck in the sky.

Janet said: "Justin kept his plane at Redondo Beach."

"That's what took them so long," said Duke-Holmquist. "Damaso! Get the things out." He grinned at the company, once again self-confident at the prospect of violent action. "Stand by to repel boarders!"

The seaplane grew, soared overhead, turned, and came down with a smack on the waves. It taxied up astern of the yawl.

As it approached, they could see Justin Lane-Walsh climbing out on the left wing. His mouth opened and moved, but they could not hear him against the wind and the whir of the propeller. The seaplane swung to one side and came up abreast of them to windward. The other Strombergs climbed out, too. Lane-Walsh yelled, this time audibly: "Heave to, you!"

Duke-Holmquist said: "Do you see that pistol anywhere?"

"No," said everybody after looking.

Ryan added: "Maybe they lost it, or emptied it breaking the lock of that door."

"Fine," said Duke-Holmquist. He put his hands to his mouth and bellowed: "Keep off or we'll sink you!"

"Haw haw," roared the Strombergs.

The yawl pounded ahead through the swells, and the breeze blew the seaplane astern of them again. The pilot gave the motor more juice, and the machine crept up alongside once more.

Duke-Holmquist called: "Let 'em have it, Damaso!"

DAMASO, standing on the forward deck with his feet spread, was doing a curious thing. He was whirling around his head a length of rope to the end of which was tied a block of wood. He gave a fast whirl and let fly. The block flew toward the plane, the rope snaking after it.

The Strombergs saw it coming, and evidently thought those

in the yawl were throwing them a rope to make fast. A couple braced themselves and spread their hands as if to catch it. But such was not Damaso's intention. The block hit the propeller with a terrific clank; splinters flew; the propeller stopped turning with a jar that shook the seaplane. The propeller was seen to have one blade sharply bent, and to have meters of rope tangled around its hub.

The Strombergs set up a howl of rage. Some of them climbed out on the left wing as if ready to jump down into the yawl, toward which the wind was swiftly blowing them. The seaplane tipped alarmingly. The pilot yelled. A couple of Strombergs crawled out on the other wing to balance the craft.

Damaso hurried aft with a boathook.

Duke-Holmquist said: "Get ready to jab a hole in their float at the water line."

Damaso poised himself. The Strombergs, yelling threats, clustered at the end of the wing. At the tip was Justin Lane-Walsh.

For a breathless thirty seconds the parties glared at each other, as the two craft bobbed closer and closer. Duke-Holmquist spun the wheel a little, the yawl nosed downwind a few points.

"They're going to drift astern of us," said Juniper-Hallett.

Duke-Holmquist laughed shortly. "Don't you think I ever ran a boat before?"

The wind pressure on the seaplane's rudder had swung the craft into the wind like a weather vane, so that, though it was drifting astern of them, its left wing was still toward them. Justin Lane-Walsh gathered himself to jump; but they were not quite close enough.

"Hey," said Juniper-Hallett, "we need that bird!"

He snatched the boathook from Damaso and shot the business end up to the seaplane wing. He caught the hook in Lane-Walsh's starspangled pants and yanked. Lane-Walsh's legs went out from under him; he sat down on the wing tip, bounced, and smacked the water. A cloud of spray rose, and was instantly blown down against the receding seaplane.

Juniper-Hallett caught a glimpse of a head of copper-wire hair, but it was already out of reach of his hook. Duke-Holmquist nodded and brought the boat around in a big circle. They came upon Lane-Walsh, swimming heavily in his clothes toward the seaplane, which was drifting swiftly in the general direction of Ensenada. They hauled him aboard. The chatter of his teeth came clearly over the puttering of the engine. The Pacific off sunny southern California is icy in February.

Juniper-Hallett explained: "I just remembered that he was with me in the Crypt the night we made our raid, and recognized several of the Ayesmy members. He'd have made trouble for them if we'd left him here."

"Good work, boy," said Duke-Holmquist.

JUNIPER-HALLETT winced at the "boy." If being married didn't make one a full-grown man, entitled to the respect accorded to such, what did?

He asked: "Are we safe now, sir?"

"No," said Duke-Holmquist. "They'll radio their company, and the company will appeal to the Board of Control to order the navy out to stop us."

"Then it's useless to try to get away?"

"We'll see."

Ryan climbed out of the cabin, whither he and Damaso had taken Lane-Walsh to change his clothes. Juniper-Hallett asked him: "How do you fit into this, sir?"

Ryan's smooth brown face smiled, and the wind ruffled his stiff gray hair. He said: "I was to be a go-between for the Ayesmy and the Hawaiians. The Hawaiians wanted to back the Ayesmy in upsetting the Corporate system, because it would end the siege of the Islands. But they wanted somebody they could trust, not having any agents on the mainland. I was the only one, and I was in a hibernine sleep.

"Then that Stromberg engineer discovered the effect of strontium bromide, and the Strombergs stole me from the Crypt to try to get the secret of the Hawaiians' power from me. It was developed back before I went to sleep, you know. Of course, the Stromberg engineers who were also Ayesmies knew about the theft, and arranged to have the Ayesmy rescue me."

"How did the Ayesmy communicate with the Hawaiians? I'd think their messages would be intercepted."

"They would have been, if they had been sent the normal

way. But people used to communicate with the Islands, centuries ago, by undersea cables, and those cables are still there. The mainland end of one of them is in a museum in Frisco. The Ayesmy spliced a lead into it and used the ancient dot-dash method."

"What is the Hawaiian power?"

"Maxwell demons, sir," said Arnold Ryan.

"What?"

"Special bacteria. Bacteria are the only things that can break the second law of thermodynamics, you know. They can, for instance, separate levulose from fructose, though the molecules of these sugars are identical except that one is a mirror image of the other. Starting with these bacteria, the Hawaiians have developed strains that will build up hydrocarbons out of water and carbon dioxide, taking their energy directly from the heat of the solution. So the solution gets cold, and has to be brought back to outside temperatures to keep the reaction going. But they have the whole Pacific Ocean to warm it up with. It's like putting a lump of ice in a highball, and instead of the ice's melting, having the ice get colder and the highball hotter."

Juniper-Hallett did not understand much of this. He asked: "Then are all these plans for breaking the Corporate system finished?"

"Not quite. The Antarctic coal fields will run out in a couple of years, and we'll be able to dictate our own terms to the Empires. Meanwhile we'll sit in the sun in the Islands and take life easy. You'll like it, I think. We Hawaiians haven't such an elaborate code as the mainlanders, but we stick better to the one we have." He shaded his eyes. "That is, you'll like it if we get there alive. Here comes the navy now."

THEY all looked back toward the mainland. The air was full of a deep throbbing sound which grew to the roar of one of the giant flying boats.

The monster thundered past them, seeming to skim the waves, though it actually was a good thirty meters up. A gun cracked, and a 10.5-centimeter shell crashed in front of them.

"That means heave to," said Duke-Holmquist. His red face

got redder and he shook a fist. He made no move to stop the boat.

The machine came back on the opposite side, between them and Santa Catalina Island. Another shell crashed, this time closer. It sent up a tall finger of water, which hung for an unreasonable time before collapsing.

Juniper-Hallett asked: "Will they try to board us?"

"Not if I know the navy," said Duke-Holmquist. "They'd like a little target practice on a live target."

The machine banked ponderously astern of them. This time, as it passed, it let loose a full broadside.

"Duck!" yelled Duke-Holmquist, doing so.

The air was suddenly full of noises like a train wreck and six shells hit all around them. Splinters whined overhead; a couple crashed through the yawl's planking; one of the columns of water toppled onto their deck, drenching them.

The yawl staggered, but kept on. The next time, Juniper-Hallett thought, they'll blow us to pieces. He hugged Janet, and heard Ryan's voice in his ear: "Sorry we got you kids into this—didn't have time to warn you—"

The navy ship thundered past again. Juniper-Hallett held his breath. It was coming—

Their engine stopped with a wheeze. Duke-Holmquist bounded to his feet with an inhuman scream. "They did it!" he yelled, dancing and waving his big fists.

"Did what?" asked Juniper-Hallett. Then he realized that the rumble of the flying boat's propellers had ceased. The only sounds were those of wind and water. He looked over the lee gunwale to see the flying boat glide silently down to the surface and settle like a big duck a kilometer or two away. He repeated: "Did what?"

"The Hawaiians got their thing that multiplies the terrestrial magnetic field turned on, so that there's a strip all along the coast that nothing can get through but a sailboat or rowboat. That's what I was wiring about from the Crypt. Now do you see why we started out in this little thing? Damaso! Damn it, come out of that cabin; the war's over. Fix those holes in the woodwork. Arnold, do you know how to get the sails up? Here, boy, take the wheel while I'm helping Ryan."

THE deck was now sharply canted to the brisk northeast breeze.

The sun was half below the horizon ahead of them. When they crested a swell, a broad highway of golden reflection glared in their faces.

Horace Juniper-Hallett and his wife sat bundled in sweaters and things, their feet braced, watching for flying fish and ducking the cold spray. The navy flying boat was out of sight, even from the tops of the swells.

Janet gave up trying to wax her nose to the proper degree of shininess, and turned to Juniper-Hallett. She said. "Horace! I just remembered my cat! My little Dolores!"

"Dolores'll have a nice home—in the zoo."

She sighed. "I suppose so. Anyway we're alone at last, dearest."

Juniper-Hallett looked around the little yawl, which was very much occupied by its seven passengers. The cabin seemed to be half full of canned goods, and the other half full of a morose, blanket-wrapped Justin Lane-Walsh. Obviously everyone would be very much in everyone else's hair for many days.

"Not quite, sweetheart," Juniper-Hallett replied. "But we shall be. We shall be."

The Fifth-Dimension Tube

By Murray Leinster

CHAPTER I
The Tube

THE generator rumbled and roared, building up to its maximum speed. The whole laboratory quivered from its vibration. The dynamo hummed and whined and the night silence outside seemed to make the noises within more deafening. Tommy Reames ran his eyes again over the power-leads to the monstrous, misshapen coils. Professor Denham bent over one of them, straightened, and nodded. Tommy Reames nodded to Evelyn, and she threw the heavy multiple-pole switch.

There was a flash of jumping current. The masses of metal on the floor seemed to leap into ungainly life. The whine of the dynamo rose to a scream and its brushes streaked blue flame. The metal things on the floor flicked together and were a tube, three feet and more in diameter. That tube writhed and twisted. It began to form itself into an awkward and seemingly impossible shape, while metal surfaces sliding on each other produced screams that cut through the din of the motor and dynamo. The writhing tube strained and wriggled. Then there was a queer, inaudible *snap* and something gave. A part of the tube quivered into nothingness. Another part hurt the eyes that looked upon it.

And then there was the smell of burned insulation and a wire was arcing somewhere while thick rubbery smoke arose. A fuse blew out with a thunderous report, and Tommy Reames leaped to the suddenly racing motor-generator. The motor died amid gasps and rumblings. And Tommy Reames looked anxiously at the Fifth-Dimension Tube.

It was important, that Tube. Through it, Tommy Reames and Professor Denham had reason to believe they could travel to another universe, of which other men had only dreamed. And it was important in other ways, too. At the moment Evelyn Denham threw the switch, last-edition newspapers in Chicago were showing headlines about "King" Jacaro's forfeiture of two hundred thousand dollars' bail by failing to appear in court. King Jacaro was a lord of racketeerdom.

While Tommy inspected the Tube anxiously, a certain chief of police in a small town upstate was telling feverishly over the telephone of a posse having killed a monster lizard by torchlight, having discovered it in the act of devouring a cow. The lizard was eight feet high, walked on its hind legs, and had a collar of solid gold about its neck. And jewel importers, in New York, were in anxious conference about a flood of untraced jewels upon the market. Their origin was unknown. The Fifth-Dimension Tube ultimately affected all of those affairs, and the Death Mist as well. And—though it was not considered dangerous then—everybody remembers the Death Mist now.

But at the moment, Professor Denham stared at the Tube concernedly, his daughter Evelyn shivered from pure excitement as she looked at it, and a red-headed man named Smithers looked impassively from the Tube to Tommy Reames and back again. He'd done most of the mechanical work on the Tube's parts, and he was as anxious as the rest. But nobody thought of the world outside the laboratory.

Professor Denham moved suddenly. He was nearest to the open end of the Tube. He sniffed curiously and seemed to listen. Within seconds the others became aware of a new smell in the laboratory. It seemed to come from the Tube itself, and it was a warm, damp smell that could only be imagined as coming from a jungle in the tropics. There were the rich odors of feverishly growing things; the heavy fragrance of unknown tropic blossoms, and a background of some curious blend of scents and smells which was alien and luring and exotic. The whole was like the smell of another planet, of the jungles of a strange world which men had never trod. And then, definitely coming out of the Tube, there was a hollow, booming noise.

IT had been echoed and re-echoed amid the twistings of the Tube, but only an animal could have made it. It grew louder, a monstrous roar. Then yells sounded suddenly above it—human yells, wild yells, insane, half-gibbering yells of hysterical excitement and blood lust. The beast-thing bellowed and an ululating chorus of joyous screams arose. The laboratory reverberated with the thunderous noise. Then there was the sound of crashing and of paddings, and abruptly the noise was diminishing as if its source were moving farther away. The beast-thing roared and bellowed as if in agony, and the yelling noise seemed to show that men were following close upon its flanks.

Those in the laboratory seemed to awaken as if from a bad dream. Denham was kneeling before the mouth of the Tube, an automatic rifle in his hands. Tommy Reames stood grimly before Evelyn. He'd snatched up a pair of automatic pistols. Smithers clutched a spanner and watched the mouth of the Tube with a strained attention. Evelyn stood shivering behind Tommy.

Tommy said with a hint of grim humor:

"I don't think there's any doubt about the Tube having gotten through. That's the Fifth-Dimension planet, all right."

He smiled at Evelyn. She was deathly pale.

"I—remember—hearing noises like that. . . ."

Denham stood up. He painstakingly slipped on the safety of his rifle and laid it on a bench with the other guns. There was a small arsenal on a bench at one side of the laboratory. The array looked much more like arms for an expedition into dangerous territory than a normal part of apparatus for an experiment in rather abstruse mathematical physics. There were even gas masks on the bench, and some of those converted brass Very pistols now used only for discharging tear- and sternutatory gas bombs.

"The Tube wasn't seen, anyhow," said Professor Denham briskly. "Who's going through first?"

Tommy slung a cartridge belt about his waist and a gas mask about his neck.

"I am," he said shortly. "We'll want to camouflage the mouth of the Tube. I'll watch a bit before I get out."

He crawled into the mouth of the twisted pipe.

THE Tube was nearly three feet across, each section was five feet long, and there were gigantic solenoids at each end of each section.

It was not an experiment made at random, nor was the world to which it reached an unknown one to Tommy or to Denham. Months before, Denham had built an instrument which would bend a ray of light into the Fifth Dimension, and had found that he could fix a telescope to the device and look into a new and wholly strange cosmos. He had seen tree-fern jungles and a monstrous red sun, and all the flora and fauna of a planet in the carboniferous period of development. More, by the accident of its placing he had seen the towers and the pinnacles of a city whose walls and towers seemed plated with gold.

Having gone so far, he had devised a catapult which literally flung objects to the surface of that incredible world. Insects, birds, and at last a cat had made the journey unharmed, and he had built a steel globe in which to attempt the journey in person. His daughter Evelyn had demanded to accompany him, and he believed it safe. The trip had been made in security, but return was another matter. A laboratory assistant, Von Holtz, had sent them into the Fifth Dimension, only to betray them. One King Jacaro, lord of Chicago racketeers, was convinced by him of the existence of the golden city of that other world, and that it was full of delectable loot. He offered a bribe past envy for the secret of Denham's apparatus. And Von Holtz had removed the apparatus for Denham's return before working the catapult to send him on his strange journey. He wanted to be free to sell full privileges of rapine and murder to Jacaro.

The result was unexpected. Von Holtz could not unravel the secret of the catapult he himself had operated. He could not sell the secret for which he had committed a crime. In desperation he called in Tommy Reames—rather more than an amateur in mathematical physics—showed him Evelyn and her father marooned in a tree-fern jungle, and hypocritically asked for aid.

Tommy's enthusiastic efforts soon became more than merely enthusiastic. The men of the Golden City remained invisible, but there were strange, half-mad outlaws of the jungles who hated the city. Tommy Reames had watched helplessly as they hunted for the occupants of the steel globe. He had worked frenziedly to achieve a rescue. In the course of his labor he discovered the treachery of Von Holtz as well as the secret of the catapult, and with the aid of Smithers—who had helped to build the original catapult—he made a new small device to achieve the original end.

THE whole affair came to an end on one mad afternoon when the Ragged Men captured first an inhabitant of the Golden City, and then Denham and Evelyn in a forlorn attempt at rescue. Tommy Reames went mad. He used a tiny sub-machine gun upon the Ragged Men through the model magnetic catapult he had made, and contrived communication with Denham afterward. Instructed by Denham, he brought about the return of father and daughter to Earth just before Ragged Men and Earthlings alike would have perished in a vengeful gas cloud from the Golden City. Even then, though, his triumph was incomplete because Von Holtz had gotten word to Jacaro, and nattily-dressed gunmen raided the laboratory and made off with the model catapult, leaving three bullets in Tommy and one in Smithers as souvenirs.

Now, using the principle developed in the catapult, Tommy and Denham had built a large Tube, and as Tommy climbed along its corrugated interior he knew a good part of what he should expect at the other end. A steady current of air blew past him. It was laden with a myriad unfamiliar scents. The Tube was a tunnel from one set of dimensions to another, a permanent way from Earth to a strange, carboniferous-period planet on which a monstrous dull-red sun shone hotly. Tommy should come out into a tree-fern forest whose lush vegetation would hide the sky, and which furnished a lurking place not only for strange reptilian monsters akin to those of the long-dead past of Earth, but for the bands of ragged, half-mad human beings who were outlaws from the civilization of which Denham and Evelyn had seen proofs.

TOMMY reached the third bend in the Tube. By now he had lost all sense of orientation. An object may be bent through one right angle only in two dimensions, and a second perfect right angle—at ninety degrees to all former paths—only in three dimensions. It follows that a third perfect right angle requires four dimensions for existence, and four perfect right angles five. The Tube bent itself through four perfect right angles, and since no human being can ever have experience of more than three dimensions, plus time, it followed that Tommy was experiencing other dimensions than those of Earth as soon as he passed the third bend. In short, he was in another cosmos.

There was a moment of awful sickness as he passed the third bend. He was hideously dizzy when he passed the fourth. For a time he felt as if he had no weight at all. But then, quite abruptly, he was climbing vertically upward and the soughing of tree-fern fronds was loud in his ears, and suddenly the end of the Tube was under his fingers and he stared out into the world of the Fifth Dimension.

Now a gentle wind blew in his face. Tree-ferns rose to incredible heights above his head, and now and again by the movements of their fronds he caught stray glimpses of unfamiliar stars. There were red stars, and blue ones, and once he caught sight of a clearly distinguishable double star, of which each component was visible to the naked eye. And very, very far away he heard the beastly yellings he knew must be the outlaws, the Ragged Men, feasting horribly on half-scorched flesh torn from the quivering, yet-living flanks of a monstrous reptile.

Something moved, whimpered—and fled suddenly. It sounded like a human being. And Tommy Reames was struck with the utterly impossible conviction that he had heard just that sound before. It was not dangerous, in any case, and he watched, and listened, and presently he slipped from the mouth of the Tube and by the glow of a flashlight stripped foliage from nearby growths and piled it about the Tube's mouth. And then, because the purpose of the Tube was not adventure but science, he went back down into the laboratory.

THE three men, with Evelyn, worked until dawn at the rest of their preparations for the use of the Tube. All that time the laboratory was filled with the heavy fragrance of a tree-fern jungle upon an unknown planet. The heavy, sickly-sweet scents of closed jungle blossoms filled their nostrils. The reek of feverishly growing green things saturated the air. A steady wind blew down the Tube, and it bore innumerable unfamiliar odors into the laboratory. Once a gigantic moth bumped and blundered into the Tube, and finally crawled heavily out into the light. It was scaled, and terrible because of its monstrous size, but it had broken a wing and could not fly. So it crawled with feverish haste toward a brilliant electric light. Its eyes were especially horrible because they were not compound like the moths of Earth. They were single, like those of a man, and were fixed in an expression of utter, fascinated hypnosis. The thing looked horribly human with those eyes staring from an insect's head, and Smithers killed it in a flash of nerve-racked horror. None of them was able to go on with their work until the thing and its fascinated, staring eyes had been put out of sight. Then they labored on with the smell of the jungles of that unnamed planet thick about them, and noises now and then coming down the Tube. There were roars, and growlings, and once there was a thin high sound which seemed like the far-distant, death-startled scream of a man.

CHAPTER II

The Death Mist

TOMMY Reames saw the red sun rise while he was on guard at the mouth of the Tube. The tree-ferns above him came into view as vague gray outlines. The many-colored stars grew pale. And presently a bit of crimson light peeped through the jungle somewhere. It moved along the horizon and very slowly grew higher. For a moment, Tommy saw the huge, dull-red ball that was the sun of this alien planet. Queer mosses took form and color in the daylight, displaying colors never seen on Earth. He saw flying things dart among the tree-fern fronds, and some were scaled and some were not, but none of them was feathered.

Then a tiny buzzing noise. The telephone that now rested below the lip of the Tube was being used from the laboratory.

"Smithers will relieve you," said Denham's voice in the receiver. "Come on down. We're not the only people experimenting with the Fifth Dimension. Jacaro's been working, and all hell's loose!"

Tommy slid down the Tube in an instant. The four right-angled turns made him sick and dizzy again, but he came out with his jaw set grimly. There was good reason for Tommy's interest in Jacaro. Besides three bullet wounds, Tommy owed Jacaro something for stealing the first model Tube.

He emerged in the laboratory on his hands and knees as the size of the Tube made necessary. Smithers smiled placidly at him and crawled in to take his place.

"What the devil's happened?" demanded Tommy.

Denham was bitter. He held a newspaper before him. Evelyn had brought coffee and the morning paper to the laboratory. She seemed rather pale.

"Jacaro's gotten through too!" snapped Denham. "He's gotten in a pack of trouble. And he's loosed the devil on Earth. Here—look!" He jabbed his finger at one headline. "And here—and here!" He thrust at others. "Here's proof."

The first headline read: "KING JACARO FORFEITS BOND." Smaller headings beneath it read: "Racketeer Missing for Income Tax Trial. $200,000 Bail Forfeited." The second headline was in smaller type: "Monster Lizard Killed! Giant Meat Eater Brought Down by Riflemen. Akin to Ancient Dinosaurs, Say Scientists."

"JACARO'S missing," said Denham harshly. "This article says he's vanished, and with him a dozen of his most prominent gunmen. You know he had a model catapult to duplicate—the one he got from you. Von Holtz could arrange the construction of a big Tube for him. And he knew about the Golden City. Look!"

His finger, trembling, tapped on the flashlight picture of the giant lizard of which the story told. And it was a giant. A rope had upheld a colossal, leering, reptilian head while men with rifles posed self-consciously beside the dead creature. It was as big as a horse, and at first glance its kinship to the extinct dinosaurs of Earth was plain. Huge teeth in sharklike rows. A long, trailing tail. But there was a collar about the beast-thing's neck.

"It had killed and was devouring a cow when they shot it," said Denham bitterly. "There've been reports of these creatures for days—so the news story says. They weren't printed because nobody believed them. But there are a couple of people missing. A searching party was hunting for them. They found this!"

Tommy Reames stared at the picture. His face went grimmer still. He thought of sounds he had heard beyond the Tube, not long since.

"There's no question where they came from. The Fifth Dimension. But if Jacaro brought them back, he's a fool."

"Jacaro's missing," said Denham savagely. "Don't you understand? He could get through to the Golden City. These beast-things are proof somebody did. And these things came down the Tube that somebody traveled through. Jacaro wouldn't send them, but somebody did. They've got collars around their necks! Who sent them? And why?"

TOMMY'S eyes narrowed.

"If civilized man found the mouth of a Tube, it would seem like the mouth of an artificial tunnel or a cave—"

"And if annoying vermin, like Jacaro's gunmen"—Denham's voice was brittle—"had come out of it, why, intelligent men might send something living and deadly down it, as men on Earth will send ferrets down a rat-hole! To wipe out the breed! That's what's happened! Jacaro's gone through and attacked the Golden City. They've found his Tube. And they've sent these things down. . . ."

"If we found rats coming from a rat-hole," said Tommy very

quietly, "and ferrets went down and didn't come up, we'd gas them."

"And so," Denham told him, "so would the Golden City."

He pointed to a boxed double-paragraph news story under a leaded twenty-point headline: "Poisonous Fog Kills Wild Life."

The story was not alarming. It said merely that state game wardens had found numerous dead game animals in a thinly-settled district near Coltsville, N.Y., and on investigation had found a bank of mist, all of half a mile across, which seemed to have caused the trouble. State chemists and biologists were investigating the phenomenon. Curiously, the bank of mist seemed not to dissipate in a normal fashion. Samples of the fog were being analyzed. It was probably akin to the Belgian fogs which on several occasions had caused much loss of life. The mist was especially interesting because in sunlight it displayed prismatic colorings. State troopers were warning the inhabitants of the neighborhood.

"The gassing's started," said Denham savagely. "I know a gas that shows rainbow colors. The Golden City uses it. So we've got to find Jacaro's Tube and seal it, or only God knows what will come out of it next. I'm going off, Tommy. You and Smithers guard our Tube. Blow it up, if necessary. It's dangerous. I'll get some authority in Albany, and we'll find Jacaro's Tube and blast it shut."

Tommy nodded, his eyes keen and thoughtful. Denham hurried out.

MINUTES later, only, they heard the roar of a car motor going down the long lane away from the laboratory. Evelyn tried to smile at Tommy.

"It seems terrible, dangerous."

Tommy considered and shrugged.

"This news is old," he observed. "This paper was printed last night. I think I'll make a couple of long-distance calls. If the Golden City's had trouble with Jacaro, it's going to make things bad for us."

He swept his eyes about and frowningly loaded a light rifle. He put it convenient to Evelyn's hand and made for the dwelling-house and the telephone. It was odd that as he emerged into the open air, the familiar smells of Earth struck his nostrils as strange and unaccustomed. The laboratory was redolent of the tree-fern forest into which the Tube extended. And Smithers was watching amid those dank, incredible carboniferous-period growths now.

Tommy put through calls, seeing all his and Denham's plans for a peaceful exploration party and amicable contact with the civilization of that other planet utterly shattered by presumed outrages by Jacaro. He made call after call, and his demands for information grew more urgent as he got closer to the source of trouble. His cause for worry was verified long before he had finished. Even as he made the first call, New York newspapers had crowded a second-grade murder off their front pages to make room for the white mist upstate.

THE early-morning editions had termed it a "poisonous fog." The breakfast editions spoke of it as a "poison fog." But it grew and moved and by the time Tommy had a clear line to get actual information about it, a tabloid had christened it the "Death Mist" and there were three chartered planes circling about it for the benefit of their newspapers. State troopers were being reinforced. At ten o'clock it was necessary to post extra traffic police to take care of the cars headed upstate to look at the mystery. At eleven it began to move! Sluggishly, to be sure, and rather raggedly, but it undoubtedly moved, and as undoubtedly it moved independently of the wind.

It was at twelve-thirty that the first casualty occurred. Before that time, the police had frantically demanded that the flood of sightseers be stopped. The Death Mist covered a square mile or more. It clung to the ground, nowhere more than fifty or sixty feet high, and glittered with all the colors of the rainbow. It moved with a velocity of anywhere from ten to twenty miles an hour. In its path were a myriad small tragedies—nesting birds stiff and still, and rabbits and other small furry bodies contorted in queer agonized postures. But until twelve-thirty no human beings were known to be its victims.

Then, though, it was moving blindly across the wind with a thin trailing edge behind it and a rolling billow of descending mist as its forefront. It rolled up to and across a concrete highway, watched by perspiring motor cops who had performed miracles in clearing a path for it among the horde of sightseeing cars. It swept on into a spindling pine wood. Behind it lay a thinning sheet of vapor—thick white mist which seemed to rise and move more swiftly to overtake the main body. It lay across the highway in a sheet which was ten feet deep, then thinned to six, to three. . . .

THE mist was no more than a foot thick when a party of motorists essayed to drive through it as through a sheet of water. They dodged a swearing motorcycle cop and, yelling hilariously, plunged forward. It happened that they had not more than a hundred yards to go, so the whole thing was plainly seen.

The car was ten yards across the sheet of mist before the effect of its motion was apparent. Then the mist, torn by the car-eddy, swirled madly in their wake. The motorists yelled delightedly. There is a picture extant, taken at just this moment. It shows the driver with a foolish grin on his face, clutching the wheel and very obviously stepping on the accelerator. A pandemonium of triumphant, hilarious shouting—and then a very sudden silence.

The car roared on. The road curved slightly. The car did not. It went off the road, turned over, and its engine shrieked itself into silence. The Death Mist went on, draining from the roadway to follow the tall, prismatically-colored cloud. It moved swiftly and blindly. To the circling planes above it, it seemed like a blind thing imagining itself confined, and searching for the edges of its prison. It gave an uncanny impression of being directed by intelligence. But the Death Mist, itself, was not alive.

Neither were the occupants of the motor car.

When Tommy got back to the laboratory after his last call for news, he found Evelyn in the act of starting to fetch him.

"Smithers called," she said uneasily. "He says something's moving about—" The buzzer of the telephone was humming stridently. Tommy answered quickly.

"Just want you handy," said Smithers' calm voice. "I might have to duck. Some Ragged Men are chasin' something. Get set, will ya?"

"Ready for anything," Tommy assured him.

Then he made it true: rifles handy, a sub-machine gun, grenades, gas masks. He handed one to Evelyn. Smithers had one already. Then Tommy waited, grimly ready by the Tube-mouth.

THE warm, scent-laden breeze blew upon him. Straining his ears, he could hear the sound of tree-fern fronds clashing in the wind. He heard the louder sounds made by Smithers, stirring ever so slightly in the Tube. And then he caught a vague, distant uproar. It would have been faint and confused at best, but the Tube was partly blocked by Smithers' body, and there were the multiple bends further to complicate the echoes. It was no more than a formless tumult through which faint yells came occasionally. It drew nearer and nearer. Tommy heard Smithers stir suddenly, almost as if he had jumped. Then there were scrapings which could only mean one thing: Smithers was climbing out of the Tube into the jungle of the Fifth-Dimension world.

The noise rose abruptly to a roar as the muffling effect of Smithers' body was removed. The yells were sharp and savage and half mad. There was a sudden crackling sound and a voice screamed:

"Gott!"

The hair rose at the back of Tommy's neck. Then there came the deafening report of an automatic pistol roaring itself empty above the end of the Tube. Smithers' voice, vastly calm:

"It's a'right, Mr. Reames. Don't worry."

A second pistol took up the fusillade. Yells and howls and screams arose. Men fled. Something came crashing to the mouth of the Tube. Smithers' voice again, with a purring note in it: "Get down there. I'll hold 'em off." Then single, deliberately spaced shots, while something came stumbling, fumbling, squirming down through the Tube, so filling it that Smithers' shooting was muted.

THEN came the subtly different explosions of the Very pistols, discharging gas bombs. And Tommy drew back, his jaw set, and he stood with his weapons very ready indeed, and a scratched, bleeding, exhausted, panting, terror-stricken human being in the tattered costume of Earth crawled from the Tube and groveled on the floor before him.

Evelyn gave a little exclamation, partly of disgust and partly of horror. Because this man, who had come from the world of the Fifth Dimension, was wholly familiar. He was tall, and he was lean, emaciated now; he wept sobbingly behind thick-lensed spectacles, and his lips were far too full and red. His name was Von Holtz; he had once been laboratory assistant to Professor Denham, and he had betrayed Evelyn and her father to the most ghastly of possible fates for a bribe offered him by Jacaro. Now he groveled. He was horrible to look at. Where he was not scratched and torn his flesh was reddened as if by fire. He was exhausted, and trembling with an awful terror, and he gasped out abject, placatory ejaculations and suddenly collapsed into a sobbing mass on the floor.

Smithers emerged from the Tube with a look of unpleasant satisfaction on his face.

"I chased off the Ragged Men with sneeze gas," he observed with a vast calmness. "They ain't comin' back for a while. An' I always wanted to break this guy's neck. I think I'll do it now."

"Not till I've questioned him," said Tommy savagely. "He and Jacaro have started hell to popping, with that Tube design they stole from me. He's got to stay alive and tell us how to stop it. Von Holtz, talk! And talk quick, or back you go through the Tube for the Ragged Men to work on!"

CHAPTER III

The Tree-Fern Jungle

TOMMY watched Smithers drive away. The sun was sinking low toward the west, and the car stirred up a cloud of light-encarmined dust as it sped down the long, narrow lane to the main road. The laboratory had intentionally been built in an isolated spot, but at the moment Tommy would have given a good deal for a few men nearby. Smithers was taking Von Holtz to Albany to add his information to Denham's pleas. Denham had ordered it, when they reached him by phone after hours of effort. Smithers had to go, to guard against Von Holtz's escape, even sick and ill as he was. And Evelyn had refused to go with him.

"If I stay in the laboratory," she insisted fiercely, "you can slip down and I can blow up the Tube after you, if the Ragged Men don't stay away. But by yourself . . ."

Tommy did not consent, but he was helpless. There was danger from the Tube. Not only from ghastly animals which might come through, but from men. Smithers had fought the Ragged Men above it. He had chased them off, but they would come back. Perhaps they would come very soon, perhaps not until Denham and Smithers had returned. If they could be held off, the as yet unknown dangers from the other Tube—of which only the lizards and the Death Mist were certainties—might be counteracted. In any case, the Tube must not be destroyed until its defense was hopeless.

Tommy made up a grim bundle to go through the Tube with him: the sub-machine gun, extra drums of shells, more gas bombs and half a dozen grenades. He hung the various objects about himself. Evelyn watched him miserably.

"You—you'll be careful, Tommy?"

"Nothing else but," said Tommy. He grinned reassuringly. "There's nothing to it, really. Just sitting still, listening. If I pop off some fireworks I'll just have to sit down and watch them run."

HE settled his gas mask about his neck and started to enter the Tube. Evelyn touched his arm.

"I'm—frightened, Tommy."

"Shucks!" said Tommy. "Also a couple of tut-tuts." He stood up, put his arms about her, and kissed her until she smiled. "Feel better now?" he asked interestedly.

"Y-yes. . . ."

"Fine!" said Tommy, and grinned again. "When you feel scared again, ring me on the phone and I'll give you another treatment."

But her smile faded as, beaming at her, he crawled into the first section of the Tube. And his own expression grew serious enough when she could see him no longer. The situation was not comfortable. Evelyn intended to marry him and he had to keep her cheerful, but he wished she were well away from here.

He tried to move cautiously through the Tube, but his bundles bumped and rattled. It seemed hours before he was climbing up the last section into the tree-fern jungle. He was caution itself as he peered over the edge. It was already night upon Earth, but here the monstrous, dull-red sun was barely sinking. It moved slowly along the horizon as it dipped, but presently a gray cast came over the colorings in the forest. Flying things came clattering homeward through the masses of fern-fronds overhead. He saw a projectile-like thing with a lizard's head and jaws go darting through an incredibly small opening. It seemed to have no wings at all. But then, in one instant, a vast wing-surface flashed out, made a single gigantic flap—and the thing was a projectile again, darting through a *chevaux-de-frise* of interlaced fronds without a sign of wings to support it.

TOMMY inspected his surroundings with an infinite care. As the darkness deepened he meditatively taped a flashlight below the barrel of the sub-machine gun. Turned on, it would cast a pitiless light upon his target, and the sights would be silhouetted against the thing to be killed. He hung his grenades in a handy row just inside the mouth of the Tube and set his gas bombs conveniently in place, then settled down to watch.

It was assuredly necessary. Von Holtz's story confirmed his own and Denham's guesses and made their worst fears seem optimistic. Von Holtz had made a Tube for Jacaro, working from the model of Tommy's own construction. It had been completed nearly a month before. But no jungle odors had seeped through that other Tube on its completion. It opened in a subcellar of a structure in the Golden City itself, the city of towers and soaring spires Denham had glimpsed long months before. By sheer fortune it opened upon a rarely-used storeroom where improbable small animals—the equivalent of rats—played obscenely in the light of ever-glowing panels in the wall.

For two days of the Fifth-Dimension world, Jacaro and his gunmen lay quiet. During two nights they made infinitely cautious reconnaissance. The second night it was necessary to kill two men who sighted the tiny exploring party. But the killing was done with silenced automatics, and there was no alarm. The third night they lay still, fearing an ambush. The fourth night Jacaro struck.

HE and his men fled back to their Tube with plunder and precious gems. Their loot was vast even beyond their hopes, though they had killed other men in gathering it. The Golden City was rich beyond belief. The very crust of the Fifth-Dimension world seemed to be composed of other substances than those of Earth. The common metals of Earth were rare or even unknown. The rarer metals of Earth were the commonplace ones in the Golden City. Even the roofs seemed plated with gold, but Jacaro's gunmen saw not one particle of iron save in a ring they took from a dead man's finger. There, an acid-etched plate of steel was set as if to be used for a signet.

Von Holtz had accompanied the raiders perforce on every journey. Jeweled bearings for motors; objects of commonest use, made of gold beat thin for lightness; huge ingots of silver for industry; once a queer-shaped spool of platinum wire that it took two men to carry—these things made up the loot they scurried back to their rathole with. Five raids they made, and twenty men they shot down before they came upon disaster. On the sixth raid an outcry rose and an ambush fell upon them.

Flashes of incredibly vivid actinic flame leaped from queer engines that opened upon them. Curious small truncheonlike weapons spat paralyzing electric shocks upon them. The twelve gangsters fought with the desperation of cornered rats, with notched and explosive bullets and with streams of lead from tommy-guns.

A chance bullet blew something up. One of the flame weapons flew to bits, spouting what seemed to be liquid thermit upon friend and foe alike. The way of the gangsters back to their Tube was barred. The route they knew was a chaos of scorched bodies and melting metal. The thermit flowed in all directions, seeming to grow in volume as it flamed. Jacaro and his gangsters fled. They broke through the shaken remnants of the ambush. The six of them who survived the fighting found a man somnolently driving a ground vehicle with two wheels. They burst upon him and, with their seared faces constituting threats in themselves, forced him to drive them out of the Golden City. They fled along aluminum roads into the tree-fern forests, while the sky behind them seemed to flame as the city woke to the tumult in its ways.

They killed the driver of their vehicle when he refused to take them farther, and it was that murder which saved their lives. It was seen by Ragged Men, the outlaws of the jungle, and it proved their enmity to the Golden City. The Ragged Men greeted them joyously and fed them, and enlisted their aid in a savage attack on a land-convoy on the way to the city. Their weapons carried the convoy, and they watched wounded prisoners killed with excruciating tortures. . . .

They were with the Ragged Men now, Von Holtz believed. He had fled a week or more before, when Jacaro—already learning the language of his half-mad allies—began to plan a grandiose attack upon the Golden City. Von Holtz was born a coward, and he knew where Tommy Reames and Denham would shortly thrust a Tube through. It would come out just where the catapult had flung Evelyn and Denham, months before, the same spot where he had marooned them. He searched desperately for that Tube, and failed to find it. He was chased by carnivores, scratched by thorns, and at last pursued by a yelling horde of human devils who were fired into by Smithers from the mouth of the just-finished Tube.

TOMMY debated the story grimly as he stood guard in the Tube in the humid jungle night. Many-colored stars winked fitfully through the thatch of giant ferns overhead. The wind soughed unsteadily above the jungle. There were queer creakings, and once or twice there were distant cries, and when the wind died down there was a deep-toned croaking audible somewhere which sounded rather like the croaking of unthinkably monstrous frogs. But it could not be that, of course. And once there was the sound of dainty movement and something passed nearby. Tommy Reames saw the shadowy outline of a bulk so vast that it turned him cold to think about it, and it did not seem fair for any creature as huge as that to move so quietly.

Then there was a little scuffling noise beneath him. A hand touched his foot.

"It's—it's me, Tommy." Evelyn crowded up beside him and

whispered shakenly: "It—it was so lonesome down there, so quiet."

Tommy frowned unhappily in the darkness. If he sent her back, she would know it was because he knew danger lurked here. Then she would worry. If he did not send her back . . .

"I'll—I'll go back the minute you tell me," she insisted forlornly. "Honestly. But—I was lonesome."

Tommy slipped his arm about her.

"Woman," he said sternly, "I'm going to let you stay ten minutes, so you can brag to our grandchildren that you were the first Earth-girl ever to be kissed in the Fifth Dimension. But I want you down in the laboratory so you won't be in my way if I start running!"

His tone was the right one. She even laughed a little, softly, as he pressed her to him. Then she clung to his hand and tried eagerly to pierce the darkness all about them.

"You'll be able to see something presently," he assured her in a low tone. "Just keep quiet, now."

SHE gazed up at the stars, then around in the so-nearly complete obscurity. Tommy answered her comments abstractedly, after a little. He was not quite sure that certain irregular sounds, yet far distant, were not actually quite regular ones. The Ragged Men Smithers had shot into had run away. But they would come back, and they might come with Jacaro and his gunmen as allies. If those distant sounds were men . . .

She withdrew her hand from his. Her back was toward him then, as she tried to pierce the darkness with her eyes. Tommy listened uneasily to the distant sound. Suddenly he felt Evelyn bump against his shoulder. He turned sharply—and she was out of the Tube! She was walking steadily off into the darkness!

"Evelyn! Evelyn!"

She did not falter or turn. He switched on the flashlight beneath his gun barrel and leaped out of the Tube himself. The light swept about. Evelyn's little figure kept moving away from him. Then his heart stood still. There were eyes beyond her in the darkness, huge, monstrous, steady eyes, half a yard apart in a head like something out of hell. And he could not fire because Evelyn was between the Thing and himself. Its eyes glowed unholily—fascinating, hypnotic, insane. . . .

EVELYN swayed . . . and the Thing moved! Tommy leaped like a madman, shouting. As his feet struck the ground a mass of solid-seeming fungus gave way beneath him. He fell sprawling, but clutching the gun fast. The spreading beam of the flashlight showed him Evelyn turning, her face filled with a wakening horror—the horror of one released from the fascination of a snake. She screamed his name.

Then a huge lizard paw swept forward and seized her body. A second gripped her as she screamed again. And Tommy Reames was deathly, terribly cold. The whole thing had happened in seconds only. He was submerged in slimy, sticky ooze which was the crushed fungus that had tripped him. But he cleared the gun. The flashlight limned a ghastly, obscenely fat body and a long tapering tail. Tommy aimed at the base of that tail and pulled the trigger, praying frenziedly.

A stream of flame leaped from the gun-muzzle. Explosive bullets uttered their queer cracking noise. The thing screamed horribly. Its cry was hoarsely shrill. The flashlight showed it swinging ponderously about, with Evelyn held fast against its body in a fashion horribly reminiscent of a child holding a doll.

Tommy was scrambling upright. Jaws clamped, cold horror filling him, he aimed again, at the sharp-toothed head above Evelyn's body. He could not try a heart shot with her in the way. Again the gun spat out a burst of explosive lead. And Tommy should have been sickened by the effect of the detonating missiles. The thing's lower jaw was shattered, half severed, made useless. It should have been killed a dozen times over.

But it screamed again until the jungle rang with the uproar, and then it fled, still screaming and still holding Evelyn clutched fast against its scaly breast.

CHAPTER IV

The Fifth-Dimension World

TOMMY flung himself in pursuit, despairing. Evelyn cried out once more as the lumbering thing fled with her, giving utterance to shrieking outcries at which the tree-fern jungle shook. It leaped once, upon monstrous hind legs, but came crashing heavily to the ground. Tommy's explosive bullets had shattered the bones which supported the balancing tail. Now that huge fleshy member dragged uselessly. The thing could not progress in its normal fashion of leaps covering many yards. It began to waddle clumsily, shrieking, with Evelyn clasped close. Its jaw was a shattered horror. It went marching insanely through the blackness of the jungle, and with it went the unholy din of its anguish, and behind it Tommy Reames came flinging himself frenziedly in pursuit.

Normally, the thing should have distanced him in seconds. Even crippled as it was, it moved swiftly. The scaly, duck-shaped head reared a good twenty feet above the fallen tree-fern fronds which carpeted the jungle. The monstrous splayed feet stretched a good yard and a half from front to rear upon the ground. Even its waddling footprints were yards apart, and it moved in terror.

Tommy tripped, fell, and got to his feet again, and the shrieking tumult was farther away. He raced madly toward the sound, the flashlight beam cutting swordlike through the blackness. He caught sight of the warty, scaly bulk of the monster at the extreme limit of the rays. It was moving faster than he could travel. He sobbed helpless curses at the thing and put forth superhuman exertions. He leaped fallen tree-fern trunks, he splashed through shallow ponds—later, when he knew something of the inhabitants of such pools, Tommy would turn cold at that memory—and raced on, gasping for breath while the shrieking of the thing that bore Evelyn grew more and more distant.

IN five minutes he was almost strangling and the thing was half a mile ahead of him. In ten, he was exhausted, and the shrieking noise it made as it waddled away was distinctly fainter. In fifteen minutes he only heard its hooting scream between the harsh laboring rasps of his own breath as he drew it into tortured lungs. But he ran on. He leaped and climbed and ran in a terrible obliviousness to all dangers the jungle might hold.

He leaped down from one toppled tree-trunk upon what seemed to be another. But the thing he landed upon gave beneath his boots in the unmistakable fashion of yielding flesh. Something vast and angry stirred and hissed furiously. Something—a head, perhaps—whipped toward him among the fallen fern-fronds. But he was racing on, sobbing, cursing, praying all at once.

Then suddenly he broke out into a profuse sweat. His breathing became easier, and then he was running lightly. His second wind had come to him. He was no longer exhausted. He felt as if he could run forever, and ran on more swiftly still. Suddenly the flashlight beam showed him a deep furrow in the rotting vegetation underfoot, and something glistened. A musky reek filled his nostrils. The thing's trail—the furrow left by its dragging tail! That musky reek was the thing's blood. It was bleeding from the wounds the explosive bullets had made. It was spouting whatever filthy fluid ran in its veins even as it waddled onward, screaming.

Five minutes more, and he felt that he was gaining on it. Ten, and he was sure of it. But it was half an hour before he actually overtook the injured monster marching like a mad machine, its mutilated ducklike head held high, its colossal feet lifting one after the other in a heavy, slowing waddle, and its hoarse screams re-echoing in a senseless uproar of agony.

TOMMY'S hands were shaking, but his brain was cool with a vast coolness. He raced past the shrieking monster, and halted in its path. He saw Evelyn, a huddled bundle, clasped still to the creature's scaly breast. And Tommy sent a burst of explosive bullets into a gigantic, foot-thick ankle-joint.

The monster toppled, and flung out its prehensile lizard claws in an instinctive effort to catch itself. Evelyn was thrown clear. And Tommy, standing alone in the blackness of a carboniferous jungle upon an alien planet, sent bullet after bullet into the shaking, obscenely flabby body of the thing. The bullets penetrated, and exploded. Great masses of flesh upheaved and fell away. Great gouts of awful-smelling fluid were flung out and blown to mist by the explosions. The thing did not so much die as disintegrate under the storm of detonating missiles.

Then Tommy went to Evelyn. He was wild with grief. He had no faintest hope that she could still be living. But as he picked her up she moaned softly, and when he cried her name she clung to him, pressing close in an agony of thankfulness almost as devastating as her fear had been.

It was minutes before either of them could think of anything other than her safety and the fact that they were together again. But then Tommy said, in a shaken effort to be himself again:

"I—I'd have done better if—if I'd had roller skates, maybe." His grin was wholly unconvincing. "Why'd you get out of the Tube?"

"It's eyes!" Evelyn shuddered, her own eyes hidden against Tommy's shoulder. "I saw them suddenly, looking at me. And I—hadn't any will. I felt myself getting out of the Tube and walking toward it. It was like the way a snake fascinates—hypnotizes—a bird. . . ."

A vagrant wind-eddy submerged them in the foul reek of the dead thing's flesh. Tommy stirred.

"Ugh! Let's get out of this. There'll be things coming to feed on that carcass. They'll smell it."

Evelyn tried to stand, and succeeded. She clung to his hand.

"Do you think you can find the Tube again?"

Tommy was already thinking of that. He grimaced.

"Probably. Back-trail the damned thing, if the flashlight battery holds out. Its tail left plenty of sign for us to follow."

THEY started. And Evelyn had literally been forgotten in its agony by the monster which had carried her. Its body, though scaled and warty, was flabby and soft. Pressed against its breast she had been half strangled, but had no injuries beyond huge, purple bruises which had not yet reached the point of stiffness. She followed Tommy gamely, and the need for action kept her from yielding to the reaction from her terror.

For a long, long time they back-trailed. Less than fifteen minutes after leaving the carcass of the thing Tommy had killed, they heard beast-roarings and the sound of fighting. But that noise died away as they traveled. Presently they reached the spot where Tommy had leaped upon a huge living thing. It was gone, now, but the impress of a body the thickness of a barrel remained upon the rotted vegetation of the jungle floor. Evelyn shivered when Tommy pointed it out.

"It was large," said Tommy ruefully. "I didn't even get a good look at the thing. Probably just as well, though. I might have been—er—delayed. Good Lord! What's that?"

A light had sprung into being somewhere. It was bright. It was blinding in its brilliance. Coming through the tangled jungle growth, it seemed as if spears of flame shot through the air, irradiating stray patches of scabrous tree-trunk with unbearable light. For an instant the illumination held. Then there was a distant, cracking detonation. The unmistakable explosion of gun-cotton split the air, and its echoes rolled and reverberated through the jungle. The light went out. Then came a thin, high yelling sound which, faint as it was, had something of the quality of hysterical glee. That crazy ululation kept up for several minutes. Evelyn shivered.

"The Ragged Men," said Tommy very quietly. "They sneaked up on the Tube. They flung blazing thermit, or something like it, with a weapon captured from the Golden City. That explosion was the grenades going off. I'm afraid the Tube's blown up, Evelyn."

She caught her breath, looking mutely up at him.

"Here's a pistol," he said briefly, "and shells. There's no use our going to the Tube to-night. It would be dangerous. We'll do our investigating at dawn."

HE found a crevice where tree-fern trunks grew close together and closed in three sides of a sort of roofless cave. He seated himself grimly at the opening to wait for daybreak. He was not easy in his mind. There had been two Tubes to the Fifth-Dimension world. One had been made by Jacaro for his gunmen. That was now held by the men of the Golden City, as was proved by carnivorous lizards and the Death Mist that had come down it. The other was now blown up or, worse, in the hands of the Ragged Men. In any case Tommy and Evelyn were isolated upon a strange planet in a strange universe. To fall into the hands of the Ragged Men was to die horribly, and the Golden City would not now welcome inhabitants of the world Jacaro and his men had come from. To the civilized men of this world, Jacaro's raids would seem invasion. They would seem acts of war on the part of the people of Earth. And the people of Earth, all of them, would seem enemies. Jacaro would never be identified as an unauthorized invader. He would seem to be a scout, an advance guard, a spy, for hordes of other invaders yet to come.

As the long night wore away, Tommy's grim hopelessness intensified. The Ragged Men would hunt them for sport and out of hatred for all sane human beings. The men of the Golden City would be merciless to compatriots of Jacaro's gunmen. And Tommy had Evelyn to look out for.

WHEN dawn came, his face was drawn and lined. Evelyn woke with a little gasp, staring affrightedly about her. Then she tried gamely to smile.

"Morning, Tommy," she said shakily. She added in a brave attempt at levity: "Where do we go from here?"

"We look at the Tube," said Tommy heavily. "There's a bare chance . . ."

He led the way as on the night before, with his gun held ready. They traveled for half an hour through the awakening jungle. Then for long, long minutes Tommy searched for a sign of living men before he ventured forth to look at the wreckage of the Tube. He found no live men, and only two dead ones. But a glimpse of their bestial, vice-ridden faces was enough to remove any regret for their deaths.

The Tube was shattered. Its mouth was belled out and broken by the explosion of the grenades hung within it. A part of the metal was molten—from the thermit, past question. There was a veritable crater fifteen feet across where the Tube had come through, and there were only shattered shreds of metal where the first bend had been. Tommy regarded the wreckage grimly. A pair of oxidized copper wires, their insulation burnt off, stung his eyes as he traced them to where they vanished in torn-up earth. He took them in his bare hands. The tingling sting of a low-voltage current made his heart leap. Then he smiled grimly. He touched them to each other. Dot-dot-dot—dash-dash-dash—dot-dot-dot. SOS! If there was anybody in the laboratory, that would tell them.

His hands stung sharply. Someone was there, ringing the phone! Evelyn came toward him, her face resolutely cheerful.

"No hope, Tommy?" she asked. "I just saw the telephone, all battered up. I guess we're pretty badly off."

"Get it!" said Tommy feverishly. "For Heaven's sake, get it! The phone wires weren't broken. If we can make it work . . ."

THE instrument was a wreck. It was crumpled and torn and apparently useless. The diaphragm of the receiver was punctured. The transmitter seemed to have been crushed. But Tommy worked desperately over them, and twisted the earth-wires into place.

"Hello, hello, hello!"

The voice that answered was Smithers', strained and fearful:

"Mr. Reames! Thank Gawd! What's happened? Is Miss Evelyn all right?"

"So far," said Tommy. "Listen!" He told curtly just what had happened. "Now, what's happened on Earth?"

"Hell!" panted Smithers bitterly. "Hell's been poppin'! The Death Mist's two miles across an' still growin' an' movin'. Four townships under martial law an' movin' out the people. It got thirty of 'em this mornin'. An' they think the professor's crazy an' nobody'll listen to him!"

"Damn!" said Tommy. He considered, grimly. "Look here, Von Holtz ought to convince them."

"He caved in, outa his head, before I got to Albany. He's in hospital now, ravin'. He's got some kinda fever the doctors don't know nothin' about. Sick as hell!"

Tommy compressed his lips. Matters were more desperate even than he had believed. He informed his helper measuredly:

"Evelyn and I can't stay around here, Smithers. The Ragged Men may come back, and it'll be weeks before you and the professor can get another Tube through. I'm going to make for the Golden City and work on them there to cut off the Death Mist."

There was an inarticulate sound from Smithers.

"Tell the professor. If he can find Jacaro's Tube, he'll work out some way to communicate through it. We've got to stop that Death Mist somehow. And we don't know what else they may try."

Smithers tried to speak, and could not. He merely made grief-stricken noises. He worshipped Evelyn, and she was isolated in a hostile world which was vastly more unreachable than could be measured by millions or trillions of miles. But at last he said unsteadily:

"We'll be comin', Mr. Reames. We'll come, if we have t' blow half the world apart!"

Tommy said grimly: "Then hunt up the Golden City and bring extra ammunition. Mostly explosive bullets. Good-by."

HE untwisted the wires from the shattered phone units and thrust them in his pocket. Evelyn was picking up stray small objects from the ground.

"I've found some cartridges, Tommy," she said constrainedly, "and a pistol I think will work."

"Then listen for visitors," commanded Tommy, "while I look for more."

For half an hour he scoured the area around the shattered Tube. He found where some clumsy-wheeled thing had been pushed to a spot near the Tube—undoubtedly the machine which had sprayed the flaming stuff upon it. He found two pockets full of shells. He found an extra magazine for the submachine gun. It was nearly full and only a little bent. That was all.

"Now," he said briskly, "we'll start. I've got a hunch the jungle thins out over that way. We'll find a clearing, try to locate the Golden City either by seeing it or by watching for aircraft flying to it, and then make for it. They're making war on Earth, there. They don't understand. We've got to make them understand. O. K.?"

Evelyn nodded. She put out her hand suddenly, a brave slender figure amid the incredible growths about her.

"I'm glad, Tommy," she said slowly, "that if—if anything happens, it will be the—the two of us. Funny, isn't it?"

Tommy kissed the twisted little smile from her face.

"And now that that's over," he observed, ashamed of his own emotion, "let's go!"

THEY went. Tommy watched the sun and kept approximately a straight line. They traveled three miles, and the jungle broke abruptly. Before them was a spongy surface neither solid earth nor marsh. It shelved gently down to a vast and steaming morass upon which the dull-red sun shone hotly. It was vast, that marsh, and a steaming haze hung over it, and it seemed to reach to the world's end. But vaguely, through the attenuating upper layers of the steamy haze, they saw the outlines of a city beyond: tall towers and soaring spires, buildings of a grace and perfection of outline unknown upon the Earth. And faint golden flashes came from the walls and pinnacles of that city. They were reflections of this planet's monster sun, upon walls and roofs of plated gold.

"The Golden City," said Tommy heavily. He looked at the horrible marsh between. His heart sank.

And then there was a sudden screaming ululation nearby. A half-naked man was running out of sight. Two others danced and capered and yelled in insane glee, pointing at Tommy and at Evelyn. The running man's outcry was echoed from far away. Then it was taken up and repeated here and there in the jungle.

"They saw our tracks near the Tube," snapped Tommy bitterly. "Oh, what a fool I am! Now they'll ring us in."

He seized Evelyn's hand and began to run. There was a little rise in the ground a hundred yards away, with a clump of leafy ferns to shade it. They reached it as other half-naked, wholly mad human forms burst out of the jungle to yell and caper and make derisive and horrible gestures at the fugitives.

"Here we fight," said Tommy grimly. "The ground's open, anyhow. We fight here, and very probably we die here. But first . . ."

He knelt down and drew the finest of fine beads upon a bearded man who carried a glittering truncheonlike club which, by the way it was carried, was more than merely a bludgeon. He pulled the trigger for a single shot.

The bullet struck the capering Ragged Man fairly in the chest. And it exploded.

CHAPTER V

The Fight in the Marsh

TWICE, within the next two hours, the Ragged Men mustered the courage to charge. They came racing across the semi-solid ooze like the madmen they were. Their yells and shouts were maniacal howls of blood-lust or worse. And twice Tommy broke their rush with a savage ruthlessness. The sub-machine gun's first magazine was nearly empty. It was an unhandy weapon for single-shot work, but it was loaded with explosive shells. The second rush he stopped with an automatic pistol. There were half-naked bodies partly buried in the ooze all the way from the jungle's edge to within ten yards of the hillock on which he and Evelyn had taken refuge.

It was hot there, terribly hot. The air was stifling. It fairly reeked of moisture, and the smells from the swamp behind them were sickening. Tommy began to transfer the shells from the spare bent magazine to the one he had carried with the gun.

"We've a couple of reasons to be thankful," he observed. "One is that there's a bit of shade overhead. The other is that we had the big magazines for this gun. We still have nearly ninety shells, besides the ones for the pistols."

Evelyn said soberly:

"We're going to be killed, don't you think, Tommy?"

Tommy frowned.

"I'm rather afraid we are," he said irritably. "Confound it, and I'd thought of such excellent arguments to use in the City back yonder! Smithers said the Death Mist was two miles across, to-day, and still growing. The people in the city are still pouring the stuff down through Jacaro's Tube."

Evelyn smiled faintly. She touched his hand.

"Trying to keep me from worrying? Tommy. . . ." She hesitated until he growled a question. "Please—remember that when Daddy and I were in the jungle before, we saw what these Ragged Men do to prisoners they take. I just want you to promise that—well, you won't wait too long, in hopes of somehow saving me."

Tommy stared at her. Then he decisively reached forward and put his hand over her mouth.

"Keep quiet," he said gently. "They shan't capture you. I promise that. Now keep quiet."

THERE was only silence for a long time. Now and again a hidden figure screamed in rage at them. Now and again some flapping thing sped toward the jungle's edge. Once a naked arm thrust one of the golden truncheons from behind its cover, pointing at a flying thing a few yards overhead. The flying thing suddenly toppled, turning over and over before it crashed to the ground. There were howls of glee.

"They seem mad," said Tommy meditatively, "and they act like lunatics, but I've got a hunch of some sort about them. But what?"

Sunlight gleamed on something golden beyond the jungle's edge. Naked figures were running to the spot. An exultant tumult arose.

"Now they try another trick," Tommy observed dispassionately. "I remember that at the Tube they had pushed something on wheels. . . ."

The sub-machine gun was unhandy for accurate single shots, and no pistol can be used to effect at long ranges. To conserve ammunition, Tommy had been shooting only at relatively close targets, allowing the Ragged Men immunity at over two hundred yards. But now he flung over the continuous-fire stud. He watched grimly.

The foliage at the edge of the jungle parted. A crude wagon appeared. Its axles were lesser tree-trunks. Its wheels were clumsy and crude beyond belief. But mounted upon it there was a queer mass of golden metal which looked strangely beautiful and strangely deadly.

"That's the thing," said Tommy dispassionately, "which made the flare of light last night. It blew up the Tube. And Von Holtz told me—hm—his friends, in the City. . . ."

He sighted carefully. The wagon and its contents were surrounded by a leaping, capering mob. They shook their fists in an insane hatred.

A storm of bullets burst upon them. Tommy was traversing the little gun with the trigger pressed down. His lips were set tightly. And suddenly it seemed as if the solid earth burst asunder! There had been an instant in which the bullet-bursts were visible. They tore and shattered the howling mob of Ragged Men. But then they struck the golden weapon. A sheet of blue-white flame leaped skyward and round about. A blast of blistering, horrible heat smote upon the beleaguered pair. The moisture of the ooze between them and the jungle flashed into steam. A section of the jungle itself, a hundred yards across, shriveled and died.

STEAM shot upward in a monstrous cloud—miles high, it seemed. Then, almost instantly, there was nothing left of the Ragged Men about the golden weapon, or of the weapon itself, but an unbearable blue-white light which poured away and trickled here and there and seemed to grow in volume as it flamed.

From the rest of the jungle a howl arose. It was a howl of such loss, and of such unspeakable rage, that the hair at the back of Tommy's neck lifted, as a dog's hackles lift at sight of an enemy.

"Keep your head down, Evelyn," said Tommy composedly. "I have an idea that that burning stuff gives off a lot of ultra-violet. Von Holtz was badly burned, you remember."

Naked figures flashed forward from the jungle beyond the burned area. Tommy shot them down grimly. He discarded the sub-machine gun with its explosive shells for the automatics. Some of his targets were only wounded. Those wounded men dragged themselves forward, screaming their rage. Tommy felt sickened, as if he were shooting down madmen. A voice roared a rage-thickened order from the jungle. The assault slackened.

Five minutes later it began again, and this time the attackers waded out into the softer ooze and flung themselves down, and then began a half-swimming, half-crawling progress behind bits of tree-fern stump, or merely pushing walls of the jellylike mud before them. The white light expanded and grew huge—but it dulled as it expanded, and presently seemed no hotter than molten steel, and later still it was no more than a dull-red heat, and later yet. . . .

Tommy shot savagely. Some of the Ragged Men died. More did not.

"I'm afraid," he said coolly, "they're going to get us. It seems rather purposeless, but I'm afraid they're going to win."

Evelyn thrust a shaking hand skyward. "There, Tommy!"

A strange, angular flying thing was moving steadily across the marsh, barely above the steamlike haze that hung in thinning layers about its foulness. The flying thing moved with a machinelike steadiness, and the sun twinkled upon something bright and shining before it.

"A flying machine," said Tommy shortly. His mind leaped ahead and his lips parted in a mirthless smile. "Get your gas mask ready, Evelyn. The explosion of that thermit-thrower made them curious in the City. They sent a ship to see."

The flying thing grew closer, grew distinct. A wail arose from the Ragged Men. Some of them leaped to their feet and fled. A man came out into the open and shook his fists at the angular thing in the air. He screamed at it, and such ghastly hatred was in the sound that Evelyn shuddered.

Tommy could see it plainly, now. Its single wing was thick and queerly unlike the air-foils of Earth. A framework hung below it, but it had no balancing tail. And there was a glittering something before it that obviously was its propelling mechanism, but as obviously was not a screw propeller. It swept overhead, with a man in it looking downward. Tommy watched coolly. It was past him, sweeping toward the jungle. It swung sharply to the right, banking steeply. Smoking things dropped from it, which expanded into columns of swiftly-descending vapor. They reached the jungle and blotted it out. The flying machine swung again and swept back to the left. More smoking things dropped. Ragged Men erupted from the jungle's edge in screaming groups, only to writhe and fall and lie still. But a group of five of them sped toward Tommy, shrieking their rage upon him as the cause of disaster. Tommy held his fire, looking upward. A hundred yards, fifty yards, twenty-five. . . .

THE flying machine soared in easy, effortless circles. The man in it was watching, making no effort to interfere.

Tommy shot down the five men, one after the other, with a curiously detached feeling that their vice-brutalized faces would haunt him forever. Then he stood up.

The flying machine banked, turned, and swept toward him, and a smoking thing dropped toward the earth. It was a gas bomb like those that had wiped out the Ragged Men. It would strike not ten yards away.

"Your mask!" snapped Tommy.

He helped Evelyn adjust it. The billowing white cloud rolled around him. He held his breath, clapped on his mask, exhaled until his lungs ached, and was breathing comfortably. The mask was effective protection. And then he held Evelyn comfortably close.

For what seemed a long, long while they were surrounded by the white mist. The cloud was so dense, indeed, that the light about them faded to a gray twilight. But gradually, bit by bit, the mist grew thinner. Then it moved aside. It drifted before the wind toward the tree-fern forest and was lost to sight.

The flying machine was circling and soaring silently overhead. As the mist drew aside, the pilot dived down and down. And Tommy emptied his automatic at the glittering thing which drew it. There was a crashing bolt of blue light. The machine canted, spun about with one wing almost vertical, that wing-tip struck the marsh, and it settled with a monstrous splashing of mud. All was still.

Tommy reloaded, watching it keenly.

"The framework isn't smashed up, anyhow," he observed grimly. "The pilot thinks we're some of Jacaro's gang. My guns were proof, to him. So, since the Ragged Men didn't get us, he gassed us." He watched again, his eyes narrow. The pilot was utterly still. "He may be knocked out. I hope so! I'm going to see."

AUTOMATIC held ready, Tommy moved toward the crashed machine. It had splashed into the ooze less than a hundred yards away. Tommy moved cautiously. Twenty yards away, the pilot moved feebly. He had knocked his head against some part of his machine. A moment later he opened his eyes and stared about. The next instant he had seen Tommy and moved convulsively. A glittering thing appeared in his hand—and Tommy fired. The glittering thing flew to one side and the pilot clapped his hand to a punctured forearm. He went white, but his jaw set. He stared at Tommy, waiting for death.

"For the love of Pete," said Tommy irritably, "I'm not going to kill you! You tried to kill me, and it was very annoying, but I have some things I want to tell you."

He stopped and felt foolish because his words were, of

course, unintelligible. The pilot was staring amazedly at him. Tommy's tone had been irritated, certainly, but there was neither hatred nor triumph in it. He waved his hand.

"Come on and I'll bandage you up and see if we can make you understand a few things."

Evelyn came running through the muck.

"He didn't hurt you, Tommy?" she gasped. "I saw you shoot—"

The pilot fairly jumped. At first glance he had recognized her as a woman. Tommy growled that he'd had to "shoot the damn fool through the arm." The pilot spoke, curiously. Evelyn looked at his arm and exclaimed. He was holding it above the wound to stop the bleeding. Evelyn looked about helplessly for something with which to bandage it.

"Make pads with your handkerchief," grunted Tommy. "Take my tie to hold them in place."

The prisoner looked curiously from one to the other. His color was returning. As Evelyn worked on his arm he seemed to grow excited at some inner thought. He spoke again, and looked at once puzzled and confirmed in some conviction when they were unable to comprehend. When Evelyn finished her first-aid task he smiled suddenly, flashing white teeth at them. He even made a little speech which was humorously apologetic, to judge by its tone. When they turned to go back to their fortress he went with them without a trace of hesitation.

"Now what?" asked Evelyn.

"They'll be looking for him in a little while," said Tommy curtly. "If we can convince him we're not enemies, he'll keep them from giving us more gas."

THE pilot was fumbling at a belt about the curious tunic he wore. Tommy watched him warily. But a pad of what seemed to be black metal came out, with a silvery-white stylus attached to it. The pilot sat down the instant they stopped and began to draw in white lines on the black surface. He drew a picture of a man and an angular flying machine, and then a sketchy, impressionistic outline of a city's towers. He drew a circle to enclose all three drawings and indicated himself, the machine, and the distant city. Tommy nodded comprehension as the pilot looked up. Then came a picture of a half-naked man shaking his fists at the three encircled sketches. The half-naked man stood beneath a roughly indicated tree-fern.

"Clever," said Tommy, as a larger circle enclosed that with the city and the machine. "He's identifying himself, and saying the Ragged Men are enemies of himself and his Golden City, too. That much is not hard to get."

He nodded vigorously as the pilot looked up again. And then he watched as a lively, tiny sketch grew on the black slab, showing half a dozen men, garbed almost as Tommy was, using weapons which could only be sub-machine guns and automatic pistols. They were obviously Jacaro's gangsters. The pilot handed over the plate and watched absorbedly as Tommy fumbled with the stylus. He drew, not well but well enough, an outline of the towers of New York. The difference in architecture was striking. There followed tiny figures of himself and Evelyn—with a drily murmured, "This isn't a flattering portrait of you, Evelyn!"—and a circle enclosing them with the towers of New York.

The pilot nodded in his turn. And then Tommy encircled the previously drawn figures of the gangsters with New York, just as the Ragged Men had been linked with the other city. And a second circle linked gangsters and Ragged Men together.

"I'M saying," observed Tommy, "that Jacaro and his mob are the Ragged Men of our world, which may not be wrong, at that."

There was no question but that the pilot took his meaning. He grinned in a friendly fashion, and winced as his wounded arm hurt him. Ruefully, he looked down at his bandage. Then he pressed a tiny stud at the top of the black-metal pad and all the white lines vanished instantly. He drew a new circle, with tree-ferns scattered about its upper third—a tiny sketch of a city's towers. He pointed to that and to the city visible through the mist—a second city, and a third, in other places. He waved his hand vaguely about, then impatiently scribbled over the middle third of the circle and handed it back to Tommy.

Tommy grinned ruefully.

"A map," he said amusedly. "He's pointed out his own city and a couple of others, and he wants us to tell him where we come from. Evelyn—er—how are we going to explain a trip through five dimensions in a sketch?"

Evelyn shook her head. But a shadow passed over their heads. The pilot leaped to his feet and shouted. There were three planes soaring above them, and the pilot in the first was in the act of releasing a smoking object over the side. At the grounded pilot's shout, he flung his ship into a frantic dive, while behind him the smoking thing billowed out a thicker and thicker cloud. His plane was nearly hidden by the vapor when he released it. It fell two hundred yards and more away, and the white mist spread and spread. But it fell short of the little hillock.

"QUICK thinking," said Tommy coolly. "He thought we had this man a prisoner, and he'd be better off dead. But—"

Their captive was shouting again. His head thrown back, he called sentence after sentence aloft while the three ships soared back and forth above their heads, soundless as bats. One of the three rose steeply and soared away toward the city. Their captive, grinning, turned and nodded his head satisfiedly. Then he sat down to wait.

Twenty minutes later a monstrous machine with ungainly flapping wings came heavily over the swamp. It checked and settled with a terrific flapping and an even more terrific din. Half a dozen armed men waited warily for the three to approach. The golden weapons lifted alertly as they drew near. The wounded man explained at some length. His explanation was dismissed brusquely. A man advanced and held out his hands for Tommy's weapons.

"I don't like it," growled Tommy, "but we've got to think of Earth. If you get a chance, hide your gun, Evelyn."

He pushed on the safety catches and passed over his guns. The pilot he had shot down led them onto the fenced-in deck of the monstrous ornithopter. Machinery roared. The wings began to beat. They were nearly invisible from the speed of their flapping when the ship lifted vertically from the ground. It rose straight up for fifty feet, the motion of the wings changed subtly, and it swept forward.

It swung in a vast half circle and headed back across the

marsh for the Golden City. Five minutes of noisy flight during which the machine flapped its way higher and higher above the marsh—which seemed more noisome and horrible still from above—and then the golden towers of the city were below. Strange and tapering and beautiful, they were. No single line was perfectly straight, nor was any form ungraceful. These towers sprang upward in clean-soaring curves toward the sky. Bridges between them were gossamerlike things that seemed lace spun out in metal. And as Tommy looked keenly and saw the jungle crowding close against the city's metal walls, the flapping of the ornithopter's wings changed again and it seemed to plunge downward like a stone toward a narrow landing place amid the great city's towering buildings.

CHAPTER VI

The Golden City

THE thing that struck Tommy first of all was the scarcity of men in the city, compared to its size. The next thing was the entire absence of women. The roar of machines smote upon his consciousness as a bad third, though they made din enough. Perhaps he ignored the machine noises because the ornithopter on which they had arrived made such a racket itself.

They landed on a paved space perhaps a hundred yards by two hundred, three sides of which were walled off by soaring towers. The fourth gave off on empty space, and he realized that he was still at least a hundred feet above the ground. The ornithopter landed with a certain skilful precision and its wings ceased to beat. Behind it, the two fixed-wing machines soared down, leveled, hovered, and settled upon amazingly inadequate wheels. Their pilots got out and began to push them toward one side of the landing area. Tommy noticed it, of course. He was noticing everything, just now. He said amazedly:

"Evelyn! They launch these planes with catapults like those our battleships use! They don't take off under their own power!"

The six men on the ornithopter put their shoulders to their machine and trundled it out of the way. Tommy blinked at the sight.

"No field attendants!" He gazed out across the open portion of the land area and saw an elevated thoroughfare below. Some sort of vehicle, gleaming like gold, moved swiftly on two wheels. There was a walkway in the center of the street with room for a multitude. But only two men were in sight upon it. "Lord!" said Tommy. "Where are the people?"

There was brief talk among the crew of the ornithopter. Two of them picked up Tommy's weapons, and the pilot he had wounded made a gesture indicating that he should follow. He led the way to an arched door in the nearest tower. A little two-wheeled car was waiting. They got into it and the pilot fumbled with the controls. As he worked at it—rather clumsily on account of his arm—the rest of the ornithopter's crew came in. They wheeled out another vehicle, climbed into it, and shot away down a sloping passage.

THEIR own vehicle followed and emerged upon the paved and nearly empty thoroughfare. Tall buildings rose all about them, with curved walls soaring dizzily skyward. There was every sign of a populous city, including the dull drumming roar of many machines, but the streets were empty. The little machine moved swiftly for minutes. Twice it swung aside and entered a sloping incline. Once it went up. The other time it dived down seventy feet on a four-hundred-foot ramp. Then it swung sharply to the right, meandered into a street-level way leading into the heart of a monster building, and stopped. And in all its travel it had not passed fifty people.

The pilot-turned-chauffeur turned and grinned amiably, and led the way again. Steps—twenty or thirty of them. Then they emerged suddenly into a vast room. It must have been a hundred and fifty feet long, fifty wide, and nearly as high. It was floored with alternate blocks of what seemed to be an iron-hard black wood and the omnipresent golden metal. Columns and pilasters about the place gave forth the same subdued deep golden glow. Light streamed from panels inset in the wall and ceiling—a curious saffron-red light. There was a massive table of the hard black wood. Chairs with curiously designed backs were ranged about it. They were benches, really, but they served the purpose of chairs. Each was too narrow to hold more than one person. The room was empty.

They waited. After a long time a man in a blue tunic came into the room and sat down at one of the benches. A long time later, another man came in, in red; and another and another, until there were a dozen in all. They regarded Tommy and Evelyn with a weary suspicion. One of them—an old man with a white beard—asked questions. The pilot answered them. At a word, the two men with Tommy's weapons placed them on the table. They were inspected casually, as familiar things. They probably were, since some of Jacaro's gunmen had been killed in a fight in this city. Another question.

The pilot explained briefly and offered Tommy the black-metal pad again. It still contained the incomplete map of a hemisphere, and was obviously a repetition of the question of where he came from.

TOMMY took it, frowning thoughtfully. Then an idea struck him. He found the little stud which, pressed by the pad's owner, had erased the previous drawings. He pressed it and the lines disappeared. And Tommy drew, crudely enough, that complicated diagram which is supposed to represent a cube which is a cube in four dimensions: a tesseract. Upon one surface of the cube he indicated the curving towers of the Golden City. Upon a surface representing a plane beyond the three dimensions of normal experience, he repeated the angular tower structures of New York. He shrugged rather hopelessly as he passed it over, but to his amazement it was understood at once.

The little black pad passed from hand to hand and an animated discussion took place. One rather hard-faced man was the most animated of all. The bearded old man demurred. The hard-faced man insisted. Tommy could see that his pilot's expression was becoming uneasy. But then a compromise seemed to be arrived at. The bearded man spoke a single, ceremonial phrase and the twelve men rose. They moved toward various doors and one by one left, until the room was empty.

But the pilot looked relieved. He grinned cheerfully at Tommy and led the way back to the two-wheeled vehicle. The two men with Tommy's weapons vanished. And again there was a swift, cyclonelike passage along empty ways with the throbbing of machinery audible everywhere. Into the base of a second building, up endless stairs, past innumerable doors. It seemed to Tommy that he heard voices behind some of them, and they were women's voices.

At a private, triple knock a door opened wide, and the pilot led the way into a room, closed and locked the door behind him, and called. A woman's voice cried out in astonishment. Through an inner arch a woman came running eagerly. Her face went blank at sight of Tommy and Evelyn, and her hand flew to a tiny golden object at her waist. Then, at the pilot's chuckle, she flushed vividly.

HOURS later, Tommy and Evelyn were able to talk it over. They were alone then, and could look out an oval window upon the Golden City all about them. It was dark, but saffron-red panels glowed in building walls all along the thoroughfares, and tiny glowing dots in the soaring spires of gold told of people within other dwellings like this.

"As I see it," said Tommy restlessly, "the Council—and it must have been that in the big room to-day—put us in our friend's hands to learn the language. He's been working with me four hours, drawing pictures, and I've been writing down words I've learned. I must have several hundred of them. But we do our best talking with pictures. And, Evelyn, this city's in a bad fix."

Evelyn said irrelevantly: "Her name is Ahnya, Tommy, and she's a dear. We got along beautifully. I'll bet I found out things you don't even guess at."

"You probably have," admitted Tommy, frowning. "Check up on this: our friend's name is Aten, and he's an air-pilot and also has something to do with growing food-stuffs in some special towers where they grow crops by artificial light only. Some of the plants he sketched look amazingly like wheat, by the way. The name of the town is"—he looked at his notes—"Yugna. There are some other towns, ten or twelve of them. Rahn is the nearest, and it's worse off than this one."

"Of course," said Evelyn, smiling. "They use *cuyal* openly, there!"

"How'd you learn all that?" demanded Tommy.

"Ahnya told me. We made gestures and smiled at each other.

We understood perfectly. She's crazy about her husband, and I —well, she knows I'm going to marry you, so. . . ."

Tommy grunted.

"I suppose she explained with a smile and gestures just how much of a strain it is, simply keeping the city going?"

"Of course," said Evelyn calmly. "The city's fighting against the jungle, which grows worse all the time. They used to grow their foodstuffs in the open fields. Then within the city. Now they use empty towers and artificial light. I don't know why."

TOMMY grunted again.

"This planet's just had, or is having, a change of geologic period," he explained, frowning. "The plants people used to live on aren't adapted to the new climate and new plants fit for food are scarce. They have to grow food under shelter, now, and their machines take an abnormal amount of supervision—I don't know why. The air-conditioners for the food plants; the machines that fight back the jungle creepers which thrive in the new climate and try to crawl into the city to smother it; the power machines; the clothing machines—a million machines have to be kept going to keep back the jungle and fight off starvation and just hold on doggedly to the bare fact of civilization. And they're short-handed. The law of diminishing returns seems to operate. They're trying to maintain a civilization higher than their environment will support. They work until they're ready to drop, just to stay in the same place. And the monotony and the strain makes some of them take to *cuyal* for relief."

He surveyed the city from the oval window, frowning in thought.

"It's a drug which grows wild," he added slowly. "It peps them up. It makes the monotony and the weariness bearable. And then, suddenly, they break. They hate the machines and the city and everything they ever knew or did. It's a sort of delayed-action psychosis which goes off with a bang. Some of them go amuck in the city, using their belt-weapons until they're killed. More of them bolt for the jungle. The city loses better than one per cent of its population a year to the jungle. And then they're Ragged Men, half mad at all times and wholly mad as far as the city and its machines are concerned."

Evelyn linked her arm in his.

"Somehow," she told him, smiling, "I think one Thomas Reames is working out ways and means to help a city named Yugna."

"Not yet," said Tommy grimly. "We have to think of Earth. Not everybody in the Council approved of us. Aten told me one chap argued that we ought to be shoved out into the jungle again as compatriots of Jacaro. And the machines were especially short-handed today because of a diversion of labor to get ready something monstrous and really deadly to send down the Tube to Earth. We've got to find out what that is, and stop it."

BUT on the second day afterward, when he and Evelyn were summoned before the Council again, he still had not found out. During those two days he learned many other things, to be sure: that Aten, for instance, was relieved from duty at the machines only because he was wounded; that the power of the main machines came from a deep bore which brought up superheated steam from the source of boiling springs long since built over; that iron was a rare metal, and consequently there was no dynamo in the city and magnetism was practically an unknown force; that electrokinetics was a laboratory puzzle—or had been, when there was leisure for research—while the science of electrostatics had progressed far past its state on Earth. The little truncheonlike weapons carried a stored-up static charge measurable only in hundreds of thousands of volts, which could be released in flashes which were effective up to a hundred feet or more.

And he learned that the thermit-throwers actually spat out in normal operation tiny droplets of matter Aten could not describe clearly, but which seemed to be radioactive with a period of five minutes or less; that in Rahn, the nearest other city, *cuyal* was taken openly, and the jungle was growing into the town with no one to hold it back; that two generations since there had been twenty cities like this one, but that a bare dozen still survived; that there was a tradition that human beings had come upon this planet from another world where other human beings had harried them, and that in that other world there were diverse races of humanity, of different colors, whereas in the world of the Golden City all mankind was one race; that Tommy's declaration that he came from another group of dimensions had been debated and, on re-examination of Jacaro's Tube, accepted, and that there was keen argument going on as to the measures to be taken concerning it.

THESE things Tommy had learned, and he and Evelyn went to their second interrogation by the city's Council armed with written vocabularies of nearly a thousand words, which they had sorted out and made ready for use. But they were still ignorant of the weapons the Golden City might use against Earth.

The Council meeting took place in the same hall, with its alternating black-and-gold flooring and the saffron-red lighting panels casting a soft light everywhere. This was a scheduled meeting, foreseen and arranged for. The twelve chairs above the heavy table were all occupied from the first. But Tommy realized that the table had been intended to seat a large number of councilors. There were guards stationed formally behind the chairs. There were spectators, auditors of the deliberations of the Council. They were dressed in a myriad colors, and they talked quietly among themselves; but it seemed to Tommy that nowhere had he seen weariness, as an ingrained expression, upon so many faces.

Tommy and Evelyn were led to the foot of the council table. The bearded old man in blue began the questioning. As Keeper of Foodstuffs—according to Aten—he was a sort of presiding officer.

Tommy answered the questions crisply. He had known what they would be, and he had developed a vocabulary to answer them. He told them of Earth, of Professor Denham, of his and the professor's experiments. He outlined the first experiment with the Fifth-Dimension catapult and the result of it—when the Golden City had sent the Death Mist to wipe out a band of Ragged Men who had captured a citizen, and after him Evelyn and her father.

THIS they remembered. Nods went around the table. Tommy told them of Jacaro, stressing the fact that Jacaro was an outlaw, a criminal upon Earth. He explained the theft of the model Tube, and how it was that their first contact with Earth had been with the dregs of Earth humanity. On behalf of his countrymen he offered reparation for all the damage Jacaro and his men had done. He proposed a peaceful commerce between worlds, to the infinite benefit of both.

There was silence until he finished. The faces before him were immobile. But a hawk-faced man in brown asked dry questions. Were there more races than one upon Earth? Were they of diverse colors? Did they ever war among themselves? At Tommy's answers the atmosphere seemed to change. And the hawk-faced man rose to speak.

Tommy and Evelyn, he conceded caustically, had certainly come from another world. Their own most ancient legends described just such a world as his: a world of many races of many colors, who fought many wars among themselves. Their ancestors had fled from such a world, according to legend through a twisting cavern which they had sealed behind them. The conditions Tommy described had been the cause of their ancestor's flight. They, the people of Yugna, would do well to follow the example of their forebears: strip these Earth folk of their weapons, exile them to the jungles, destroy the Tube through which the Mist of Many Colors had been sent. All should be as in the past ages.

TOMMY opened his mouth to answer, but another man sprang to his feet. His face alone was not weary and worn. As he stood up, Aten murmured *"Cuyal!"* and Tommy understood that this man used the drug which was destroying the city's citizens, but gave a transient energy to its victims. He spoke in fiery phrases, urging action which would be drastic and certain. He spoke confidently, persuasively. There was a rustling among those who watched and listened to the debate. He had caught at their imagination.

Evelyn, exerting every faculty to understand, saw Tommy's lips set grimly.

"What—what is it?" she whispered. "I—I don't understand. . . ."

Tommy spoke in a savage growl.

"He says," he told her bitterly, "that in one blow they can defeat both the jungle and the invaders from Earth. In past ages their ancestors were faced by enemies they could not defeat. They fled to this world. Now they are faced by jungles they cannot defeat. He proposes that they flee to our world. The Death Mist is a toy, he reminds them, compared with gases they know. There is a gas of which one part in ten hundred million is fatal! In a hundred of their days they can make and send through the Tube enough of it to kill every living thing on Earth. They've figures on the Earth's size and atmosphere from me, damn 'em! And he reminds them that that deadly gas changes of itself into a harmless substance. He urges them to gas Earth humanity out of existence, call upon the other cities of this world, and presently move through the Tube to Earth. They'll carry their food-plants, rebuild their cities, and abandon this planet to the jungles and the Ragged Men. And the hell of it is, they can do it!"

A sudden approving buzz went through the council hall.

CHAPTER VII

The Fleet from Rahn

THE approval of the citizens of Yugna was not enthusiastic. It was desperate. Their faces were weary. Their lives were warped. They had been fighting since birth against the encroachment of the jungle, which until the days of their grandparents had been no menace at all. But for two generations these people had been foredoomed, and they knew it. Nearly half the cities of their race were overwhelmed and their inhabitants reduced to savage hunters in the victorious jungles. Now the people of Yugna saw a chance to escape from the jungle. They were offered rest. Peace. Relaxation from the desperate need to serve insatiable machines. Sheer desperation impelled them. In their situation, the people of Earth would annihilate a solar system for relief, let alone the inhabitants of a single planet.

Shouts began to be heard above the uproar in the Council hall—approving shouts, demands that one be appointed to conduct the operation which was to give them a new planet on which to live, where their food-plants would thrive in the open, where jungles would no longer press on them.

Tommy's face went savage and desperate, itself. He clenched and unclenched his hands, struggling among his meagre supply of words for promises of help from Earth, which promises would tip the scales for peace again. He raised his voice in a shout for attention. He was unheard. The Council hall was in an uproar of desperate approval. The orator stood flushed and triumphant. The Council members looked from eye to eye, and slowly the old, white-bearded Keeper of Foodstuffs placed a golden box upon the table. He touched it in a certain fashion, and handed it to the next man. That second man touched it, and passed it to a third. And that man . . .

A hush fell instantly. Tommy understood. The measure was being decided by solemn vote. The voting device had reached the fifth man when there was a frantic clatter of footsteps, a door burst in, and babbling men stood in the opening, white-faced and stammering and overwhelmed, but trying to make a report.

Consternation reigned, incredulous, amazed consternation. The bearded old man rose dazedly and strode from the hall with the rest of the Council following him. A pause of stunned stupefaction, and the spectators in the hall rushed for other doors.

"Stick to Aten," snapped Tommy. "Something's broken, and it has to be our way. Let's see what it is."

He clung alike to Evelyn and to Aten as their air-pilot fought to clear a way. The doors were jammed. It was minutes before they could make their way through and plunge up the interminable steps Aten mounted, only to fling himself out to the open air. Then they were upon a flying bridge between two of the towers of the city. All about the city human figures were massing, staring upward.

And above the city swirled a swarm of aircraft. Tommy counted three of the clumsy ornithopters, high and motelike. There were twenty or thirty of the small, one-man craft. There were a dozen or more two-man planes. And there were at least forty giant single-wing ships which looked as if they had been made for carrying freight. They soared and circled above the city in soundless confusion. Before each of them glittered something silvery, like glass, which was not a screw propeller but somehow drew them on.

The Council was massed two hundred yards away. A single-seater dived downward, soared and circled noiselessly fifty yards overhead, and its pilot shouted a message. Then he climbed swiftly and rejoined his fellows. The men about Tommy looked stunned, as if they could not believe their ears. Aten seemed stricken beyond the passability of reaction.

"I got part of it," snapped Tommy, to Evelyn's whispered question. "I think I know the rest. Aten!" He snapped question after question in his inadequate phrasing of the city's tongue. Evelyn saw Aten answer dully, then bitterly, and then, as Tommy caught his arm and whispered savagely to him, Aten's eyes caught fire. He nodded violently and turned on his heel.

"Come on!" And Tommy seized Evelyn's arm again.

They followed closely as Aten wormed his way through the crowd. They raced behind him downstairs and through a door into a dusty and unvisited room. It was a museum. Aten pointed grimly.

Here were the automatic pistols taken from those of Jacaro's men who had been killed, a nasty sub-machine gun which had been Tommy's, and grenades—Jacaro's. Tommy checked shell calibres and carried off a ninety-shot magazine full of explosive bullets, and a repeating rifle.

"I can do more accurate work with this than the machine gun," he said cryptically. "Let's go!"

It was not until they were racing away from the Council building in one of the two-wheeled vehicles that Evelyn spoke again.

"I—understand part," she said unsteadily. "Those planes overhead are from Rahn. And they're threatening—"

"Blackmail," said Tommy between clenched teeth. "It sounds like a perfectly normal Earth racket. A fleet from Rahn is over Yugna, loaded with the Death Mist. Yugna pays food and goods and women or it's wiped out by gas. Further, it surrenders its aircraft to make further collections easier. Rahn refuses to die, though it's let in the jungle. It's turned pirate stronghold. Fed and clothed by a few other cities like this one, it should be able to hold out. It's a racket, Evelyn. A stick-up. A hijacking of a civilized city. Sounds like Jacaro."

THE little vehicle darted madly through empty highways, passing groups of men staring dazedly upward at the soaring motes overhead. It darted down this inclined way, up that one. It shot into a building and around a winding ramp. It stopped with a jerk and Aten was climbing out. He ran through a doorway, Tommy and Evelyn following. Planes of all sizes, still and lifeless, filled a vast hall. And Aten struggled with a door mechanism and a monster valve swung wide. Then Tommy threw his weight with Aten's to roll out the plane he had selected. It was a small, triangular ship, with seats for three, but it was heavy. The two men moved it with desperate exertion. Aten pointed, panting, to a slide-rail and it took them five minutes to get the plane about that rail and engage a curious contrivance in a slot in the ship's fuselage.

"Tommy," said Evelyn, "you're not going to—"

"Run away? Hardly!" said Tommy. "We're going up. I'm going to fight the fleet with bullets. They don't have missile-weapons here, and Aten will know the range of their electric-charge outfits."

"I'm coming too," said Evelyn desperately.

Tommy hesitated, then agreed.

"If we fail they'll gas the city anyway. One way or the other. . . ."

There was a sudden rumble as Evelyn took her place. The plane shot forward with a swift smooth acceleration. There was no sound of any motor. There was no movement of the glittering thing at the forepart of the plane. But the ship reached the end of the slide and lifted, and then was in mid-air, fifty feet above the vehicular way, a hundred feet above the ground.

TOMMY spoke urgently. Aten nodded. The ship had started to climb. He leveled it out and darted straight forward. He swung madly to dodge a soaring tower. He swept upward a little to avoid a flying bridge. The ship was traveling with an enormous speed, and the golden walls of the city flashed past below them and they sped away across feathery jungle.

"If we climbed at once," observed Tommy shortly, "they'd

think we meant to fight. They might start their gassing. As it is, we look like we're running away."

Evelyn said nothing. For five miles the plane fled as if in panic. Evelyn clung to the filigree side of the cockpit. The city dwindled behind them. Then Aten climbed steeply. Tommy was looking keenly at the glittering thing which propelled the ship. It seemed like a crystal gridwork, like angular lace contrived of glass. But a cold blue flame burned in it and Tommy was obscurely reminded of a neon tube, though the color was wholly unlike. A blast of air poured back through the grid. Somehow, by some development of electro-statics, the "static jet" which is merely a toy in Earth laboratories had become usable as a means of propelling aircraft.

Back they swept toward the Golden City, five thousand feet or more aloft. The ground was partly obscured by the hazy, humid atmosphere, but glinting sun-reflections from the city guided them. Soaring things took shape before them and grew swiftly nearer. Tommy spoke again, busily loading the automatic rifle with explosive shells.

Aten swung to follow a vast dark shape in its circular soaring, a hundred feet above it and a hundred yards behind. Wind whistled, rising to a shriek. Tommy fired painstakingly.

THE other plane zoomed suddenly as a flash of blue flame spouted before it. It dived, then, fluttering and swooping, began to drift helplessly toward the spires of the city below it.

"Good!" snapped Tommy. "Another one, Aten."

Aten made no reply. He flung his ship sidewise and dived steeply before a monstrous freight carrier. Tommy fired deliberately as they swept past. The propelling grid flashed blue flame in a vast, crashing flame. It, too, began to flutter down.

Tommy did not miss until the fifth time, and Aten turned with a grimace of disappointment. Tommy's second shot burst in a freight compartment and a man screamed. His voice carried horribly in the silence of these heights. But Tommy shot again, and again, and there was a satisfying blue flash as a fifth big ship went fluttering helplessly down.

Aten began to circle for height. Tommy refilled the magazine.

"I'm bringing 'em down," he explained unnecessarily to Evelyn, "by smashing their propellers. They have to land, and when they land they're hostages—I hope!"

Confusion became apparent among the hostile planes. The one Yugna ship was identified as the source of disaster. Tommy worked his rifle with a cold fury. He aimed at no man, but the propelling grids were large. For a one-man ship they were five feet in diameter, and for the big freight ships they were circles fifteen feet across. They were perfect targets, and Aten seemed to grasp the necessary tactics almost instantly. Dead ahead or from straight astern, Tommy would not miss a shot. The fleet of Rahn went fluttering downward. Fifteen of the biggest were down, and six of the two-man planes. A sixteenth and seventeenth flashed at their bows and drifted helplessly. . . .

THEN the one-man ships attacked. Six of them at once. Aten grinned and dived for all of them. One by one, Tommy smashed their crystal grids and watched them sinking unsteadily toward the towers of the city. As his own ship drove over them, little golden flashes licked out. Electric-charge weapons. One flash struck the wingtip of their plane and flame burst out, but Aten flung the ship into a mad whirl in which the blaze was blown out.

Another freight ship helpless—and another. Then the air fleet of Rahn turned and fled. The ornithopters winged away in heavy, creaking terror. The other dived for speed and flattened out hardly above the tree-fern jungle. They streaked away in ignominious panic. Aten darted and circled above them and, as Tommy failed to fire, turned and went racing back toward the city.

"After the first ones went down," observed Tommy, "they knew that if they gassed the city we'd shoot them down into their own gas cloud. So they ran away. I hope this gives us a pull."

The city's towers loomed before them. The lacy bridges swarmed with human figures. Somewhere a fight was in progress about a grounded plane from Rahn. Others seemed to have surrendered sullenly on alighting. For the first time Tommy saw the city as a thronging mass of humanity, and for the first time he realized how terrible must be the strain upon the city if with so large a population so few could be free for leisure in normal times.

The little plane settled down and landed lightly. There were a dozen men on the landing platform now, and they were herding disarmed men from Rahn away from a big ship Tommy had brought down. Tommy looked curiously at the prisoners. They seemed freer than the inhabitants of Yugna. Their faces showed no such signs of strain. But they did not seem well-fed, nor did they appear as capable or as resolute.

"Cuyal!" said Aten in an explanatory tone, seeing Tommy's expression. He put his shoulder to the big ship, to wheel it back into its shed.

"You son of a gun," grunted Tommy, "it's all in the day's work to you, fighting an invading fleet!"

A messenger came panting through the doorway. Tommy grinned.

"The Council wants us, Evelyn. Now maybe they'll listen."

THE atmosphere of the resumed Council meeting was, as a matter of fact, considerably changed. The white-bearded Keeper of Foodstuffs thanked them with dignity. He invited Tommy to offer advice, since his services had proved so useful.

"Advice?" said Tommy, in the halting, fumbling phrases he had slaved to acquire. "I would put the prisoners from Rahn to work at the machines, releasing citizens." There was a buzz of approval, and he added drily in English: "I'm playing politics, Evelyn." Again in the speech of Yugna he added: "And I would have the fleet of Yugna soar above Rahn, not to demand tribute as that city did, but to disable all its aircraft, so that such piracy as to-day may not be tried again!" There was a second buzz of approval. "And third," said Tommy earnestly, "I would communicate with Earth, rather than assassinate it. I would acquire the science of Earth for the benefit of this world, rather than use the science of this world to annihilate that! I—"

For the second time the council meeting was interrupted. An armed messenger came pounding into the room. He reported swiftly. Tommy grasped Evelyn's wrist in what was almost a painful grip.

"Noises in the Tube!" he told her sharply. "Earth-folk doing something in the Tube Jacaro came through. Your father . . ."

There was an alert silence in the Council hall. The white-bearded old man had listened to the messenger. Now he asked a grim question of Tommy.

"They may be my friends, or your enemies," said Tommy briefly. "Mass thermit-throwers and let me find out!"

IT was the only possible thing to do. Tommy and Evelyn went with the Council, in a body, in a huge wheeled vehicle that raced across the city. Lingering groups still searched the sky above them, now blessedly empty again. But the Council's vehicle dived down and down to ground level, where the rumble of machines was loud indeed, and then turned into a tunnel which went down still farther. There was feverish activity ahead, where it stopped, and a golden thermit-thrower came into sight upon a dull-colored truck.

Questions. Feverish replies. The white-bearded man touched Tommy on the shoulder, regarding him with a peculiarly noncommittal gaze, and pointed to a doorway that someone was just opening. The door swung wide. There was a confusion of prismatically-colored mist within it, and Tommy noticed that tanks upon tanks were massed outside the metal wall of that compartment, and seemingly had been pouring something into the room.

The mist drew back from the door. Saffron-red lighting panels appeared dimly, then grew distinct. There were small, collapsed bundles of fur upon the floor of the storeroom being exposed to view. They were, probably, the equivalent of rats. And then the last remnant of mist vanished with a curiously wraithlike abruptness, and the end of Jacaro's Tube came into view.

Tommy advanced, Evelyn clinging to his sleeve. There were clanking noises audible in this room even above the dull rumble of the city's machines. The noises came from the Tube's mouth. It was four feet and more across, and it projected at a crazy angle out of a previously solid wall.

"Hello!" shouted Tommy. "Down the Tube!"

THE clattering noise stopped, then continued at a faster rate.

"The gas is cut off!" shouted Tommy again. "Who's there?"

A voice gasped from the Tube's depths:

"It's him!" The tone was made metallic by echoing and re-echoing in the bends of the Tube, but it was Smithers. "We're comin', Mr. Reames."

"Is—is Daddy there?" called Evelyn eagerly. "Daddy!"

"Coming," said a grim voice.

The clattering grew nearer. A goggled, gas-masked head appeared, and a body followed it out of the Tube, laden with a multitude of burdens. A second climbed still more heavily after the first. The brightly-colored citizens of the Golden City reached quietly to the weapons at their waists. A third voice came up the Tube, distant and nearly unintelligible. It roared a question.

Smithers ripped off his gas mask and said distinctly:

"Sure we're through. Go ahead. An' go to hell!"

Then there was a thunderous detonation somewhere down in the Tube's depths. The visible part of it jerked spasmodically and cracked across. A wisp of brownish smoke puffed out of it, and the stinging reek of high explosive tainted the air. Then Evelyn was clinging close to her father, and he was patting her comfortingly, and Smithers was pumping both of Tommy's hands, his normal calmness torn from him for once. But after a bare moment he had gripped himself again. He unloaded an impressive number of parcels from about his person. Then he regarded the citizens of the Golden City with an impersonal, estimating gaze, ignoring twenty weapons trained upon him.

"Those damn fools back on Earth," he observed impassively, "decided the professor an' me was better off of it. So they let us come through the Tube before they blew it up. We brought the explosive bullets, Mr. Reames. I hope we brought enough."

And Tommy grinned elatedly as Denham turned to crush his hands in his own.

CHAPTER VIII

"Those Devils Have Got Evelyn!"

THAT night the three of them talked, on a high terrace with most of the Golden City spread out below them. Over their heads, lights of many colors moved and shifted slowly in the sky. There were a myriad glowing specks of saffron-red about the ways of the city, and the air was full of fragrant odors. The breath of the jungle reached them even a thousand feet above ground. And the dull, persistent roar of the machines reached them too. There were five people on the terrace: Tommy, Denham, Smithers, Aten and the white-bearded old Keeper of Foodstuffs. He looked on as the Earthmen talked.

"We're marooned," Tommy was saying crisply, "and for the time being we've got to throw in with these people. I believe they came from Earth originally. Four, five thousand years ago, perhaps. Their tale is of a cave they sealed up behind them. It might have been a primitive Tube, if such a thing can be imagined."

Denham filled his pipe and lighted it meditatively.

"Half the American Indian tribes," he observed drily, "had legends of coming originally from an underworld. I wonder if Tubes are less your own invention than we thought?"

Tommy shrugged.

"In any case, Earth is safe."

"Is it?" insisted Denham. "You say they understood at once when you talked of dimension-travel. Ask the old chap there."

TOMMY frowned, then labored with the question. The bearded old man spoke gravely. At his answer, Tommy grimaced.

"Datl's gone looking for the cave their legends tell of," he said reluctantly. "He's the lad who wanted the city to gas Earth with some ghastly stuff they know of, and move over when the gas was harmless again. But the cave has been lost for centuries, and it's in the torrid zone—which *is* torrid! We're near the North Pole of this planet, and it's tropic here. It must be mighty hot at the equator. Datl took a ship and supplies and sailed off. He may be killed. In any case it'll be some time before he's dangerous. Meanwhile, as I said, we're marooned."

"And more," said Denham deliberately. "By the time the authorities halfway believed me, and Von Holtz could talk, there were more deaths from the Death Mist. It wiped out a village, clean. So when it was realized that I'd caused it—or that was their interpretation—and was the only man who could cause it again, why, the authorities thought it a splendid idea for me to come through the Tube. They invited me to commit suicide. My knowledge was too dangerous for a man to have. So," he added grimly, "I have committed suicide. We will not be welcomed back on Earth, Tommy."

Tommy made an impatient gesture.

"Worry about that later," he said impatiently. "Right now there's a war on. Rahn's desperate, and the prisoners we took this morning say Jacaro and his gunmen are there, advising them. Ragged Men have joined in to help kill civilized humans. And they've still got aircraft."

"Which can still bombard this city," observed Denham. "Can't they?"

Tommy pointed to the many-colored beams of light playing through the sky overhead.

"No. Those lights were invented to guide night-flying planes back home. They're static lights—cold lights, by the way—and they register powerfully when a static-discharge propeller comes within range of them. If Rahn tries a night attack, Aten and I take off and shoot them down again. That's that. But we've got to design gas masks for these people, and I think I can persuade the Council to send over and take all Rahn's aircraft away to-morrow. But the real emergency is the jungle."

HE expounded the situation of the city as he understood it. He labored painstakingly to make his meaning clear while Denham blew meditative smoke rings and Smithers listened quietly. But when Tommy had finished, Smithers said in a vast calm:

"Say, Mr. Reames, y'know I asked you to get somebody to take me through some o' these engine rooms. That's kinda my specialty. An' these folks are good, no question! There's engines—even steam engines—we couldn't build on Earth. But, my Gawd, they're dumb! There ain't a piece of automatic machinery on the place. There's one man to every motor, handlin' the controls or the throttle. They got stuff we couldn't come near, but they never thought of a steam governor."

Tommy turned kindling eyes upon him. "Go on!"

"Hell," said Smithers, "gimme some tools an' I'll go through one shop an' cut the workin' force in half, just slammin' governors, reducin' valves, an' automatic cut-offs on the machines I understand!"

Tommy jumped to his feet. He paced up and down, then halted and began to spout at Aten and the Keeper of Foodstuffs. He gesticulated, fumbling for words, and hunted absurdly for the ones he wanted among his written lists, and finally was drawing excitedly on Aten's black-metal tablet. Smithers got up and looked over his shoulder.

"That ain't it, Mr. Reames," he said slowly. "Maybe I . . ."

TOMMY pressed the stud that erased the page. Smithers took the tablet and began to draw painstakingly. Aten, watching, exclaimed suddenly. Smithers was drawing an actual machine, actually used in the Golden City, and he was making a working sketch of a governor so that it would operate without supervision while the steam pressure continued. Aten began to talk excitedly. The Keeper of Foodstuffs took the tablet and examined it. He looked blank, then amazed, and as the utterly foreign idea of a machine which controlled itself struck home, his hands shook and color deepened in his cheeks.

He gave an order to Aten, who dashed away. In ten minutes other men began to arrive. They bent over the drawing. Excited comments, discussions and disputes began. A dawning enthusiasm manifested itself. Two of them approached Smithers respectfully, with shining eyes. They drew their tablets from their belts, rather skilfully drew the governor he had indicated in larger scale, and by gestures asked for more detailed plans. Smithers stood up to go with them.

"You're a hero, now, Smithers," Tommy informed him exultantly. "They'll work you to death and call you blessed!"

"Yes, sir," said Smithers. "These fellas are right good mechanics. They just happened to miss this trick." He paused. "Uh—where's Miss Evelyn?"

"With Aten's—wife," said Tommy. This was no time to discuss the marital system of Yugna. "We were prisoners until this morning. Now we're guests of honor. Evelyn's talking to a lot of women and trying to boost our prestige."

SMITHERS went over to the gesticulating group of draftsmen. He settled down to explain by drawings, since he had not a word of their language. In a few minutes a group went rushing away with the sketch tablets held jealously to their breasts, bound for workshops. Other men appeared to present new problems. A wave of sheer enthusiasm was in being. A new idea which would lessen the demands of the machines was a godsend to these folk.

Then Denham blew a smoke ring and said meditatively:

"I think I've got something too, Tommy. Ultra-sonic vibrations. Sound waves at two to three hundred thousand per second. Air won't carry them. Liquids will. They use 'em to sterilize milk, killing the germs by sound waves carried through the fluid. I think we can start some ultra-sonic generators out there that will go through the wet soil and kill all vegetation within a given range. We might clear away the jungle for half a mile or so and then use ultra-sonic beams to keep it clear while new food-plants are tried out."

Tommy's eyes glowed.

"You've given yourself a job! We'll turn this planet upside down."

"We'll have to," said Denham drily. "This city may believe in you, but there are others, and these folk are a little too clever. There's no reason why some other city shouldn't attack Earth, if they seriously attack the problem of building a Tube."

Tommy ground his teeth, frowning. Then he started up. There was a new noise down in the city. A sudden flare of intolerable illumination broke out. There was an explosion, many screams, then the yelling tumult of men in deadly battle.

EVERY man on the tower terrace was facing toward the noise, staring. The white-bearded man gave an order, deliberately. Men rushed. But as they swarmed toward an exit, a green beam of light appeared near the uproar. It streaked upward, wavering from side to side and making the golden walls visible in a ghostly fashion. It shivered in a hasty rhythm.

Aten groaned, almost sobbed. There was another flash of that unbearable actinic flame. A thermit-thrower was in action. Then a third flash. This was farther away. The tumult died suddenly, but the green light-beam continued its motion.

Tommy was snapping questions. Aten spoke, and choked upon his words. Tommy swore in a sudden raging passion and then turned a chalky face toward the other two men from Earth.

"The prisoners!" he said in a hoarse voice. "The men from Rahn! They broke loose. They rushed an arsenal. With hand weapons and a thermit-thrower they fought their way to a place where the big vehicles are kept. They raided a dwelling-tower on the way and seized women. They've gone off on the metal roads through the jungle!" He tried to ease his collar. Aten, still watching the green beam, croaked another sentence. "Those devils have got Evelyn!" cried Tommy hoarsely. "My god! Aten's wife, and his. . . ." He jerked a hand toward the Councilor. "Fifty women—gone through the jungle with them, toward Rahn! Those devils have got Evelyn!"

He whirled upon Aten, seizing his shoulder, shaking the man as he roared questions.

"No chance of catching them." Far away, in the jungle, the infinitely vivid actinic flame blazed for several seconds. "They've sprayed thermit on the road. It's melted and ruined. It'd take hours to haul the ground vehicles past the gap. They've got arms and lights. They can fight off the beasts and Ragged Men. They'll make Rahn. And then"—he shook with the rage that possessed him—"Jacaro's there with those gunmen of his and his friends the Ragged Men!"

HE seemed to control himself with a terrific effort. He turned to the white-bearded Councilor, whose bearing was that of a man stunned by disaster. Tommy spoke measuredly, choosing words with a painstaking care, clipping the words crisply as he spoke.

The Councilor stiffened. Old as he was, an undeniable fighting light came into his eyes. He barked orders right and left. men woke from the paralysis of shock and fled upon errands of his command. And Tommy turned to Denham and Smithers.

"The women will be safe until dawn," he said evenly. "Our late prisoners can't lose the way—aluminum roads that are no longer much used lead between all the cities—but they won't dare stop in the jungles. They'll go straight on through. They should reach Rahn at dawn or a little before. And at dawn our air fleet will be over the city and they'll give back the women, unharmed, or we'll turn their own trick on them, by God! It'd be better for Evelyn to die of gas than as—as the Ragged Men would kill her!"

His hands were clenched and he breathed noisily for an instant. Then he swallowed and went on in the same unnatural calm:

"Smithers, you're going to stay behind, with part of the air fleet. You'll get aloft before dawn and shoot down any strange aircraft. They might try to stalemate us by repeating their threat, with our guns over Rahn. I'll give orders."

He turned again to the Councilor, who nodded, glanced at Smithers, and repeated the command.

"You, sir," he spoke to Denham, "you'll come with me. It's your right, I suppose. And we'll go down and get ready."

He led the way steadily toward a door. But he reached up to his collar, once, as if he were choking, and ripped away collar and coat and all, unconscious of the resistance of the cloth.

THAT night the Golden City made savage preparation for war. Ships were loaded and ranged in order. Crews armed themselves, and helped in the loading and arming of other ships. Oddly enough, it was to Tommy that men came to ask if the directing apparatus for the Death Mist should be carried. The Death Mist could, of course, be used as a gas alone, drifting with the wind, or it could be directed from a distance. This had been done on Earth, with the directional impulses sent blindly down the Tube merely to keep the Mist moving always. The controlling apparatus could be carried in a monster freight plane. Tommy ordered it done. Also he had the captured planes from Rahn refitted for flight by replacing their smashed propelling grids. Fresh crews of men for these ships organized themselves.

When the fleet took off there was only darkness in all the world. The unfamiliar stars above shone bright and very near as Tommy's ship, leading, winged noiselessly up and down and straight away from the play of prismatic lights above the city. Behind him, silhouetted against that many-colored glow, were the angular shapes of many other noiseless shadows. The ornithopters with their racket would start later, so the planes would be soaring above Rahn before their presence was even suspected. The rest of the fleet flew in darkness.

THE flight above the jungle would have been awe-inspiring at another time. There were the stars above, nearer and brighter than those of Earth. There was no Milky Way in the firmament of this universe. The stars were separate and fewer in number. There was no moon. And below there was only utter, unrelieved darkness from which now and again beast-sounds arose. They were clearly audible on board the silent air fleet. Roarings, bellowings, and hoarse screamings. Once the ships passed above a tumult as of unthinkable monsters in deadly battle, when for an instant the very clashing of monstrous jaws was audible and a hissing sound which seemed filled with deadly hate.

Then lights—few of them, and dim ones. Then blazing fires —Ragged Men, camped without the walls of Rahn or in some gold-walled courtyard where the jungle thrust greedy, invading green tentacles. The air fleet circled noiselessly in a huge batlike cloud. Then things came racing from the darkness, down below, and there was a tumult and a shouting, and presently the hilarious, insanely gleeful uproar of the Ragged Men. Tommy's face went gray. These were the escaped prisoners, arrived actually after the air fleet which was to demand the return of their captives.

Tommy wet his lips and spoke grimly to his pilot. There were six men and many Death-Mist bombs in his ship. He was asking if communication could be had with the other ships. It was wise to let Rahn know at once that avengers lurked overhead for the captives just delivered there.

For answer, a green signal-beam shot out. It wavered here and there. Tommy commanded again. And as the signal-beam flickered, he somehow sensed the obedience of the invisible ships about him. They were sweeping off to right and left. Bombs of the Death Mist were dropping in the darkness. Even in the starlight, Tommy could see great walls of pale vapor building themselves up above the jungle. And a sudden confused noise of yapping defiance and raging hatred came up from the city of Rahn. But before dawn came there was no other sign that their presence was known.

THE ornithopters came squeaking and rattling in their heavy flight just as the dull-red sun of this world peered above the horizon. The tree-fern fronds waved languidly in the morning breeze. The walls and towers of Rahn gleamed bright gold, in parts, and in parts they seemed dull and scabrous with some creeping fungus stuff, and on one side of the city the wall was overwhelmed by a triumphant tide of green. There the jungle had crawled over the ramparts and surged into the city. Three of the towers had their bases in the welter of growing things, and creepers had climbed incredibly and were still climbing to enter and then destroy the man-made structures.

But about the city there now reared a new rampart, rising above the tree-fern tops: there was a wall of the Death Mist encompassing the city. No living thing could enter or leave the city without passing through that cloud. And at Tommy's order it moved forward to the very encampments of the Ragged Men.

He spoke, beginning his ultimatum. But a movement below checked him. On a landing stage that was spotted with molds and lichens, women were being herded into clear view. They were the women of the Golden City. Tommy saw a tiny figure in khaki—Evelyn! Then there was a sudden uproar from an encampment of the Ragged Men. His eyes flicked there, and he saw the Ragged Men running into and out of the tall wall of Death Mist. And they laughed uproariously and ran into and out of the Mist again.

His pilot dived down. The Ragged Men yelled and capered and howled derisively at him. He saw that they removed masklike things from their faces in order to shout, and donned them again before running again into the Mist. At once he understood. The Ragged Men had gas masks!

Then, a sudden cracking noise. Three men had opened fire with rifles from below. Their garments were drab-colored, in contrast to the vivid tints of the clothing of the inhabitants of Rahn. They were Jacaro's gunmen. And a great freight carrier from Yugna veered suddenly, and a bluish flash burst out before it, and it began to flutter helplessly down into the city beneath.

The weapons of Tommy's fleet were useless, since the citizens of Rahn were protected by gas masks. And Tommy's fighting ships were subject to the same rifle fire against their propelling grids that had defeated the fleet from Rahn. The only thing the avenging fleet could now accomplish was the death of the women it could not save.

CHAPTER IX

War!

A huge ornithopter came heavily out on the landing stage in the city of Rahn. Its crew took their places. With a creaking and rattling noise it rose toward the invading fleet. From its filigree cockpit sides, men waved green branches. A green light wavered from the big plane that carried the bearded Council man and Denham. That plane swept forward and hovered above the ornithopter. The two flying things seemed almost fastened together, so closely did their pilots maintain that same speed and course. A snaky rope went coiling down into the lower ship's cockpit. A burly figure began to climb it hand over hand. A second figure followed. A third figure, in the drab clothing that distinguished Jacaro's men from all others, wrapped the rope about himself and was hauled up bodily. And Tommy had seen Jacaro but once, yet he was suddenly grimly convinced that this was Jacaro himself.

The two planes swept apart. The ornithopter descended toward the landing stage of Rahn. The freight plane swept toward the ship that carried Tommy. Again the snaky rope coiled down. And Tommy swung up the fifteen feet that alone separated the two soaring planes, and looked into the hard, amused eyes of Jacaro where he sat between two other emissaries of Rahn. One of them was half naked and savage, with the light of madness in his eyes. A Ragged Man. The other was lean and desperate, despite the colored tunic of a civilized man that he wore.

"HELLO," said Jacaro blandly. "We come up to talk things over."

Tommy gave him the briefest of nods. He looked at Denham —who was deathly white and grim—and the bearded Councilor.

"I' been givin' 'em the dope," said Jacaro easily. "We got the whip hand now. We got gas masks, we got guns just the same as you have, an' we got the women."

"You haven't ammunition," said Tommy evenly, "or damned little. Your men brought down one ship, and stopped. If you had enough shells, would you have stopped there?"

Jacaro grinned.

"You got arithmetic, Reames," he conceded. "That's so. But —I'm sayin' it again—we got the women. Your girl, for one! Now, how about throwin' in with me, you an' the professor?"

"No," said Tommy.

"In a coupla months, Rahn'll be runnin' this planet," said Jacaro blandly, "and I'm runnin' Rahn! I didn't know how easy the racket'd be, or I'd've let Yugna alone. I'd've come here first. Now get it! Rahn runnin' the planet, with a couple guys runnin' Rahn an' passin' down through a Tube any little thing we want, like a few million bucks in solid gold. An' Rahn an' the other cities for kinda country homes for us an' our friends. All the women we want, good liquor, an' a swell time!"

"Talk sense," said Tommy, without even contempt in his tone.

JACARO snarled.

"No sense actin' too big!" But the snarl encouraged Tommy, because it proved Jacaro less confident than he tried to seem. His next change of tone proved it. "Aw, hell!" he said placatingly. "This is what I'm figurin' on. These guys ain't used to fighting, but they got the stuff. They got gases that are hell-roarin'. They got ships can beat any we got back home. Figure out the racket. A coupla big Tubes, that'll let a ship—maybe folded—go through. A fleet of 'em floatin' over N'York, loaded with gas—that white stuff y' can steer wherever y' want it. Figure the shake-down. We could pull a hundred million from Chicago! We c'd take over the whole United States! Try that on y' piano! Me, King Jacaro, King of America!" His dark eyes flashed. "I'll give y' Canada or Mexico, whichever y' want. Name y' price, guy. A coupla months organizin' here, buildin' a big Tube, then. . . ."

Tommy's expression did not change.

"If it were that easy," he said drily, "you wouldn't be bargaining. I'm not altogether a fool, Jacaro. We want those women back. You want something we've got, and you want it badly. Cut out the oratory and tell me the real price for the return of the women, unharmed."

Jacaro burst into a flood of profanity.

"I'd rather Evelyn died from gas," said Tommy, "than as your filthy Ragged Men would kill her. And you know I mean it." He switched to the language of the cities to go on coldly: "If one woman is harmed, Rahn dies. We will shoot down every ship that rises from her stages. We will spray burning thermit through her streets. We will cover her towers with gas until her people starve in the gas masks they've made!"

The lean man in the tunic of Rahn snarled bitterly: "What matter? We starve now!"

Tommy turned upon him as Jacaro whirled and cursed him bitterly for the revealing outburst.

"We will ransom the women with food," said Tommy coldly—and then his eyes flamed, "and thrash you afterwards for fools!"

HE made a gesture to the Keeper of Foodstuffs. It was unconsciously an authoritative gesture, though the Keeper of Foodstuffs was in the state of affairs in Yugna the head of the Council. But that old man spoke deliberately. The man from Rahn snarled his reply. And Tommy turned aside as the bargaining went on. He could see Evelyn down below, a tiny speck of khaki amid the rainbow-colored robes of the other women. This had been a savage expedition to rescue or to avenge. It had deteriorated into a bargain. Tommy heard, dully, amounts of unfamiliar weights and measures of foodstuffs he did not recognize. He heard the time and place of payment named: the gate of Yugna, the third dawn hence. He hardly looked up as at some signal one of their own ornithopters slid below and the three ambassadors of Rahn prepared to go over the side. But Jacaro snarled out of one corner of his mouth.

"These guys are takin' each other's words. Maybe that's all right, but I'm warnin' you, if there's any double-crossin'. . . ."

He was gone. The Keeper of Foodstuffs touched Tommy's shoulder.

"Our flier," he said slowly, "will make sure our women are as yet unharmed. We are to deliver the foods at our own city gate, and after the women have been returned. Rahn dares not keep them or harm them. We of Yugna keep our word. Even in Rahn they know it."

"But they won't keep theirs," said Tommy heavily. "Not with a man of Earth to lead them."

HE watched with his heart in his mouth as the ornithopter alighted near the assembled women of Yugna. As the three ambassadors climbed out, he could hear the faint murmur of voices. The men of Yugna, under truce, called across the landing stage to the women of their own city, and the women replied to them. Then the crew of the one grounded freighter arrived on the landing stage and the flapping flier rose slowly and rejoined the fleet. Its crew shouted a shamefaced reassurance to the flagship.

"I suppose," said Tommy bitterly, "we'd better go back—if you're sure the women are safe."

"I am sure," said the old man unhappily, "or I had not agreed to pay half the foodstuffs in Yugna for their return."

He withdrew into a troubled silence as the fleet swept far from triumphantly for him. Denham had not spoken at all, though his eyes had blazed savagely upon the men of Rahn. Now he spoke, dry-throatedly:

"Tommy—Evelyn—"

"She is all right so far," said Tommy bitterly. "She's to be ransomed by foodstuffs, paid at the gates of Yugna. And Jacaro bragged he's running Rahn—and they've got gas masks. We'd better be ready for trouble after the women are returned."

Denham nodded grimly. Tommy reached out and took one of the black tablets from the man beside him. He began to draw carefully, his eyes savage.

"What's that?"

"There's high-pressure steam in Yugna," said Tommy coldly. "I'm designing steam guns. Gravity feed of spherical projectiles. A jet of steam instead of gunpowder. They'll be low-velocity, but we can use big-calibre balls for shock effect, and with long barrels they ought to serve for a hundred yards or better. Smooth bore, of course."

Denham stirred. His lips were pinched.

"I'll design a gas mask," he said restlessly, "and Smithers and I, between us, will do what we can."

THE air fleet went on over the waving tree-fern jungle in an unvarying monotony of bitterness. Presently Tommy wearily explained his design to the bearded Councilor who, with the quick comprehension of mechanical design apparently instinctive in these folk, grasped it immediately. He selected three of the six-man crew and passed Tommy's drawings to them. While the jungle flowed beneath the fleet they studied the sketches, made other drawings, and showed them eagerly to Tommy. When the fleet soared down to the scattered landing stages, not only was the design understood but apparently plans for production had been made. It did not take the men of the Golden City long to respond.

Tommy flung himself savagely into the work he had taken upon himself. It did not occur to him to ask for authority. He knew what had to be done and he set to work to do it, commanding men and materials as if there could be no question of disobedience. As a matter of fact, he yielded impatiently to an order of the Council that he should present himself in the Council hall, and, since no questions were asked him, continued his organizing in the very presence of the Council, sending for information and giving orders in a low tone while the council deliberated. A vote was taken by the voting machine. At its end, he was solemnly informed that, though not a native of Yugna, he was entrusted with the command of the defense forces of the city. His skill in arms—as evidenced by his defeat of the fleet of Rahn—and his ability in command—when he met the gas-mask defense of Rahn with a threat of starvation —moved the Council to that action. He accepted the command almost abstractedly, and hurried away to pick gun emplacements.

WITHIN four hours after the return of the fleet, the first steam gun was ready for trial. Smithers appeared, sweat-streaked and vastly calm, to announce that others could be turned out in quantity.

"These guys have got the stuff," he said steadily. "Instead o' castin' their stuff, they shoot it on a core in a melted spray. They ain't got steel, an' copper's scarce, but they got some alloys that are good an' tough. One's part tungsten or I'm crazy."

Tommy nodded.

"Turn out all the guns you can," he said. "I look for fighting."

"Yeah," said Smithers. "Miss Evelyn's still all right?"

"Up to three hours ago," said Tommy grimly. "Every three hours one of our ships lands in Rahn and reports. We give the Rahnians their stuff at our own city gates. I've warned Jacaro that we've mounted thermit-throwers on our food stores. If he manages to gas us by surprise, nevertheless our foodstuffs can't be captured. They've got to turn over Evelyn and cart off their food before they dare to fight, else they'll starve."

"But—uh—there're other cities they could stick up, ain't there?"

"We've warned them," said Tommy curtly. "They've got thermit-throwers mounted on their food supplies, too. And they're desperate enough to keep Rahn off. They're willing enough to let Yugna do the fighting, but they know what Rahn's winning will mean."

Smithers turned away, then turned back.

"Uh—Mr. Reames," he said heavily, "those fellas've gone near crazy about governors an' reducing valves an' such. They're inventin' ways to use 'em on machines I don't make head or tail of. We got three-four hundred men loose from machines already, an' they're turnin' out these steam guns as soon as you check up. There'll be more loose by night. I had 'em spray some castin's for another Tube, too. Workin' like they do, an' with the tools they got, they make speed."

Tommy responded impatiently: "There's no steel, no iron for magnets."

"I know," admitted Smithers. "I'm tryin' steam cylinders to —uh—energize the castin's, instead o' coils. It'll be ready by morning. I wish you'd look it over, Mr. Reames. If Miss Evelyn gets safe into the city, we could send her down the Tube to Earth until the fightin's over."

"I'll try to see it," said Tommy impatiently. "I'll try!"

HE turned back to the set-up steam gun. A flexible pipe from a heavily insulated cylinder ran to it. A hopper dropped metallic balls down into a bored-out barrel, where they were sucked into the blast of superheated steam from the storage cylinder. At a touch of the trigger a monstrous cloud of steam poured out. It was six feet from the gun muzzle before it condensed enough to be visible. Then a huge white cloud developed: but the metal pellets went on with deadly force. Half an inch in diameter, they carried seven hundred yards at extreme elevation. Point-blank range was seventy-five yards. They would kill at three hundred, and stun or disable beyond that. At a hundred yards they would tear through a man's body.

Tommy was promised a hundred of the weapons, with their boilers, in two days. He selected their emplacements. He directed that a disabling device be inserted, so if rushed they could not be turned against their owners. He inspected the gas masks being turned out by the women, who in this emergency worked like the men. Though helpless before machinery, it seemed, they could contrive a fabric device like a gas mask.

The second day the work went on more desperately still. But Smithers' work in releasing men was telling. There were fifteen hundred governors, or reducing valves, or automatic cutouts in operation now. And fifteen hundred men were released from the machines, which had to be kept going to keep the city alive. With that many men, intelligent mechanics all, Tommy and Smithers worked wonders. Smithers drove them mercilessly, using profanity and mechanical drawings instead of speech. Denham withdrew twenty men and labored on top of one of the towers. Toward sunset of the second day, vast clouds of steam bellied out from it at odd, irregular intervals. Nothing else manifested itself. Those irregular belchings of steam continued until dark, but Tommy paid no attention to them. He was driving the gunners of the machine guns to practice. He was planning patrols, devising a reserve, mounting thermit-throwers and arranging for the delivery of the promised ransom at the specified city gate. So far, there was no sign of anything unusual in Rahn. Messengers from Yugna saw the captive women regularly, once every three hours. The last to leave had reported them being loaded into great ground vehicles under a defending escort, to travel through the dark jungle roads to Yugna. A vast concourse of empty vehicles was trailing into the jungle after them, to bring back the food which would keep Rahn from starving, for a while. It all seemed wholly regular.

AT dawn, the remaining ships of the air fleet of Rahn were soaring silently above the jungle about the Golden City. They made no threat. They offered no affront. But they soared, and soared. . . .

A little after dawn, glitterings in the jungle announced the arrival of the convoy. Messengers, in advance, shouted the news. Men from Yugna went out to inspect. The atmosphere grew tense. The air fleet of Rahn drew closer.

Slowly, a great golden gateway yawned. Four ground vehicles rolled forward, and under escort of the Rahnians entered the city. Half the captive women from Yugna were within them. They alighted, weeping for joy, and were promptly whisked away. Evelyn was not among them. Tommy ground his teeth. An explanation came. When one half the promised ransom was paid, the others would be forthcoming.

Tommy gave grim orders. Half the foodstuffs were taken to the city gate—half, no more. At his direction, it was explained gently to the Rahnians that the rest of the ransom remained under guard of the thermit-throwers. It would not be exposed to capture until the last of the captives were released. There was argument, expostulation. The rest of the women appeared. Aten, at Tommy's express command, piled Evelyn and his own wife into a ground vehicle and came racing madly to the tower from which Tommy could see all the circuit of the city.

"You're all right?" asked Tommy. At Evelyn's speechless nod, he put his hand heavily on her shoulder. "I'm glad," he managed to say. "Put on that gas mask. Hell's going to pop in a minute."

He watched, every muscle tense. There was confusion about the city gate. Ground vehicles, loaded with foodstuffs, poured out of the gate and back toward the jungle. Other vehicles with improvised enlargements to their carrying platforms—making them into huge closed boxes—rolled up to the gate. The loaded vehicles rolled back and back and back, and ever more apparently empty ones crowded about the city gate waiting for admission.

Then there was a sudden flare of intolerable light. A wild yell arose. Clouds of steam shot up from the ready steam guns. But the circling air fleet turned as one ship and plunged for the city. The leaders began to drop smoking things that turned into monstrous pillars of prismatically-colored mist. A wave of deadly vapor rolled over the ramparts of the city. And then there was a long-continued ululation and the noise of battle. Ragged Men, hidden in the jungle, had swarmed upon the walls with ladders made of jungle reeds. They came over the parapet in a wave of howling madness. And they surged into the city, flinging gas bombs as they came.

CHAPTER X

The Fight

THE city was pandemonium. Tommy, looking down from his post of command, swore softly under his breath. The Death Mist was harmless to the defenders of Yugna as a gas, because of their gas masks. But it served as a screen. It blotted out the waves of attackers so the steam guns could not be aimed save at the shortest of short ranges. His precautions were taking effect, to be sure. Two thirds of the attackers were Ragged Men drawn from about half the surviving cities, and against such a horde Yugna could not have held out at all but for his preparations. Now the defenders took a heavy toll. Swarms of men came racing toward the open gate, their truncheons aglow in the sunlight. The ring of Death Mist was contracting as if to strangle the city, and it left the ramparts bare again. And from more than one point upon the battlements the roaring clouds of steam burst out again. A dozen guns concentrated on the racing men of Rahn, plunging from the jungle to enter by the gate. They were racing forward, without order but at top speed, to share in the fighting and loot. Then streams of metal balls tore into them. The front of the irregular column was wiped out utterly. Wide swathes were cut in the rest. The survivors ran wildly forward over a litter of dead and dying men. Electric-charge weapons sent crackling discharges among them. Their contorted figures reeled and fell or leaped convulsively to lie forever still where they struck. And then the steam guns turned about to fire into the rear of the men who had charged past them.

The steam guns had literally blasted away the line of Ragged Men where they stood. But the line went on, with great ragged gaps in it, to be sure, but still vastly outnumbering the defenders of the city. Here and there a steam gun was silent, its gun crew dead. And presently those that were left were useless, immobile upon the ramparts in the rear of the attack.

DOWN in the ways of the city the fight rose to a riotous clamor. At Tommy's order the women of the city had been concentrated into a few strong towers. The machines of the city were left undefended for a time. A few strong patrols of fighting men, strategically placed, flung themselves with irresistible force upon certain bands of maddened Ragged Men. But where a combat raged, there the Ragged Men swarmed howling. Their hatred impelled them to suicidal courage and to unspeakable atrocities. From his tower, Tommy saw a man of Yugna, evidently a prisoner. Four Ragged Men surrounded him, literally tearing him to pieces like the maniacs they were. Then he saw dust spurting up in a swift-advancing line, and all four Ragged Men twitched and collapsed on top of their victim. A steam gun had done that. A fighting patrol of the men of Yugna swept fiercely down a paved way in one of the Golden City's vehicles. There was the glint of gold from it. A solid, choked mass of invaders rushed upon it. Without slackening speed, without a pause, the vehicle raced ahead. Intolerable flashes of light appeared. A thermit-thrower was mounted on the machine. It drove forward like a flaming meteor, and as electric-charge weapons flashed upon it men screamed and died. It tore into a vast cloud of the Death Mist and the unbearable flames of its weapon could only be seen as illuminations of that deadly vapor.

A part of the city was free of defenders, save the isolated steam gunners left behind upon the walls. Ragged Men, drunk with success, ran through its ways, slashing at the walls, battering at the lightpanels, pounding upon the doorways of the towers. Tommy saw them hacking at the great doorway of a tower. It gave. They rushed within. Almost instantly thereafter the opening spouted them forth again and after them, leaping upon them, snapping and biting and striking out with monstrous paws and teeth, were green lizard-things like the one that had been killed—years back, it seemed—on Earth. A deadly combat began instantly. But when the last of the fighting creatures was down, no more than a dozen were left of the three score who had begun the fight.

BUT this was not the main battle. The main battle was hidden under the Death-Mist cloud, concentrated in a vast thick mass in the very center of the city. Tommy watched that grimly. Perhaps eight thousand men had assailed the city. Certainly two thousand of them were represented by the still or twitching forms in queer attitudes here and there, in single dots or groups. There were seven hundred corpses before the city gate alone, where the steam guns had mowed down a reinforcing column. And there were others scattered all about. The defenders had lost heavily enough, but Tommy's defense behind the line of the ramparts was soundly concentrated in strong points, equipped with steam guns and mostly armed with thermit-throwers as well. From the center of the city there came only a vast, unorganized tumult of battle and death.

Then a huge winged thing came soaring down past Tommy's tower. It landed with a crash on the roofs below, spilling its men like ants. Tommy strained his eyes. There was a billowing outburst of steam from the tower where Denham had been working the night before. A big flier burst into the weird bright flame of the thermit fluid. It fell, splitting apart as it dropped. Again the billowing steam. No result—but beyond the city walls showed a flash of thermit flame.

"Denham!" muttered Tommy. "He's got a steam cannon; he's shooting shells loaded with thermit! They smash when they hit. Good!"

He dispatched a man with orders, but a messenger was panting his way up as the runner left. He thrust a scribbled bit of paper into Tommy's hand.

"I'm trying to bring down the ship that's controlling the Death Mist. I'll shell those devils in the middle of town as soon as our controls can handle the Mist.

Denham."

Tommy began to snap out his commands. He raced downward toward the street. Men seemed to spring up like magic about him. A ship with one wing aflame was tottering in midair, and another was dropping like a plummet.

Then Tommy uttered a roar of pure joy. The huge globe of beautiful, deadly vapor was lifting! Its control-ship was shattered, and men of the Golden City had found its setting. The Mist rose swiftly in a single vast globule of varicolored reflections. And the situation in the center of the city was clear. Two towers were besieged. Dense masses of the invaders crowded about them, battering at them. Steam guns opened from their windows. Thermit-throwers shot out flashes of deadly fire.

Tommy led five hundred men in savage assault, cleaving the mass of invaders like a wedge. He cut off a hundred men and wiped them out, while a rear guard poured electric charges into the main body of the enemy. More men of Yugna came leaping from a dozen doorways and joined them. Tommy found Smithers by his side, powder-stained and sweat-streaked.

"MISS Evelyn's all right?" Smithers asked in a great calm.

"She is," growled Tommy. "On the top floor of a tower, with a hundred men to guard her."

"You didn't look at the Tube I made," said Smithers impassively; "but I turned on the steam. Looks like it worked. It's ready to go through, anyways. It's the same place the other one was, down in that cellar. I'm tellin' you in case anything happens."

He opened fire with a magazine rifle into the thick of the mob that assailed the two towers. Tommy left him with fifty men to block a highway and led his men again into the mass of mingled Ragged Men and Rahnians. His followers saw his tactics now. They split off a section of the mob and fell upon it ferociously. There were sudden awful screams. Thermit flame was rising from two places in the very thick of the mob. It burst up from a third, and fourth, and fifth. . . . Denham, atop his tower, had the range with his steam cannon, and was flinging heavy shells into the attackers of the two central buildings. And then there was a roaring of steam and a ground vehicle came to a stop not fifty feet away. A gun crew of Yugnans had shifted their unwieldy weapon and its insulated steam boiler to a freight-carrying vehicle. Now the gunner pulled trigger and traversed his weapon into the thick of the massed invaders, while his companions worked desperately to keep the hopper full of projectiles.

The invaders melted away. Steam guns in the towers, thermit projectiles from the cannon far away; now this. . . . And the concealing cloud of Death Mist was rising still, headed straight up toward the zenith. It looked like a tiny, dwindling pearl.

THE assault upon Yugna had been a mad one, a frantic one. But the flight from Yugna was the flight of men trying to escape from hell. Wild panic characterized the fleeing men. They threw aside their weapons and ran with screams of terror no whit less horrible than their howls of triumph had been. And Tommy would have stopped the slaughter, but there was no way to send orders to the rampart gunners in time. As the fugitives swarmed toward the walls again, the storms of steam-propelled missiles mowed them down. Even those who scrambled down to the ground outside and fled sobbing for the jungle were pursued by hails of bullets. Of the eight thousand men who assailed Yugna, less than one in five escaped.

Pursuit was still in progress. Here and there, through the city, the sound of isolated combats still went on. Denham came down from his tower, looking rather sick as he saw the carnage about him. A strong escort brought Evelyn. Aten was grinning proudly, as though he had in person defeated the enemy. And as Evelyn shakingly put out her hand to touch Tommy's arm—it was only later that he realized he had been wounded in half a dozen minor ways—a shadow roared over their heads. The crackle of firearms came from it.

"Jacaro!" snarled Tommy. He leaped instinctively to pursue. But the flying thing was bound for a landing in an open square, the same one which not long since had seen the heaviest fighting. It alighted there and toppled askew on contact.

Figures tumbled out of it, in torn and ragged garments fashioned in the style of the very best tailors of the Earth's underworld.

Men of Yugna raced to intercept them. Firearms spat and bellowed luridly. In a close-knit, flame-spitting group, the knot of men raced over fallen bodies and hurtled areas where the pavement had cooled to no more than a dull-red heat where a thermit shell had struck. One man, two, three men fell under the small-arms fire. The gangsters went racing on, firing desperately. They dived into a tunnel and disappeared.

"THE Tube!" roared Smithers. "They' goin' for the Tube!"

He plunged forward, and Tommy seized his arm.

"They'll go through your Tube," he said curtly. "It looks like the one they came through. They'll think it is. Let 'em!"

Smithers tried to tear free.

"But they'll get back to Earth!" he raged. "They'll get off clear!"

The sharp, cracking sound of a gun-cotton explosion came out of the doorway into which Jacaro and his men had dived. Tommy smiled very grimly indeed.

"They've gone through," he said drily, "and they've blown up the Tube behind them. But—I didn't tell you—I took a look at your castings. Your pupils were putting them together, ready for the steam to go in, in place of the coils I used. But—er—Smithers! You'd discarded one pair of castings. They didn't satisfy you. Your pupils forgot that. They hooked them all together."

Smithers gulped.

"Instead of four right-angled bends," said Tommy grimly, "you have six connected together. You turned on the steam in a hurry, not noticing. And I don't know how many series of dimensions there are in this universe of ours. We know of two. There may be any number. But Jacaro and his men didn't go back to Earth. God only knows where they landed, or what it's like. Maybe somewhere a million miles in space. Nobody knows. The main thing is that Earth is safe now. The Death Mist has faded out of the picture."

He turned and smiled warmly at Evelyn. He was a rather

horrible sight just then, though he did not know it. He was bloody and burned and wounded. He ignored all matters but success, however.

"I think," he said drily, "we have won the confidence of the Golden City, Evelyn, and that there'll be no more talk of gassing Earth. As soon as the Council meets again, we'll make sure. And then—well, I think we can devote a certain amount of time to our personal affairs. You are the first Earth-girl to be kissed in the Fifth Dimension. We'll have to see if you can't distinguish yourself further."

AGAIN the Council hall in the tower of government in the Golden City of Yugna. Again the queer benches about the black wood table—though two of the seats that had been occupied were now empty. Again the guards behind the chairs, and the crowd of watchers—visitors, citizens of Yugna attending the deliberations of the Council. The audience was a queer one, this time. There were bandages here and there. There were men who were wounded, broken, bent and crippled in the fighting. But a warmly welcoming murmur spread through the hall as Tommy came in, himself rather extensively patched. He was wearing the tunic and breeches of the Golden City, because his own clothes were hopelessly beyond repair. The bearded old Councilor gathered the eyes of his fellows. They rose. The Council seated itself as one man.

Quiet, placid formalities. The Keeper of Foodstuffs murmured that the ransom paid to Rahn had been recaptured after the fight. The Keeper of Rolls reported with savage satisfaction the number of enemies who had been slain in battle. He added that the loss to Yugna was less than one man to ten of the enemy. And he added with still greater emphasis that the shops being fitted with automatic controls had released now—it had grown so much—two thousand men from the necessary day-and-night working force, and further releases were to be expected. The demands of the machines were lessened already beyond the memory of man. Eyes turned to Tommy. There was an expectant pause for his reply.

"I have been Commander of Defense Forces," he told them slowly, "in this fighting. I have given you weapons. My two friends have done more. The machines will need fewer and fewer attendants as the hints they have given you are developed by yourselves. And there is some hope that one of my friends may show you, in ultra-sonic vibrations, a weapon against the jungle itself. My own work is finished. But I ask again for friendship for my planet Earth. I ask that no war be made on my own people. I ask that what benefits you receive from us be passed to the other surviving cities on the same terms. And since there can be no further fighting on this scale, I give back my commission as Commander of Defense."

There was a little murmur among the men of Yugna, looking on. It rose to a protesting babble, to a shout of denial. The bearded old Keeper of Foodstuffs smiled.

"It is proposed that the appointment as Commander of Defense Forces be permanent," he said mildly.

He produced the queer black box and touched it in a certain fashion. He passed it to the next man, and the next and next. It went around the table. It passed a second time, but this time each man merely looked at the top.

"You command the defense forces of Yugna for always," said the bearded old man, gently. "Now give orders that your requests become laws."

TOMMY stared blankly. He was suddenly aware of Aten in the background, smiling triumphantly and very happily at him. There was something like a roar of approval from the men of Yugna, assembled.

"Just what," demanded Tommy, "does this mean?"

"For many years," said a hawk-faced man ungraciously, "we have had no Commander of Defense. We have had no wars. But we see it is needful. We have chosen you, with all agreeing. The Commander of Defense"—he sniffed a little, pugnaciously —"has the authority the ancient kings once owned."

Tommy leaned back in the curious benchlike chair, his eyes narrow and thoughtful. This would simplify matters. No danger of trouble to Earth. A free hand for Denham and Smithers to help these folk, and for Denham to learn scientific facts—in the sciences they had developed—which would be of inestimable value to Earth. And it could be possible to open a peaceful traffic with the nations of Earth without any danger of war. And maybe . . .

He smiled suddenly. It widened almost into a grin.

"All right. I'll settle down here for a while. But—er—just how does one set about getting married here?"

The Shadow Out of Time

By H. P. Lovecraft

AFTER twenty-two years of nightmare and terror, saved only by a desperate conviction of the mythical source of certain impressions, I am unwilling to vouch for the truth of that which I think I found in Western Australia on the night of July 17–18, 1935. There is reason to hope that my experience was wholly or partly an hallucination—for which, indeed, abundant causes existed. And yet, its realism was so hideous that I sometimes find hope impossible.

If the thing did happen, then man must be prepared to accept notions of the cosmos, and of his own place in the seething vortex of time, whose merest mention is paralyzing. He must, too, be placed on guard against a specific, lurking peril which, though it will never engulf the whole race, may impose monstrous and unguessable horrors upon certain venturesome members of it.

It is for this latter reason that I urge, with all the force of my being, a final abandonment of all the attempts at unearthing those fragments of unknown, primordial masonry which my expedition set out to investigate.

Assuming that I was sane and awake, my experience on that night was such as has befallen no man before. It was, moreover, a frightful confirmation of all I had sought to dismiss as myth and dream. Mercifully there is no proof, for in my fright I lost the awesome object which would—if real and brought out of that noxious abyss—have formed irrefutable evidence.

When I came upon the horror I was alone—and I have up to now told no one about it. I could not stop the others from digging in its direction, but chance and the shifting sand have so far saved them from finding it. Now I must formulate some definitive statement—not only for the sake of my own mental balance, but to warn such others as may read it seriously.

These pages—much in whose earlier parts will be familiar to close readers of the general and scientific press—are written in the cabin of the ship that is bringing me home. I shall give them to my son, Professor Wingate Peaslee of Miskatonic University—the only member of my family who stuck to me after my queer amnesia of long ago, and the man best informed on the inner facts of my case. Of all living persons, he is least likely to ridicule what I shall tell of that fateful night.

I did not enlighten him orally before sailing, because I think he had better have the revelation in written form. Reading and rereading at leisure will leave with him a more convincing picture than my confused tongue could hope to convey.

He can do anything that he thinks best with this account—showing it, with suitable comment, in any quarters where it will be likely to accomplish good. It is for the sake of such readers as are unfamiliar with the earlier phases of my case that I am prefacing the revelation itself with a fairly ample summary of its background.

MY name is Nathaniel Wingate Peaslee, and those who recall the newspaper tales of a generation back—or the letters and articles in psychological journals six or seven years ago—will know who and what I am. The press was filled with the details of my strange amnesia in 1908–13, and much was made of the traditions of horror, madness, and witchcraft which lurked behind the ancient Massachusetts town then and now forming my place of residence. Yet I would have it known that there is nothing whatever of the mad or sinister in my heredity and early life. This is a highly important fact in view of the shadow which fell so suddenly upon me from *outside* sources.

It may be that centuries of dark brooding had given to crumbling, whisper-haunted Arkham a peculiar vulnerability as regards such shadows—though even this seems doubtful in the light of those other cases which I later came to study. But the chief point is that my own ancestry and background are altogether normal. What came, came from *somewhere else*—where, I even now hesitate to assert in plain words.

I am the son of Jonathan and Hannah (Wingate) Peaslee, both of wholesome old Haverhill stock. I was born and reared in Haverhill—at the old homestead in Boardman Street near Golden Hill—and did not go to Arkham till I entered Miskatonic University as instructor of political economy in 1895.

For thirteen years more my life ran smoothly and happily. I married Alice Keezar of Haverhill in 1896, and my three children, Robert, Wingate and Hannah were born in 1898, 1900, and 1903, respectively. In 1898 I became an associate professor, and in 1902 a full professor. At no time had I the least interest in either occultism or abnormal psychology.

It was on Thursday, May 14, 1908, that the queer amnesia came. The thing was quite sudden, though later I realized that certain brief, glimmering visions of several hours previous—chaotic visions which disturbed me greatly because they were so unprecedented—must have formed premonitory symptoms. My head was aching, and I had a singular feeling—altogether new to me—that some one else was trying to get possession of my thoughts.

The collapse occurred about 10:20 a. m., while I was conducting a class in Political Economy VI—history and present tendencies of economics—for juniors and a few sophomores. I began to see strange shapes before my eyes, and to feel that I was in a grotesque room other than the classroom.

My thoughts and speech wandered from my subject, and the students saw that something was gravely amiss. Then I slumped down, unconscious, in my chair, in a stupor from which no one could arouse me. Nor did my rightful faculties again look out upon the daylight of our normal world for five years, four months, and thirteen days.

It is, of course, from others that I have learned what followed. I showed no sign of consciousness for sixteen and a half hours, though removed to my home at 27 Crane Street, and given the best of medical attention.

At 3 a. m. May 15th my eyes opened and I began to speak, but before long the doctors and my family were thoroughly frightened by the trend of my expression and language. It was clear that I had no remembrance of my identity and my past, though for some reason I seemed anxious to conceal this lack of knowledge. My eyes gazed strangely at the persons around me, and the flections of my facial muscles were altogether unfamiliar.

EVEN my speech seemed awkward and foreign. I used my vocal organs clumsily and gropingly, and my diction had a curiously stilted quality, as if I had laboriously learned the English language from books. The pronunciation was barbarously alien, whilst the idiom seemed to include both scraps of curious Archaism and expressions of a wholly incomprehensible cast.

Of the latter, one in particular was very potently—even terrifiedly—recalled by the youngest of the physicians twenty years afterward. For at that late period such a phrase began to have an actual currency—first in England and then in the United States—and though of much complexity and indisputable newness, it reproduced in every least particular the mystifying words of the strange Arkham patient in 1908.

Physical strength returned at once, although I required an odd amount of reeducation in the use of my hands, legs, and bodily apparatus in general. Because of this and other handicaps inherent in the mnemonic lapse, I was for some time kept under strict medical care.

When I saw that my attempts to conceal the lapse had failed, I admitted it openly, and became eager for information of all sorts. Indeed, it seemed to the doctors that I lost interest in my proper personality as soon as I found the case of amnesia accepted as a natural thing.

They noticed that my chief efforts were to master certain

points in history, science, art, language, and folklore—some of them tremendously abstruse, and some childishly simple—which remained, very oddly in many cases, outside my consciousness.

At the same time they noticed that I had an inexplicable command of many almost unknown sorts of knowledge—a command which I seemed to wish to hide rather than display. I would inadvertently refer, with casual assurance, to specific events in dim ages outside the range of accepted history—passing off such references as a jest when I saw the surprise they created. And I had a way of speaking of the future which two or three times caused actual fright.

These uncanny flashes soon ceased to appear, though some observers laid their vanishment more to a certain furtive caution on my part than to any waning of the strange knowledge behind them. Indeed, I seemed anomalously avid to absorb the speech, customs, and perspectives of the age around me; as if I were a studious traveler from a far, foreign land.

As soon as permitted, I haunted the college library at all hours; and shortly began to arrange for those odd travels, and special courses at American and European Universities, which evoked so much comment during the next few years.

I did not at any time suffer from a lack of learned contacts, for my case had a mild celebrity among the psychologists of the period. I was lectured upon as a typical example of secondary personality—even though I seemed to puzzle the lecturers now and then with some bizarre symptom or some queer trace of carefully veiled mockery.

Of real friendliness, however, I encountered little. Something in my aspect and speech seemed to excite vague fears and aversions in every one I met, as if I were a being infinitely removed from all that is normal and healthful. This idea of a black, hidden horror connected with incalculable gulfs of some sort of *distance* was oddly widespread and persistent.

My own family formed no exception. From the moment of my strange waking my wife had regarded me with extreme horror and loathing, vowing that I was some utter alien usurping the body of her husband. In 1910 she obtained a legal divorce, nor would she ever consent to see me, even after my return to normality in 1913. These feelings were shared by my elder son and my small daughter, neither of whom I have ever seen since.

ONLY my second son, Wingate, seemed able to conquer the terror and repulsion which my change aroused. He indeed felt that I was a stranger, but though only eight years old held fast to a faith that my proper self would return. When it did return he sought me out, and the courts gave me his custody. In succeeding years he helped me with the studies to which I was driven, and to-day, at thirty-five, he is a professor of psychology at Miskatonic.

But I do not wonder at the horror I caused—for certainly, the mind, voice, and facial expression of the being that awaked on May 15, 1908, were not those of Nathaniel Wingate Peaslee.

I will not attempt to tell much of my life from 1908 to 1913, since readers may glean all the outward essentials—as I largely had to do—from files of old newspapers and scientific journals.

I was given charge of my funds, and spent them slowly and on the whole wisely, in travel and in study at various centers of learning. My travels, however, were singular in the extreme, involving long visits to remote and desolate places.

In 1909 I spent a month in the Himalayas, and in 1911 aroused much attention through a camel trip into the unknown deserts of Arabia. What happened on those journeys I have never been able to learn.

During the summer of 1912 I chartered a ship and sailed in the arctic, north of Spitzbergen, afterward showing signs of disappointment.

Later in that year I spent weeks alone beyond the limits of previous or subsequent exploration in the vast limestone caverns system of western Virginia—black labyrinths so complex that no retracing of my steps could even be considered.

My sojourns at the universities were marked by abnormally rapid assimilation, as if the secondary personality had an intelligence enormously superior to my own. I have found, also, that my rate of reading and solitary study was phenomenal. I could master every detail of a book merely by glancing over it as fast as I could turn the leaves; while my skill at interpreting complex figures in an instant was veritably awesome.

At times there appeared almost ugly reports of my power to influence the thoughts and acts of others, though I seemed to have taken care to minimize displays of this faculty.

Other ugly reports concerned my intimacy with leaders of occultist groups, and scholars suspected of connection with nameless bands of abhorrent elder-world hierophants. These rumors, though never proved at the time, were doubtless stimulated by the known tenor of some of my reading—for the consultation of rare books at libraries cannot be effected secretly.

There is tangible proof—in the form of marginal notes—that I went minutely through such things as the Comte d'Erlette's *Cultes des Goules,* Ludvig Prinn's *De Vermis Mysteriis,* the *Unaussprechlichen Kulten* of von Junzt, the surviving fragments of the puzzling *Book of Eibon,* and the dreaded *Necronomicon* of the mad Arab Abdul Alhazred. Then, too, it is undeniable that a fresh and evil wave of underground cult activity set in about the time of my odd mutation.

IN the summer of 1913 I began to display signs of ennui and flagging interest, and to hint to various associates that a change might soon be expected in me. I spoke of returning memories of my earlier life—though most auditors judged me insincere, since all the recollections I gave were casual, and such as might have been learned from my old private papers.

About the middle of August I returned to Arkham and reopened my long-closed house in Crane Street. Here I installed a mechanism of the most curious aspect, constructed piecemeal by different makers of scientific apparatus in Europe and America, and guarded carefully from the sight of any one intelligent enough to analyze it.

Those who did see it—a workman, a servant, and the new housekeeper—say that it was a queer mixture of rods, wheels, and mirrors, though only about two feet tall, one foot wide, and one foot thick. The central mirror was circular and convex. All this is borne out by such makers of parts as can be located.

On the evening of Friday, September 26, I dismissed the housekeeper and the maid until noon of the next day. Lights burned in the house till late, and a lean, dark, curiously foreign-looking man called in an automobile.

It was about one a. m. that the lights were last seen. At 2:15 a. m. a policeman observed the place in darkness, but with the stranger's motor still at the curb. By 4 o'clock the motor was certainly gone.

It was at 6 o'clock that a hesitant, foreign voice on the telephone asked Dr. Wilson to call at my house and bring me out of a peculiar faint. This call—a long-distance one—was later traced to a public booth in the North Station in Boston, but no sign of the lean foreigner was ever unearthed.

When the doctor reached my house he found me unconscious in the sitting room—in an easy-chair with a table drawn up before it. On the polished table top were scratches showing where some heavy object had rested. The queer machine was gone, nor was anything afterward heard of it. Undoubtedly the dark, lean foreigner had taken it away.

In the library grate were abundant ashes, evidently left from the burning of every remaining scrap of paper on which I had written since the advent of the amnesia. Dr. Wilson found my breathing very peculiar, but after an hypodermic injection it became more regular.

At 11:15 a. m., September 27th, I stirred vigorously, and my hitherto masklike face began to show signs of expression. Dr. Wilson remarked that the expression was not that of my secondary personality, but seemed much like that of my normal self. About 11:30 I muttered some very curious syllables—syllables which seemed unrelated to any human speech. I appeared, too, to struggle against something. Then, just after noon—the housekeeper and the maid having meanwhile returned—I began to mutter in English:

> "—of the orthodox economists of that period, Jevons typifies the prevailing trend toward scientific correlation. His attempt to link the commercial cycle of prosperity and depression with the physical cycle of the solar spots forms perhaps the apex of—"

Nathaniel Wingate Peaslee had come back—a spirit in whose time scale it was still that Thursday morning in 1908, with the economics class gazing up at the battered desk on the platform.

II.

MY reabsorption into normal life was a painful and difficult process. The loss of over five years creates more complications than can be imagined, and in my case there were countless matters to be adjusted.

What I heard of my actions since 1908 astonished and disturbed me, but I tried to view the matter as philosophically as I could. At last, regaining custody of my second son, Wingate, I settled down with him in the Crane Street house and endeavored to resume my teaching—my old professorship having been kindly offered me by the college.

I began work with the February 1914 term, and kept at it just a year. By that time I realized how badly my experience had shaken me. Though perfectly sane—I hoped—and with no flaw in my original personality, I had not the nervous energy of the old days. Vague dreams and queer ideas continually haunted me, and when the outbreak of the World War turned my mind to history I found myself thinking of periods and events in the oddest possible fashion.

My conception of *time*—my ability to distinguish between consecutiveness and simultaneousness—seemed subtly disordered; so that I formed chimerical notions about living in one age and casting one's mind all over eternity for knowledge of past and future ages.

The War gave me strange impressions of remembering some of its far off consequences—as if I knew how it was coming out and could look *back* upon it in the light of future information. All such quasi memories were attended with much pain, and with a feeling that some artificial psychological barrier was set against them.

When I diffidently hinted to others about my impressions, I met with varied responses. Some persons looked uncomfortably at me, but men in the mathematics department spoke of new developments in those theories of relativity—then discussed only in learned circles—which were later to become so famous. Dr. Albert Einstein, they said, was rapidly reducing time to the status of a mere dimension.

But the dreams and disturbed feelings gained on me, so that I had to drop my regular work in 1915. Certain of the impressions were taking an annoying shape—giving me the persistent notion that my amnesia had formed some unholy sort of exchange; that the secondary personality had indeed been an intruding force from unknown regions, and that my own personality had suffered displacement.

Thus I was driven to vague and frightful speculations concerning the whereabouts of my true self during the years that another had held my body. The curious knowledge and strange conduct of my body's late tenant troubled me more and more as I learned further details from persons, papers, and magazines.

Queerness that had baffled others seemed to harmonize terribly with some background of black knowledge which festered in the chasms of my subconsciousness. I began to search feverishly for every scrap of information bearing on the studies and travels of that other one during the dark years.

Not all of my troubles were as semi-abstract as this. There were the dreams—and these seemed to grow in vividness and concreteness. Knowing how most would regard them, I seldom mentioned them to any one but my son or certain trusted psychologists, but eventually I commenced a scientific study of other cases in order to see how typical or nontypical such visions might be among amnesia victims.

My results, aided by psychologists, historians, anthropologists, and mental specialists of wide experience, and by a study that included all records of split personalities from the days of demoniac-possession legends to the medically realistic present, at first bothered me more than they consoled me.

I soon found that my dreams had, indeed, no counterpart in the overwhelming bulk of true amnesia cases. There remained, however, a tiny residue of accounts which for years baffled and shocked me with their parallelism to my own experience. Some of them were bits of ancient folklore; others were case histories in the annals of medicine; one or two were anecdotes obscurely buried in standard histories.

It thus appeared that, while my special kind of affliction was prodigiously rare, instances of it had occurred at long intervals ever since the beginning of men's annals. Some centuries might contain one, two, or three cases, others none—or at least none whose record survived.

The essence was always the same—a person of keen thoughtfulness seized with a strange secondary life and leading for a greater or lesser period an utterly alien existence typified at first by vocal and bodily awkwardness, and later by a wholesale acquisition of scientific, historic, artistic, and anthropological knowledge; an acquisition carried on with feverish zest and with a wholly abnormal absorptive power. Then a sudden return of the rightful consciousness, intermittently plagued ever after with vague unplaceable dreams suggesting fragments of some hideous memory elaborately blotted out.

And the close resemblance of those nightmares to my own—even in some of the smallest particulars—left no doubt in my mind of their significantly typical nature. One or two of the cases had an added ring of faint, blasphemous familiarity, as if I had heard of them before through some cosmic channel too morbid and frightful to contemplate. In three instances there was specific mention of such an unknown machine as had been in my house before the second change.

Another thing that worried me during my investigation was the somewhat greater frequency of cases where a brief, elusive glimpse of the typical nightmares was afforded to persons not visited with well-defined amnesia.

These persons were largely of mediocre mind or less—some so primitive that they could scarcely be thought of as vehicles for abnormal scholarship and preternatural mental acquisitions. For a second they would be fired with alien force—then a backward lapse, and a thin, swift-fading memory of unhuman horrors.

There had been at least three such cases during the past half century—one only fifteen years before. Had something been groping blindly through time from some unsuspected abyss in nature? Were these faint cases monstrous, sinister experiments of a kind and authorship utterly beyond sane belief?

Such were a few of the formless speculations of my weaker hours—fancies abetted by myths which my studies uncovered. For I could not doubt but that certain persistent legends of immemorial antiquity, apparently unknown to the victims and physicians connected with recent amnesia cases, formed a striking and awesome elaboration of memory lapses such as mine.

OF the nature of the dreams and impressions which were growing so clamorous I still almost fear to speak. They seemed to savor of madness, and at times I believed I was indeed going mad. Was there a special type of delusion afflicting those who had suffered lapses of memory? Conceivably, the efforts of the subconscious mind to fill up a perplexing blank with pseudomemories might give rise to strange imaginative vagaries.

This, indeed—though an alternative folklore theory finally seemed to me more plausible—was the belief of many of the alienists who helped me in my search for parallel cases, and who shared my puzzlement at the exact resemblances sometimes discovered.

They did not call the condition true insanity, but classed it rather among neurotic disorders. My course in trying to track it down and analyze it, instead of vainly seeking to dismiss or forget it, they heartily endorsed as correct according to the best psychological principles. I especially valued the advice of such physicians as had studied me during my possession by the other personality.

My first disturbances were not visual at all, but concerned the more abstract matters which I have mentioned. There was, too, a feeling of profound and inexplicable horror concerning myself. I developed a queer fear of seeing my own form, as if my eyes would find it something utterly alien and inconceivably abhorrent.

When I did glance down and behold the familiar human shape in quiet gray or blue clothing, I always felt a curious relief, though in order to gain this relief I had to conquer an infinite dread. I shunned mirrors as much as possible, and was always shaved at the barber's.

It was a long time before I correlated any of these disappointed feelings with the fleeting visual impressions which began to develop. The first such correlation had to do with the odd sensation of an external, artificial restraint on my memory.

I felt that the snatches of sight I experienced had a profound and terrible meaning, and a frightful connection with myself, but that some purposeful influence held me from grasping that meaning and that connection. Then came that queerness about the element of time, and with it desperate efforts to place the fragmentary dream glimpses in the chronological and spatial pattern.

The glimpses themselves were at first merely strange rather than horrible. I would seem to be in an enormous vaulted chamber whose lofty stone groinings were well nigh lost in the shadows overhead. In whatever time or place the scene might be, the principle of the arch was known as fully and used as extensively as by the Romans.

There were colossal, round windows and high, arched doors, and pedestals or tables each as tall as the height of an ordinary room. Vast shelves of dark wood lined the walls, holding what seemed to be volumes of immense size with strange hieroglyphs on their backs.

The exposed stonework held curious carvings, always in curvilinear mathematical designs, and there were chiseled inscriptions in the same characters that the huge books bore. The dark granite masonry was of a monstrous megalithic type, with lines of convex-topped blocks fitting the concave-bottomed courses which rested upon them.

There were no chairs, but the tops of the vast pedestals were littered with books, papers, and what seemed to be writing materials—oddly figured jars of a purplish metal, and rods with stained tips. Tall as the pedestals were, I seemed at times able to view them from above. On some of them were great globes of luminous crystal serving as lamps, and inexplicable machines formed of vitreous tubes and metal rods.

The windows were glazed, and latticed with stout-looking bars. Though I dared not approach and peer out them, I could see from where I was the waving tops of singular fernlike growths. The floor was of massive octagonal flagstones, while rugs and hangings were entirely lacking.

LATER, I had visions of sweeping through Cyclopean corridors of stone, and up and down gigantic, inclined planes of the same monstrous masonry. There were no stairs anywhere, nor was any passageway less than thirty feet wide. Some of the structures through which I floated must have towered in the sky for thousands of feet.

There were multiple levels of black vaults below, and never-opened trapdoors, sealed down with metal bands and holding dim suggestions of some special peril.

I seemed to be a prisoner, and horror hung broodingly over everything I saw. I felt that the mocking curvilinear hieroglyphs on the walls would blast my soul with their message were I not guarded by a merciful ignorance.

Still later my dreams included vistas from the great round windows, and from the titanic flat roof, with its curious gardens, wide barren area, and high, scalloped parapet of stone, to which the topmost of the inclined planes led.

There were almost endless leagues of giant buildings, each in its garden, and ranged along paved roads fully two hundred feet wide. They differed greatly in aspect, but few were less than five hundred feet square or a thousand feet high. Many seemed so limitless that they must have had a frontage of several thousand feet, while some shot up to mountainous altitudes in the gray, steamy heavens.

They seemed to be mainly of stone or concrete, and most of them embodied the oddly curvilinear type of masonry noticeable in the building that held me. Roofs were flat and garden-covered, and tended to have scalloped parapets. Sometimes there were terraces and higher levels, and wide, cleared spaces amidst the gardens. The great roads held hints of motion, but in the earlier visions I could not resolve this impression into details.

In certain places I beheld enormous dark cylindrical towers which climbed far above any of the other structures. These appeared to be of a totally unique nature and showed signs of prodigious age and dilapidation. They were built of a bizarre type of square-cut basalt masonry, and tapered slightly toward their rounded tops. Nowhere in any of them could the least traces of windows or other apertures save huge doors be found. I noticed also some lower buildings—all crumbling with the weathering of aeons—which resembled these dark, cylindrical towers in basic architecture. Around all these aberrant piles of square-cut masonry there hovered an inexplicable aura of menace and concentrated fear, like that bred by the sealed trapdoors.

THE omnipresent gardens were almost terrifying in their strangeness, with bizarre and unfamiliar forms of vegetation nodding over broad paths lined with curiously carven monoliths. Abnormally vast fernlike growths predominated—some green, and some of a ghastly, fungoid pallor.

Among them rose great spectral things resembling Calamites, whose bamboo-like trunks towered to fabulous heights. Then there were tufted forms like fabulous cycads, and grotesque dark-green shrubs and trees of coniferous aspect.

Flowers were small, colorless, and unrecognizable, blooming in geometrical beds and at large among the greenery.

In a few of the terrace and roof-top gardens were larger and more-vivid blossoms of almost offensive contours and seeming to suggest artificial breeding. Fungi of inconceivable size, outlines, and colors speckled the scene in patterns bespeaking some unknown but well-established horticultural tradition. In the larger gardens on the ground there seemed to be some attempt to preserve the irregularities of nature, but on the roofs there was more selectiveness, and more evidences of the topiary art.

The skies were almost always moist and cloudy, and sometimes I would seem to witness tremendous rains. Once in a while, though, there would be glimpses of the Sun—which looked abnormally large—and of the Moon, whose markings held a touch of difference from the normal that I could never quite fathom. When—very rarely—the night sky was clear to any extent, I beheld constellations which were nearly beyond recognition. Known outlines were sometimes approximated, but seldom duplicated; and from the position of the few groups I could recognize, I felt I must be in the Earth's southern hemisphere, near the Tropic of Capricorn.

The far horizon was always steamy and indistinct, but I could see that great jungles of unknown tree ferns, Calamites, Lepidodendron, and sigillaria lay outside the city, their fantastic frontage waving mockingly in the shifting vapors. Now and then there would be suggestions of motion in the sky, but these my early visions never resolved.

By the autumn of 1914 I began to have infrequent dreams of strange floatings over the city and through the regions around it. I saw interminable roads through forests of fearsome growths with mottled, fluted, and banded trunks, and past other cities as strange as the one which persistently haunted me.

I saw monstrous constructions of black or iridescent stone in glades and clearings where perpetual twilight reigned, and traversed long causeways over swamps so dark that I could tell but little of their moist, towering vegetation.

Once I saw an area of countless miles strewn with age-blasted basaltic ruins whose architecture had been like that of the few windowless, round-topped towers in the haunting city.

And once I saw the sea—a boundless, steamy expanse beyond the colossal stone piers of an enormous town of domes and arches. Great shapeless suggestions of shadow moved over it, and here and there its surface was vexed with anomalous spoutings.

III.

AS I have said, it was not immediately that these wild visions began to hold their terrifying quality. Certainly, many persons have dreamed intrinsically stranger things—things compounded of unrelated scraps of daily life, pictures, and reading, and arranged in fantastically novel forms by the unchecked caprices of sleep.

For some time I accepted the visions as natural, even though I had never before been an extravagant dreamer. Many of the vague anomalies, I argued, must have come from trivial sources too numerous to track down; while others seemed to reflect a common textbook knowledge of the plants and other conditions of the primitive world of a hundred and fifty million years ago—the world of the Permian or Triassic Age.

In the course of some months, however, the element of terror did figure with accumulating force. This was when the dreams began so unfailingly to have the aspect of memories, and when my mind began to link them with my growing abstract disturbances—the feeling of mnemonic restraint, the curious impressions regarding time, the sense of a loathsome exchange with my secondary personality of 1908–13, and, considerably later, the inexplicable loathing of my own person.

As certain definite details began to enter the dreams, their horror increased a thousandfold—until by October, 1915, I felt I must do something. It was then that I began an intensive study of other cases of amnesia and visions, feeling that I might thereby objectivize my trouble and shake clear of its emotional grip.

However, as before mentioned, the result was at first almost exactly opposite. It disturbed me vastly to find that my dreams had been so closely duplicated; especially since some of the accounts were too early to admit of any geological knowledge—and therefore of any idea of primitive landscapes—on the subjects' part.

What is more, many of these accounts supplied very horrible details and explanations in connection with the visions of great buildings and jungle gardens—and other things. The actual sights and vague impressions were bad enough, but what was hinted or asserted by some of the other dreamers savored of madness and blasphemy. Worst of all, my own pseudomemory was aroused to wilder dreams and hints of coming revelations. And yet most doctors deemed my course, on the whole, an advisable one.

I studied psychology systematically and under the prevailing stimulus my son Wingate did the same—his studies leading eventually to his present professorship. In 1917 and 1918 I took special courses at Miskatonic. Meanwhile, my examination of medical, historical, and anthropological records became indefatigable, involving travels to distant libraries, and finally including even a reading of the hideous books of forbidden elder lore in which my secondary personality had been so disturbingly interested.

Some of the latter were the actual copies I had consulted in my altered state, and I was greatly disturbed by certain marginal notations and ostensible *corrections* of the hideous text in a script and idiom which somehow seemed oddly unhuman.

These markings were mostly in the respective languages of the various books, all of which the writer seemed to know with equal, though obviously, academic facility. One note appended to von Junzt's *Unaussprechlichen Kulten,* however, was alarmingly otherwise. It consisted of certain curvilinear hieroglyphs in the same ink as that of the German corrections, but following no recognized human pattern. And these hieroglyphs were closely and unmistakably akin to the characters constantly met with in my dreams—characters whose meaning I would sometimes momentarily fancy I knew, or was just on the brink of recalling.

To complete my black confusion, many librarians assured me that, in view of previous examinations and records of consultation of the volumes in question, all of these notations must have been made by myself in my secondary state. This despite the fact that I was and still am ignorant of three of the languages involved.

PIECING together the scattered records, ancient and modern, anthropological and medical, I found a fairly consistent mixture of myth and hallucination whose scope and wildness left me utterly dazed. Only one thing consoled me: the fact that the myths were of such early existence. What lost knowledge could have brought pictures of the Paleozoic or Mesozoic landscape into these primitive fables, I could not even guess; but the pictures had been there. Thus, a basis existed for the formation of a fixed type of delusion.

Cases of amnesia no doubt created the general myth pattern—but afterward the fanciful accretions of the myths must have reacted on amnesia sufferers and colored their pseudomemories. I myself had read and heard all the early tales during my memory lapse—my quest had amply proved that. Was it not natural, then, for my subsequent dreams and emotional impressions to become colored and molded by what my memory subtly held over from my secondary state?

A few of the myths had significant connections with other cloudy legends of the prehuman world, especially those Hindu tales involving stupefying gulfs of time and forming part of the lore of modern theosophists.

Primal myth and modern delusion joined in their assumption that mankind is only one—perhaps the least—of the highly evolved and dominant races of this planet's long and largely unknown career. Things of inconceivable shape, they implied, had reared great towers to the sky and delved into every secret of nature before the first amphibian forbear of man had crawled out of the hot sea three hundred million years ago.

Some had come down from the stars; a few were as old as the cosmos itself; others had risen swiftly from terrane germs as far behind the first germs of our life cycle as those germs are behind ourselves. Spans of thousands of millions of years, and linkages of other galaxies and universes, were freely spoken of. Indeed, there was no such thing as time in its humanly accepted sense.

But most of the tales and impressions concerned a relatively late race, of a queer and intricate shape, resembling no life form known to science, which had lived till only fifty million years before the advent of man. This, they indicated, was the greatest race of all because it alone had conquered the secret of time.

It had learned all things that ever were known or ever would be known on the Earth, through the power of its keener minds to project themselves into the past and future, even through gulfs of millions of years, and study the lore of every age. From the accomplishments of this race arose all legends of prophets, including those in human mythology.

In its vast libraries were volumes of texts and pictures holding the whole of Earth's annals—histories and descriptions of every species that had ever been or that ever would be, with full records of their arts, their achievements, their languages, and their psychologies.

With this aeon-embracing knowledge, the Great Race chose from every era and life form such thoughts, arts, and processes as might suit its own nature and situation. Knowledge of the past, secured through a kind of mind casting outside the recognized senses, was harder to glean than knowledge of the future.

In the latter case the course was easier and more material. With suitable mechanical aid a mind would project itself forward in time, feeling its dim, extra-sensory way till it approached the desired period. Then, after preliminary trials, it would seize on the best discoverable representative of the highest of that period's life forms. It would enter the organism's brain and set up therein its own vibrations, while the displaced mind would strike back to the period of the displacer, remaining in the latter's body till a reverse process was set up.

The projected mind, in the body of the organism of the future, would then pose as a member of the race whose outward form it wore, learning as quickly as possible all that could be learned of the chosen age and its massed information and techniques.

MEANWHILE the displaced mind, thrown back to the displacer's age and body, would be carefully guarded. It would be kept from harming the body it occupied, and would be drained of all its knowledge by trained questioners. Often it could be questioned in its own language, when previous quests into the future had brought back records of that language.

If the mind came from a body whose language the Great Race could not physically reproduce, clever machines would be made, on which the alien speech could be played as on a musical instrument.

The Great Race's members were immense rugose cones ten feet high, and with head and other organs attached to foot-thick, distensible limbs spreading from the apexes. They spoke by the clicking or scraping of huge paws or claws attached to the end of two of their four limbs, and walked by the expansion and contraction of a viscous layer attached to their vast, ten-foot bases.

When the captive mind's amazement and resentment had worn off, and when—assuming that it came from a body vastly different from the Great Race's—it had lost its horror at its unfamiliar, temporary form, it was permitted to study its new environment and experience a wonder and wisdom approximating that of its displacer.

With suitable precautions, and in exchange for suitable services, it was allowed to rove all over the habitable world in titan airships or on the huge boatlike, atomic-engined vehicles which traversed the great roads, and to delve freely into the libraries containing records of the planet's past and future.

This reconciled many captive minds to their lot; since none was other than keen, and to such minds the unveiling of hidden mysteries of Earth—closed chapters of inconceivable pasts and dizzying vortices of future time which include the years ahead of their own natural ages—forms always, despite the abysmal horrors often unveiled, the supreme experience of life.

Now and then certain captives were permitted to meet other captive minds seized from the future—to exchange thoughts with consciousness living a hundred or a thousand or a million years before or after their own ages. And all were urged to write copiously in their own languages of themselves and their respective periods, such documents to be filed in the great central archives.

It may be added that there was one special type of captive whose privileges were far greater than those of the majority. These were the dying *permanent* exiles, whose bodies in the future had been seized by keen-minded members of the Great Race who, faced with death, sought to escape mental extinction.

Such melancholy exiles were not as common as might be expected, since the longevity of the Great Race lessened its love of life—especially among those superior minds capable of projection. From cases of the permanent projection of elder minds arose many of those lasting changes of personality noticed in later history—including mankind's.

As for the ordinary cases of exploration—when the displacing mind had learned what it wished in the future, it would build an apparatus like that which had started its flight and reverse the process of projection. Once more it would be in its own body in its own age, while the lately captive mind would return to that body of the future to which it properly belonged.

Only when one or the other of the bodies had died during the exchange was this restoration impossible. In such cases, of course, the exploring mind had—like those of the death escapers—to live out an alien-bodied life in the future; or else the captive mind—like the dying permanent exiles—had to end its days in the form and past age of the Great Race.

THIS fate was least horrible when the captive mind was also of the Great Race—a not infrequent occurrence, since in all its periods that race was intensely concerned with its own future. The number of dying permanent exiles of the

Great Race was very slight—largely because of the tremendous penalties attached to displacements of future Great Race minds by the moribund.

Through projection, arrangements were made to inflict these penalties on the offending minds in their new future bodies—and sometimes forced reexchanges were effected.

Complex cases of the displacement of exploring or already captive minds by minds in various regions of the past had been known and carefully rectified. In every age since the discovery of mind projection, a minute but well-recognized element of the population consisted of Great Race minds from past ages, sojourning for a longer or shorter while.

When a captive mind of alien origin was returned to its own body in the future, it was purged by an intricate mechanical hypnosis of all it had learned in the Great Race Age—this because of certain troublesome consequences inherent in the general carrying forward of knowledge in large quantities.

The few existing instances of clear transmission had caused, and would cause at known future times, great disasters. And it was largely in consequence of two cases of the kind—said the old myths—that mankind had learned what it had concerning the Great Race.

Of all things surviving physically and directly from that aeon-distant world, there remained only certain ruins of great stones in far places and under the sea, and parts of the text of the frightful Pnakotic Manuscripts.

Thus, the returning mind reached its own age with only the faintest and most fragmentary visions of what it had undergone since its seizure. All memories that could be eradicated were eradicated, so that in most cases only a dream-shadowed blank stretched back to the time of the first exchange. Some minds recalled more than others, and the chance joining of memories had at rare times brought hints of the forbidden past to future ages.

There probably never was a time when groups or cults did not secretly cherish certain of these hints. In the *Necronomicon* the presence of such a cult among human beings was suggested—a cult that sometimes gave aid to minds voyaging down the aeons from the days of the Great Race.

And, meanwhile, the Great Race itself waxed well-nigh omniscient, and turned to the task of setting up exchanges with the minds of other planets, and of exploring their pasts and futures. It sought likewise to fathom the past years and origin of that black, aeon-dead orb in far space whence its own mental heritage had come—for the mind of the Great Race was older than its bodily form.

The beings of a dying elder world, wise with the ultimate secrets, had looked ahead for a new world and species wherein they might have long life, and had sent their minds *en masse* into that future race best adapted to house them—the cone-shaped things that peopled our Earth a billion years ago.

Thus the Great Race came to be, while the myriad minds sent backward were left to die in the horror of strange shapes. Later the race would again face death, yet would live through another forward migration of its best minds into the bodies of others who had a longer physical span ahead of them.

SUCH was the background of intertwined legend and hallucination. When, around 1920, I had my researches in coherent shape, I felt a slight lessening of the tension which their earlier stages had increased. After all, and in spite of the fancies prompted by blind emotions, were not most of my phenomena readily explainable? Any chance might have turned my mind to dark studies during the amnesia—and then I read the forbidden legends and met the members of ancient and ill-regarded cults. That, plainly, supplied the material for the dreams and disturbed feelings which came after the return of memory.

As for the marginal notes in dream hieroglyphs and languages unknown to me, but laid at my door by librarians—I might easily have picked up a smattering of the tongues during my secondary state, while the hieroglyphs were doubtless coined by my fancy from descriptions in old legends, and afterward woven into my dreams. I tried to verify certain points through conversations with known cult leaders, but never succeeded in establishing the right connections.

At times the parallelism of so many cases in so many distant ages continued to worry me as it had at first, but on the other hand I reflected that the excitant folklore was undoubtedly more universal in the past than in the present.

Probably all the other victims whose cases were like mine had had a long and familiar knowledge of the tales I had learned only when in my secondary state. When these victims had lost their memory, they had associated themselves with the creatures of their household myths—the fabulous invaders supposed to displace men's minds—and had thus embarked upon quests for knowledge which they thought they could take back to a fancied, nonhuman past.

Then, when their memory returned, they reversed the associative process and thought of themselves as the former captive minds instead of as the displacers. Hence the dreams and pseudomemories following the conventional myth pattern.

Despite the seeming cumberousness of these explanations, they came finally to supersede all others in my mind—largely because of the greater weakness of any rival theory. And a substantial number of eminent psychologists and anthropologists gradually agreed with me.

The more I reflected, the more convincing did my reasoning seem; till in the end I had a really effective bulwark against the visions and impressions which still assailed me. Suppose I did see strange things at night? These were only what I had heard and read of. Suppose I did have odd loathings and perspectives and pseudomemories? These, too, were only echoes of myths absorbed in my secondary state. Nothing that I might dream, nothing that I might feel, could be of any actual significance.

Fortified by this philosophy, I greatly improved in nervous equilibrium, even though the visions—rather than the abstract impressions—steadily became more frequent and more disturbingly detailed. In 1922 I felt able to undertake regular work again, and put my newly gained knowledge to practical use by accepting an instructorship in psychology at the university.

My old chair of political economy had long been adequately filled—besides which, methods of teaching economics had changed greatly since my heyday. My son was at this time just entering on the post-graduate studies leading to his present professorship, and we worked together a great deal.

IV.

I continued, however, to keep a careful record of the *outré* dreams which crowded upon me so thickly and vividly. Such a record, I argued, was of genuine value as a psychological document. The glimpses still seemed damnably like memories, though I fought off this impression with a goodly measure of success.

In writing, I treated the phantasmata as things seen; but at all other times I brushed them aside like any gossamer illusions of the night. I had never mentioned such matters in common conversation; though reports of them, filtering out as such things will, had aroused sundry rumors regarding my mental health. It is amusing to reflect that these rumors were confined wholly to laymen, without a single champion among physicians or psychologists.

Of my visions after 1914 I will here mention only a few, since fuller accounts and records are at the disposal of the serious student. It is evident that with time the curious inhibitions somewhat waned, for the scope of my visions vastly increased. They have never, though, become other than disjointed fragments seemingly without clear motivation.

Within the dreams I seemed gradually to acquire a greater and greater freedom of wandering. I floated through many strange buildings of stone, going from one to the other along mammoth underground passages which seemed to form the common avenues of transit. Sometimes I encountered those gigantic sealed trapdoors in the lowest level, around which such an aura of fear and forbiddenness clung.

I saw tremendous tessellated pools, and rooms of curious and inexplicable utensils of myriad sorts. Then there were colossal caverns of intricate machinery whose outlines and purpose were wholly strange to me, and whose sound manifested itself only after many years of dreaming. I may here remark that sight and sound are the only senses I have ever exercised in the visionary world.

The real horror began in May, 1915, when I first saw the living things. This was before my studies had taught me what, in view of the myths and case histories, to expect. As mental barriers wore down, I beheld great masses of thin vapor in various parts of the building and in the streets below.

These steadily grew more solid and distinct, till at last I could trace their monstrous outlines with uncomfortable ease. They seemed to be enormous, iridescent cones, about ten feet high and ten feet wide at the base, and made up of some ridgy, scaly, semielastic matter. From their apexes projected four flexible, cylindrical members, each a foot thick, and of a ridgy substance like that of the cones themselves.

These members were sometimes contracted almost to nothing, and sometimes extended to any distance up to about ten feet. Terminating two of them were enormous claws or nippers. At the end of a third were four red, trumpetlike appendages. The fourth terminated in an irregular yellowish globe some two feet in diameter and having three great dark eyes ranged along its central circumference.

Surmounting this head were four slender gray stalks bearing flower-like appendages, whilst from its nether side dangled eight greenish antennae or tentacles. The great base of the central cone was fringed with a rubbery, gray substance which moved the whole entity through expansion and contraction.

THEIR actions, though harmless, horrified me even more than their appearance—for it is not wholesome to watch monstrous objects doing what one had known only human beings to do. These objects moved intelligently about the great rooms, getting books from the shelves and taking them to the great tables, or *vice versa,* and sometimes writing diligently with a peculiar rod gripped in the greenish head tentacles. The huge nippers were used in carrying books and in conversation—speech consisting of a kind of clicking and scraping.

The objects had no clothing, but wore satchels or knapsacks suspended from the top of the conical trunk. They commonly carried their head and its supporting member at the level of the cone top, though it was frequently raised or lowered.

The other three great members tended to rest downward at the sides of the cone, contracted to about five feet each, when not in use. From their rate of reading, writing, and operating their machines—those on the tables seemed somehow connected with thought—I concluded that their intelligence was enormously greater than man's.

Afterward I saw them everywhere; swarming in all the great chambers and corridors, tending monstrous machines in vaulted crypts, and racing along the vast roads in gigantic, boat-shaped cars. I ceased to be afraid of them, for they seemed to form supremely natural parts of their environment.

Individual differences amongst them began to be manifest, and a few appeared to be under some kind of restraint. These latter, though showing no physical variation, had a diversity of gestures and habits which marked them off not only from the majority, but very largely from one another.

They wrote a great deal in what seemed to my cloudy vision a vast variety of characters—never the typical curvilinear hieroglyphs of the majority. A few, I fancied, used our own familiar alphabet. Most of them worked much more slowly than the general mass of the entities.

All this time my own part in the dreams seemed to be that of a disembodied consciousness with a range of vision wider than the normal, floating freely about, yet confined to the ordinary avenues and speeds of travel. Not until August, 1915, did any suggestions of bodily existence begin to harass me. I say harass, because the first phase was a purely abstract, though infinitely terrible, association of my previously noted body loathing with the scenes of my visions.

For a while my chief concern during dreams was to avoid looking down at myself, and I recall how grateful I was for the total absence of large mirrors in the strange rooms. I was mightily troubled by the fact that I always saw the great tables—whose height could not be under ten feet—from a level not below that of their surfaces.

And then the morbid temptation to look down at myself became greater and greater, till one night I could not resist it. At first my downward glance revealed nothing whatever. A moment later I perceived that this was because my head lay at the end of a flexible neck of enormous length. Retracting this neck and gazing down very sharply, I saw the scaly, rugose, iridescent bulk of a vast cone ten feet tall and ten feet wide at the base. That was when I waked half of Arkham with my screaming as I plunged madly up from the abyss of sleep.

ONLY after weeks of hideous repetition did I grow half reconciled to these visions of myself in monstrous form. In the dreams I now moved bodily among the other unknown entities, reading terrible books from the endless shelves and writing for hours at the great tables with a stylus managed by the green tentacles that hung down from my head.

Snatches of what I read and wrote would linger in my memory. There were horrible annals of other worlds and other universes, and of stirrings of formless life outside of all universes. There were records of strange orders of beings which had peopled the world in forgotten parts, and frightful chronicles of grotesque-bodied intelligences which would people it millions of years after the death of the last human being.

I learned of chapters in human history whose existence no scholar of to-day has ever suspected. Most of these writings were in the language of the hieroglyphs; which I studied in a queer way with the aid of droning machines, and which was evidently an agglutinative speech with root systems utterly unlike any found in human languages.

Other volumes were in other unknown tongues learned in the same queer way. A very few were in languages I knew. Extremely clever pictures, both inserted in the records and forming separate collections, aided me immensely. And all the time I seemed to be setting down a history of my own age in English. On waking, I could recall only minute and meaningless scraps of the unknown tongues which my dream self had mastered, though whole phases of the history stayed with me.

I learned—even before my waking self had studied the parallel cases or the old myths from which the dreams doubtless sprang—that the entities around me were of the world's greatest race, which had conquered time and had sent exploring minds into every age. I knew, too, that I had been snatched from my age while another used my body in that age, and that a few of the other strange forms housed similarly captured minds. I seemed to talk, in some odd language of claw clickings, with exiled intellects from every corner of the solar system.

There was a mind from the planet we know as Venus, which would live incalculable epochs to come, and one from an outer moon of Jupiter six million years in the past. Of Earthly minds there were some from the winged, star-headed, half-vegetable race of Paleogean Antarctica; one from the reptile people of fabled Valusia; three from the furry prehuman Hyperborean worshippers of Tsathoggua; one from the wholly abominable Tcho-Tchos; two from the Arachnida denizens of Earth's last age; five from the hardy Coleopterous species immediately following mankind, to which the Great Race was some day to transfer its keenest minds *en masse* in the face of horrible peril; and several from different branches of humanity.

I talked with the mind of Yiang-Li, a philosopher from the cruel empire of Tsan-Chan, which is to come in 5,000 A. D.; with that of a general of the great-headed brown people who held South Africa in 50,000 B. C.; with that of a twelfth-century Florentine monk named Bartolomeo Corsi; with that of a king of Lomar who had ruled that terrible polar land one hundred thousand years before the squat, yellow Inutos came from the west to engulf it.

I talked with the mind of Nug-Soth, a magician of the dark conquerors of 16,000 A. D.; with that of a Roman named Titus Sempronius Blaesus, who had been a quaestor in Sulla's time; with that of Khephnes, an Egyptian of the 14th Dynasty, who told me the hideous secret of Nyarlathotep; with that of a priest of Atlantis' middle kingdom; with that of a Suffolk gentleman of Cromwell's day, James Woodville. Also, with that of a court astronomer of pre-Inca Peru; with that of the Australian physicist Nevil Kingston-Brown, who will die in 2,518 A. D.; with that of the archimage of vanished Yhe in the Pacific; with that of Theodotides, a Graeco-Bactrian official of 200 B. C.; with that of an aged Frenchman of Louis XIII's time named Pierre-Louis Montagny; with that of Crom-Ya, a Cimmerian chieftain of 15,000 B. C.; and with so many others that my brain can not hold the shocking secrets and dizzying marvels I learned from them.

I awakened each morning in a fever, sometimes frantically trying to verify or discredit such information as fell within the range of modern human knowledge. Traditional facts took on new and doubtful aspects, and I marveled at the dream fancy which could invent such surprising addenda to history and science.

I shivered at the mysteries the past may conceal, and trembling at the menaces the future may bring forth. What was hinted in the speech of post-human entities of the fate of mankind produced such an effect on me that I will not set it down here.

After man there would be the mighty beetle civilization, the bodies of whose members the cream of the Great Race would seize when the monstrous doom overtook the elder world. Later, as the Earth's span closed, the transferred minds would again migrate through time and space—to another stopping place in the bodies of the bulbous vegetable entities of Mercury. But there would be races after them, clinging pathetically to the cold planet and burrowing to its horror-filled core, before the utter end.

Meanwhile, in my dreams, I wrote endlessly in that history of my own age which I was preparing—half voluntarily and half through promises of increased library and travel opportunities—for the Great Race's central archives. The archives were in a colossal subterranean structure near the city's center, which I came to know well through frequent labors and consultations. Meant to last as long as the race, and to withstand the fiercest of Earth's convulsions, this titan repository surpassed all other buildings in the massive, mountainlike firmness of its construction.

The records, written or printed on great sheets of a curiously tenacious cellulose fabric, were bound into books that opened from the top, and were kept in individual cases of a strange, extremely light rustless metal of grayish hue, decorated with mathematical designs and bearing the title in the Great Race's curvilinear hieroglyphs.

These cases were stored in tiers of rectangular vaults—like closed, locked shelves—wrought of the same rustless metal and fastened by knobs with intricate turnings. My own history was assigned a specific place in the vaults of the lowest or vertebrate level—the section devoted to the cultures of mankind and of the furry, reptilian races immediately preceding it in Terrestrial dominance.

But none of the dreams ever gave me a full picture of daily life. All were the merest misty, disconnected fragments, and it is certain that these fragments were not unfolded in their rightful sequence. I have, for example, a very imperfect idea of my own living arrangements in the dream world; though I seem to have possessed a great stone room of my own. My restrictions as a prisoner gradually disappeared, so that some of the visions included vivid travels over the mighty jungle roads, sojourns in strange cities, and explorations of some of the vast, dark, windowless ruins from which the Great Race shrank in curious fear. There were also long sea voyages in enormous, many-decked boats of incredible swiftness, and trips over wild regions in closed, projectilelike airships lifted and moved by electrical repulsion.

Beyond the wide, warm ocean were other cities of the Great Race, and on one far continent I saw the crude villages of the black-snouted, winged creatures who would evolve as a dominant stock after the Great Race had sent its foremost minds into the future to escape the creeping horror. Flatness and exuberant green life were always the keynote of the scene. Hills were low and sparse, and usually displayed signs of volcanic forces.

OF the animals I saw, I could write volumes. All were wild; for the Great Race's mechanized culture had long since done away with domestic beasts, while food was wholly vegetable or synthetic. Clumsy reptiles of great bulk floundered in steaming morasses, fluttered in the heavy air, or spouted in the seas and lakes; and among these I fancied I could vaguely recognize lesser, archaic prototypes of many forms—Dinosauria, Pterodactyls, Ichthyosauria, Labyrinthodonta, Plesiosauri, and the like—made familiar through paleontology. Of birds or mammals there was none that I could discover.

The ground and swamps were constantly alive with snakes, lizards, and crocodiles, while insects buzzed incessantly among the lush vegetation. And far out at sea, unspied and unknown monsters spouted mountainous columns of foam into the vaporous sky. Once I was taken under the ocean in a gigantic submarine vessel with searchlights, and glimpsed some living horrors of awesome magnitude. I saw also the ruins of incredible sunken cities, and the wealth of orinoid, brachiopod, coral, and ichthyic life which everywhere abounded.

Of the physiology, psychology, folkways, and detailed history of the Great Race my visions preserved but little information, and many of the scattered points I have set down were gleaned from my study of old legends and other cases rather than from my own dreaming.

For in time, of course, my reading and research caught up with and passed the dreams in many phases, so that certain dream fragments were explained in advance and formed verifications of what I had learned. This consolingly established my belief that similar reading and research, accomplished by my secondary self, had formed the source of the whole terrible fabric of pseudomemories.

The period in my dreams, apparently, was one somewhat less than 150,000,000 years ago, when the Paleozoic Age was giving place to the Mesozoic Age. The bodies occupied by the Great Race represented no surviving—or even scientifically known—line of Terrestrial evolution, but were of a peculiar, closely homogeneous, and highly specialized organic type inclining as much to the vegetable as to the animal state.

Cell action was of an unique sort almost precluding fatigue, and wholly eliminating the need of sleep. Nourishment, assimilated through the red trumpetlike appendages on one of the great flexible limbs, was always semi-fluid and in many aspects wholly unlike the food of existing animals.

The beings had but two of the senses which we recognize—sight and hearing, the latter accomplished through the flowerlike appendages on the gray stalks above their heads. Of other and incomprehensible senses—not, however, well utilizable by alien captive minds inhabitating their bodies—they possessed many. Their three eyes were so situated as to give them a range of vision wider than the normal. Their blood was a sort of deep-greenish ichor of great thickness.

They had no sex, but reproduced through seeds or spores which clustered on their bases and could be developed only under water. Great, shallow tanks were used for the growth of their young—which were, however, reared only in small numbers on account of the longevity of individuals—four or five thousand years being the common life span.

Markedly defective individuals were quickly disposed of as soon as their defects were noticed. Disease and the approach of death were, in the absence of a sense of touch or of physical pain, recognized by purely visual symptoms.

The dead were incinerated with dignified ceremonies. Once in a while, as before mentioned, a keen mind would escape death by forward projection in time; but such cases were not numerous. When one did occur, the exiled mind from the future was treated with the utmost kindness till the dissolution of its unfamiliar tenement.

THE Great Race seemed to form a single, loosely knit nation or league, with major institutions in common, though there were four definite divisions. The political and economical system of each unit was a sort of fascistic socialism, with major resources rationally distributed, and power delegated to a small governing board elected by the votes of all able to pass certain educational and psychological tests. Family organization was not overstressed, though ties among persons of common descent were recognized, and the young were generally reared by their parents.

Resemblances to human attitudes and institutions were, of course, most marked in those fields where on the one hand highly abstract elements were concerned, or, where on the other hand there was a dominance of the basic, unspecialized urges common to all organic life. A few added likenesses came through conscious adoption as the Great Race probed the future and copied what it liked.

Industry, highly mechanized, demanded but little time from each citizen; and the abundant leisure was filled with intellectual and aesthetic activities of various sorts.

The sciences were carried to an unbelievable height of development, and art was a vital part of life, though at the period of my dreams it had passed its crest and meridian. Technology was enormously stimulated through the constant struggle to survive, and to keep in existence the physical fabric of great cities, imposed by the prodigious geologic upheavals of those primal days.

Crime was surprisingly scant, and was dealt with through highly efficient policing. Punishments ranged from privilege deprivation and imprisonment to death or major emotion wrenching, and were never administered without a careful study of the criminal's motivations.

Warfare, largely civil for the last few millennia though sometimes waged against reptilian and octopodic invaders, or against the winged, star-headed old ones who centered in the antarctic, was infrequent though infinitely devastating. An enormous army, using cameralike weapons which produced tremendous electrical effects, was kept on hand for purposes seldom mentioned, but obviously connected with the ceaseless fear of the dark, windowless elder ruins and of the great sealed trapdoors in the lowest subterranean levels.

THIS fear of the basalt ruins and trapdoors was largely a matter of unspoken suggestion—or, at most, of furtive, quasi whispers. Everything specific which bore on it was significantly absent from such books as were on the common shelves. It was the one subject lying altogether under a taboo among the Great Race, and seemed to be connected alike with horrible bygone struggles, and with that future peril which would some day force the race to send its keener minds ahead *en masse* in time.

Imperfect and fragmentary as were the other things presented by dreams and legends, this matter was still more bafflingly shrouded. The vague old myths avoided it—or perhaps all allusions had for some reason been excised. And in the dreams of myself and others, the hints were peculiarly few. Members of the Great Race never intentionally referred to the matter, and what could be gleaned came only from some of the more sharply observant captive minds.

According to these scraps of information, the basis of the fear was a horrible elder race of half polypous, utterly alien entities which had come through space from immeasurably distant universes and had dominated the Earth and three other solar planets about six hundred million years ago. They were only partly material—as we understand matter—and their type of consciousness and media of perception differed widely from those of Terrestrial organisms. For example, their senses did not include that of sight; their mental world being a strange, nonvisual pattern of impressions.

They were, however, sufficiently material to use implements

of normal matter when in cosmic areas containing it; and they required housing—albeit of a peculiar kind. Though their senses could penetrate all material barriers, their substance could not; and certain forms of electrical energy could wholly destroy them. They had the power of aërial motion, despite the absence of wings or any other visible means of levitation. Their minds were of such texture that no exchange with them could be effected by the Great Race.

When these things had come to the Earth they had built mighty basalt cities of windowless towers, and had preyed horribly upon the beings they found. Thus it was when the minds of the Great Race sped across the void from that obscure, transgalactic world known in the disturbing and debatable Eltdown Shards as Yith.

The newcomers, with the instruments they created, had found it easy to subdue the predatory entities and drive them down to those caverns of inner earth which they had already joined to their abodes and begun to inhabit.

Then they had sealed the entrances and left them to their fate, afterward occupying most of their great cities and preserving certain important buildings for reasons connected more with superstition than with indifference, boldness, or scientific and historical zeal.

But as the aeons passed, there came vague, evil signs that the elder things were growing strong and numerous in the inner world. There were sporadic irruptions of a particularly hideous character in certain small and remote cities of the Great Race, and in some of the deserted elder cities which the Great Race had not peopled—places where the paths to the gulfs below had not been properly sealed or guarded.

After that greater precautions were taken, and many of the paths were closed forever—though a few were left with sealed trapdoors for strategic use in fighting the elder things if ever they broke forth in unexpected places.

THE irruptions of the elder things must have been shocking beyond all description, since they had permanently colored the psychology of the Great Race. Such was the fixed mood of horror that the very aspect of the creatures was left unmentioned. At no time was I able to gain a clear hint of what they looked like.

There were veiled suggestions of a monstrous plasticity, and of temporary lapses of visibility, while other fragmentary whispers referred to their control and military use of great winds. Singular whistling noises, and colossal footprints made up of five circular toe marks, seemed also to be associated with them.

It was evident that the coming doom so desperately feared by the Great Race—the doom that was one day to send millions of keen minds across the chasm of time to strange bodies in the safer future—had to do with a final successful irruption of the elder beings.

Mental projections down the ages had clearly foretold such a horror, and the Great Race had resolved that none who could escape should face it. That the foray would be a matter of vengeance, rather than an attempt to reoccupy the outer world, they knew from the planet's later history—for their projections showed the coming and going of subsequent races untroubled by the monstrous entities.

Perhaps these entities had come to prefer Earth's inner abysses to the variable, storm-ravaged surfaces, since light meant nothing to them. Perhaps, too, they were slowly weakening with the aeons. Indeed, it was known that they would be quite dead in the time of the post-human beetle race which the fleeing minds would tenant.

Meanwhile, the Great Race maintained its cautious vigilance, with potent weapons ceaselessly ready despite the horrified banishing of the subject from common speech and visible records. And always the shadow of nameless fear hung about the sealed trapdoors and the dark, windowless elder towers.

V.

THAT is the world of which my dreams brought me dim, scattered echoes every night. I cannot hope to give any true idea of the horror and dread contained in such echoes, for it was upon a wholly intangible quality—the sharp sense of pseudomemory—that such feelings mainly depended.

As I have said, my studies gradually gave me a defense against these feelings in the form of rational, psychological explanations; and this saving influence was augmented by the subtle touch of accustomedness which comes with the passage of time. Yet, in spite of everything, the vague, creeping terror would return momentarily now and then. It did not, however, engulf me as it had before; and after 1922 I lived a very normal life of work and recreation.

In the course of years I began to feel that my experience—together with the kindred cases and the related folklore—ought to be definitely summarized and published for the benefit of serious students; hence, I prepared a series of articles briefly covering the whole ground and illustrated with crude sketches of some of the shapes, scenes, decorative motifs, and hieroglyphs remembered from the dreams.

These appeared at various times during 1928 and 1929 in the *Journal of the American Psychological Society,* but did not attract much attention. Meanwhile, I continued to record my dreams with the minutest care, even though the growing stack of reports attained troublesomely vast proportions.

On July 10, 1934, there was forwarded to me by the Psychological Society the letter which opened the culminating and most horrible phase of the whole mad ordeal. It was postmarked Pilbarra, Western Australia, and bore the signature of one whom I found, upon inquiry, to be a mining engineer of considerable prominence. Inclosed were some very curious snapshots. I will reproduce the text in its entirety, and no reader can fail to understand how tremendous an effect it and the photographs had upon me.

I was, for a time, almost stunned and incredulous; for, although I had often thought that some basis of fact must underlie certain phases of the legends which had colored my dreams, I was none the less unprepared for anything like a tangible survival from a lost world remote beyond all imagination. Most devastating of all were the photographs—for here, in cold, incontrovertible realism, there stood out against a background of sand certain worn-down, water-ridged, storm-weathered blocks of stone whose slightly convex tops and slightly concave bottoms told their own story.

And when I studied them with a magnifying glass I could see all too plainly, amidst the batterings and pittings, the traces of those vast curvilinear designs and occasional hieroglyphs whose significance had become so hideous to me. But here is the letter, which speaks for itself:

49, Dampier St.,
Pilbarra, W. Australia,
May 18, 1934.

Prof. N. W. Peaslee,
c/o Am. Psychological Society,
30 E. 41st St.,
New York City, U. S. A.

My Dear Sir:

A recent conversation with Dr. E. M. Boyle of Perth, and some papers with your articles which he has just sent me, make it advisable for me to tell you about certain things I have seen in the Great Sandy Desert east of our gold field here. It would seem, in view of the peculiar legends about old cities with huge stonework and strange designs and hieroglyphs which you describe, that I have come upon something very important.

The blackfellows have always been full of talk about "great stones with marks on them," and seem to have a terrible fear of such things. They connect them in some way with their common racial legends about Buddai, the gigantic old man who lies asleep for ages underground with his head on his arm, and who will some day awake and eat up the world.

There are some very old and half-forgotten tales of enormous underground huts of great stones, where passages lead down and down, and where horrible things have happened. The blackfellows claim that once some warriors, fleeing in battle, went down into one and never came back, but that frightful winds began to blow from the place soon after they went down. However, there usually isn't much in what these natives say.

But what I have to tell is more than this. Two years ago, when I was prospecting about five hundred miles east in the desert, I came on a lot of queer pieces of dressed stone perhaps 3 × 2 × 2 feet in size, and weathered and pitted to the very limit.

At first I couldn't find any of the marks the blackfellows told about, but when I looked close enough I could make out some deeply carved lines in spite of the weathering. There were peculiar curves, just like what the blackfellows had tried to describe. I imagine there must have been thirty or forty blocks, some nearly buried in the sand, and all within a circle of perhaps a quarter of a mile in diameter.

When I saw some, I looked around closely for more, and made a careful reckoning of the place with my instruments. I also took pictures of ten or twelve of the most typical blocks, and will inclose the prints for you to see.

I turned my information and pictures into the government at Perth, but they have done nothing with them.

Then I met Dr. Boyle, who had read your articles in the *Journal of the American Psychological Society,* and, in time, happened to mention the stones. He was enormously interested and became quite excited when I showed him my snapshots, saying that the stones and the markings were just like those of the masonry you had dreamed about and seen described in legends.

He meant to write you, but was delayed. Meanwhile, he sent me most of the magazines with your articles and I saw at once, from your drawings and descriptions, that my stones are certainly the kind you mean. You can appreciate this from the inclosed prints. Later on you will hear directly from Dr. Boyle.

Now I can understand how important all this will be to you. Without question we are faced with the remains of an unknown civilization older than any dreamed of before, and forming a basis for your legends.

As a mining engineer I have some knowledge of geology, and can tell you that these blocks are so ancient they frighten me. They are mostly sandstone and granite, though one is almost certainly made of a queer sort of cement or concrete.

They bear evidence of water action, as if this part of the world had been submerged and come up again after long ages—all since those blocks were made and used. It is a matter of hundreds of thousands of years—or Heaven knows how much more. I don't like to think about it.

In view of your previous diligent work in tracking down the legends and everything connected with them, I cannot doubt that you will want to lead an expedition to the desert and make some archaeological excavations. Both Dr. Boyle and I are prepared to coöperate in such work if you—or organizations known to you—can furnish the funds.

I can get together a dozen miners for the heavy digging—the blackfellows would be of no use, for I've found that they have an almost maniacal fear of this particular spot. Boyle and I are saying nothing to others, for you very obviously ought to have precedence in any discoveries or credit.

The place can be reached from Pilbarra in about four days by motor tractor—which we'd need for our apparatus. It is somewhat west and south of Warburton's path of 1873, and one hundred miles southeast of Joanna Spring. We could float things up the De Grey River instead of starting from Pilbarra—but all that can be talked over later.

Roughly the stones lie at a point about 22° 3′ 14″ South Latitude, 125° 0′ 39″ East Longitude. The climate is tropical, and the desert conditions are trying.

I shall welcome further correspondence upon this subject, and am indeed keenly eager to assist in any plan you may devise. After studying your articles I am deeply impressed with the profound significance of the whole matter. Dr. Boyle will write later. When rapid communication is needed, a cable to Perth can be relayed by wireless.

Hoping profoundly for an early message,

Believe me,
Most faithfully yours,
ROBERT B. F. MACKENZIE.

OF the immediate aftermath of this letter, much can be learned from the press. My good fortune in securing the backing of Miskatonic University was great, and both Mr. Mackenzie and Dr. Boyle proved invaluable in arranging matters at the Australian end. We were not too specific with the public about our objects, since the whole matter would have lent itself unpleasantly to sensational and jocose treatment by the cheaper newspapers. As a result, printed reports were sparing; but enough appeared to tell of our quest for reported Australian ruins and to chronicle our various preparatory steps.

Professor William Dyer of the college's geology department—leader of the Miskatonic Antarctic Expedition of 1930–31—Ferdinand C. Ashley of the department of ancient history, and Tyler M. Freeborn of the department of anthropology—together with my son Wingate—accompanied me.

My correspondent, Mackenzie, came to Arkham early in 1935 and assisted in our final preparations. He proved to be a tremendously competent and affable man of about fifty, admirably well-read, and deeply familiar with all the conditions of Australian travel.

He had tractors waiting at Pilbarra, and we chartered a tramp steamer to get up the river to that point. We were prepared to excavate in the most careful and scientific fashion, sifting every particle of sand, and disturbing nothing which might seem to be in or near its original situation.

Sailing from Boston aboard the wheezy *Lexington* on March 28, 1935, we had a leisurely trip across the Atlantic and Mediterranean, through the Suez Canal, down the Red Sea, and across the Indian Ocean to our goal. I need not tell how the sight of the low, sandy West Australian coast depressed me, and how I detested the crude mining town and dreary gold fields where the tractors were given their last loads.

Dr. Boyle, who met us, proved to be elderly, pleasant and intelligent—and his knowledge of psychology led him into many long discussions with my son and me.

Discomfort and expectancy were oddly mingled in most of us when at length our party of eighteen rattled forth over the arid leagues of sand and rock. On Friday, May 31st, we forded a branch of the De Grey and entered the realm of utter desolation. A certain positive terror grew on me as we advanced to this actual site of the elder world behind the legends—a terror, of course, abetted by the fact that my disturbing dreams and pseudomemories still beset me with unabated force.

IT was on Monday, June 3rd, that we saw the first of the half-buried blocks. I cannot describe the emotions with which I actually touched—in objective reality—a fragment of Cyclopean masonry in every respect like the blocks in the walls of my dream buildings. There was a distinct trace of carving—and my hands trembled as I recognized part of a curvilinear decorative scheme made hellish to me through years of tormenting nightmare and baffling research.

A month of digging brought a total of some 1250 blocks in varying stages of wear and disintegration. Most of these were carven megaliths with curved tops and bottoms. A minority were smaller, flatter, plain-surfaced, and square or octagonally cut—like those of the floors and pavements in my dreams

—while a few were singularly massive and curved or slanted in such a manner as to suggest use in vaulting or groining, or as parts of arches or round window casings.

The deeper—and the farther north and east—we dug, the more blocks we found; though we still failed to discover any trace of arrangement among them. Professor Dyer was appalled at the measureless age of the fragments, and Freeborn found traces of symbols which fitted darkly into certain Papuan and Polynesian legends of infinite antiquity. The condition and scattering of the blocks told minutely of vertiginous cycles of time and geologic upheavals of cosmic savagery.

We had an airplane with us, and my son Wingate would often go up to different heights and scan the sand-and-rock waste for signs of dim, large-scale outlines—either differences of level or trails of scattered blocks. His results were virtually negative; for whenever he would one day think he had glimpsed some significant trend, he would on his next trip find the impression replaced by another equally insubstantial—a result of the shifting, wind-blown sand.

One or two of these ephemeral suggestions, though, affected me queerly and disagreeably. They seemed, after a fashion, to dovetail horribly with something I had dreamed or read, but which I could no longer remember. There was a terrible familiarity about them—which somehow made me look furtively and apprehensively over the abominable, sterile terrain toward the north and northeast.

Around the first week in July I developed an unaccountable set of mixed emotions about that general northeasterly region. There was horror, and there was curiosity—but more than that, there was a persistent and perplexing illusion of memory.

I tried all sorts of psychological expedients to get these notions out of my head, but met with no success. Sleeplessness also gained upon me, but I almost welcomed this because of the resultant shortening of my dream periods. I acquired the habit of taking long, lone walks in the desert late at night—usually to the north or northeast, whither the sum of my strange new impulses seemed subtly to pull me.

SOMETIMES, on these walks, I would stumble over nearly buried fragments of the ancient masonry. Though there were fewer visible blocks here than where we had started, I felt sure that there must be a vast abundance beneath the surface. The ground was less level than at our camp, and the prevailing high winds now and then piled the sand into fantastic temporary hillocks—exposing low traces of the elder stones while it covered other traces.

I was queerly anxious to have the excavations extend to this territory, yet at the same time dreaded what might be revealed. Obviously, I was getting into a rather bad state—all the worse because I could not account for it.

An indication of my poor nervous health can be gained from my response to an odd discovery which I made on one of my nocturnal rambles. It was on the evening of July 11th, when the Moon flooded the mysterious hillocks with a curious pallor.

Wandering somewhat beyond my usual limits, I came upon a great stone which seemed to differ markedly from any we had yet encountered. It was almost wholly covered, but I stooped and cleared away the sand with my hands, later studying the object carefully and supplementing the Moonlight with my electric torch.

Unlike the other very large rocks, this one was perfectly square-cut, with no convex or concave surface. It seemed, too, to be of a dark basaltic substance, wholly dissimilar to the granite and sandstone and occasional concrete of the now familiar fragments.

Suddenly I rose, turned, and ran for the camp at top speed. It was a wholly unconscious and irrational flight, and only when I was close to my tent did I fully realize why I had run. Then it came to me. The queer dark stone was something I had dreamed and read about, and which was linked with the uttermost horrors of the aeon-old legendry.

It was one of the blocks of that basaltic elder masonry which the fabled Great Race held in such fear—the tall, windowless ruins left by those brooding, half-material, alien things that festered in Earth's nether abysses and against whose windlike, invisible forces the trapdoors were sealed and the sleepless sentinels posted.

I remained awake all that night, but by dawn realized how

silly I had been to let the shadow of a myth upset me. Instead of being frightened, I should have had a discoverer's enthusiasm.

The next forenoon I told the others about my find, and Dyer, Freeborn, Boyle, my son, and I set out to view the anomalous block. Failure, however, confronted us. I had formed no clear idea of the stone's location, and a late wind had wholly altered the hillocks of shifting sand.

VI.

I come now to the crucial and the most difficult part of my narrative—all the more difficult because I cannot be quite certain of its reality. At times I feel uncomfortably sure that I was not dreaming or deluded; and it is this feeling—in view of the stupendous implications which the objective truth of my experience would raise—which impels me to make this record.

My son—a trained psychologist with the fullest and most sympathetic knowledge of my whole case—shall be the primary judge of what I have to tell.

First let me outline the externals of the matter, as those at the camp know them: On the night of July 17–18, after a windy day, I retired early but could not sleep. Rising shortly before eleven, and afflicted as usual with that strange feeling regarding the northeastward terrain, I set out on one of my typical nocturnal walks, seeing and greeting only one person—an Australian miner named Tupper—as I left our precincts.

The Moon, slightly past full, shone from a clear sky, and drenched the ancient sands with a white, leprous radiance which seemed to me somehow infinitely evil. There was no longer any wind, nor did any return for nearly five hours, as amply attested by Tupper and others who saw me walking rapidly across the pallid, secret-guarding hillocks toward the northeast.

About 3:30 a. m., a violent wind blew up, waking every one in camp and felling three of the tents. The sky was unclouded, and the desert still blazed with that leprous Moonlight. As the party saw to the tents my absence was noted, but in view of my previous walks this circumstance gave no one alarm. And yet, as many as three men—all Australians—seemed to feel something sinister in the air.

Mackenzie explained to Professor Freeborn that this was a fear picked up from blackfellow folklore—the natives having woven a curious fabric of malignant myth about the high winds which at long intervals sweep across the sands under a clear sky. Such winds, it is whispered, blow out of the great stone huts under the ground, where terrible things have happened—and are never felt except near places where the big marked stones are scattered. Close to four the gale subsided as suddenly as it had begun, leaving the sand hills in new and unfamiliar shapes.

It was just past five, with the bloated, fungoid Moon sinking in the west, when I staggered into camp—hatless, tattered, features scratched and ensanguined, and without my electric torch. Most of the men had returned to bed, but Professor Dyer was smoking a pipe in front of his tent. Seeing my winded and almost frenzied state, he called Dr. Boyle, and the two of them got me on my cot and made me comfortable. My son, roused by the stir, soon joined them, and they all tried to force me to lie still and attempt sleep.

But there was no sleep for me. My psychological state was very extraordinary—different from anything I had previously suffered. After a time I insisted upon talking—nervously and elaborately explaining my condition.

I told them I had become fatigued, and had lain down in the sand for a nap. There had, I said, been dreams even more frightful than usual—and when I was awaked by the sudden high wind my over-wrought nerves had snapped. I had fled in panic, frequently falling over half-buried stones and thus gaining my tattered and bedraggled aspect. I must have slept long—hence the hours of my absence.

Of anything strange either seen or experienced I hinted absolutely nothing—exercising the greatest self-control in that respect. But I spoke of a change of mind regarding the whole work of the expedition, and earnestly urged a halt in all digging toward the northeast.

My reasoning was patently weak—for I mentioned a dearth of blocks, a wish not to offend the superstitious miners, a possible shortage of funds from the college, and other things either untrue or irrelevant. Naturally, no one paid the least attention to my new wishes—not even my son, whose concern for my health was very obvious.

THE next day I was up and around the camp, but took no part in the excavations. Seeing that I could not stop the work, I decided to return home as soon as possible for the sake of my nerves, and made my son promise to fly me in the plane to Perth—a thousand miles to the southwest—as soon as he had surveyed the region I wished let alone.

If, I reflected, the thing I had seen was still visible, I might decide to attempt a specific warning even at the cost of ridicule. It was just conceivable that the miners who knew the local folklore might back me up. Humoring me, my son made the survey that very afternoon, flying over all the terrain my walk could possibly have covered. Yet nothing of what I had found remained in sight.

It was the case of the anomalous basalt block all over again—the shifting sand had wiped out every trace. For an instant I half regretted having lost a certain awesome object in my stark fright—but now I know that the loss was merciful. I can still believe my whole experience an illusion—especially if, as I devoutly hope, that hellish abyss is never found.

Wingate took me to Perth on July 20th, though declining to abandon the expedition and return home. He stayed with me until the 25th, when the steamer for Liverpool sailed. Now, in the cabin of the *Empress,* I am pondering long and frantically upon the entire matter, and have decided that my son, at least, must be informed. It shall rest with him whether to diffuse the matter more widely.

In order to meet any eventuality I have prepared this summary of my background—as already known in a scattered way to others—and will now tell as briefly as possible what seemed to happen during my absence from the camp that hideous night.

Nerves on edge, and whipped into a kind of perverse eagerness by that inexplicable, dread-mingled, mnemonic urge toward the northeast, I plodded on beneath the evil, burning Moon. Here and there I saw, half shrouded by the sand, those primal Cyclopean blocks left from nameless and forgotten aeons.

The incalculable age and brooding horror of this monstrous waste began to oppress me as never before, and I could not keep from thinking of my maddening dreams, of the frightful legends which lay behind them, and of the present fears of natives and miners concerning the desert and its carven stones.

And yet I plodded on as if to some eldritch rendezvous—more and more assailed by bewildering fancies, compulsions, and pseudomemories. I thought of some of the possible contours of the lines of stones as seen by my son from the air, and wondered why they seemed at once so ominous and so familiar. Something was fumbling and rattling at the latch of my recollection, while another unknown force sought to keep the portal barred.

The night was windless, and the pallid sand curved upward and downward like frozen waves of the sea. I had no goal, but somehow plowed along as if with fate-bound assurance. My dreams welled up into the waking world, so that each sand-embedded megalith seemed part of endless rooms and corridors of prehuman masonry, carved and hieroglyphed with symbols that I knew too well from years of custom as a captive mind of the Great Race.

At moments I fancied I saw those omniscient, conical horrors moving about at their accustomed tasks, and I feared to look down lest I find myself one with them in aspect. Yet all the while I saw the sand-covered blocks as well as the rooms and corridors; the evil, burning Moon as well as the lamps of luminous crystal; the endless desert as well as the waving ferns beyond the windows. I was awake and dreaming at the same time.

I do not know how long or how far—or indeed, in just what direction—I had walked when I first spied the heap of blocks bared by the day's wind. It was the largest group in one place that I had seen so far, and so sharply did it impress me that the visions of fabulous aeons faded suddenly away.

Again there were only the desert and the evil Moon and the shards of an unguessed past. I drew close and paused, and cast the added light of my electric torch over the tumbled pile. A hillock had blown away, leaving a low, irregularly round mass of megaliths and smaller fragments some forty feet across and from two to eight feet high.

From the very outset I realized that there was some utterly unprecedented quality about those stones. Not only was the mere number of them quite without parallel, but something in the sand-worn traces of design arrested me as I scanned them under the mingled beams of the Moon and my torch.

Not that any one differed essentially from the earlier specimens we had found. It was something subtler than that. The impression did not come when I looked at one block alone, but only when I ran my eye over several almost simultaneously.

Then, at last, the truth dawned upon me. The curvilinear patterns on many of those blocks were closely related—parts of one vast decorative conception. For the first time in this aeon-shaken waste I had come upon a mass of masonry in its old position—tumbled and fragmentary, it is true, but none the less existing in a very definite sense.

MOUNTING at a low place, I clambered laboriously over the heap; here and there clearing away the sand with my fingers, and constantly striving to interpret varieties of size, shape, and style, and relationships of design.

After a while I could vaguely guess at the nature of the bygone structure, and at the designs which had once stretched over the vast surfaces of the primal masonry. The perfect identity of the whole with some of my dream glimpses appalled and unnerved me.

This was once a Cyclopean corridor thirty feet wide and thirty feet tall, paved with octagonal blocks and solidly vaulted overhead. There would have been rooms opening off on the right, and at the farther end one of those strange inclined planes would have wound down to still lower depths.

I started violently as these conceptions occurred to me, for there was more in them than the blocks themselves had supplied. How did I know that this level should have been far underground? How did I know that the plane leading upward should have been behind me? How did I know that the long subterrane passage to the square of pillars ought to lie on the left one level above me?

How did I know that the room of machines and the right-ward-leading tunnel to the central archives ought to lie two levels below? How did I know that there would be one of those horrible, metal-banded trapdoors at the very bottom four levels down? Bewildered by this intrusion from the dream world, I found myself shaking and bathed in a cold perspiration.

Then, as a last, intolerable touch, I felt that faint, insidious stream of cool air trickling upward from a depressed place near the center of the huge heap. Instantly, as once before, my visions faded, and I saw again only the evil Moonlight, the brooding desert, and the spreading tumulus of Paleogean masonry. Something real and tangible, yet fraught with infinite suggestions of nighted mystery, now confronted me. For that stream of air could argue but one thing—a hidden gulf of great size beneath the disordered blocks on the surface.

My first thought was of the sinister blackfellow legends of vast underground huts among the megaliths where horrors happen and great winds are born. Then thoughts of my own dreams came back, and I felt dim pseudomemories tugging at my mind. What manner of place lay below me? What primal, inconceivable source of age-old myth cycles and haunting nightmares might I be on the brink of uncovering?

It was only for a moment that I hesitated, for more than curiosity and scientific zeal was driving me on and working against my growing fear.

I seemed to move automatically, as if in the clutch of some compelling fate. Pocketing my torch, and struggling with a strength that I had not thought I possessed, I wrenched aside first one titan fragment of stone and then another, till there welled up a strong draft whose dampness contrasted oddly with the desert's dry air. A black rift began to yawn, and at length—when I had pushed away every fragment small enough to budge—the leprous Moonlight blazed on an aperture of ample width to admit me.

I drew out my torch and cast a brilliant beam into the opening. Below me was a chaos of tumbled masonry, sloping roughly down toward the north at an angle of about forty-five degrees, and evidently the result of some bygone collapse from above.

Between its surface and the ground level was a gulf of impenetrable blackness at whose upper edge were signs of gigantic, stress-heaved vaulting. At this point, it appeared, the desert's sands lay directly upon a floor of some titan structure of Earth's youth—how preserved through aeons of geologic convulsion I could not then and cannot now even attempt to guess.

IN retrospect, the barest idea of a sudden, lone descent into such a doubtful abyss—and at a time when one's whereabouts were unknown to any living soul—seems like the utter apex of insanity. Perhaps it was—yet that night I embarked without hesitancy upon such a descent.

Again there was manifest that lure and driving of fatality which had all along seemed to direct my course. With torch flashing intermittently to save the battery, I commenced a mad scramble down the sinister, Cyclopean incline below the opening—sometimes facing forward as I found good hand and foot holds, and at other times turning to face the heap of megaliths as I clung and fumbled more precariously.

In two directions beside me, distant walls of carven, crumbling masonry loomed dimly under the direct beams of my torch. Ahead, however, was only unbroken blackness.

I kept no track of time during my downward scramble. So seething with baffling hints and images was my mind that all objective matters seemed withdrawn to incalculable distances. Physical sensation was dead, and even fear remained as a wraithlike, inactive gargoyle leering impotently at me.

Eventually I reached a level floor strewn with fallen blocks, shapeless fragments, of stone, and sand and detritus of every kind. On either side—perhaps thirty feet apart—rose massive walls culminating in huge groinings. That they were carved I could just discern, but the nature of the carvings was beyond my perception.

What held me most was the vaulting overhead. The beam from my torch could not reach the roof, but the lower parts of the monstrous arches stood out distinctly. And so perfect was their identity with what I had seen in countless dreams of the elder world, that I trembled actively for the first time.

Behind and high above, a faint luminous blur told of the distant Moonlighted world outside. Some vague shred of caution warned me that I should not let it out of my sight, lest I have no guide for my return.

I now advanced toward the wall at my left, where the traces of carving were plainest. The littered floor was nearly as hard to traverse as the downward heap had been, but I managed to pick my difficult way.

At one place I heaved aside some blocks and kicked away the detritus to see what the pavement was like, and shuddered at the utter, fateful familiarity of the great octagonal stones whose buckled surface still held roughly together.

Reaching a convenient distance from the wall, I cast the searchlight slowly and carefully over its worn remnants of carving. Some bygone influx of water seemed to have acted on the sandstone surface, while there were curious incrustations which I could not explain.

In places the masonry was very loose and distorted, and I wondered how many aeons more this primal, hidden edifice could keep its remaining traces of form amidst Earth's heavings.

BUT it was the carvings themselves that excited me most. Despite their time-crumbled state, they were relatively easy to trace at close range; and the complete, intimate familiarity of every detail almost stunned my imagination. That the major attributes of this hoary masonry should be familiar, was not beyond normal credibility.

Powerfully impressing the weavers of certain myths, they had become embodied in a stream of cryptic lore which, somehow, coming to my notice during the amnesic period, had evoked vivid images in my subconscious mind.

But how could I explain the exact and minute fashion in which each line and spiral of these strange designs tallied with what I had dreamed for more than a score of years? What obscure, forgotten iconography could have reproduced each subtle shading and *nuance* which so persistently, exactly, and unvaryingly besieged my sleeping vision night after night?

For this was no chance or remote resemblance. Definitely and absolutely, the millennially ancient, aeon-hidden corridor in which I stood was the original of something I knew in sleep as intimately as I knew my own house in Crane Street,

Arkham. True, my dreams showed the place in its undecayed prime; but the identity was no less real on that account. I was wholly and horribly oriented.

The particular structure I was in was known to me. Known, too, was its place in that terrible elder city of dream. That I could visit unerringly any point in that structure or in that city which had escaped the changes and devastations of uncounted ages, I realized with hideous and instinctive certainty. What in Heaven's name could all this mean? How had I come to know what I knew? And what awful reality could lie behind those antique tales of the beings who had dwelt in this labyrinth of primordial stone?

Words can convey only fractionally the welter of dread and bewilderment which ate at my spirit. I knew this place. I knew what lay below me, and what had lain overhead before the myriad towering stories had fallen to dust and débris and the desert. No need now, I thought with a shudder, to keep that faint blur of Moonlight in view.

I was torn betwixt a longing to flee and a feverish mixture of burning curiosity and driving fatality. What had happened to this monstrous megalopolis of old in the millions of years since the time of my dreams? Of the subterrane mazes which had underlain the city and linked all the titan towers, how much had still survived the writhings of Earth's crust?

Had I come upon a whole buried world of unholy archaism? Could I still find the house of the writing master, and the tower where S'gg'ha, the captive mind from the star-headed vegetable carnivores of antarctica, had chiseled certain pictures on the blank spaces of the walls?

Would the passage at the second level down, to the hall of the alien minds, be still unchoked and traversable? In that hall the captive mind of an incredible entity—a half-plastic denizen of the hollow interior of an unknown trans-Plutonian planet eighteen million years in the future—had kept a certain thing which it had modeled from clay.

I shut my eyes and put my hand to my head in a vain, pitiful effort to drive these insane dream fragments from my consciousness. Then, for the first time, I felt acutely the coolness, motion, and dampness of the surrounding air. Shuddering, I realized that a vast chain of aeon-dead black gulfs must indeed be yawning somewhere beyond and below me.

I thought of the frightful chambers and corridors and inclines as I recalled them from my dreams. Would the way to the central archives still be open? Again that driving fatality tugged insistently at my brain as I recalled the awesome records that once lay cased in those rectangular vaults of rustless metal.

There, said the dreams and legends, had reposed the whole history, past and future, of the cosmic space-time continuum—written by captive minds from every orb and every age in the solar system. Madness, of course—but had I not now stumbled into a nighted world as mad as I?

I thought of the locked metal shelves, and of the curious knob twistings needed to open each one. My own came vividly into my consciousness. How often had I gone through that intricate routine of varied turns and pressures in the Terrestrial vertebrate section on the lowest level! Every detail was fresh and familiar.

If there were such a vault as I had dreamed of, I could open it in a moment. It was then that madness took me utterly. An instant later, and I was leaping and stumbling over the rocky débris toward the well-remembered incline to the depths below.

VII.

FROM that point forward my impressions are scarcely to be relied on—indeed, I still possess a final, desperate hope that they all form parts of some demoniac dream or illusion born of delirium. A fever raged in my brain, and everything came to me through a kind of haze—sometimes only intermittently.

The rays of my torch shot feebly into the engulfing blackness, bringing phantasmal flashes of hideously familiar walls and carvings, all blighted with the decay of ages. In one place a tremendous mass of vaulting had fallen, so that I had to clamber over a mighty mound of stones reaching almost to the ragged, grotesquely stalactited roof.

It was all the ultimate apex of nightmare, made worse by that blasphemous tug of pseudomemory. One thing only was unfamiliar, and that was my own size in relation to the monstrous masonry. I felt oppressed by a sense of unwonted smallness, as if the sight of these towering walls from a mere human body was something wholly new and abnormal. Again and again I looked nervously down at myself, vaguely disturbed by the human form I possessed.

Onward through the blackness of the abyss I leaped, plunged and staggered—often falling and bruising myself, and once nearly shattering my torch. Every stone and corner of that demoniac gulf was known to me, and at many points I stopped to cast beams of light through choked and crumbling, yet familiar, archways.

Some rooms had totally collapsed, others were bare, or débris-filled. In a few I saw masses of metal—some fairly intact, some broken, and some crushed or battered—which I recognized as the colossal pedestals or tables of my dreams. What they could in truth have been, I dared not guess.

I found the downward incline and began its descent—though after a time halted by a gaping, ragged chasm whose narrowest point could not be much less than four feet across. Here the stonework had fallen through, revealing incalculable inky depths beneath.

I knew there were two more cellar levels in this titan edifice, and trembled with fresh panic as I recalled the metal-clamped trapdoor on the lowest one. There could be no guards now—for what had lurked beneath had long since done its hideous work and sunk into its long decline. By the time of the post-human beetle race it would be quite dead. And yet, as I thought of the native legends, I trembled anew.

It cost me a terrible effort to vault that yawning chasm, since the littered floor prevented a running start—but madness drove me on. I chose a place close to the left-hand wall—where the rift was least wide and the landing spot reasonably clear of dangerous débris—and after one frantic moment reached the other side in safety.

At last, gaining the lower level, I stumbled on past the archway of the room of machines, within which were fantastic ruins of metal, half buried beneath fallen vaulting. Everything was where I knew it would be, and I climbed confidently over the heaps which barred the entrance of a vast transverse corridor. This, I realized, would take me under the city to the central archives.

Endless ages seemed to unroll as I stumbled, leaped, and crawled along that débris-cluttered corridor. Now and then I could make out carvings on the age-stained walls—some familiar, others seemingly added since the period of my dreams. Since this was a subterrane house-connecting highway, there were no archways save when the route led through the lower levels of various buildings.

At some of these intersections I turned aside long enough to look down well-remembered corridors and into well-remembered rooms. Twice only did I find any radical changes from what I had dreamed of—and in one of these cases I could trace the sealed-up outlines of the archway I remembered.

I shook violently, and felt a curious surge of retarding weakness as I steered a hurried and reluctant course through the crypt of one of those great windowless, ruined towers whose alien, basalt masonry bespoke a whispered and horrible origin.

This primal vault was round and fully two hundred feet across, with nothing carved upon the dark-hued stonework. The floor was here free from anything save dust and sand, and I could see the apertures leading upward and downward. There were no stairs nor inclines—indeed, my dreams had pictured those elder towers as wholly untouched by the fabulous Great Race. Those who had built them had not needed stairs or inclines.

In the dreams, the downward aperture had been tightly sealed and nervously guarded. Now it lay open—black and yawning, and giving forth a current of cool, damp air. Of what limitless caverns of eternal night might brood below, I would not permit myself to think.

Later, clawing my way along a badly heaped section of the corridor, I reached a place where the roof had wholly caved in. The débris rose like a mountain, and I climbed up over it, passing through a vast, empty space where my torchlight could reveal neither walls nor vaulting. This, I reflected, must be the cellar of the house of the metal purveyors, fronting on the third square not far from the archives. What had happened to it I could not conjecture.

I found the corridor again beyond the mountain of detritus and stone, but after a short distance encountered a wholly choked place where the fallen vaulting almost touched the perilously sagging ceiling. How I managed to wrench and tear aside enough blocks to afford a passage, and how I dared disturb the tightly packed fragments when the least shift of equilibrium might have brought down all the tons of superincumbent masonry to crush me to nothingness, I do not know.

It was sheer madness that impelled and guided me—if, indeed, my whole underground adventure was not—as I hope—a hellish delusion or phase of dreaming. But I did make—or dream that I made—a passage that I could squirm through. As I wriggled over the mound of débris—my torch, switched continuously on, thrust deeply in my mouth—I felt myself torn by the fantastic stalactites of the jagged floor above me.

I was now close to the great underground archival structure which seemed to form my goal. Sliding and clambering down the farther side of the barrier, and picking my way along the remaining stretch of corridor with hand-held, intermittently flashing torch, I came at last to a low, circular crypt with arches—still in a marvelous state of preservation—opening off on every side.

The walls, or such parts of them as lay within reach of my torchlight, were densely hieroglyphed and chiseled with typical curvilinear symbols—some added since the period of my dreams.

This, I realized, was my fated destination, and I turned at once through a familiar archway on my left. That I could find a clear passage up and down the incline to all the surviving levels, I had, oddly, little doubt. This vast, Earth-protected pile, housing the annals of all the solar system, had been built with supernal skill and strength to last as long as that system itself.

Blocks of stupendous size poised with mathematical genius and bound with cements of incredible toughness, had combined to form a mass as firm as the planet's rocky core. Here, after ages more prodigious than I could sanely grasp, its buried bulk stood in all its essential contours, the vast, dust-drifted floors scarce sprinkled with the litter elsewhere so dominant.

THE relatively easy walking from this point onward went curiously to my head. All the frantic eagerness hitherto frustrated by obstacles now took itself out in a kind of febrile speed, and I literally raced along the low-roofed, monstrously well-remembered aisles beyond the archway.

I was past being astonished by the familiarity of what I saw. On every hand the great hieroglyphed metal shelf doors loomed monstrously; some yet in place, others sprung open, and still others bent and buckled under bygone geological stresses not quite strong enough to shatter the titan masonry.

Here and there a dust-covered heap beneath a gaping, empty shelf seemed to indicate where cases had been shaken down by Earth tremors. On occasional pillars were great symbols and letters proclaiming classes and subclasses of volumes.

Once I paused before an open vault where I saw some of the accustomed metal cases still in position amidst the omnipresent gritty dust. Reaching up, I dislodged one of the thinner specimens with some difficulty, and rested it on the floor for inspection. It was titled in the prevailing curvilinear hieroglyphs, though something in the arrangement of the character seemed subtly unusual.

The odd mechanism of the hooked fastener was perfectly well known to me, and I snapped up the still rustless and workable lid and drew out the book within. The latter, as expected, was some twenty by fifteen inches in area, and two inches thick; the thin metal covers opening at the top.

Its tough cellulose pages seemed unaffected by the myriad cycles of time they had lived through, and I studied the queerly pigmented, brush-drawn letters of the text—symbols unlike either the usual curved hieroglyphs or any alphabet known to human scholarship—with a haunting, half-aroused memory.

It came to me that this was the language used by a captive mind I had known slightly, in my dreams—a mind from a large asteroid on which had survived much of the archaic life and lore of the primal planet whereof it formed a fragment. At the same time I recalled that this level of the archives was devoted to volumes dealing with the non-Terrestrial planets.

As I ceased poring over this incredible document I saw that the light of my torch was beginning to fail, hence quickly inserted the extra battery I always had with me. Then, armed with the stronger radiance, I resumed my feverish racing through unending tangles of aisles and corridors—recognizing now and then some familiar shelf, and vaguely annoyed by the acoustic conditions which made my footfalls echo incongruously in these catacombs.

The very prints of my shoes behind me in the millennially untrodden dust made me shudder. Never before, if my mad dreams held anything of truth, had human feet pressed upon those immemorial pavements.

Of the particular goal of my insane racing, my conscious mind held no hint. There was, however, some force of evil potency pulling at my dazed will and buried recollection, so that I vaguely felt I was not running at random.

I came to a downward incline and followed it to profounder depths. Floors flashed by me as I raced, but I did not pause to explore them. In my whirling brain there had begun to beat a certain rhythm which set my right hand twitching in unison. I wanted to unlock something, and felt that I knew all the intricate twists and pressures needed to do it. It would be like a modern safe with a combination lock.

Dream or not, I had once known and still knew. How any dream—or any scrap of unconsciously absorbed legend—could have taught me a detail so minute, so intricate, and so complex, I did not attempt to explain to myself. I was beyond all coherent thought. For was not this whole experience—this shocking familiarity with a set of unknown ruins, and this monstrously exact identity of everything before me with what only dreams and scraps of myth could have suggested—a horror beyond all reason?

Probably it was my basic conviction then—as it is now during my saner moments—that I was not awake at all, and that the entire buried city was a fragment of febrile hallucination.

Eventually, I reached the lowest level and struck off to the right of the incline. For some shadowy reason I tried to soften my steps, even though I lost speed thereby. There was a space I was afraid to cross on this last, deeply buried floor.

As I drew near it I recalled what thing in that space I feared. It was merely one of the metal-barred and closely guarded trapdoors. There would be no guards now, and on that account I trembled and tiptoed as I had done in passing through that black basalt vault where a similar trapdoor had yawned.

I felt a current of cool, damp air as I had felt there, and wished that my course led in another direction. Why I had to take the particular course I was taking, I did not know.

When I came to the space I saw that the trapdoor yawned widely open. Ahead, the shelves began again, and I glimpsed on the floor before one of them a heap very thinly covered with dust, where a number of cases had recently fallen. At the same moment a fresh wave of panic clutched me, though for some time I could not discover why.

Heaps of fallen cases were not uncommon, for all through the aeons this lightless labyrinth had been racked by the heavings of Earth and had echoed at intervals to the deafening clatter of toppling objects. It was only when I was nearly across the space that I realized why I shook so violently.

Not the heap, but something about the dust of the level floor, was troubling me. In the light of my torch it seemed as if that dust were not as even as it ought to be—there were places where it looked thinner, as if it had been disturbed not many months before. I could not be sure, for even the apparently thinner places were dusty enough; yet a certain suspicion of regularity in the fancied unevenness was highly disquieting.

When I brought the torchlight close to one of the queer places I did not like what I saw—for the illusion of regularity became very great. It was as if there were regular lines of composite impressions—impressions that went in threes, each slightly over a foot square and consisting of five nearly circular three-inch prints, one in advance of the other four.

These possible lines of foot-square impressions appeared to lead in two directions, as if something had gone somewhere and returned. They were, of course, very faint, and may have been illusions or accidents; but there was an element of dim, fumbling terror about the way I thought they ran. For at one end of them was the heap of cases which must have clattered down not long before, while at the other end was the ominous trapdoor with the cool, damp wind, yawning unguarded down to abysses past imagination.

VIII.

THAT my strange sense of compulsion was deep and overwhelming is shown by its conquest of my fear. No rational motive could have drawn me on after that hideous suspicion of prints and the creeping dream memories it excited. Yet my right hand, even as it shook with fright, still twitched rhythmically in its eagerness to turn a lock it hoped to find. Before I knew it I was past the heap of lately fallen cases and running on tiptoe through aisles of utterly unbroken dust toward a point which I seemed to know morbidly, horribly well.

My mind was asking itself questions whose origin and relevancy I was only beginning to guess. Would the shelf be reachable by a human body? Could my human hand master all the aeon-remembered motions of the lock? Would the lock be undamaged and workable? And what would I do—what dare I do —with what—as I now commenced to realize—I both hoped and feared to find? Would it prove the awesome, brain-shattering truth of something past normal conception, or show only that I was dreaming?

The next I knew I had ceased my tiptoed racing and was standing still, staring at a row of maddeningly familiar hieroglyphed shelves. They were in a state of almost perfect preservation, and only three of the doors in this vicinity had sprung open.

My feelings toward these shelves cannot be described—so utter and insistent was the sense of old acquaintance. I was looking high up at a row near the top and wholly out of my reach, and wondering how I could climb to best advantage. An open door four rows from the bottom would help, and the locks of the closed doors formed possible holds for hands and feet. I would grip the torch between my teeth, as I had in other places where both hands were needed. Above all I must make no noise.

How to get down what I wished to remove would be difficult, but I could probably hook its movable fastener in my coat collar and carry it like a knapsack. Again I wondered whether the lock would be undamaged. That I could repeat each familiar motion I had not the least doubt. But I hoped the thing would not scrape or creak—and that my hand could work it properly.

Even as I thought these things I had taken the torch in my mouth and begun to climb. The projecting locks were poor supports; but, as I had expected, the opened shelf helped greatly. I used both the swinging door and the edge of the aperture itself in my ascent, and managed to avoid any loud creaking.

Balanced on the upper edge of the door, and leaning far to my right, I could just reach the lock I sought. My fingers, half numb from climbing, were very clumsy at first; but I soon saw that they were anatomically adequate. And the memory rhythm was strong in them.

Out of unknown gulfs of time the intricate, secret motions had somehow reached my brain correctly in every detail—for after less than five minutes of trying there came a click whose familiarity was all the more startling because I had not consciously anticipated it. In another instant the metal door was slowly swinging open with only the faintest grating sound.

DAZEDLY I looked over the row of grayish case ends thus exposed, and felt a tremendous surge of some wholly inexplicable emotion. Just within reach of my right hand was a case whose curving hieroglyphs made me shake with a pang infinitely more complex than one of mere fright. Still shaking, I managed to dislodge it amidst a shower of gritty flakes, and ease it over toward myself without any violent noise.

Like the other case I had handled, it was slightly more than twenty by fifteen inches in size, with curved mathematical designs in low relief. In thickness it just exceeded three inches.

Crudely wedging it between myself and the surface I was climbing, I fumbled with the fastener and finally got the hook free. Lifting the cover, I shifted the heavy object to my back, and let the hook catch hold of my collar. Hands now free, I awkwardly clambered down to the dusty floor and prepared to inspect my prize.

Kneeling in the gritty dust, I swung the case around and rested it in front of me. My hands shook, and I dreaded to draw out the book within almost as much as I longed—and felt compelled—to do so. It had very gradually become clear to me what I ought to find, and this realization nearly paralyzed my faculties.

If the thing were there—and if I were not dreaming—the implications would be quite beyond the power of the human spirit to bear. What tormented me most was my momentary inability to feel that my surroundings were a dream. The sense of reality was hideous—and again becomes so as I recall the scene.

At length I tremblingly pulled the book from its container and stared fascinatedly at the well-known hieroglyphs on the cover. It seemed to be in prime condition, and the curvilinear letters of the title held me in almost as hypnotized a state as if I could read them. Indeed, I cannot swear that I did not actually read them in some transient and terrible access of abnormal memory.

I do not know how long it was before I dared to lift that thin metal cover. I temporized and made excuses to myself. I took the torch from my mouth and shut it off to save the battery. Then, in the dark, I collected my courage—finally lifting the cover without turning on the light. Last of all, I did indeed flash the torch upon the exposed page—steeling myself in advance to suppress any sound no matter what I should find.

I looked for an instant, then almost collapsed. Clenching my teeth, however, I kept silent. I sank wholly to the floor and put a hand to my forehead amidst the engulfing blackness. What I dreaded and expected was there. Either I was dreaming, or time and space had become a mockery.

I must be dreaming—but I would test the horror by carrying this thing back and showing it to my son if it were indeed a reality. My head swam frightfully, even though there were no visible objects in the unbroken gloom to swirl about me. Ideas and images of the starkest terror—excited by the vistas which my glimpse had opened up—began to throng in upon me and cloud my senses.

I thought of those possible prints in the dust, and trembled at the sound of my own breathing as I did so. Once again I flashed on the light and looked at the page as a serpent's victim may look at his destroyer's eyes and fangs.

Then, with clumsy fingers, in the dark, I closed the book, put it in its container, and snapped the lid and the curious, hooked fastener. This was what I must carry back to the outer world if it truly existed—if the whole abyss truly existed—if I, and the world itself, truly existed.

JUST when I tottered to my feet and commenced my return I cannot be certain. It came to me oddly—as a measure of my sense of separation from the normal world—that I did not even once look at my watch during those hideous hours underground.

Torch in hand, and with the ominous case under one arm, I eventually found myself tiptoeing in a kind of silent panic past the draft-giving abyss and those lurking suggestions of prints. I lessened my precautions as I climbed up the endless inclines, but could not shake off a shadow of apprehension which I had not felt on the downward journey.

I dreaded having to repass through that black basalt crypt that was older than the city itself, where cold drafts welled up from unguarded depths. I thought of that which the Great Race had feared, and of what might still be lurking—be it ever so weak and dying—down there. I thought of those five-circle prints and of what my dreams had told me of such prints—and of strange winds and whistling noises associated with them. And I thought of the tales of the modern blackfellows, wherein the horror of great winds and nameless subterrane ruins was dwelt upon.

I knew from a carven wall symbol the right floor to enter, and came at last—after passing that other book I had examined—to the great circular space with the branching archways. On my right, and at once recognizable, was the arch through which I had arrived. This I now entered, conscious that the rest of my course would be harder because of the tumbled state of the masonry outside the archive building. My new metal-cased burden weighed upon me, and I found it harder and harder to be quiet as I stumbled among débris and fragments of every sort.

Then I came to the ceiling-high mound of débris through which I had wrenched a scanty passage. My dread at wriggling through again was infinite, for my first passage had made some noise, and I now—after seeing those possible prints—dreaded sound above all things. The case, too, doubled the problem of traversing the narrow crevice.

But I clambered up the barrier as best I could, and pushed the case through the aperture ahead of me. Then, torch in mouth, I scrambled through myself—my back torn as before by stalactites.

As I tried to grasp the case again, it fell some distance ahead of me down the slope of the débris, making a disturbing clatter and arousing echoes which sent me into a cold perspiration. I lunged for it at once, and regained it without further noise—but a moment afterward the slipping of blocks under my feet raised a sudden and unprecedented din.

That din was my undoing. For, falsely or not, I thought I heard it answered in a terrible way from spaces far behind me. I thought I heard a shrill, whistling sound, like nothing else on Earth, and beyond any adequate verbal description. If so, what followed has a certain grim irony—since, save for the panic of this thing, the second thing might never have happened.

As it was, my frenzy was absolute and unrelieved. Taking my torch in my hand and clutching feebly at the case, I leaped and bounded wildly ahead with no idea in my brain beyond a mad desire to race out of these nightmare ruins to the waking world of desert and Moonlight which lay so far above.

I hardly knew it when I reached the mountain of débris which towered into the vast blackness beyond the caved-in roof, and bruised and cut myself repeatedly in scrambling up its steep slope of jagged blocks and fragments.

Then came the great disaster. Just as I blindly crossed the summit, unprepared for the sudden dip ahead, my feet slipped utterly and I found myself involved in a mangling avalanche of sliding masonry whose cannon-loud uproar split the black, cavern air in a deafening series of Earth-shaking reverberations.

I have no recollection of emerging from this chaos, but a momentary fragment of consciousness shows me as plunging and tripping and scrambling along the corridor amidst the clangor—case and torch still with me.

Then, just as I approached that primal basalt crypt I had so dreaded, utter madness came. For as the echoes of the avalanche died down, there became audible a repetition of that frightful alien whistling I thought I had heard before. This time there was no doubt about it—and what was worse, it came from a point not behind but *ahead of me.*

Probably I shrieked aloud then. I have a dim picture of myself as flying through the hellish basalt vault of the elder things, and hearing that damnable alien sound piping up from the open, unguarded door of limitless nether blacknesses. There was a wind, too—not merely a cool, damp draft, but a violent, purposeful blast belching savagely and frigidly from that abominable gulf whence the obscene whistling came.

There are memories of leaping and lurching over obstacles of every sort, with that torrent of wind and shrieking sound growing moment by moment, and seeming to curl and twist purposefully around me as it struck out wickedly from the spaces behind and beneath.

Though in my rear, that wind had the odd effect of hindering instead of aiding my progress; as if it acted like a noose or lasso thrown around me. Heedless of the noise I made, I clattered over a great barrier of blocks and was again in the structure that led to the surface.

I recall glimpsing the archway to the room of machines and almost crying out as I saw the incline leading down to where one of those blasphemous trapdoors must be yawning two levels below. But instead of crying out I muttered over and over to myself that this was all a dream from which I must soon wake. Perhaps I was in camp—perhaps I was at home in Arkham. As these hopes bolstered up my sanity I began to mount the incline to the higher level.

I knew, of course, that I had the four-foot cleft to recross, yet was too racked by other fears to realize the full horror until I came almost upon it. On my descent, the leap across had been easy—but could I clear the gap as readily when going uphill, and hampered by fright, exhaustion, the weight of the metal case, and the anomalous backward tug of that demon wind? I thought of these things at the last moment, and thought also of the nameless entities which might be lurking in the black abysses below the chasm.

My wavering torch was growing feeble, but I could tell by some obscure memory when I neared the cleft. The chill blasts of wind and the nauseous whistling shrieks behind me were for the moment like a merciful opiate, dulling my imagination to the horror of the yawning gulf ahead. And then I became aware of the added blasts and whistling in front of me—tides of abomination surging up through the cleft itself from depths unimagined and unimaginable.

Now, indeed, the essence of pure nightmare was upon me. Sanity departed—and, ignoring everything except the animal impulse of flight, I merely struggled and plunged upward over the incline's débris as if no gulf had existed. Then I saw the chasm's edge, leaped frenziedly with every ounce of strength I possessed, and was instantly engulfed in a pandemoniac vortex of loathsome sound and utter, materially tangible blackness.

THAT is the end of my experience, so far as I can recall. Any further impressions belong wholly to the domain of phantasmagoric delirium. Dream, madness, and memory merged wildly together in a series of fantastic, fragmentary delusions which can have no relation to anything real.

There was a hideous fall through incalculable leagues of viscous, sentient darkness, and a babel of noises utterly alien to all that we know of the Earth and its organic life. Dormant, rudimentary senses seemed to start into vitality within me, telling of pits and voids peopled by floating horrors and leading to sunless crags and oceans and teeming cities of windowless, basalt towers upon which no light ever shone.

Secrets of the primal planet and its immemorial aeons flashed through my brain without the aid of sight or sound, and there were known to me things which not even the wildest of my former dreams had ever suggested. And all the while cold fingers of damp vapor clutched and picked at me, and that eldritch, damnable whistling shrieked fiendishly above all the alternations of babel and silence in the whirlpools of darkness around.

Afterward there were visions of the Cyclopean city of my dreams—not in ruins, but just as I had dreamed of it. I was in my conical, nonhuman body again, and mingled with crowds of the Great Race and the captive minds who carried books up and down the lofty corridors and vast inclines.

Then, superimposed upon these pictures, were frightful, momentary flashes of a nonvisual consciousness involving desperate struggles, a writhing free from clutching tentacles of whistling wind, an insane, batlike flight through half-solid air, a feverish burrowing through the cyclone-whipped dark, and a wild stumbling and scrambling over fallen masonry.

Once, there was a curious, intrusive flash of half sight—a faint, diffuse suspicion of bluish radiance far overhead. Then there came a dream of wind-pursued climbing and crawling—of wriggling into a blaze of sardonic Moonlight through a jumble of débris which slid and collapsed after me amidst a morbid hurricane. It was the evil, monotonous beating of that maddening Moonlight which at last told me of the return of what I had once known as the objective, waking world.

I was clawing prone through the sands of the Australian desert, and around me shrieked such a tumult of wind as I had never before known on our planet's surface. My clothing was in rags, and my whole body was a mass of bruises and scratches.

Full consciousness returned very slowly, and at no time could I tell just where delirious dream left and true memory began. There had seemed to be a mound of titan blocks, an abyss beneath it, a monstrous revelation from the past, and a nightmare horror at the end—but how much of this was real?

My flashlight was gone, and likewise any metal case I may have discovered. Had there been such a case—or any abyss—or any mound? Raising my head, I looked behind me, and saw only the sterile, undulant sands of the desert.

The demon wind died down, and the bloated, fungoid Moon sank reddeningly in the west. I lurched to my feet and began to stagger southwestward toward the camp. What in truth had happened to me? Had I merely collapsed in the desert and dragged a dream-racked body over miles of sand and buried blocks? If not, how could I bear to live any longer?

For, in this new doubt, all my faith in the myth-born unreality of my visions dissolved once more into the hellish older doubting. If that abyss was real, then the Great Race was real—and its blasphemous reachings and seizures in the cosmos-wide vortex of time were no myths or nightmares, but a terrible, soul-shattering actuality.

HAD I, in full, hideous fact, been drawn back to a prehuman world of a hundred and fifty million years ago in those dark, baffling days of the amnesia? Had my present body been the vehicle of a frightful alien consciousness from Paleogean gulfs of time?

Had I, as the captive mind of those shambling horrors, indeed known that accursed city of stone in its primordial heyday, and wriggled down those familiar corridors in the loathsome shape of my captor? Were those tormenting dreams of more than twenty years the offspring of stark, monstrous memories?

Had I once veritably talked with minds from reachless corners of time and space, learned the universe's secrets, past and to come, and written the annals of my own world for the metal cases of those titan archives? And were those others—those shocking elder things of the mad winds and demon pipings—in truth a lingering, lurking menace, waiting and slowly weakening in black abysses while varied shapes of life drag out their multimillennial courses on the planet's age-racked surface?

I do not know. If that abyss and what it held were real, there is no hope. Then, all too truly, there lies upon this world of man a mocking and incredible shadow out of time. But, mercifully, there is no proof that these things are other than fresh phases of my myth-born dreams. I did not bring back the metal case that would have been a proof, and so far those subterrane corridors have not been found.

If the laws of the universe are kind, they will never be found. But I must tell my son what I saw or thought I saw, and let him use his judgment as a psychologist in gauging the reality of my experience, and communicating this account to others.

I have said that the awful truth behind my tortured years of dreaming hinges absolutely upon the actuality of what I thought I saw in those Cyclopean, buried ruins. It has been hard for me, literally, to set down that crucial revelation, though no reader can have failed to guess it. Of course, it lay in that book within the metal case—the case which I pried out of its forgotten lair amidst the undisturbed dust of a million centuries.

No eye had seen, no hand had touched that book since the advent of man to this planet. And yet, when I flashed my torch upon it in that frightful abyss, I saw that the queerly pigmented letters on the brittle, aeon-browned cellulose pages were not indeed any nameless hieroglyphs of Earth's youth. They were, indeed, the letters of our familiar alphabet, spelling out the words of the English language, in my own handwriting.

Bindlestiff

By James Blish

It was inevitable that, occasionally, one of the cruising cities of space would turn criminal. And they made vicious, deadly enemies!

I.

EVEN to the men of the flying city, the Rift was awesome beyond all human experience. Loneliness was natural between the stars, and starmen were used to it—the star-density of the average cluster was more than enough to give a veteran Okie claustrophobia; but the enormous empty loneliness of the Rift was unique.

To the best of Mayor Amalfi's knowledge, no Okie city had ever crossed the Rift before. The City Fathers, who knew everything, agreed. Amalfi was none too sure that it was wise, for once, to be a pioneer.

Ahead and behind, the walls of the Rift shimmered, a haze of stars too far away to resolve into individual points of light. The walls curved gently toward a starry floor, so many parsecs "beneath" the keel of the city that it seemed to be hidden in a rising haze of star dust.

"Above," there was nothing; a nothing as final as the slamming of a door—it was the intergalactic gap.

The Rift was, in effect, a valley cut in the face of the galaxy. A few stars swam in it, light-millennia apart—stars which the tide of human colonization could never have reached. Only on the far side was there likely to be any inhabited planet, and, consequently, work for a migratory city.

On the near side there were the Earth police. They would not chase Amalfi's city across the Rift; they were busy consolidating their conquests of Utopia and the Duchy of Gort, barbarian planets whose ties with Earth were being forcibly reestablished. But they would be happy to see the city turn back —there was a violation of a Vacate order still on the books, and a little matter of a trick—

Soberly, Amalfi contemplated the oppressive chasm which the screens showed him. The picture came in by ultrawave from a string of proxy-robots, the leader of which was already parsecs out across the gap. And still the far wall was featureless, just beginning to show a faintly granular texture which gave promise of resolution into individual stars at top magnification.

"I hope the food holds out," he muttered. "I never expected the cops to chase us this far."

Beside him, Mark Hazleton, the city manager, drummed delicately upon the arm of his chair. "No reason why it shouldn't," he said lazily. "Of course the oil's low, but the *Chlorella* crop is flourishing. And I doubt that we'll be troubled by mutation in the tanks. Aren't ultronic nexi supposed to vary directly with star-density?"

"Sure," Amalfi said, irritated. "We won't starve if everything goes right. If we hadn't been rich enough to risk crossing, I'd of let us be captured and paid the fine instead. But we've never been as long as a year without planet-fall before, and this crossing is going to take all of the four years the Fathers predicted. The slightest accident, and we'll be beyond help."

"There'll be no accident," Hazleton said confidently.

"There's fuel decomposition—we've never had a flash-fire

but there's always a first time. And if the Twenty-third Street spindizzy conks out again—"

He stopped abruptly. Through the corner of his eye, a minute pinprick of brightness poked insistently into his brain. When he looked directly at the screen, it was still there. He pointed.

"Look—is that a cluster? No, it's too small. If that's a free-floating star, it's close."

He snatched up a phone. "Give me Astronomy. Hello, Jake. Can you figure me the distance of a star from the source of an ultraphone broadcast?"

"Why, yes," the phone said. "Wait, and I'll pick up your image. Ah—I see what you mean; something at 10:00 o'clock center, can't tell what yet. Dinwiddie pickups on your proxies? Intensity will tell the tale." The astronomer chuckled like a parrot on the rim of a cracker barrel. "Now if you'll just tell me how many proxies you have, and how far they—"

"Five. Full interval."

"Hm-m-m. Big correction." There was a long, itching silence. "Amalfi?"

"Yeah."

"About ten parsecs, give or take 0.4. I'd say you've found a floater, my boy."

"Thanks." Amalfi put the phone back and drew a deep breath. "What a relief."

"You won't find any colonists on a star that isolated," Hazleton reminded him.

"I don't care. It's a landing point, possibly a fuel or even a food source. Most stars have planets; a freak like this might not, or it might have dozens. Just cross your fingers."

He stared at the tiny sun, his eyes aching from sympathetic strain. A star in the middle of the Rift—almost certainly a wild star, moving at four hundred or five hundred k.p.s. It occurred to him that a people living on a planet of that star might remember the moment when it burst through the near wall and embarked upon its journey into the emptiness.

"There might be people there," he said. "The Rift was swept clean of stars once, somehow. Jake claims that that's an overdramatic way of putting it, that the mean motions of the stars probably opened the gap naturally. But either way that sun must be a recent arrival, going at quite a clip, since it's moving counter to the general tendency. It could have been colonized while it was still passing through a populated area. Runaway stars tend to collect hunted criminals as they go by, Mark."

"Possibly," Hazleton admitted. "By the way, that image is coming in from your lead proxy, 'way out across the valley. Don't you have any outriggers? I ordered them sent."

"Sure. But I don't use them except for routine. Cruising the Rift lengthwise would be suicide. We'll take a look if you like."

He touched the board. On the screen, the far wall was wiped away. Nothing was left but thin haze; down at that end, the Rift turned, and eventually faded out into a rill of emptiness, soaking into the sands of the stars.

"Nothing there. Lots of nothing."

Amalfi moved the switch again.

On the screen, apparently almost within hallooing distance, a city was burning.

SPACE flight got its start, as a war weapon, amid the collapse of the great Western culture of Earth. In the succeeding centuries it was almost forgotten. The new culture, that vast planar despotism called by historiographers the Bureaucratic State, did not think that way.

Not that the original Soviets or their successors forbade space travel. They simply never thought of it. Space flight had been a natural, if late, result of Western thought-patterns, which had always been ambitious for the infinite, but the geometrically flat dialectic of the succeeding culture could not include it. Where the West had soared from the rock like a sequoia, the Soviets spread like lichens, tightening their grip, satisfied to be at the very bases of the pillars of sunlight the West had sought to ascend.

The coming of the spindizzy—the antigravity generator, or gravitron—spelled the doom of the flat culture, as the leveling menace of the nuclear reactor had cut down the soaring West. Space flight returned; not, this time, as a technique of tiny ships and individual adventure, but as a project of cities.

There was no longer any reason why a man-carrying vehicle to cross space needed to be small, cramped, organized fore-and-aft, penurious of weight. The spindizzy could lift anything, and protect it, too. Most important, its operation was rooted in a variation of the value of *c* as a limit. The overdrive, the meteor screen, and antigravity had all arrived in one compact package, labeled "$G = (2PC)^2/(BU)^2$."

Every culture has its characteristic mathematic, in which historiographers can see its inevitable form. This one, couched in the algebra of the Magian culture, pointing toward the matrix-mechanics of the new Nomad era, was a Western discovery. Blackett had found the essential relationship between gravity and magnetism, and Dirac had explained why it had not been detected before. Yet despite all of the minority groups butchered or "concentrated" by the Bureaucratic State, only the pure mathematicians went unsuspected about the destruction of that State, innocent even in their own minds of revolutionary motives.

The exodus began.

At first it was logical enough. The Aluminum Trust, the Thorium Trust, the Germanium Trust put their plants aloft bodily, to mine the planets. The Steel Trust made it possible for the rest, for it had turned Mars into the Pittsburgh of the solar system, and lulled the doubts of the State.

But the Thorium Trust's Plant No. 8 never came back. The revolution against the planar culture began as simply as that.

The first of the Okie cities soared away from the solar system, looking for work among the colonists—colonists left stranded among the stars by the ebb tide of Western civilization. The new culture began among these nomad cities, and before long Earth was virtually deserted.

But Earth laws, though much changed, survived. It was still possible to make a battleship, and the Okies were ungainly. Steam shovels, by and large, had been more characteristic of the West than tanks had been, but in a fight between the two the outcome was predictable; that situation never changed. The cities were the citizens—but there were still police.

AND in the Rift, where there were no police, a city was burning. It was all over in a few minutes. The city bucked and toppled in a maelstrom of lightning. Feeble flickers of resistance spat around its edges—and then it no longer had any edges. Sections of it broke off, and melted like wraiths. From its ardent center, a few hopeless life ships shot out into the gap; whatever was causing the destruction let them go. No conceivable life ship could live long enough to cross the Rift.

Amalfi cut in the audio circuit, filling the control room with a howl of static. Far behind the wild blasts of sound, a tiny voice was shouting desperately:

"Rebroadcast if anyone hears us. Repeat: we have the fuelless drive. We're destroying our model and evacuating our passenger. Pick him up if you can. We're being blown up by a bindlestiff. Rebroadcast if—"

Then there was nothing left but the skeleton of the city, glowing whitely, evaporating in the blackness. The pale, innocent light of the guide-beam for a Bethe blaster played over it, but it was still impossible to see who was wielding the weapon. The Dinwiddie circuits in the proxy were compensating for the glare, so that nothing was coming through to the screen that did not shine with its own light.

The terrible fire died slowly, and the stars brightened. As the last spark flared and went out, a shadow loomed against the distant starwall. Hazleton drew his breath in sharply.

"*Another* city! So some outfits really do go bindlestiff. And we thought we were the first out here!"

Amalfi nodded, feeling a little sick. That one city should destroy another was bad enough. But it was even more of a wrench to realize that the whole scene was virtually ancient history. Ultrawave transmission was faster than light, but by no means instantaneous; the dark city had destroyed its smaller counterpart nearly two years ago, and must now be beyond pursuit. It was even beyond identification, for no orders could be sent now to the proxy which would result in any action until another two years had passed.

"You'd think some heavy thinker on Earth would've figured out a way to make Diracs compact enough to be mounted in a proxy," he grumbled. "They haven't got anything better to do back there."

Hazleton had no difficulty in penetrating to the speech's real meaning. He said, "Maybe we can still smoke 'em out, boss."

"Not a chance. We can't afford a side jaunt."

"Well, I'll send out a general warning on the Dirac," Hazleton said. "It's barely possible that the cops will be able to invest the Rift before the 'stiff gets out."

"That'll trap *us* neatly, won't it? Besides, that bindlestiff isn't going to leave the Rift."

"Eh? How do you know?"

"Did you hear what the SOS said about a fuelless drive?"

"Sure," Hazleton said uneasily, "but the guy who knows how to build it must be dead by now, even if he escaped the burning."

"We can't be sure of that—and that's the one thing that the 'stiff has to make sure of. If they get ahold of it, 'stiffs won't be a rarity any more. There'll be widespread piracy throughout the galaxy!"

"That's a big statement, Amalfi."

"Think, Mark. Pirates died out a thousand years ago on Earth when sailing ships were replaced by fueled ships. The fueled ships were faster—but couldn't themselves become pirates, because they had to touch civilized ports regularly to coal up. We're in the same state. But if that bindlestiff can actually get its hands on a fuelless drive—"

Hazleton stood up, kneading his hands uneasily. "I see what you mean. Well, there's only one place where a life ship could go out here, and that's the wild star. So the 'stiff is probably there, too, by now." He looked thoughtfully at the screen, now glittering once more only with anonymous stars. "Shall I send out the warning or not?"

"Yes, send it out. It's the law. But I think it's up to us to deal with the 'stiff; we're familiar with ways of manipulating strange cultures, whereas the cops would just smash things up if they did manage to get here in time."

"Check. Our course as before, then."

"Necessarily."

Still the city manager did not go. "Boss," he said at last, "that outfit is heavily armed. They could muscle in on us with no trouble."

"Mark, I'd call you yellow if I didn't know you were just lazy," Amalfi growled. He stopped suddenly and peered up the length of Hazleton's figure to his long, horselike face. "Or are you leading up to something?"

Hazleton grinned like a small boy caught stealing jam.

"Well, I did have something in mind. I don't like 'stiffs, especially killers. Are you willing to entertain a small scheme?"

"Ah," Amalfi said, relaxing. "That's better. Let's hear it."

II.

THE wild star, hurling itself through the Rift on a course that would not bring it to the far wall for another ten thousand Earth years, carried with it six planets, of which only one was even remotely Earthlike. That planet shone deep, chlorophyll green on the screens long before it had grown enough to assume a recognizable disk shape. The proxies called in now, arrived one by one, circling the new world like a swarm of ten-meter footballs, eying it avidly.

It was everywhere the same: savagely tropical, in the throes of a geological period roughly comparable to Earth's Carboniferous era. Plainly, the only planet would be nothing but a way station; there would be no work for pay there.

Then the proxies began to pick up weak radio signals.

Nothing, of course, could be made of the language; Amalfi turned that problem over to the City Fathers at once. Nevertheless, he continued to listen to the strange gabble while he warped the city into an orbit. The voices sounded ritualistic, somehow.

The City Fathers said: "THIS LANGUAGE IS A VARIANT OF PATTERN G, BUT THE SITUATION IS AMBIGUOUS. GENERALLY WE WOULD SAY THAT THE RACE WHICH SPEAKS IT IS INDIGENOUS TO THE PLANET, A RARE CASE BUT BY NO MEANS UNHEARD OF. HOWEVER, THERE ARE TRACES OF FORMS WHICH MIGHT BE DEGENERATES OF ENGLISH, AS WELL AS STRONG EVIDENCES OF DIALECT MIXTURES SUGGESTING A TRIBAL SOCIETY. THIS LATTER FACT IS NOT CONSONANT WITH THE POSSESSION OF RADIO NOR WITH THE UNDERLYING SAMENESS OF THE PATTERN. UNDER THE CIRCUMSTANCES WE MUST POSITIVELY FORBID ANY MACHINATIONS BY MR. HAZLETON ON THIS VENTURE."

"I didn't ask them for advice," Amalfi said. "And what good is a lesson in etymology at this point? Still, Mark, watch your step—"

"'Remember Thor V,'" Hazleton said, mimicking the mayor's father-bear voice to perfection. "All right. Do we land?"

For answer, Amalfi grasped the space stick, and the city began to settle. Amalfi was a true child of space, a man with an intuitive understanding of the forces and relationships which were involved in astronautics; in delicate situations he invariably preferred to dispense with instruments. Sensitively he sidled the city downward, guiding himself mainly by the increasingly loud chanting in his earphones.

At four thousand meters there was a brief glitter from amid the dark-green waves of the treetops. The proxies converged upon it slowly, and on the screens a turreted roof showed; then two, four, a dozen. There was a city there—a homebody, grown from the earth. Closer views showed it to be walled, the wall standing just inside a clear ring where nothing grew; the greenery between the towers was camouflage.

At three thousand, a flight of small ships burst from the city like frightened birds, trailing feathers of flame. "Gunners!" Hazleton snapped into his mike. "Posts!"

Amalfi shook his head, and continued to bring his city closer to the ground. The fire-tailed birds wheeled around them, dipping and flashing, weaving a pattern in smoky plumes; yet an Earthman would have thought, not of birds, but of the nuptial flight of drone bees.

Amalfi, who had never seen a bird or a bee, nevertheless sensed the ceremony in the darting cortege. With fitting solemnity he brought the city to a stop beside its jungle counterpart, hovering just above the tops of the giant cycads. Then, instead of clearing a landing area with the usual quick scythe of the mesotron rifles, he polarized the spindizzy screen.

The base and apex of the Okie city grew dim. What happened to the giant ferns and horsetails directly beneath it could not be seen—they were flattened into synthetic fossils in the muck in a split second—but those just beyond the rim of the city were stripped of their fronds and splintered, and farther out, in a vast circle, the whole forest bowed low away from the city to a clap of sunlit thunder.

Unfortunately, the Twenty-third Street spindizzy, always the weakest link, blew out at the last minute and the city dropped the last five meters in free fall. It arrived on the surface of the planet rather more cataclysmically than Amalfi had intended. Hazleton hung on to his bucket seat until City Hall had stopped swaying, and then wiped blood from his nose with a judicious handkerchief.

"That," he said, "was one dramatic touch too many. I'd best go have that spindizzy fixed again, just in case."

Amalfi shut off the controls with a contented gesture. "If that bindlestiff should show," he said, "they'll have a tough time amassing any prestige *here* for a while. But go ahead, Mark, it'll keep you busy."

THE mayor eased his barrel-shaped bulk into the lift shaft and let himself be slithered through the friction fields to the street. Outside, the worn facade of City Hall shone with sunlight, and the City's motto—MOW YOUR LAWN, LADY? —was clear even under its encrustation of verdigris. Amalfi was glad that the legend could not be read by the local folk—it would have spoiled the effect.

Suddenly he was aware that the chanting he had been hearing for so long through the earphones was thrilling through the air around him. Here and there, the sober, utilitarian faces of the Okie citizens were turning to look down the street, and traces of wonder, mixed with amusement and an unaccountable sadness, were in those faces. Amalfi turned.

A procession of children was coming toward him: children wound in mummylike swatches of cloth down to their hips, the strips alternately red and white. Several free-swinging panels of many-colored fabric, as heavy as silk, swirled about their legs as they moved.

Each step was followed by a low bend, hands outstretched and fluttering, heads rolling from shoulder to shoulder, feet moving in and out, toe-heel-toe, the whole body turning and turning again. Bracelets of objects like dried pods rattled at wrists and bare ankles. Over it all the voices chanted like water flutes.

Amalfi's first wild reaction was to wonder why the City Fathers had been puzzled about the language. *These were human children.* Nothing about them showed any trace of alienage.

Behind them, tall black-haired men moved in less agile procession, sounding in chorus a single word which boomed through the skirl and pitter of the children's dance at wide-spaced intervals. The men were human, too; their hands, stretched immovably out before them, palms up, had five fingers, with fingernails on them; their beards had the same topography as human beards; their chests, bared to the sun by a symbolical rent which was torn at the same place in each garment, and marked identically by a symbolical wound rubbed on with red chalk, showed ribs where ribs ought to be, and the telltale tracings of clavicles beneath the skin.

About the women there might have been some doubt. They came at the end of the procession, all together in a huge cage drawn by lizards. They were all naked and filthy and sick, and could have been any kind of animal. They made no sound, but only stared out of purulent eyes, as indifferent to the Okie city and its owners as to their captors. Occasionally they scratched, reluctantly, wincing from their own claws.

The children deployed around Amalfi, evidently picking him out as the leader because he was the biggest. He had expected as much; it was but one more confirmation of their humanity. He stood still while they made a circle and sat down, still chanting and shaking their wrists. The men, too, made a circle, keeping their faces toward Amalfi, their hands outstretched. At last that reeking cage was drawn into the double ring, virtually to Amalfi's feet. Two male attendants unhitched the docile lizards and led them away.

Abruptly the chanting stopped. The tallest and most impressive of the men came forward and bent, making that strange gesture with fluttering hands over the street. Before Amalfi quite realized what was intended, the stranger had straightened, placed some heavy object in his hand, and retreated, calling aloud the single word the men had been intoning before. Men and children responded together in one terrific shout, and then there was silence.

Amalfi was alone in the middle of the circle, with the cage. He looked down at the thing in his hand.

It was—a key.

MIRAMON shifted nervously in the chair, the great black sawtoothed feather stuck in his topknot bobbing uncertainly. It was a testimony of his confidence in Amalfi that he sat in it at all, for in the beginning he had squatted, as was customary on his planet. Chairs were the uncomfortable prerogatives of the gods.

"I myself do not believe in the gods," he explained to Amalfi, bobbing the feather. "It would be plain to a technician, you understand, that your city was simply a product of a technology superior to ours, and you yourselves to be men such as we are. But on this planet religion has a terrible force, a very immediate force. It is not expedient to run counter to public sentiment in such matters."

Amalfi nodded. "From what you tell me, I can believe that. Your situation is unique. What, precisely, happened 'way back then?"

Miramon shrugged. "We do not know," he said. "It was nearly eight thousand years ago. There was a high civilization here then—the priests and the scientists agree on that. And the climate was different; it got cold regularly every year, I am told, although how men could survive such a thing is difficult to understand. Besides, there were many more stars—the ancient drawings show *thousands* of them, though they fail to agree on the details."

"Naturally. You're not aware that your sun is moving at a terrific rate?"

"Moving?" Miramon laughed shortly. "Some of our more mystical scientists have that opinion—they maintain that if the planets move, so must the sun. It is an imperfect analogy, in my opinion. Would we still be in this trough of nothingness if we were moving?"

"Yes, you would—you are. You underestimate the size of the Rift. It's impossible to detect any parallax at this distance, though in a few thousand years you'll begin to suspect it. But while you were actually among the stars, your ancestors could see it very well, by the changing positions of the neighboring suns."

Miramon looked dubious. "I bow to your superior knowledge, of course. But, be that as it may—the legends have it that for some sin of our people, the gods plunged us into this starless desert, and changed our climate to perpetual heat. This is why our priests say that we are in Hell, and that to be put back among the cool stars again, we must redeem our sins. We have no Heaven as you have defined the term—when we die, we die damned; we must win 'salvation' right here in the mud. The doctrine has its attractive features, under the circumstances."

Amalfi meditated. It was reasonably clear, now, what had happened, but he despaired of explaining it to Miramon—hard common sense sometimes has a way of being impenetrable. This planet's axis had a pronounced tilt, and the concomitant amount of libration. That meant that, like Earth, it had a Draysonian cycle: every so often, the top wabbled, and then resumed spinning at a new angle. The result, of course, was a disastrous climatic change. Such a thing happened on Earth roughly once every twenty-five thousand years, and the first one in recorded history had given birth to some extraordinary silly legends and faiths—sillier than those the Hevians entertained, on the whole.

Still, it was miserable bad luck for them that a Draysonian overturn had occurred almost at the same time that the planet had begun its journey across the Rift. It had thrown a very high culture, a culture entering its ripest phase, back forcibly into the Interdestructional phase without the slightest transition.

The planet of He was a strange mixture now. Politically the regression had stopped just before barbarism—a measure of the lofty summits this race had scaled at the time of the catastrophe—and was now in reverse, clawing through the stage of warring city-states. Yet the basics of the scientific techniques of eight thousand years ago had not been forgotten; now they were exfoliating, bearing "new" fruits.

Properly, city-states should fight each other with swords, not with missile weapons, chemical explosives, and supersonics—and flying should be still in the dream stage, a dream of flapping wings at that; not already a jet-propelled fact. Astronomical and geological accident had mixed history up for fair.

"WHAT would have happened to me if I'd unlocked that cage?" Amalfi demanded suddenly.

Miramon looked sick. "Probably you would have been killed —or they would have tried to kill you, anyhow," he said, with considerable reluctance. "That would have been releasing Evil again upon us. The priests say that it was women who brought about the sins of the Great Age. In the bandit cities, to be sure, that savage creed is no longer maintained—which is one reason why we have so many deserters to the bandit cities. You can have no idea of what it is like to do your duty to the race each year as our law requires. Madness!"

He sounded very bitter. "This is why it is hard to make our people see how suicidal the bandit cities are. Everyone on this world is weary of fighting the jungle, sick of trying to rebuild the Great Age with handfuls of mud, of maintaining social codes which ignore the presence of the jungle—but most of all, of serving in the Temple of the Future. In the bandit cities the women are clean, and do not scratch one."

"The bandit cities don't fight the jungle?" Amalfi asked.

"No. They prey on those who do. They have given up the religion entirely—the first act of a city which revolts is to slay its priests. Unfortunately, the priesthood is essential; and our beast-women must be borne, since we cannot modify one tenet without casting doubt upon all—or so they tell us. It is only the priesthood which keeps us fighting, only the priesthood which teaches us that it is better to be men than mud-puppies. So we —the technicians—follow the rituals with great strictness, stupid though some of them are, and consider it a matter of no moment that we ourselves do not believe in the gods."

"Sense in that," Amalfi admitted. Miramon, in all conscience, was a shrewd apple. If he was representative of as large a section of Hevian thought as he believed himself to be, much might yet be done on this wild and untamed world.

"It amazes me that you knew to accept the key as a trust," Miramon said. "It was precisely the proper move—but how could you have guessed that?"

Amalfi grinned. "That wasn't hard. I know how a man looks when he's dropping a hot potato. Your priest made all the gestures of a man passing on a sacred trust, but he could hardly wait until he'd got it over with. Incidentally, some of those women are quite presentable now that Dee's bathed 'em and Medical has taken off the under layers. Don't look so alarmed, we won't tell your priests—I gather that we're the foster fathers of He from here on out."

"You are thought to be emissaries from the Great Age," Miramon agreed gravely. "What you *actually* are, you have not said."

"True. Do you have migratory workers here? The phrase comes easily in your language; yet I can't see how—"

"Surely, surely. The singers, the soldiers, the fruit-pickers—all go from city to city, selling their services." Suddenly the Hevian got it. "Do you . . . do you imply . . . that your resources are *for sale?* For sale to *us?*"

"Exactly, Miramon."

"But how shall we pay you?" Miramon gasped. "All of what we call wealth, all that we have, could not buy a length of the cloth in your sash!"

Amalfi thought about it, wondering principally how much of the real situation Miramon could be expected to understand. It occurred to him that he had persistently underestimated the Hevian so far; it might be profitable to try the full dose—and hope that it wasn't lethal.

"IT'S this way," Amalfi said. "In the culture we belong to, a certain metal, called germanium, serves for money. You have enormous amounts of it on your planet, but it's very hard to obtain, and I'm sure you've never even detected it. One of the things we would like is your permission to mine for that metal."

Miramon's pop-eyed skepticism was comical. "Permission?" he squeaked. "Please, Mayor Amalfi—is your ethical code as foolish as ours? Why do you not mine this metal without permission and be done with it?"

"Our law enforcement agencies would not allow it. Mining your planet would make us rich—almost unbelievably rich. Our assays show, not only fabulous amounts of germanium, but also the presence of certain drugs in your jungle—drugs which are known to be anti-agapics—"

"Sir?"

"Sorry, I mean that, used properly, they cure death."

Miramon rose with great dignity.

"You are mocking me," he said. "I will return at a later date and perhaps we may talk again."

"Sit down, please," Amalfi said contritely. "I had forgotten that death is not everywhere known to be a disease. It was conquered so long ago—before space flight, as a matter of fact. But the pharmaceuticals involved have always been in very short supply, shorter and shorter as man spread throughout the galaxy. Less than a two-thousandth of one percent of our present population can get the treatment now, and an ampoule of any anti-agapic, even the most inefficient ones, can be sold for the price the seller asks. Not a one of the anti-agapics has ever been synthesized, so if we could harvest here—"

"That is enough, it is not necessary that I understand more," Miramon said. He squatted again, reflectively. "All this makes me wonder if you are not from the Great Age after all. Well—this is difficult to think about reasonably. Why would your culture object to your being rich?"

"It wouldn't, as long as we got it honestly. We shall have to show that we worked for our riches. We'll need a written agreement. A permission."

"That is clear," Miramon said. "You will get it, I am sure. I cannot grant it myself. But I can predict what the priests will ask you to do to earn it."

"What, then? This is just what I want to know. Let's have it."

"First of all, you will be asked for the secret of this . . . this cure for death. They will want to use it on themselves, and hide it from the rest of us. Wisdom, perhaps; it would make for more desertions otherwise—but I am sure they will want it."

"They can have it, but we'll see to it that the secret leaks out. The City Fathers know the therapy. What next?"

"You must wipe out the jungle."

Amalfi sat back, stunned. Wipe out the jungle! Oh, it would be easy enough to lay waste almost all of it—even to give the Hevians energy weapons to keep those wastes clear—but sooner or later, the jungle would come back. The weapons would disintegrate in the eternal moisture, the Hevians would not take proper care of them, would not be able to repair them—how would the brightest Greek have repaired a shattered X-ray tube, even if he had known how? The technology didn't exist.

No, the jungle would come back. And the cops would come to He to see whether or not the Okie city had fulfilled its contract—and would find the planet as raw as ever. Good-by to riches.

This was jungle climate. There would be jungles here until the next Draysonian catastrophe, and that was that.

"Excuse me," he said, and reached for the control helmet. "Give me the City Fathers," he said into the mouthpiece.

"SPEAK," the spokesman vodeur said after a while.

"How would you go about wiping out a jungle?"

There was a moment's silence. "SODIUM FLUOSILICATE SPRAY WOULD SERVE. IN A WET CLIMATE IT WOULD CREATE FATAL LEAF-BLISTER. ALSO THERE IS A FORGOTTEN COMPOUND, 2,4-D WHICH WOULD SERVE FOR STUBBORN SECTIONS. OF COURSE THE JUNGLE WOULD RETURN."

"That's what I meant. Any way to make the job stick?"

"NO, UNLESS THE PLANET EXHIBITS DRAYSONIANISM."

"What?"

"NO, UNLESS THE PLANET EXHIBITS DRAYSONIANISM. IN THAT CASE ITS AXIS MIGHT BE REGULARIZED. IT HAS NEVER BEEN TRIED, BUT THEORETICALLY IT IS QUITE SIMPLE; A BILL TO REGULARIZE EARTH'S AXIS WAS DEFEATED BY THREE VOTES IN THE EIGHTY-SECOND COUNCIL, OWING TO THE OPPOSITION OF THE CONSERVATION LOBBY."

"Could the city handle it?"

"NO. THE COST WOULD BE PROHIBITIVE. *MAYOR AMALFI, ARE YOU CONTEMPLATING TIPPING THIS PLANET? WE FORBID IT!* EVERY INDICATION SHOWS—"

Amalfi tore the helmet from his head and flung it across the room. Miramon jumped up in alarm.

"Hazleton!"

The city manager shot through the door as if he had been kicked through it on roller skates. "Here, boss—what's the—"

"Get down below and turn off the City Fathers—*fast,* before they catch on and do something! Quick, man—"

Hazleton was already gone. On the other side of the control room, the phones of the helmet squawked dead data in italic capitals.

Then, suddenly, they went silent.

The City Fathers had been turned off, and Amalfi was ready to move a world.

III.

THE fact that the City Fathers could not be consulted—for the first time in two centuries—made the job more difficult than it need have been, barring their conservatism. Tipping the planet, the crux of the job, was simple enough in essence; the spindizzy could handle it. But the side-effects of the medicine might easily prove to be worse than the disease.

The problem was seismological. Rapidly whirling objects have a way of being stubborn about changing their positions. If that energy were overcome, it would have to appear somewhere else—the most likely place being multiple earthquakes.

Too, very little could be anticipated about the gravitics of the task. The planet's revolution produced, as usual, a sizable magnetic field. Amalfi did not know how well that field would take to being tipped with relation to the space-lattice which it distorted, nor just what would happen when the spindizzies polarized the whole gravity field. During "moving day" the planet would be, in effect, without magnetic moment of its own, and since the Calculator was one of the City Fathers, there was no way of finding out where the energy would reappear, in what form, or in what intensity.

He broached the latter question to Hazleton. "If we were dealing with an ordinary case, I'd say it would show up as velocity," he pointed out. "In which case we'd be in for an involuntary junket. But this is no ordinary case. The mass involved is . . . well, it's planetary, that's all. What do you think, Mark?"

"I don't know what to think," Hazleton admitted. "When we move the city, we change the magnetic moment of its component atoms; but the city itself doesn't revolve, and doesn't have a *gross* magnetic moment. Still—we could control velocity; suppose the energy reappears as heat, instead? There'd be nothing left but a cloud of gas."

Amalfi shook his head. "That's a bogey. The gyroscopic resistance may show up as heat, sure, but not the magnetogravitic. I think we'd be safe to expect it to appear as velocity, just as in ordinary spindizzy operation. Figure the conversation equivalency and tell me what you get."

Hazleton bent over his slide rule, the sweat standing out

along his forehead and above his mustache in great heavy droplets. Amalfi could understand the eagerness of the Hevians to get rid of the jungle and its eternal humidity—his own clothing had been sopping ever since the city had landed here.

"Well," the city manager said finally, "unless I've made a mistake somewhere, the whole kit and kaboodle will go shooting away from here at about half the speed of light. That's not too bad—less than cruising speed for us. We could always loop around and bring it back into its orbit."

"Ah, but could we? Remember, we don't control it! It appears automatically when we turn on the spindizzies. We don't even know in which direction we're going to move."

"Yes we do," Hazleton objected. "Along the axis of spin, of course."

"Cant? And torque?"

"No problem—yet there is. I keep forgetting we're dealing with a planet instead of electrons." He applied the slipstick again. "No soap. Can't be answered without the Calculator and he's turned off. But if we can figure a way to control the flight, it won't matter in the end. There'll be perturbations of the other planets when this one goes massless, whether it moves or not, but nobody lives there anyhow."

"All right, go figure a control system. I've got to get the Geology men to—"

The door slid back suddenly, and Amalfi looked over his shoulder. It was Anderson, the perimeter sergeant. The man was usually blasé in the face of all possible wonders, unless they threatened the city. "What's the matter?" Amalfi said, alarmed.

"Sir, we've gotten an ultrawave from some outfit claiming to be refugees from another Okie—claim they hit a bindlestiff. They've crashlanded on this planet up north and they're being mobbed by one of the local bandit towns. They were holding 'em off and yelling for help, and then they stopped transmitting."

Amalfi heaved himself to his feet. "Did you get a bearing?" he demanded.

"Yes, sir."

"Give me the figures. Come on, Mark. We need those boys."

THEY grabbed a cab to the edge of the city, and went the rest of the way on foot, across the supersonics-cleared strip of bare turf which surrounded the Hevian town. The turf felt rubbery; Amalfi suspected that some rudimentary form of friction-field was keeping the mud in a state of stiff gel. He had visions of foot-soldiers sinking suddenly into liquid ooze as defenders turned off the fields, and quickened his pace.

Inside the gates, the guards summoned a queer, malodorous vehicle which seemed to be powered by the combustion of hydrocarbons, and they were shot through the streets toward Miramon. Throughout the journey, Amalfi clung to a cloth strap in an access of nervousness. He had never traveled right *on* the surface at any speed before, and the way things zipped past him made him jumpy.

"Is this bird out to smash us up?" Hazleton demanded petulantly. "He must be doing all of four hundred kilos an hour."

"I'm glad you feel the same way," Amalfi said, relaxing a little. "Actually I'll bet he's doing less than two hundred. It's just the way the—"

The driver, who had been holding his car down to a conservative fifty out of deference to the strangers, wrenched the machine around a corner and halted neatly before Miramon's door. Amalfi got out, his knees wobbly. Hazleton's face was a delicate puce.

"I'm going to figure a way to make our cabs operate outside the city," he muttered. "Every time we make a new planet-fall, we have to ride in ox carts, on the backs of bull kangaroos, in hot-air balloons, steam-driven airscrews, things that drag you feet first and face down through tunnels, or whatever else the natives think is classy transportation. My stomach won't stand much more."

Amalfi grinned and raised his hand to Miramon, whose expression suggested laughter smothered with great difficulty.

"What brings you here?" the Hevian said. "Come in. I have no chairs, but—"

"No time," Amalfi said. He explained the situation quickly. "We've got to get those men out of there, if they're still alive. This bindlestiff is a bandit city, like the ones you have here, but it has all the stuff we have and more besides. It's vital to find out what these survivors know about it. Can you locate the town that's holding them? We have a fix on it."

Miramon went back into his house—actually, like all the other living quarters in the town, it was a dormitory housing twenty-five men of the same trade or profession—and returned with a map. The map-making conventions of He were anything but self-explanatory, but after a while Hazleton figured out the symbolism involved. "That's your city, and here's ours," he said, pointing. "Right? And this peeled orange is a butterfly grid. I've always claimed that was a lot more faithful to spherical territory than our parabolic projection, boss."

"Easier still to express what you want to remember as a topological relation," Amalfi grunted. "Show Miramon where the signals came from."

"Up here, on this wing of the butterfly."

Miramon frowned. "That can only be Fabr-Suithe. A very bad place to approach, even in the military sense. However, we shall have to try. Do you know what the end result will be?"

"No; what?"

"The bandit cities will come out in force to hinder the Great Work. They do not fear you now—they fear nothing, we think they take drugs—but they have seen no reason to risk probable huge losses by attacking you. When *you* attack one of them, they will have that reason; they learn hatred very quickly."

Amalfi shrugged. "We'll chance it. We'll pick our own town up and go calling; if they don't want to deliver up these Okies—"

"Boss—"

"Eh?"

"How are you going to get us off the ground?"

Amalfi could feel his ears turning red, and swore. "I forgot that Twenty-third Street machine. And we can't get anything suitable into a Hevian rocket—a pile would fit easily enough, but a frictionator or a dismounted spindizzy wouldn't, and there'd be no point in taking popguns—Maybe we could gas them."

"Excuse me," Miramon said, "but it is not certain that the priests will authorize the use of the rockets. We had best drive over to the temple directly and ask."

"Belsen and bebop!" Amalfi said. It was the oldest oath in his repertoire.

TALK, even with electrical aid, was impossible in the rocket. The whole machine roared like a gigantic tam-tam to the vibration of the jets. Morosely Amalfi watched Hazleton connecting the mechanism in the nose with the power-leads from the pile—no mean balancing feat, considering the way the rocket pitched in its passage through the tortured Hevian air currents. The reactor itself had not been filled all the way, since its total capacity could not have been used, and the heavy water sloshed and foamed in the transparent cube.

There had been no difficulty with the priests about the little rocket task force itself. To the end of his life Amalfi was sure that the straightfaced Miramon had invented the need for religious permission, just to get the two Okies back into the ground car again. Still, the discomforts of that ride were small compared to this one.

The pilot shifted his feet on the treadles and the deck pitched. Metal rushed back under Amalfi's nose, and he found himself looking through misty air at a crazily canted jungle. Something long, thin, and angry flashed over it and was gone. At the same instant there was a piercing inhuman shriek, sharp enough to dwarf for a long instant the song of the rocket.

Then there were more of the same: *ptsouiiirrr! ptsouiiirrr! ptsouiiirrr!* The machine jerked to each one and now and then shook itself violently, twisting and careening across the jungle-top. Amalfi had never felt so helpless before in his life. He did not even know what the noise was; he could only be sure that it was ill-tempered. The coarse *blaam* of high explosive, when it began, was recognizable—the city had often had occasion to blast on jobs—but nothing in his experience went *kerchowkerchowkerchowkerchowkerchow* like a demented vibratory drill, and the invisible thing that screamed its own pep-yell as it flew—*eeeeeeeeyowKRCHKackackarackarackaracka*—seemed wholly impossible.

He was astonished to discover that the hull around him was stippled with small holes, real holes with the slipstream fluting over them. It took him what seemed to be three weeks to realize that the whooping and cheer-leading which meant nothing to him was riddling the ship and threatening to kill him any second.

Someone was shaking him. He lurched to his knees, trying to unfreeze his eyeballs.

"Amalfi! Amalfi!" The voice, though it was breathing on his ear, was parsecs away. "Pick your spot, quick! They'll have us shot down in a—"

Something burst outside and threw Amalfi to the deck. Doggedly he crawled to the port and peered down through the shattered plastic. The bandit Hevian city swooped past, upside down. He was sick suddenly, and the city was lost in a web of tears. The second time it came he managed to see which building had the heaviest guard, and pointed, choking.

The rocket threw its tailfeathers over the nearest cloud and bored beak-first for the ground. Amalfi hung on to the edge of the suddenly-blank deck port, his own blood spraying back in a fine mist into his face from his cut fingers.

"Now!"

Nobody heard, but Hazleton saw his nod. A blast of pure heat blew through the upended cabin as the pile blew off the shielded nose of the rocket. Even through the top of his head, the violet-white light of that soundless concussion nearly blinded Amalfi, and he could feel the irradiation of his shoulders and chest. He would have no colds for the next two or three years, anyhow—every molecule of histamine in his blood must have been detoxified at that instant.

The rocket yawed wildly, and then came under control again. The ordnance noises had already quit, cut off at the moment of the flash.

The bandit city was blind.

The sound of the jets cut off, and Amalfi understood for the first time what an "aching void" might be. The machine fell into a steep glide, the air howling dismally outside it. Another rocket, under the guidance of one of Hazleton's assistants, dived down before it, scything a narrow runway in the jungle with a mesotron rifle—for the bandit towns kept no supersonic no-plant's-land between themselves and the rank vegetation.

The moment the rocket stopped moving, Amalfi and a handpicked squad of Okies and Hevians were out of it and slogging through the muck. From inside the bandit city drifted a myriad of screams—human screams now, screams of agony and terror, from men who thought themselves blinded for life. Amalfi had no doubt that many of them were. Certainly anyone who had had the misfortune to be looking at the sky when the pile had converted itself into photons would never see again.

But the law of chance would have protected most of the renegades, so speed was vital. The mud built up heavy pads under his shoes, and the jungle did not thin out until they hit the town's wall itself.

The gates had been rusted open years ago, and were choked with greenery. The Hevians hacked their way through it with practiced knives and cunning.

Inside, the going was still almost as thick. The city proper presented a depressing face of proliferating despair. Most of the buildings were completely enshrouded in vines, and many were halfway toward ruins. Iron-hard tendrils had thrust their way between stones, into windows, under cornices, up drains and chimney funnels. Poison-green, succulent leaves plastered themselves greedily upon every surface, and in shadowed places there were huge blood-colored fungi which smelled like a man six days dead; the sweetish taint hung heavily in the air. Even the paving blocks had sprouted—inevitably, since, whether by ignorance or laziness, most of them had been cut from green wood.

The screaming began to die into whimpers. Amalfi did his best to keep from inspecting the inhabitants. A man who believes he has just been blinded permanently is not a pretty sight, even when he is wrong. Yet it was impossible not to notice the curious mixture of soiled finery and gleamingly clean nakedness; it was as if two different periods had mixed in the city, as if a gathering of Hruntan nobles had been sprinkled with Noble Savages. Possibly the men who had given in completely to the jungle had also slid back far enough to discover the pleasures of bathing—if so, they would shortly discover the pleasures of the mud-wallow, too, and would not look so noble after that.

"Amalfi, here they are—"

The mayor's suppressed pity for the blinded men evaporated when he got a look at the imprisoned Okies. They had been systematically mauled to begin with, and after that sundry little attentions had been paid to them which combined the best features of savagery and decadence. One of them, mercifully, had been strangled by his comrades early in the "trial." Another, a basket case, should have been rescued, for he could still talk rationally, but he pleaded so persistently for death that Amalfi had him shot in a sudden fit of sentimentality. Of the other three men, all could walk and talk, but two were mad. The catatonic was carried out on a stretcher, and the manic was gagged and led gingerly away.

"How did you do it?" asked the rational man in Russian, the dead universal language of deep space. He was a human skeleton, but he radiated a terrific personal force. He had lost his tongue early in the "questioning," but had already taught himself to talk by the artifical method—the result was inhuman, but it was intelligible. "They were coming down to kill us as soon as they heard your jets. Then there was a sort of a flash, and they all started screaming—a pretty sound, let me tell you."

"I'll bet," Amalfi said. "That 'sort of a flash' was a photon explosion. It was the only way we could figure on being sure of getting you out alive. We thought of trying gas, but if they had had gas masks they would have been able to kill you anyhow."

"I haven't seen any masks, but I'm sure they have them. There are traveling volcanic gas clouds in this part of the planet, they say; they must have evolved some absorption device—charcoal is well known here. Lucky we were so far underground, or we'd be blind, too, then. You people must be engineers."

"More or less," Amalfi agreed. "Strictly, we're miners and petroleum geologists, but we've developed a lot of sidelines since we've been aloft—like any Okie. Here's our rocket—crawl in. It's rough, but it's transportation. How about you?"

"Agronomists. Our mayor thought there was a field for it out here along the periphery—teaching the abandoned colonies and the offshoots how to work poisoned soil and manage low-yield crops without heavy machinery. Our sideline was waxmans."

"What are those?" Amalfi said, adjusting the harness around the wasted body.

"Soil-source antibiotics. It was those the bindlestiff wanted—and got. The filthy swine. They can't bother to keep a reasonably sanitary city; they'd rather pirate some honest outfit for drugs when they have an epidemic. Oh, and they wanted germanium, too, of course. They blew us up when they found we didn't have any—we'd converted to a barter economy as soon as we got out of the last commerce lanes."

"What about your passenger?" Amalfi said with studied nonchalance.

"Dr. Beetle? Not that that was his name, I couldn't pronounce *that* even when I had my tongue. I don't imagine he survived; we had to keep him in a tank even in the city, and I can't quite see him living through a life-ship journey. He was a Myrdian, smart cookies all of them, too. That no-fuel drive of his—"

Outside, a shot cracked, and Amalfi winced. "We'd best get off—they're getting their eyesight back. Talk to you later. Hazleton, any incidents?"

"Nothing to speak of, boss. Everybody stowed?"

"Yep. Kick off."

There was a volley of shots, and then the rocket coughed, roared, and stood on its tail. Amalfi pulled a deep sigh loose from the acceleration and turned his head toward the rational man.

He was still securely strapped in, and looked quite relaxed. A brassnosed slug had come through the side of the ship next to him and had neatly removed the top of his skull.

IV.

WORKING information out of the madmen was a painfully long, anxious process. The manic was a three-hundred-fifty-hour case, and even after he had been returned to a semblance of rationality he could contribute very little.

The life ship had not come to He because of the city's Dirac warning, he said. The life ship and the burned Okie had not had any Dirac equipment. The life ship had come to He, as Amalfi had predicted, because it was the only possible planetfall in the desert of the Rift. Even so, the refugees had had to use deep-sleep and strict starvation rationing to make it.

"Did you see the 'stiff again?"

"No, sir. If they heard your Dirac warning, they probably figured the police had spotted them and scrammed—or maybe they thought there was a military base or an advanced culture here on the planet."

"You're guessing," Amalfi said gruffly. "What happened to Dr. Beetle?"

The man looked startled. "The Myrdian in the tank? He got blown up with the city, I guess."

"He wasn't put off in another life ship?"

"Doesn't seem very likely. But I was only a pilot. Could be that they took him out in the mayor's gig for some reason."

"You don't know anything about his no-fuel drive?"

"First I heard of it."

Amalfi was far from satisfied; he suspected that there was still a short circuit somewhere in the man's memory. The city's auditors insisted that he had been cleared, however, and Amalfi had to accept the verdict. All that remained to be done was to get some assessment of the weapons available to the bindlestiff; on this subject the manic was ignorant, but the city's analyst said cautiously that something might be extracted from the catatonic within a month or two.

Amalfi accepted the figure, since it was the best he had. With Moving Day so close, he couldn't afford to worry overtime about another problem. He had already decided that the simplest answer to vulcanism, which otherwise would be inevitable when the planet's geophysical balance was changed, was to reinforce the crust. All over the surface of He, drilling teams were sinking long, thin, slanting shafts, reaching toward the stress-fluid of the world's core. The shafts interlocked intricately, and thus far only one volcano had been created by the drilling—in general the lava-pockets which had been tapped had already been anticipated and the flow had been bled off into half a hundred intersecting channels without ever reaching the surface. After the molten rock had hardened, the clogged channels were drilled again, with mesotron rifles set to the smallest possible dispersion.

None of the shafts had yet tapped the stress fluid; the plan was to complete them all simultaneously. At that point, specific areas, riddled with channel-intersections, would give way, and immense plugs would be forced up toward the crust, plugs of iron, connected by ferrous cantilevers through the channels between. The planet of He would wear a cruel corset, permitting not the slightest flexure—it would be stitched with threads of steel, steel that had held even granite in solution for millennia.

The heat problem was tougher, and Amalfi was not sure whether or not he had hit upon the solution. The very fact of structural resistance would create high temperatures, and any general formation of shearplanes would cut the imbedded girders at once. The method being prepared to cope with that was rather drastic, and its after-effects unknown.

On the whole, however, the plans were simple, and putting them into effect had seemed heavy but relatively simple labor. Some opposition, of course, had been expected from the local bandit towns.

But Amalfi had not expected to lose nearly twenty percent of his crews during the first month.

It was Miramon who brought in the news of the latest camp found slaughtered. Amalfi was sitting under a tree fern on high ground overlooking the city, watching a flight of giant dragonflies and thinking about heat-transfer in rock.

"You are sure they were adequately protected?" Miramon asked cautiously. "Some of our insects—"

Amalfi thought the insects, and the jungle, almost disturbingly beautiful. The thought of destroying it all occasionally upset him. "Yes, they were," he said shortly. "We sprayed out the camp areas with dicoumarins and fluorine-substituted residuals. Besides—do any of your insects use explosives?"

"Explosives! There was dynamite used? I saw no evidence—"

"No. That's what bothers me. I don't like all those felled trees you describe. We used to use TDX to get a cutting blast; it has a property of exploding in a flat plane."

Miramon goggled. "Impossible. An explosion has to expand evenly in the open."

"Not if it's a piperazo-hexybitrate built from polarized carbon atoms. Such atoms can't move in any direction but at right angles to the gravity radius. That's what I mean. You people are up to dynamite, but not to TDX."

He paused, frowning. "Of course some of our losses have just been by bandit raids, with arrows and crude bombs—your friends from Fabr-Suithe and their allies. But these camps where there was an explosion and no crater to show for it—"

He fell silent. There was no point in mentioning the gassed corpses. It was hard even to think about them. Somebody on this planet had a gas which was a regurgitant, a sternutatory and a vesicant all in one. The men had been forced out of their masks—which had been designed solely to protect them from volcanic gases—to vomit, had taken the stuff into their lungs by convulsive sneezing, and had blistered into great sacs of serum inside and out. That, obviously, had been the multiple-benzene ring Hawkesite; very popular in the days of the Hruntan Empire, when it had been called "polybathroom-floorine" for no discoverable reason. But what was it doing on He?

There was only one possible answer, and for a reason which he did not try to understand, it made Amalfi breathe a little easier. All around him, the jungle sighed and swayed, and humming clouds of gnats made rainbows over the dew-laden pinnae of the fern. The jungle, almost always murmurously quiet, had never seemed like a real enemy; now Amalfi knew that that intuition had been right. The real enemy had declared itself, stealthily, but with a stealth which was naïveté itself in comparison with the ancient guile of the jungle.

"Miramon," Amalfi said tranquilly, "we're in a spot. That city I told you about—the bindlestiff—is already here. It must have landed before we arrived, long enough ago to hide itself thoroughly. Probably it came down at night in some taboo area. The men in it have leagued themselves with Fabr-Suithe, anyhow, that much is obvious."

A moth with a two-meter wingspread blundered across the clearing, piloted by a gray-brown nematode which had sunk its sucker above the ganglion between the glittering creature's pinions. Amalfi was in a mood to read parables into things, and the parasitism reminded him anew of how greatly he had underestimated the enemy. The bindlestiff evidently knew, and was skillful at, the secret of manipulating a new culture; a shrewd Okie never attempts to overwhelm a civilization, but instead pilots it, as indetectably as possible, doing no apparent harm, adding no apparent burden, but turning history deftly and tyrannically aside at the crucial instant—

Amalfi snapped the belt switch of his ultraphone. "Hazleton?"

"Here, boss." Behind the city manager's voice was the indistinct rumble of heavy mining. "What's up?"

"Nothing yet. Are you having any trouble out there?"

"No. We're not expecting any, either, with all this artillery."

"Famous last words," Amalfi said. "The 'stiff's here, Mark."

There was a short silence. In the background, Amalfi could hear the shouts of Hazleton's crew. When the city manager's voice came in again, it was moving from word to word very carefully, as if it expected each one to break under its weight. "You imply that the 'stiff was already on He when our Dirac broadcast went out. Right? I'm not sure these losses of ours can't be explained some other way, boss; the theory . . . uh . . . lacks elegance."

Amalfi grinned tightly. "A heuristic criticism," he said. "Go to the foot of the class, Mark, and think it over. Thus far they've out-thought us six ways for Sunday. We may be able to put your old plan into effect yet, but if it's to work, we'll have to provoke open conflict."

"How?"

"Everybody here knows that there's going to be a drastic change when we finish what we're doing, but we're the only ones who know exactly what we're going to do. The 'stiffs will have to stop us, whether they've got Dr. Beetle or not. So I'm forcing their hand. Moving Day is hereby advanced by one thousand hours."

"What! I'm sorry, boss, but that's flatly impossible."

Amalfi felt a rare spasm of anger. "That's as may be," he growled. "Nevertheless, spread it around; let the Hevians hear it. And just to prove that I'm not kidding, Mark, I'm turning the City Fathers back on at that time. If you're not ready to spin by then, you may well swing instead."

The click of the belt-switch to the "Off" position was unsatisfying. Amalfi would much have preferred to conclude the interview with something really final—a clash of cymbals, for instance. He swung suddenly on Miramon.

"What are you goggling at?"

The Hevian shut his mouth, flushing. "Your pardon. I was hoping to understand your instructions to your assistant, in the hope of being of some use. But you spoke in such incomprehensible terms that it sounded like a theological dispute. As for me, I never argue about politics or religion." He turned on his heel and stamped off through the trees.

Amalfi watched him go, cooling off gradually. This would never do. He must be getting to be an old man. All during the conversation he had felt his temper getting the better of his judgment, yet he had felt sodden and inert, unwilling to make the effort of opposing the momentum of his anger. At this rate, the City Fathers would soon depose him and appoint some stable character to the mayoralty—not Hazleton, certainly, but some unpoetic youngster who would play everything by empirics. Amalfi was in no position to be threatening anyone else with liquidation, even as a joke.

He walked toward the grounded city, heavy with sunlight, sunk in reflection. He was now about a thousand years old, give or take fifty; strong as an ox, mentally alert and "clear," in good hormone balance, all twenty-eight senses sharp, his own special psi faculty—orientation—still as infallible as ever, and all in all as sane as a compulsively peripatetic star man could be. The anti-agapics would keep him in this shape indefinitely, as far as anyone knew—but the problem of *patience* had never been solved.

The older a man became, the more quickly he saw answers to tough questions; and the less likely he was to tolerate slow thinking among his associates. If he were sane, his answers were generally right answers; if he were unsane, they were not; but what mattered was the speed of the thinking itself. In the end, both the sane and the unsane became equally dictatorial.

It was funny; before death had been conquered, it had been thought that memory would turn immortality into a Greek gift, because not even the human brain could remember a practical infinity of accumulated facts. Nowadays, however, nobody bothered to remember many *things*. That was what the City Fathers and like machines were for; they stored facts. Living men memorized nothing but processes, throwing out obsolete ones for new ones as invention made it necessary. When they needed facts, they asked the machines.

In some cases, even processes were thrown out, if there were simple, indestructible machines to replace them—the slide rule, for instance. Amalfi wondered suddenly if there were a single man in the city who could multiply, divide, take square root, or figure pH in his head or on paper. The thought was so novel as to be alarming—as alarming as if an ancient astrophysicist had seriously wondered how many of his colleagues could run an abacus.

No, memory was no problem. But it was very hard to be patient after a thousand years.

The bottom of a port drifted into his field of view, plastered with brown tendrils of mud. He looked up. The port was a small one, and in a part of the perimeter of the city a good distance away from the section where he had intended to go on board. Feeling like a stranger, he went in.

Inside, the corridor rang with bloodcurdling shrieks. It was as if someone were flaying a live dinosaur, or, better, a pack of them. Underneath the awful noises there was a sound like water being expelled under high pressure, and someone was laughing madly. Alarmed, Amalfi hunched his bull shoulders and burst through the nearest door.

SURELY there had never been such a place in the city. It was a huge, steamy chamber, walled with some ceramic substance placed in regular tiles. The tiles were slimy, and stained; hence, old—very old.

Hordes of nude women ran aimlessly back and forth in it, screaming, battering at the wall, dodging wildly, or rolling on the mosaic floor. Every so often a thick stream of water caught one of them, bowling her howling away or driving her helplessly. Amalfi was soaking wet almost at once. The laughter got louder. Overhead, long banks of nozzles sprayed needles of mist into the air.

The mayor bent quickly, threw off his muddy shoes, and stalked the laughter, his toes gripping the slippery mosaic. The heavy column of water swerved toward him, then was jerked away again.

"John! Do you need a bath so badly? Come join the party!"

It was Dee Hazleton, the Utopian girl who had become the city manager's companion shortly before the crossing of the Rift had been undertaken. She was as nude as any of her victims, and was gleefully plying an enormous hose.

"Isn't this fun? We just got a new batch of these creatures. I got Mark to connect the old fire hose and I've been giving them their first wash."

It did not sound much like the old Dee, who had been full of solemn thoughts about politics—she had been a veritable commissar when Amalfi had first met her. He expressed his opinions of women who had lost their inhibitions so drastically. He went on at some length, and Dee made as if to turn the hose on him again.

"No, you don't," he growled, wresting it from her. It proved extremely hard to manage. "Where is this place, anyhow? I don't recall any such torture chamber in the plans."

"It was a public bath, Mark says. It's in the oldest part of the city, and Mark says it must have been just shut off when the city went aloft for the first time. I've been using it to sluice off these women before they're sent to Medical. The water is pumped in from the river to the west, so there's no waste involved."

"Water for bathing!" Amalfi said. "The ancients certainly were wasteful. Still I'd thought the static jet was older than that."

He surveyed the Hevian women, who were now huddling, temporarily reprieved, in the warmest part of the echoing chamber. None of them shared Dee's gently curved ripeness, but, as usual, some of them showed promise. Hazleton was prescient; it had to be granted. Of course it had been expectable that the Hevian would turn out to be human, for only eleven nonhuman civilizations had ever been discovered, and of these only the Lyrans and the Myrdians had any brains to speak of.

But to have had the Hevians turn over complete custody of their women to the Okies, without so much as a conference, at first contact—after Hazleton had proposed using any possible women as bindlestiff-bait—a proposal advanced before it had been established that there even was such a place as He—

Well, that was Hazelton's own psi-gift—not true clairvoyance, but an ability to pluck workable plans out of logically insufficient data. Time after time only the seemingly miraculous working-out of Hazleton's plans had prevented his being shot by the blindly logical City Fathers.

"Dee, come to Astronomy with me," Amalfi said with sudden energy. "I've got something to show you. And for my sake put on something, or the men will think I'm out to found a dynasty."

"All right," Dee said reluctantly. She was not yet used to the odd Okie standards of exposure, and sometimes appeared nude when it wasn't customary—a compensation, Amalfi supposed, for her Utopian upbringing, where she had been taught that nudity had a deleterious effect upon the purity of one's politics. The Hevian women moaned and hid their heads while she put on her shorts—most of them had been stoned for inadvertently covering themselves at one time or another, for in Hevian society women were not people but reminders of damnation, doubly evil for the slightest secrecy.

History, Amalfi thought, would be more instructive a teacher if it were not so stupefyingly repetitious. He led the way up the corridor, searching for a lift, Dee's wet soles padding cheerfully behind him.

In Astronomy, Jake was as usual peering wistfully at a nebula somewhere out on the marches of no-when, trying to make ellipses out of spirals without recourse to the Calculator. He looked up as Amalfi and the girl entered.

"Hello," he said, dismally. "Amalfi, I really need some help here. How can a man work without facts? If only you'd turn the City Fathers back on—"

"Shortly. How long has it been since you looked back the way we came, Jake?"

"Not since we started across the Rift. Why, should I have? The Rift is just a scratch in a saucer; you need real distance to work on basic problems."

"I know that. But let's take a look. I have an idea that we're not as alone in the Rift as we thought."

Resignedly, Jake went to his control desk and thumbed buttons. "What do you expect to find?" he demanded, his voice petulant. "A haze of iron filings, or a stray meson? Or a fleet of police cruisers?"

"Well," Amalfi said, pointing to the screen, "those aren't wine bottles."

The police cruisers, so close that the light of He's sun twinkled on their sides, shot across the screen in a brilliant stream, long tails of false photons striping the Rift behind them.

"So they aren't," Jake said, not much interested. "Now may I have my scope back, Amalfi?"

Amalfi only grinned. Cops or not cops, he felt young again.

HAZLETON was mud up to the thighs. Long ribands of it trailed behind him as he hurtled up the lift shaft to the control tower. Amalfi watched him coming, noting the set whiteness of the city manager's face as he looked up at Amalfi's bending head.

"What's this about cops?" Hazleton demanded while still in flight. "The message didn't get to me straight. We were raided, all hell's broken loose everywhere. I nearly didn't get here straight myself." He sprang into the chamber, his boots shedding gummy clods.

"I saw the fighting. Looks like the Moving Day rumor reached the 'stiffs, all right."

"Sure. What's this about cops?"

"The cops are here. They're coming in from the northwest quadrant, already off overdrive, and should be here day after tomorrow."

"Surely they're not after us," Hazleton said. "And I can't see why they should come all this distance after the 'stiffs. They must have had to use deep-sleep to make it. And we didn't say anything about the no-fuel drive in our alarm 'cast—"

"We didn't have to," Amalfi said. "Some day I must tell you the parable of the diseased bee—as soon as I figure out what a bee is. In the meantime things are breaking fast. We have to keep an eye on everything, and be able to jump in any direction no matter which item on the agenda comes up first. How bad is the fighting?"

"Very bad. At least five of the local bandit towns are in on it, including Fabr-Suithe, of course. Two of them mount heavy stuff, about contemporary with the Hruntan Empire in its heyday . . . ah, I see you know that already. Well, it's supposed to be a holy war on us. We're meddling with the jungle and interfering with their chances for salvation-through-suffering, or something—I didn't stop to dispute the point."

"That's bad; it will convince some of the civilized towns, too—I doubt that Fabr-Suithe really believes the religious line, they've thrown all that overboard, but it makes wonderful propaganda."

"You're right there. Only a few of the civilized towns, the ones that have been helping us from the beginning, are putting up a stiff fight. Almost everyone else, on both sides, is sitting it out waiting for us to cut each other's throat. Our handicap is that we lack mobility. If we could persuade all the civilized towns to come in on our side we wouldn't need it, but so many of them are scared."

"The enemy lacks mobility, too, until the bindlestiff is ready to take a direct hand," Amalfi said thoughtfully. "Have you seen any signs that the tramps are in on the fighting?"

"Not yet. But it can't be long now. And we don't even know where they are!"

"They'll be forced to locate themselves today or tomorrow, I'm certain. Right now I want you to muster all the rehabilitated women we have on hand and get ready to spring your scheme. As soon as I get a fix on the bindlestiff I'll locate the nearest participating bandit town, and you can do the rest."

Hazleton's eyes, very weary until now, began to glitter with amusement. "And how about Moving Day?" he said. "You know, of course—you know everything—that not one of your stress-fluid plugs is going to hold with the work this incomplete."

"I'm counting on it," Amalfi said tranquilly. "We'll spin when the time comes. If a few plugs spring high, wide, and tall, I won't weep."

"How—"

The Dinwiddie Watch blipped sharply, and both men turned to look at the screen. There was a fountain of green dots on it. Hazleton took three quick steps and turned on the coordinates, which he had had readjusted to the butterfly grid.

"Well, where are they?" Amalfi demanded.

"Right smack in the middle of the southwestern continent, in that vine-jungle where the little chigger-snakes nest—the ones that burrow under your fingernails. There's supposed to be a lake of boiling mud on that spot."

"There probably is—they could be under it with a medium-light screen."

"All right, we've got them placed—but what are they shooting up?"

"Mines, I suspect," Amalfi said.

"That's dandy," Hazleton said bitterly. "They'll leave an escape lane for themselves, of course, but we'll never be able to find it. They've got us under a plutonium umbrella, Amalfi."

"We'll get out. Go plant your women, Mark. And—put some clothes on 'em first. They'll make more of a show that way."

"You bet they will," the city manager said feelingly. He went out.

AMALFI went out on the balcony. At moments of crisis, his old predilection for seeing and hearing and breathing the conflict, with his senses unfiltered and unheightened by any instruments, became too strong to resist. There was good reason for the drive, for that matter; for excitement of the everyday senses had long ago been shown to bring his orientation-sense to its best pitch.

From the balcony of City Hall, most of the northwest quadrant of the perimeter was visible. There was plenty of battle noises rattling the garish tropical sunset there, and even an occasional tiny toppling figure. The city had adopted the local dodge of clearing and gelling the mud at its rim, and had returned the gel to the morass state at the first sign of attack; but the jungle men had broad skis, of some metal no Hevian could have fashioned so precisely. Disks of red fire marked bursting TDX shells, scything the air like death's own winnows. No gas was in evidence, but Amalfi knew that there would be gas before long.

The city's retaliatory fire was largely invisible, since it emerged below the top of the perimeter. There was a Bethé fender out, which would keep the wall from being scaled—until one of the projectors was knocked out; and plenty of heavy rifles were being kept hot. But the city had never been designed for warfare, and many of its most efficient destroyers had their noses buried in the earth, since their intended function was only to clear a landing area. Using an out-and-out Bethé blaster was, of course, impossible where there was an adjacent planetary mass.

He sniffed the scarlet edges of the struggle appraisingly. Under his fingers on the balcony railing were three buttons, which he had had placed there four hundred years ago. They had set in motion different things at different times. But each time, they had represented choices of action which he would have to make when the pinch came; he had never had reason to have a fourth button installed.

Rockets screamed overhead. Bombs followed, crepitating bursts of noise and smoke and flying metal. He did not look up; the very mild spindizzy screen would fend off anything moving that rapidly. Only slow-moving objects, like men, could sidle through a polarized gravitic field. He looked out to the horizon, touching the buttons very delicately.

Suddenly the sunset snuffed itself out. Amalfi, who had never seen a tropical sunset before coming to He, felt a vague alarm, but as far as he could see the abrupt darkness was natural, if startling. The fighting went on, the flying disks of TDX much more lurid now against the blackness.

After a while there was a dog-fight far aloft, identifiable mostly by traceries of jet trails and missiles. The jungle jammered derision and fury without any letup.

Amalfi stood, his senses reaching out slowly, feeling the positions of things. It was hard work, for he had never tried to grasp a situation at such close quarters before, and the trajectory of every shell tried to capture his attention.

About an hour past midnight, at the height of the heaviest raid yet, he felt a touch at his elbow.

"Boss—"

Amalfi heard the word as if it had been uttered at the bottom of the Rift. The still-ascending fountain of space mines had just been touched, and he was trying to reach the top of it; somewhere up there the trumpet flattened into a shell encompassing the whole of He, and it was important to know how high up that network of orbits began.

But the utter exhaustion of the voice touched something deeper. He said, "Yes, Mark."

"It's done. We lost almost everybody. But we caused a very

nice riot." A ghost of animation stirred in the voice for a moment. "You should have been there."

"I'm—almost there now. Good . . . work, Mark. Get . . . some rest."

"Sure. But—"

Something very heavy described a searing hyperbola in Amalfi's mind, and then the whole city was a scramble of magnesium-white and ink. As the light faded, there was a formless spreading and crawling, utterly beyond any detection but Amalfi's.

"Gas alarm, Mark," he heard himself saying. "Hawkesite . . . barium suits for everybody."

"Yes. Right. Boss, you'll kill yourself running things this way."

Amalfi found that he could not answer. He had found the town where the women had been dropped. Nothing clear came through, but there was certainly a riot there, and it was not entirely within the town itself. Tendrils of movement were being turned back from the Okie city, and were weaving out from places where there had been no sign of activity before.

At the base of the mine fountain, something else new was happening. A mass rose slowly, and there was a thick flowing around it. Then it stopped, and there was a sense of doors opening, heavy potentials moving out into tangled desolation. The tramps were leaving their city. The unmistakable, slightly nauseating sensation of a spindizzy field under medium drive domed the boiling of the lake of mud.

Dawn coming now. The riot in the town where the women were still would not come clear, but it was getting worse rather than better. Abruptly there was no town there at all, but a boiling, mushrooming pillar of radioactive gas—the place had been bombed. The struggle moved back toward the area of tension that marked the location of the bindlestiff.

Amalfi's own city was shrouded in sick orange mist, lit with flashes of no-color. The gas could not pass the spindizzy screen in a body, but it diffused through, molecule by heavy molecule. He realized suddenly that he had not heeded his own gas warning, and that there was probably some harm coming to him; but he could not localize it. He moved slightly, and instantly felt himself incased. What—

Barium paste. Hazleton had known that Amalfi could not leave the balcony, and evidently had plastered him with the stuff in default of trying to get a suit on him. Even his eyes were covered, and a feeling of distension in his nostrils bespoke a Kolman respirator.

The emotional and gravitic tensions in the bindlestiff city continued to gather; it would soon be unbearable. Above, just outside the space mines, the first few police vessels were sidling in cautiously. The war in the jungle had already fallen into meaninglessness. The abduction of the women from the Hevian town by the tramps had collapsed all Hevian rivalry; bandits and civilized towns alike were bent now upon nothing but the destruction of Fabr-Suithe and its allies. Fabr-Suithe could hold them off for a long time, but it was clearly time for the bindlestiff to leave—time for it to make off with its women and its anti-agapics and its germanium, time for it to lose itself in the Rift before the Earth police could invest all of He.

The tension knotted suddenly, painfully, and rose away from the boiling mud. The 'stiff was taking off. Amalfi pressed the button—the only one, this time, that had been connected to anything.

Moving Day began.

V.

IT began with six pillars of glaring white, forty miles in diameter, that burst through the soft soil at every compass point of He. Fabr-Suithe had sat directly over the site of one of them. The bandit town was nothing but a flake of ash in a split second, a curled flake borne aloft on the top of a white-hot piston.

The pillars lunged roaring into the heavens, fifty, a hundred, two hundred miles, and burst at their tops like popcorn. The sky burned thermite-blue with steel meteors. Outside, the space mines, cut off from the world of which they had been satellites by the greatest spin-dizzy screen of all time, fled into the Rift.

And when the meteors had burned away, the sun was growing.

The world of He was on over-drive, its magnetic moment transformed, expressed as momentum; it was the biggest city ever flown. There was no time to feel alarmed. The sun flashed by and was dwindling to a point before the fact could be grasped. It was gone. The far wall of the Rift began to swell, and separate into individual points of light.

Appalled, Amalfi fought to grasp the scale of speed. He failed. The planet of He was moving, that was all he could comprehend; its speed gulped light-years like gnats. Even to think of controlling so stupendous a flight was ridiculous.

Stars began to wink past He like fireflies. Then they were all behind.

The surface of the saucer that was the galaxy receded.

"Boss, we're going out of the—"

"I know it. Get me a fix on the Hevian sun before it's too late."

Hazleton worked feverishly. It took him only three minutes, but during those three minutes, the massed stars receded far enough so that the gray scar of the Rift became plain, as a definite mark on a spangled ground. The Hevian sun was less than an atom in it.

"Got it. But we can't swing the planet back. It'll take us two thousand years to cross to the next galaxy. We'll have to abandon He, boss, or we're sunk."

"All right. Get us aloft. Full drive."

"Our contract—"

"Fulfilled—take my word for it. Spin!"

The city screamed and sprang aloft. The planet of He did not dwindle—it simply vanished, snuffed out in the intergalactic gap. It was the first of the pioneers.

Amalfi took the controls, the barium casing cracking and falling away from him as he moved. The air still stank of Hawkesite, but the concentration of the gas already had been taken down below the harmful level by the city's purifiers. The mayor began to edge the city away from the vector of He's movement and the city's own, back toward the home lens.

Hazleton stirred restlessly.

"Your conscience bothering you, Mark?"

"Maybe," Hazleton said. "Is there some escape clause in our contract that lets us run off like this? If there is I missed it, and I read the fine print pretty closely."

"No, no escape clause," Amalfi said, shifting the space stick delicately. "The Hevians won't be hurt. The spindizzy screen will protect them from loss of heat and atmosphere—their volcanoes will supply more heat than they'll need, and their technology is up to artificial UV generation. But they won't be able to put out enough UV to keep the jungle alive. By the time they reach the Andromedan star that suits them, they'll understand the spindizzy principle well enough to set up a proper orbit. Or maybe they'll like roaming better by then, and decide to be an Okie planet. Either way, we did what we promised to do, fair and square."

"We didn't get paid," the city manager pointed out. "And it'll take our last reserves to get back to any part of our own galaxy. The bindlestiff got off, and got carried 'way out of range of the cops in the process—with plenty of dough, women, everything."

"No, they didn't," Amalfi said. "They blew up the moment we moved He."

"All right," Hazleton said resignedly. "You could detect that; I'll take your word for it. But you'd better be able to explain it."

"It's not hard to explain. The 'stiffs had captured Dr. Beetle. I was pretty sure they would. They came to He for no other reason. They needed the fuelless drive, and they knew Dr. Beetle had it, because of the agronomists' SOS. So they snatched him when he landed—notice how they made a big fuss about the *other* agronomist life ship, to divert our attention?—and worked the secret out of him."

"So?"

"So," Amalfi said, "they forgot that any Okie city always has passengers like Dr. Beetle—people with big ideas only partially worked out, ideas that need the finishing touches that can only be provided by some other culture. After all, a man doesn't take passage on an Okie city unless he's a third-rate sort of person, hoping to make his everlasting fortune on some planet where the people know less than he does."

Hazleton scratched his head ruefully. "That's right. We had the same experience with the Lyran invisibility machine. It didn't work, until we took that Hruntan physicist on board; he had the necessary extra knowledge—but he couldn't have discovered the principle himself, either."

"Exactly. The 'stiffs were in too much of a hurry. They didn't carry their stolen fuelless drive with them until they found some culture which could perfect it. They tried to use it right away—they were lazy. And they tried to use it inside the biggest spindizzy field ever generated. It blew up. If we hadn't left them parsecs behind in a split second, it would have blown up He at the same time."

Hazleton sighed and began to plot the probable point at which the city would return to its own galaxy. It turned out to be a long way away from the Rift, in an area that, after a mental wrench to visualize it backwards from the usual orientation, promised a fair population.

"Look," he said, "we'll hit about where the last few waves of the Acolytes settled—remember the Night of Hadjjii?"

Amalfi didn't, since he hadn't been born then, nor had Hazleton; but he remembered the history, which was what the city manager had meant. With a sidelong glance, he leaned forward, resumed the helmet he had cast aside a year ago, and turned on the City Fathers.

The helmet phone shrilled with alarm. "All right, all right," he growled. "What is it?"

"MAYOR AMALFI, HAVE YOU TIPPED THIS PLANET?"

"No," Amalfi said. "We sent it on its way as it was."

There was a short silence, humming with computation. "VERY WELL. WE MUST NOW SELECT THE POINT AT WHICH WE LEAVE THE RIFT. STAND BY FOR DETERMINATION."

Amalfi and Hazleton grinned at each other. Amalfi said, "We're coming in on the last Acolyte stars. Give us a determination for the present setup there, please—"

"YOU ARE MISTAKEN. THAT AREA IS NOWHERE NEAR THE RIFT. WE WILL GIVE YOU A DETERMINATION FOR THE FAR RIFT WALL: STAND BY."

Amalfi removed the headset gently.

"That," he said, moving the phone away from his mouth, "was long ago—and far away."

We Have Fed Our Sea

By Poul Anderson

Perhaps the deadest of all things possible in this Universe is the dead cold core of a burned-out supernova. But Death is, of course, the ultimate trap of all living things!

THEY named her *Southern Cross* and launched her on the road whose end they would never see. Months afterward she was moving at half the speed of light; if there was to be enough reaction mass for deceleration and maneuver, the blast must be terminated. And so the long silence came. For four and a half centuries, the ship would fall.

They manned her by turns, and dreamed other ships, and launched them, and saw how a few of the shortest journeys ended. Then they died.

And other men came after them. Wars flamed up and burned out, the howling peoples dwelt in smashed cities and kindled their fires with books. Conquerors followed, and conquerors of those, an empire killed its mother aborning, a religion called men to strange hilltops, a new race and a new state bestrode the Earth. But still the ships fell upward through night, and always there were men to stand watch upon them. Sometimes the men wore peaked caps and comets, sometimes steel helmets, sometimes decorous gray cowls, eventually blue berets with a winged star; but always they watched the ships, and more and more often as the decades passed they brought their craft to new harbors.

After ten generations, the *Southern Cross* was not quite halfway to her own goal, though she was the farthest from Earth of any human work. She was showing a little wear, here a scratch, there a patch, and not all the graffiti of bored and lonely men rubbed out by their successors. But those fields and particles which served her for eye, brain, nerve still swept heaven; each man at the end of his watch took a box of microplates with him as he made the hundred light-year stride to Earth's Moon. Much of this was lost, or gathered dust, in the century when Earthmen were busy surviving. But there came a time when a patient electrically seeing machine ran through many such plates from many ships. And so it condemned certain people to death.

I.

SUNDOWN burned across great waters. Far to the west, the clouds banked tall above New Zealand threw hot gold into the sky. In that direction, the sea was too bright to look upon. Eastward it faded through green and royal blue to night, where the first stars trod forth and trembled. There was just enough wind to ruffle the surface, send wavelets lapping against the hull of the ketch, flow down the idle mainsail and stir the girl's loosened pale hair.

Terangi Maclaren pointed north. "The kelp beds are that way," he drawled. "Main source of the family income, y' know. They mutate, crossbreed, and get seaweed which furnishes all kind of useful products. It's beyond me, thank the honorable ancestors. Biochemistry is an organized mess. I'll stick to something simple, like the degenerate nucleus."

The girl giggled. "And if it isn't degenerate, will you make it so?" she asked.

She was a technic like himself, of course: he would never have let a common on his boat, since a few machines were, in effect, a sizable crew. Her rank was higher than his, so high that no one in her family worked productively—whereas Maclaren was one of the few in his who did not. She was of carefully selected mutant Burmese strain, with amber skin, exquisite small features, and greenish-blond hair. Maclaren had been angling for weeks to get her alone like this. Not that General Feng, her drug-torpid null of a guardian, cared how much scandal she made, flying about the planet without so much as an amazon for chaperone. But she was more a creature of the Citadel and its hectic lights than of the sunset ocean.

Maclaren chuckled. "I wasn't swearing at the nucleus," he said. "Degeneracy is a state of matter under certain extreme conditions. Not too well understood, even after three hundred years of quantum theory. But I wander, and I would rather wonder. At you, naturally."

He padded barefoot across the deck and sat down by her. He was a tall man in his early thirties, slender, with wide shoulders and big hands, dark-haired and brown-skinned like all Oceanians; but there was an aquiline beak on the broad high-cheeked face, and some forgotten English ancestor looked out of hazel eyes. Like her, he wore merely an informal sarong and a few jewels.

"You're talking like a scholar, Terangi," she said. It was not a compliment. There was a growing element in the richest families who found Confucius, Plato, Einstein, and the other classics a thundering bore.

"Oh, but I am one," said Maclaren. "You'd be amazed how parched and stuffy I can get. Why, as a student—"

"But you were the amateur swim-wrestling champion!" she protested.

"True. I could also drink any two men under the table and knew every dive on Earth and the Moon. However, d' you imagine my father, bless his dreary collection of old-fashioned virtues, would have subsidized me all these years if I didn't bring some credit to the family? It's kudos, having an astrophysicist for a son. Even if I am a rather expensive astrophysicist." He grinned through the gathering dusk. "Every so often, when I'd been on a particularly outrageous binge, he would threaten to cut my allowance off. Then I'd have no choice but to come up with a new observation or a brilliant new theory, or at least a book."

She snuggled a little closer. "Is that why you are going out to space now?" she asked.

"Well, no," said Maclaren. "That's purely my own idea. My notion of fun. I told you I was getting stuffy in my dotage."

"WE haven't seen you very often in the Citadel, the last few years," she agreed. "And you were so busy when you did show."

"Politics, of a sort. The ship's course couldn't be changed without an order from a reluctant Exploration Authority, which meant bribing the right people, heading off the opposition, wheedling the Protector himself . . . d' you know, I discovered it was fun. I might even take up politics as a hobby, when I get back."

"How long will you be gone?" she asked.

"Can't say for certain, but probably just a month. That ought to furnish me with enough material for several years of study. Might dash back to the ship at odd moments for the rest of my life, of course. It'll take up permanent residence around that star."

"Couldn't you come home . . . every night?" she murmured.

"Don't tempt me," he groaned. "I can't. One month is the standard minimum watch on an interstellar vessel, barring emergencies. You see, every transmission uses up a Frank tube, which costs money."

"Well," she pouted, "if you think so much of an old dead star—"

"You don't understand, your gorgeousness. This is the first chance anyone has ever had, in more than two centuries of space travel, to get a close look at a truly burned-out star. There was even some argument whether the class existed. Is the universe old enough for any sun to have used up its nuclear *and* gravitational energy? By the ancestors, it's conceivable this one is left over from some previous cycle of creation!"

He felt a stiffening in her body, as if she resented his talk of what she neither understood nor cared about. And for a moment he resented her. She didn't really care about this boat either, or him, or anything except her own lovely shell. Why was he wasting time in the old worn routines, when he should be studying and preparing? He knew precisely why.

And then her rigidity melted in a little shudder. He glanced at her, she was a shadow with a palely glowing mane, in the deep blue twilight. The last embers of sun were almost gone, and one star after another woke overhead, soon the sky would be crowded with their keenness.

Almost, she whispered: "Where is this spaceship, now?"

A bit startled, he pointed at the first tracing of the *Southern Cross*. "That way," he said. "She was originally bound for Alpha Crucis, and hasn't been diverted very far off that course. Since she's a good thirty parsecs out, we wouldn't notice the difference if we could see that far."

"But we can't. Not ever. The light would take a hundred years, and I . . . we would all be dead—No!"

He soothed her, a most pleasant proceeding which became still more pleasant as the night went on. And they were on his yacht, which had borne his love from the first day he took the tiller, in a calm sea, with wine and small sandwiches, and she even asked him to play his guitar and sing. But somehow it was not the episode he had awaited. He kept thinking of this or that preparation, what had he overlooked, what could he expect to find at the black sun; perhaps he was indeed under the subtle tooth of age, or of maturity if you wanted a euphemism, or perhaps the *Southern Cross* burned disturbingly bright overhead.

II.

WINTER lay among the Outer Hebrides. Day was a sullen glimmer between two darknesses, often smothered in snow. When it did not fling itself upon the rocks and burst in freezing spume, the North Atlantic rolled in heavy and gnawing. There was no real horizon, leaden waves met leaden sky and misty leaden light hid the seam. "Here there is neither land nor water nor air, but a kind of mixture of them," wrote Pytheas.

The island was small. Once it had held a few fishermen, whose wives kept a sheep or two, but that was long ago. Now only one house remained, a stone cottage built centuries back and little changed. Down at the landing was a modern shelter for a sailboat, a family submarine, and a battered aircar; but it was of gray plastic and fitted into the landscape like another boulder.

David Ryerson put down his own hired vehicle there, signaled the door to open, and rolled through. He had not been on Skula for half a decade: it touched him, in a way, how his hands remembered all the motions of steering into this place and how the dank interior was unaltered. As for his father— He bit back an inward fluttering, helped his bride from the car, and spread his cloak around them both as they stepped into the wind.

It howled in from the Pole, striking them so they reeled and Tamara's black locks broke free like torn banners. Ryerson thought he could almost hear the wind toning in the rock underfoot. Surely the blows of the sea did, crash after crash through a bitter drift of flung scud. For a moment's primitive terror, he thought he heard his father's God, whom he had denied, roar in the deep. He fought his way to the cottage and laid numbed fingers on the anachronism of a corroded bronze knocker.

Magnus Ryerson opened the door and waved them in. "I'd not expected you yet," he said, which was as close as he would ever come to an apology. When he shut out the wind, there was a quietness which gaped.

This main room, brick-floored, whitewashed, irregular and solid, centered about a fireplace where peat burned low and blue. The chief concessions to the century were a radi-globe and a stunning close-up photograph of the Sirian binary. One did not count the pilot's manuals or the stones and skins and gods brought from beyond the sky; after all, any old sea captain would have kept his Bowditch and his souvenirs. The walls were lined with books as well as microspools. Most of the full-size volumes were antique, for little was printed in English these days.

Magnus Ryerson stood leaning on a cane of no Terrestrial wood. He was a huge man, two meters tall in his youth and not greatly stooped now, with breadth and thickness to match. His nose jutted craggily from a leather skin, shoulder-length white hair, breast-length white beard. Under tangled brows, the eyes were small and frost-blue. He wore the archaic local dress, a knitted sweater and canvas trousers. It came as a shock to realize after several minutes that his right hand was artificial.

"Well," he rumbled at last, in fluent Interhuman, "so this is the bride. Tamara Sumito Ryerson, eh? Welcome, girl." There was no great warmth in his tone.

She bent her face to folded hands. "I greet you most humbly, honorable father." She was Australian, a typical high-class common of that province, fine-boned, bronze-hued, with blue-black hair and oblique brown eyes; but her beauty was typical nowhere. She had dressed with becoming modesty in a long white gown and a hooded cloak, no ornaments save a wedding band with the Ryerson monogram on it.

Magnus looked away from her, to his son. "Professor's daughter, did you say?" he murmured in English.

"Professor of symbolics," said David. He made his answer a defiance by casting it in the Interhuman which his wife understood. "We . . . Tamara and I . . . met at his home. I needed a background in symbolics to understand my own specialty and—"

"You explain too much," said Magnus dryly. "Sit."

He lowered himself into a chair. After a moment, David followed. The son was just turned twenty years old, a slender boy of average height with light complexion, thin sharp features, yellow hair, and his father's blue eyes. He wore the tunic of a science graduate, with insignia of gravitics, self-consciously, but not so used to it that he would change for an ordinary civilian blouse.

TAMARA made her way into the kitchen and began preparing tea. Magnus looked after her. "Well-trained, anyhow," he grunted in English. "So I suppose her family is at least heathen, and not any of these latter-day atheists. That's somewhat."

David felt the island years, alone with his widower father, return to roost heavy upon him. He stifled an anger and said, also in English: "I couldn't have made any better match. Even from some swinish practical standpoint. Not without marrying into a technic family, and—Would you want me to do that? I'll gain technic rank on my own merits!"

"If you stay on Earth," said Magnus. "Who notices a colonial?"

"Who notices an Earthling, among ten billion others?" snapped David. "On a new planet . . . on Rama . . . a man can be himself. These stupid hereditary distinctions won't even matter."

"There is room enough right here," said Magnus. "As a boy you never used to complain Skula was crowded. On the contrary!"

"And I would settle down with some illiterate beefy-faced good Christian fishwife you picked for me and breed more servants for the Protectorate, all my life!"

The words had come out before David thought. Now, in a kind of dismay, he waited for his father's reaction. This man had ordered him out into a winter gale, or supperless to bed, for fifteen years out of twenty. In theory the grown son was free of him, free of everyone save contractual overlords and whatever general had most recently seized the title of Protector. In practice it was not so easy. David knew with a chill that he would never have decided to emigrate without Tamara's unarrogant and unbendable will to stiffen his. He would probably never even have married her, without more than her father's consent, against the wish of his own—David gripped the worn arms of his chair.

Magnus sighed. He felt about after a pipe and tobacco pouch. "I would have preferred you to maintain residence on Earth," he said with a somehow shocking gentleness. "By the time the quarantine on Washington 5584 has been lifted, I'll be dead."

David locked his mouth. *You hoary old fraud,* he thought, *if you expect to hook me that way—*

"It's not as if you would be penned on one island all your

days," said Magnus. "Why did I spend all I had saved, to put my sons through the Academy? So they could be spacemen, as I was and my father and grandfather before me. Earth isn't a prison. The Earthman can go as far as the farthest ships have reached. It's the colonies are the hole. Once you go there to live, you never come back here."

"Is there so much to come back to?" said David. Then, after a minute, trying clumsily for reconciliation: "And father, I'm the last. Space ate them all. Radiation killed Tom, a meteor got Ned, Eric made a falling star all by himself, Ian just never returned from wherever it was. Don't you want to preserve our blood in me, at least?"

"So you mean to save your own life?"

"Now, wait! You know how dangerous a new planet can be. That's the reason for putting the initial settlers under thirty years of absolute quarantine. If you think I—"

"No," said Magnus. "No, you're no coward, Davy, where it comes to physical things. When you deal with people, though . . . I don't know what you're like. You don't yourself. Are you running away from man, as you've been trying to run from the Lord God Jehovah? Not so many folk on Rama as on Earth, no need to work both with and against them, as on a ship—Well." He leaned forward, the pipe smoldering in his plastic hand. "I want you to be a spaceman, aye, of course. I cannot dictate your choice. But if you would at least try it, once only, so you could honestly come back and tell me you're not born for stars and openness and a sky all around you—Do you understand? I could let you go to your planet then. Not before. I would never know, otherwise, how much I had let you cheat yourself."

Silence fell between them. They heard the wind as it mourned under their eaves, and the remote snarling of the sea.

David said at last, slowly: "So that's why you . . . yes. Did you give my name to Technic Maclaren for that dark star expedition?"

Magnus nodded. "I heard from my friends in the Authority that Maclaren had gotten the *Cross* diverted from orbit. Some of them were mickle put out about it, too. After all, she was the first one sent directly toward a really remote goal, she is farther from Earth than any other ship has yet gotten, it was like breaking a tradition." He shrugged. "God knows when anyone will reach Alpha Crucis now. But I say Maclaren is right. Alpha may be an interesting triple star, but a truly cold sun means a deal more to science. At any rate, I did pull a few wires. Maclaren needs a gravitics man to help him take his data. The post is yours if you wish it."

"I don't," said David. "How long would we be gone, a month, two months? A month from now I planned to be selecting my own estate on Rama."

"Also, you've only been wed a few weeks. Oh, yes. I understand. But you can be sent to Rama as soon as you get back; there'll be several waves of migration. You will have space pay plus exploratory bonus, some valuable experience, and," finished Magnus sardonically, "my blessing. Otherwise you can get out of my house this minute."

David hunched into his chair, as if facing an enemy.

He heard Tamara move about, slow in the unfamiliar kitchen, surely more than a little frightened of this old barbarian. If he went to space, she would have to stay here, bound by a propriety which was one of the chains they had hoped to shed on Rama. It was a cheerless prospect for her, too.

And yet, thought David, the grim face before him had once turned skyward, on a spring night, telling him the names of the stars.

III.

THE other man, Ohara, was good, third-degree black. But finally his alertness wavered. He moved in unwarily, and Seiichi Nakamura threw him with a foot sweep that drew approving hisses from the audience. Seeing his chance, Nakamura pounced, got control of Ohara from the waist down by sitting on him, and applied a strangle. Ohara tried to break it, but starving lungs betrayed him. He slapped the mat when he was just short of unconsciousness. Nakamura released him and squatted, waiting. Presently Ohara rose. So did the winner. They retied their belts and bowed to each other. The abbot, who was refereeing, murmured a few words which ended the match. The contestants sat down, closed their eyes, and for a while the room held nothing but meditation.

Nakamura had progressed beyond enjoying victory for its

own sake. He could still exult in the aesthetics of a perfect maneuver; what a delightful toy the human body is, when you know how to throw eighty struggling kilos artistically through the air! But even that, he knew, was a spiritual weakness. Judo is more than a sport, it should be a means to an end: ideally, a physical form of meditation upon the principles of Zen.

He wondered if he would ever attain that height. Rebelliously, he wondered if anyone ever had, in actual practice, for more than a few moments anyhow . . . It was an unworthy thought. A wearer of the black belt in the fifth degree should at least have ceased inwardly barking at his betters. And now enough of all the personal. It was only his mind reflecting the tension of the contest, and tension was always the enemy. His mathematical training led him to visualize fields of force, and the human soul as a differential quantity dX—where X was a function of no one knew how many variables—which applied just enough, vanishingly small increments of action so that the great fields slid over each other and—Was this a desirable analogue? He must discuss it with the abbot sometime; it seemed too precise to reflect reality. For now he had better meditate upon one of the traditional paradoxes: consider the noise made by two hands clapping, and then the noise made by *one* hand clapping.

The abbot spoke another word. The several contestants on the mat bowed to him, rose, and went to the showers. The audience, yellow-robed monks and a motley group of townspeople, left their cushions and mingled cheerfully.

When Nakamura came out, his gi rolled under one arm, his short thick-set body clad in plain gray coveralls, he saw the abbot talking to Diomed Umfando, chief of the local Protectorate garrison. He waited until they noticed him. Then he bowed and sucked in his breath respectfully.

"Ah," said the abbot. "A most admirable performance tonight."

"It was nothing, honorable sir," said Nakamura.

"What did you . . . yes. Indeed. You are leaving tomorrow, are you not?"

"Yes, master. On the *Southern Cross,* the expedition to the dark star. It is uncertain how long I shall be away." He laughed self-deprecatingly, as politeness required. "It is always possible that one does not return. May I humbly ask the honorable abbot that—"

"Of course," said the old man. "Your wife and children shall always be under our protection, and your sons will be educated here if no better place can be found for them." He smiled. "But who can doubt that the best pilot on Sarai will return as a conqueror?"

They exchanged ritual compliments. Nakamura went about saying good-by to various other friends. As he came to the door, he saw the tall blue-clad form of Captain Umfando. He bowed.

"I am walking back into town now," said the officer, almost apologetically: "May I request the pleasure of your company?"

"If this unworthy person can offer even a moment's distraction to the noble captain?"

THEY left together. The dojo was part of the Buddhist monastery, which stood two or three kilometers out of the town called Susa. A road went through grainfields, an empty road now, for the spectators were still drinking tea under the abbot's red roof. Nakamura and Umfando walked in silence for a while; the captain's bodyguard shouldered their rifles and followed unobtrusively.

Capella had long ago set. Its sixth planet, Il-Khan the giant, was near full phase, a vast golden shield blazoned with a hundred hues. Two other satellites, not much smaller than this Earth-sized Sarai on which humans dwelt, were visible. Only a few stars could shine through all that light, low in the purple sky; the fields lay drowned in amber radiance, Susa's lanterns looked feeble in the distance. Meteor trails crisscrossed heaven, as if someone wrote swift ideographs up there. On the left horizon, a sudden mountain range climbed until its peaks burned with snow. A moonbird was trilling, the fiddler insects answered, a small wind rustled in the grain. Otherwise only the scrunch of feet on gravel had voice.

"This is a lovely world," murmured Nakamura.

Captain Umfando shrugged. Wryness touched his ebony features. "I could wish it were more sociable."

"Believe me, sir, despite political differences, there is no ill will toward you or your men personally—"

"Oh, come now," said the officer. "I am not that naïve. Sarai may begin by disliking us purely as soldiers and tax collectors for an Earth which will not let the ordinary colonist even visit it. But such feelings soon envelop the soldier himself. I've been jeered at, and mudballed by children, even out of uniform."

"It is most deplorable," said Nakamura in distress. "May I offer my apologies on behalf of my town?"

Umfando shrugged. "I'm not certain that an apology is in order. I didn't have to make a career of the Protector's army. And Earth does exploit the colonies. There are euphemisms and excuses, but exploitation is what it amounts to."

He thought for a moment, and asked with a near despair: "But what else can Earth do?"

Nakamura said nothing. They walked on in silence for a while.

Umfando said at last, "I wish to put a rude question." When the flat face beside him showed no reluctance, he plowed ahead. "Let us not waste time on modesty. You know you're one of the finest pilots in the Guild. Any Capellan System pilot is—he has to be!—but you are the one they ask for when things get difficult. You've been on a dozen exploratory missions in new systems. It's not made you rich, but it has made you one of the most influential men on Sarai.

"Why do *you* treat me like a human being?"

Nakamura considered it gravely. "Well," he decided, "I cannot consider politics important enough to quarrel about."

"I see." A little embarrassed, Umfando changed the subject: "I can get you on a military transport to Batu tomorrow, if you wish. Drop you off at the 'caster station."

"Thank you, but I have already engaged passage on the regular interstellar ferry."

"Uh . . . did you ask for the *Cross* berth?"

"No. I had served a few watches on her, of course, like everyone else. A good ship. A little outmoded now, perhaps, but well and honestly made. The Guild offered me the position, and since I had no other commitments, I accepted."

Guild offers were actually assignments for the lower ranks of spacemen, Umfando knew. A man of Nakamura's standing could have refused. But maybe the way you attained such prestige was by never refusing.

"Do you expect any trouble?" he asked.

"One is never certain. The great human mistake is to anticipate. The totally relaxed and unexpectant man is the one prepared for whatever may happen: he does not have to get out of an inappropriate posture before he can react."

"Ha! Maybe judo ought to be required for all pilots."

"No. I do not think the coerced mind ever really learns an art."

Nakamura saw his house ahead. It stood on the edge of town, half screened by Terrestrial Bamboo. He had spent much time on the garden which surrounded it; many visitors were kind enough to call his garden beautiful. He sighed. A gracious house, a good and faithful wife, four promising children, health and achievement, what more could a man reasonably ask? He told himself that his remembrances of Kyoto were hazed, he had left Earth as a very young boy. Surely this serene and uncrowded Sarai offered more than poor tortured antheap Earth gave even to her overlords. And yet some mornings he woke up with the temple bells of Kyoto still chiming in his ears.

He stopped at the gate. "Will you honor my home for a cup of tea?" he asked.

"No, thanks," said Umfando, almost roughly. "You've a family to . . . to say good-by to. I will see you when—"

Fire streaked across the sky. For an instant Il-Khan himself was lost in blue flame. The bolide struck somewhere among the mountains. A sheet of pure outraged energy flared above ragged peaks. Then smoke and dust swirled up like a devil, and moments afterward thunder came banging down through the valley.

Umfando whistled. "That was a monster!"

"A . . . yes . . . most unusual . . . yes, yes." Nakamura stammered something, somehow he bowed good night and somehow he kept from running along the path to his roof. But as he walked, he began to shake.

It was only a meteorite, he told himself frantically. Only a meteorite. The space around a giant star like Capella, and especially around its biggest planet, was certain to be full of cosmic junk. Billions of meteors hit Sarai every day. Hundreds of them got through to the surface. But Sarai was as big as Earth, he told himself. Sarai had oceans, deserts, uninhabited plains and forests . . . why, even on Sarai you were more likely to be killed by lightning than by a meteorite and—and—

Oh, the jewel in the lotus! he cried out. *I am afraid. I am afraid of the black sun.*

IV.

IT was raining again, but no one on Krasna pays attention to that. They wear a few light non-absorbent garments and welcome the rain on their bodies, a moment's relief from saturated hot air. The clouds thin overhead, so that the land glimmers with watery brightness, sometimes even the uppermost clouds break apart and Tau Ceti spears a blinding reddish shaft through smoke-blue masses and silvery rain.

Chang Sverdlov rode into Dynamogorsk with a hornbeast lashed behind his saddle. It had been a dangerous chase, through the tidal marshes and up over the bleak heights of Czar Nicholas IV Range, but he needed evidence to back his story, that he had only been going out to hunt. Mukerji, the chief intelligence officer of the Protectorate garrison, was getting suspicious, God rot his brain.

Two soldiers came along the elevated sidewalk. Rain drummed on their helmets and sluiced off the slung rifles. Earth soldiers went in armed pairs on a street like Trumpet Road: for a Krasnan swamprancher, fisher, miner, logger, trapper, brawling away his accumulated loneliness, with a skinful of vodka or rice wine, a fluff-headed fille-de-joie to impress, and a sullen suspicion that the dice had been loaded, was apt to unlimber his weapons when he saw a blueback.

Sverdlov contented himself with spitting at their boots, which were about level with his head. It went unnoticed in the downpour. And in the noise, and crowding, and blinking lights, with thunder above the city's gables. He clucked to his saurian and guided her toward the middle of the slough called Trumpet Road. Its excitement lifted his anger a bit. *I'll report in,* he told himself, *and go wheedle an advance from the Guild bank, and then make up six weeks of bushranging in a way the joyhouses will remember!*

He turned off on the Avenue of Tigers and stopped before a certain inn. Tethering his lizard and throwing the guard a coin, he entered the taproom. It was as full of men and racket as usual. He shouldered up to the bar. The landlord recognized him; Sverdlov was a very big and solid young man, bullet-headed, crop-haired, with a thick nose and small brown eyes in a pockmarked face. The landlord drew a mug of kvass, spiked it with vodka, and set it out. He nodded toward the ceiling. "I will tell her you are here," he said, and left.

Sverdlov leaned on the bar, one hand resting on a pistol butt, the other holding up his drink. *I could wish it really were one of the upstairs girls expecting me,* he thought. *Do we need all this melodrama of codes, countersigns, and cell organization?* He considered the seething of near-naked men in the room. A chess game, a card game, a dirty joke, an Indian wrestling match, a brag, a wheedle, an incipient fight: his own Krasnans! It hardly seemed possible that any of those ears could have been hired by the Protector and yet . . .

The landlord came back. "She's here and ready for you," he grinned. A couple of nearby men guffawed coarsely. Sverdlov tossed off his drink, lit one of the cheap cigars he favored, and pushed through to the stairs.

At the end of a third floor corridor he rapped on a door. A voice invited him in. The room beyond was small and drably furnished, but its window looked down a straight street to the town's end and a sudden feathery splendor of rainbow trees. Lightning flimmered through the bright rain of Krasna. Sverdlov wondered scornfully if Earth had jungle and infinite promise on any doorstep.

He closed the door and nodded at the two men who sat waiting. He knew fat Li-Tsung; the gaunt Arabic-looking fellow was strange to him, and neither asked for an introduction.

Li-Tsung raised an eyebrow. Sverdlov said, "It is going well. They were having some new troubles—the aerospores were playing merry hell with the electrical insulation—but I think I worked out a solution. The Wetlanders are keeping our boys amply fed, and there is no indication anyone has betrayed them. Yet."

The thin man asked, "This is the clandestine bomb factory?"

"No," said Li-Tsung. "It is time you learned of these matters, especially when you are leaving the system today. This man has been helping direct something more important than small arms manufacture. They are tooling up out there to make interplanetary missiles."

"What for?" answered the stranger. "Once the Fellowship has seized the mattercaster, it will be years before reinforcements can arrive from any other system. You'll have time enough to build heavy armament then." He glanced inquiringly at Sverdlov. Li-Tsung nodded. "In fact," said the thin man, "my division is trying to so organize things that there will be no closer Protectorate forces than Earth itself. Simultaneous revolution on a dozen planets. Then it would be at least two decades before spaceships could reach Tau Ceti."

"Ah," grunted Sverdlov. He lowered his hairy body into a chair. His cigar jabbed at the thin man. "Have you ever thought the Earthlings are no fools? The mattercaster for the Tau Ceti System is up there on Moon Two. Sure. We seize it, or destroy it. But is it the *only* transceiver around?"

The thin man choked. Li-Tsung murmured, "This is not for the rank and file. There is enough awe of Earth already to hold the people back. But in point of fact, the Protector is an idiot if there is not at least one asteroid in some unlikely orbit, with a heavy-duty 'caster mounted on it. We can expect the Navy in our skies within hours of the independence proclamation. We must be prepared to fight!"

"But—" said the thin man. "But this means it will take years more to make ready than I thought. I had hoped—"

"The Centaurians rebelled prematurely, forty years ago," said Li-Tsung. "Let us never forget the lesson. Do you want to be lobotomized?"

There was silence for a while. Rain hammered on the roof. Down in the street, a couple of rangers just in from the Uplands were organizing an impromptu saurian fight.

"Well," said Sverdlov at last. "I'd better not stay here."

"Oh, but you should," said Li-Tsung. "You are supposedly visiting a woman, do you remember?"

Sverdlov snorted impatience, but reached for the little chess set in his pouch. "Who'll play me a quick game, then?"

"Are the bright lights that attractive?" asked Li-Tsung.

Sverdlov spoke an obscenity. "I've spent nearly my whole

leave chasing through the bush and up into the Czar," he said. "I'll be off to Thovo—or worse yet, to Krimchak or Cupra or the Belt, Thovo has a settlement at least—for weeks. Months, perhaps! Let me relax a little first."

"As a matter of fact," said Li-Tsung, "your next berth has already been assigned, and it is not to any of those places. It is outsystem." In his public *persona,* he was a minor official in the local branch of the Astronautical Guild.

"What?" Sverdlov cursed for a steady minute. "You mean I'm to be locked up for a month on some stinking ship in the middle of interstellar space, and—"

"Calmly, please, calmly. You won't be standing a routine single-handed just-in-case watch. This will be rather more interesting. You will be on the XA463, the *Southern Cross."*

SVERDLOV considered. He had taken his turn on the stellar vessels, but had no interest in them: they were a chore, one of the less desirable aspects of the spaceman's life. He had even been on duty when a new system was entered, but it had thrilled him not. Its planets turned out to be poisonous hells; he had finished his hitch and gone home before they even completed the transceiver station, the devil could drink his share of the celebration party.

"I don't know which of them that would be," he said.

"It is bound for Alpha Crucis. Or was. Several years ago, the photographs taken by its instruments were routinely robo-analyzed on Earth. There were discrepancies. Chiefly, some of the background stars were displaced, the Einstein effect of mass on light rays. A more careful study revealed there was a feeble source of long radio waves in that direction. They appear to be the dying gasp of a star."

Since Sverdlov's work involved him with the atomic nucleus, he could not help arguing: "I don't think so. The dying gasp, as you put it, would be gravitational potential energy, released as radiation when a star's own fires are all exhausted. But a thing so cold it only emits in the far radio frequencies . . . I'd say that was merely some kind of turbulence in what passes for an atmosphere. That the star isn't just dying, it's *dead."*

"I don't know," shrugged Li-Tsung. "Perhaps no one does. This expedition will be to answer such questions. They gave up on Alpha Crucis for the time being and decelerated the ship toward this black star. It is arriving there now. The next personnel will take up an orbit and make the initial studies. You are the engineer."

Sverdlov drew heavily on his cigar. "Why me?" he protested. "I'm an interplanetary man. Except for those interstellar tours, I've never even been out of the Tau Ceti System."

"That may be one reason you were picked," said Li-Tsung. "The Guild does not like its men too provincial in outlook."

"Surely," sneered Sverdlov. "We colonials can travel anywhere we please, except to Earth. Only our goods go to Earth without special permission."

"You need not recruit us into the Fellowship of Independence," said the thin man in a parched voice.

Sverdlov clamped teeth together and got out through stiff lips: "There will be Earthlings aboard, won't there? It's asking for trouble, to put me on the same ship as an Earthling."

"You will be very polite and co-operative," said Li-Tsung sharply. "There are other reasons for your assignment. I cannot say much, but you can guess that we have sympathizers, even members, in the Guild . . . on a higher level than spacehand! It is possible that something of potential military value will be learned from the dark star. Who knows? Something about force fields or—Use your own imagination. It can do no harm to have a Fellowship man on the *Cross.* It may do some good. You will report to me when you return."

"Very well, very well," grumbled Sverdlov. "I can stand a month or two of Earthlings, I suppose."

"You will get your official orders soon," Li-Tsung told him. He glanced at his watch. "I think you can run along now; you have a reputation as a, hm-m-m, fast worker. Enjoy yourself."

"And don't get talking drunk," said the thin man.

Sverdlov paused in the doorway. "I don't," he said. "I wouldn't be alive now if I did."

V.

THE Authority booked first-class passages for all expeditionary personnel, which in the case of a hop up to the Moon meant a direct ferry traveling at one gee all the way. Standing by the observation window, an untasted drink in his hand, David Ryerson remarked: "You know, this is only the third time I've been off Earth. And the other two, we transshipped at Satellite and went free-fall most of the way."

"Sounds like fun," said Maclaren. "I must try it sometime."

"You . . . in your line of work . . . you must go to the Moon quite often," said Ryerson shyly.

Maclaren nodded. "Mount Ambarzumian Observatory, on Farside. Still a little dust and gas to bother us, of course, but I'll let the purists go out to Plato Satellite and bring me back their plates."

"And—No. Forgive me." Ryerson shook his blond head.

"Go on." Maclaren, seated in a voluptuous formfit lounger, offered a box of cigarettes. He thought he knew Ryerson's type, serious, gifted, ambitious, but awe-smitten at the gimcrack fact of someone's hereditary technic rank. "Go ahead," he invited. "I don't embarrass easy."

"I was only wondering . . . who paid for all your trips . . . the observatory or—"

"Great ancestors! The observatory?" Maclaren threw back his head and laughed with the heartiness of a man who had never had to be very cautious. It rang above the low music and cultivated chatter; even the ecdysiast paused an instant on her stage.

"My dear old colleague," said Maclaren, "I not only pay my own freight, I am expected to contribute generously toward the expenses of the institution. At least," he added, "my father is. But where else would money for pure research come from? You can't tax it out of the lower commons, y' know. They haven't got it. The upper commons are already taxed to the limit, short of pushing them back down into the hand-to-mouth masses. And the Protectorate rests on a technic class serving but not paying. That's the theory, anyhow: in practice, of course, a lot of 'em do neither. But how else would you support abstract science, except by patronage? Thank the Powers for the human snob instinct, it keeps both research and art alive."

Ryerson looked alarmed; glanced about as if expecting momentary arrest, finally lowered himself to the edge of a chair and almost whispered: "Yes, sir, yes, I know, naturally. I was just not so . . . so familiar with the details of . . . financing."

"Eh? But how could you have missed learning? You trained to be a scientist, didn't you?"

Ryerson stared out at Earth, sprawling splendor across the constellations. "I set out to be a spaceman," he said, blushing. "But in the last couple of years I got more interested in gravitics, had to concentrate too much on catching up in that field to . . . well . . . also, I was planning to emigrate, so I wasn't interested in—The colonies need trained men. The opportunities—"

Pioneering is an unlimited chance to become the biggest frog, provided the puddle is small enough, thought Maclaren. But he asked aloud, politely, "Where to?"

"Rama. The third planet of Washington 5584."

"Hm-m-m? Oh, yes. The new one, the GO dwarf. Uh, how far from here?"

"Ninety-seven light-years. Rama has just passed the five-year survey test." Ryerson leaned forward, losing shyness in his enthusiasm. "Actually, sir, Rama is the most nearly terrestroid planet they have yet found. The biochemistry is so similar to Earth's that one can even eat some of the native plants and— Oh, and there are climatic zones, oceans, forests, mountains, a single big moon—"

"And thirty years of isolation," said Maclaren. "Nothing connecting you to the universe but a voice."

Ryerson reddened again. "Does that matter so much?" he asked aggressively. "Are we losing a great deal by that?"

"I suppose not," said Maclaren.

Your lives, perhaps, he thought. *Remember the Shadow Plague on New Kashmir? Or your children—there was the mutation virus on Gondwana. Five years is not long enough to learn a planet; the thirty-year quarantine is an arbitrary minimum. And, of course, there are the more obvious and spectacular things, which merely kill colonists without threatening the human race. Storms, quakes, morasses, volcanoes, meteorites. Cumulative poisoning. Wild animals. Unsuspected half-intelligent aborigines. Strangeness, loneliness, madness. It's no wonder the colonies which survive develop their own cultures. It's no wonder they come to think of Earth as a parasite on their own tedious heroisms. Of course, with ten billion people, and a great deal of once arable country sterilized by radiation, Earth has little choice.*

What I would like to know is, why does anyone emigrate in the first place? The lessons are ghastly enough; why do otherwise sensible people, like this boy, refuse to learn them?

"Oh, well," he said aloud. He signaled the waiter. "Refuel us, chop-chop."

Ryerson looked in some awe at the chit which the other man thumbprinted. He could not suppress it: "Do you always travel first-class to the Moon?"

Maclaren put a fresh cigarette between his lips and touched his lighter-ring to the end. His smile cocked it at a wry angle. "I suppose," he answered, "I have always traveled first-class through life."

THE ferry made turnover without spilling a drink or a passenger and backed down onto Tycho Port. Maclaren adjusted without a thought to Lunar gravity, Ryerson turned a little green and swallowed a pill. But even in his momentary distress, Ryerson was bewildered at merely walking through a tube to a monorail station. Third-class passengers must submit to interminable official bullying: safety regulations, queues, assignment to hostel. Now, within minutes, he was again on soft cushions, staring through crystalline panes at the saw-toothed magnificence of mountains.

When the train got under way, he gripped his hands together, irrationally afraid. It took him a while to hunt down the reason: the ghost of his father's God, ranting at pride and sloth from the tomb which the son had erected.

"Let's eat," said Maclaren. "I chose this train with malice aforethought. It's slow enough so we can enjoy our meal en route, and the chef puts his heart into the oysters won-ton."

"I'm not . . . not hungry," stammered Ryerson.

Maclaren's dark, hooked face flashed a grin. "That's what cocktails and hors d'oeuvres are for, lad. Stuff yourself. If it's true what I've heard of deep-space rations, we're in for a dreary month or two."

"You mean you've never been on an interstellar ship?"

"Of course not. Never been beyond the Moon in my life. Why should I do any such ridiculous thing?"

Maclaren's cloak swirled like fire as he led the way toward the diner. Beneath an iridescent white tunic, his legs showed muscular and hairless, down to the tooled-leather buskins; the slant of the beret on his head was pure insolence. Ryerson, trailing drably behind in spaceman's gray coveralls, felt bitterness. *What have I been dragged away from Tamara for? Does this peacock know a mass from a hole in the ground? He's hired himself a toy, is all, because for a while he's bored with wine and women . . . and Tamara is locked away on a rock with a self-righteous old beast who hates the sound of her name!*

As they sat down at their table, Maclaren went on, "But this is too good a chance to pass up. I found me a tame mathematician last year and sicced him onto the Schrödinger equation—Sugimoto's relativistic version, I mean; Yuen postulates too bloody much for my taste—anyhow, he worked it out for the quantities involved in a dark star, mass and gravitational intensities and cetera. His results make us both wonder if such a body doesn't go over to an entirely new stage of degeneracy at the core. One gigantic neutron? Well, maybe that's too fantastic. But consider—"

And while the monorail ran on toward Farside, Maclaren left the Interhuman language quite behind him. Ryerson could follow tensors, even when scribbled on a menu, but Maclaren had some new function, symbolized by a pneumatic female outline, that *reduced* to a generalized tensor under certain conditions. Ryerson stepped out on Farside, two hours later, with his brain rotating.

He had heard of the cyclopean installations which fill the whole of Yukawa Crater and spread out onto the plains beyond. Who has not? But all he saw on his first visit was a gigantic concourse, a long slideway tunnel, and a good many uniformed technicians. He made some timid mention of his disappointment to Maclaren. The New Zealander nodded: "Exactly. There's more romance, more sense of distance covered, and a devil of a lot better scenery, in an afternoon on the bay, than in a fifty light-year leap. I say space travel is overrated. And it's a fact, I've heard, that spacemen themselves prefer the interplanetary runs. They take the dull interstellar watches as a matter of duty, by turns."

Here and there the tunnel branched off, signs indicating the way to Alpha Centauri Jump, Tau Ceti Jump, Epsilon Eridani Jump, all the long-colonized systems. Those were for passengers; freight went by other beams. There was no great bustle along any of the tubes. Comparatively few Earthlings had occasion to visit outsystem on business; still fewer could afford it for pleasure, and of course no colonial came here without a grudging O.K. The Protector had trouble enough; he was not going to expose the mother planet and its restless billions to new ideas born under new skies, nor let any more colonials than he could help see first-hand what an inferior position they held. That was the real reason for the ban, every educated Terrestrial knew as much. The masses, being illiterate, swallowed a vague official excuse about trade policy.

The branches leading to Sirius Jump, Procyon Jump, and the other attained but uncolonizable systems, were almost deserted. Little came from such places—perhaps an occasional gem or exotic chemical. But relay stations had been established there, for 'casting to more useful planets.

Ryerson's heart leaped when he passed a newly activated sign: an arrow and WASHINGTON 5584 JUMP burning above. *That* tunnel would be filled, come next week!

He should have been in the line. And Tamara. Well, there would be later waves. His passage was already paid for, he had had no difficulty about transferring to another section.

To make conversation, he said through a tightness: "Where are the bulkheads?"

"Which ones?" asked Maclaren absently.

"Safety bulkheads. A receiver does fail once in a great while, you know. That's why the installations here are spread out so much, why every star has a separate 'caster. There's a vast amount of energy involved in each transmission—one reason why a 'casting is more expensive than transportation by spaceship. Even a small increment, undissipated, can melt a whole chamber."

"Oh, yes. That." Maclaren had let Ryerson get pompous about the obvious because it was plain he needed something to bolster himself. What itched the kid, anyhow? One should think that when the Authority offered a fledgling a post on an expedition as fundamental as this—Of course, it had upset Ryerson's plans of emigration. But not importantly. There was no danger he would find all the choice sites on Rama occupied if he came several weeks late: too few people had the fare as it was.

Maclaren said, "I see what you mean. Yes, the bulkheads are there, but recessed into the walls and camouflaged. You don't want to emphasize possible danger to the cash customers, eh? Some technic might get annoyed and make trouble."

"Some day," said Ryerson, "they'll reduce the energy margin needed; and they'll figure how to reproduce a Frank tube, rather than manufacture it. Record the pattern and recreate from a matter bank. Then anyone can afford to ride the beams. Interplanetary ships, even air and surface craft, will become obsolete."

Maclaren made no answer. He had sometimes thought, more or less idly, about the unrealized potentialities of matter-casting. Hard to say whether personal immortality would be a good thing or not. Not for the masses, surely! Too many of them as it was. But a select few, like Terangi Maclaren—or was it worth the trouble? Even given boats, chess, music, the No Drama, beautiful women and beautiful spectroscopes, life could get heavy.

As for matter transmission, the difficulty and hence the expense lay in the complexity of the signal. Consider an adult human. There are some 10^{14} cells in him, each an elaborate structure involving many proteins with molecular weights in the millions. You had to scan every one of those molecules—identify it structurally, ticket its momentary energy levels, and place it in proper spatio-temporal relationship to every other molecule—as nearly simultaneously as the laws of physics permitted. You couldn't take a man apart, or reassemble him, in more than a few microseconds; he wouldn't survive it. You couldn't even transmit a recognizable beefsteak in much less of a hurry.

So the scanning beam went through and through, like a blade of energy. It touched every atom in its path, was modified thereby, and flashed that modification onto the transmitter matrix. But such fury destroyed. The scanned object was reduced to gas so quickly that only an oscilloscope could watch the process. The gas was sucked into the destructor chamber and atomically condensed in the matter bank; in time it would become an incoming passenger, or incoming freight. In a sense, the man had died.

If you could record the signal which entered the transmitter matrix—you could keep such a record indefinitely, recreate the man and his instantaneous memories, thoughts, habits, prejudices, hopes and loves and hates and horrors, a thousand years afterward. You could create a billion identical men. Or, more practically, a single handmade prototype could become a billion indistinguishable copies; nothing would be worth more than any handful of dirt. Or . . . superimpose the neurone trace-patterns, memories, of a lifetime, onto a recorded twenty-year-old body, be born again and live forever!

The signal was too complex, though. An unpromising research program went on. Perhaps in a few centuries they would find some trick which would enable them to record a man, or even a Frank tube. Meanwhile, transmission had to be simultaneous with scanning. The signal went out. Probably it would be relayed a few times. Eventually the desired receiving chamber got it. The receiver matrix, powered by dying atomic nuclei, flung gases together, formed higher elements, formed molecules and cells and dreams according to the signal, in microseconds. It was designed as an energy-consuming process, for obvious reasons: packing fraction energy was dissipated in gravitic and magnetic fields, to help shape the man. (Or the beefsteak, or the spaceship, or the colonial planet's produce.) He left the receiving chamber and went about his business.

A mono-isotopic element is a simple enough signal to record, Maclaren reminded himself, *though even that requires a houseful of transistor elements. So this civilization can afford to be extravagant with metals—can use pure mercury as the raw material of a spaceship's blast, for instance. But we still eat our bread in the sweat of some commoner's brow.*

Not for the first time, but with no great indignation—life was too short for anything but amusement at the human race—Maclaren wondered if the recording problem really was as difficult as the physicists claimed. No government likes revolutions, and molecular duplication would revolutionize society beyond imagining. Just think how they had to guard the stations as it was, and stick them out here on the Moon . . . otherwise, even today, some fanatic could steal a tube of radium from a hospital and duplicate enough to sterilize a planet!

"Oh, well," he said, half aloud.

THEY reached the special exploration section and entered an office. There was red tape to unsnarl. Ryerson let Maclaren handle it, and spent the time trying to understand that soon the pattern which was himself would be embodied in newly-shaped atoms, a hundred light-years from Tamara. It wouldn't penetrate. It was only words.

Finally the papers were stamped. The transceivers to/from an interstellar spaceship could handle several hundred kilos at a time; Maclaren and Ryerson went together. They had a moment's wait because of locked safety switches on the *Southern Cross:* someone else was arriving or departing ahead of them.

"Watch that first step," said Maclaren. "It's a honey."

"What?" Ryerson blinked at him, uncomprehending.

The circuit closed. There was no sensation, the process went too fast.

The scanner put its signal into the matrix. The matrix modulated the carrier wave. But such terminology is mere slang, borrowed from electronics. You cannot have a "wave" when you have no velocity, and gravitational forces do not. (This is a more accurate rendition of the common statement that "gravitation propagates at an infinite speed.") Inconceivable energies surged within a thermonuclear fire chamber; nothing controlled them, nothing could control them, but the force fields they themselves generated. Matter pulsed in and out of existence *qua* matter, from particle to gamma ray quantum and back. Since quanta have no rest mass, the pulsations disturbed the geometry of space according to the laws of Einsteinian mechanics. Not much: gravitation is feebler than magnetism or electricity. Were it not for the resonance effect, the signal would have been smothered in "noise" a few kilometers away. Even as it was, there were many relayings across the parsecs until the matrix on the *Cross* reacted. And yet in one sense no time at all had passed; and no self-respecting mathematician would have called the "beam" by such a name. It was, however, a signal, the only signal which relativity physics allowed to go faster than light—and, after all, it did not really *go,* it simply *was.*

Despite the pill inside him, Ryerson felt as if the bottom had dropped out of the world. He grabbed for a handhold. The after-image of the transmitter chamber yielded to the coils and banks of the receiver room on a spaceship. He hung weightless, a thousand billion billion kilometers from Earth.

VI.

FORWARD of the 'casting chambers, "above" them during acceleration, were fuel deck, gyros, and air renewal plant. Then you passed through the observation deck, where instruments and laboratory equipment crowded together. A flimsy wall around the shaftway marked off the living quarters: folding bunks, galley, bath, table, benches, shelves, and lockers, all crammed into a six-meter circle.

Seiichi Nakamura wrapped one leg casually around a stanchion, to keep himself from drifting in air currents, and made a ceremony out of leafing through the log-book in his hands. It gave the others a chance to calm down, and the yellow-haired boy, David Ryerson, seemed to need it. The astrophysicist, Maclaren, achieved the unusual feat of lounging in free fall; he puffed an expensive Earth-side cigarette and wrinkled his patrician nose at the pervading smell of an old ship, two hundred years of cooking and sweat and machine oil. The big, ugly young engineer, Sverdlov, merely looked sullen. Nakamura had never met any of them before.

"Well, gentlemen," he said at last. "Pardon me, I had to check the data recorded by the last pilot. Now I know approximately where we are at." He laughed with polite self-deprecation. "Of course you are all familiar with the articles. The pilot is captain. His duty is to guide the ship where the chief scientist—Dr. Maclaren-san in this case—wishes, within the limits of safety as determined by his own judgment. In case of my death or disability, command devolves upon the engineer, ah, Sverdlov-san, and you are to return home as soon as practicable. Yes-s-s. But I am sure we will all have a most pleasant and instructive expedition together."

He felt the banality of his words. It was the law, and a wise one, that authority be defined at once if there were non-Guild personnel aboard. Some pilots contented themselves with reading the regulations aloud, but it had always seemed an unnecessarily cold procedure to Nakamura. Only . . . he saw a sick bewilderment in Ryerson's eyes, supercilious humor in Maclaren's, angry impatience in Sverdlov's . . . his attempt at friendliness had gone flat.

"We do not operate so formally," he went on in a lame fashion. "We shall post a schedule of housekeeping duties and help each other, yes? Well. That is for later. Now as to the star, we have some approximate data and estimates taken by previous watches. It appears to have about four times the mass of Sol; its radius is hardly more than twice Earth's, possibly less; it emits detectably only in the lower radio frequencies, and even that is feeble. I have here a quick reading of the spectrum which may interest you, Dr. Maclaren."

THE big dark man reached out for it. His brows went up. "Now this," he said, "is the weirdest collection of wave lengths I ever saw." He flickered experienced eyes along the column of numbers. "Seems to be a lot of triplets, but the lines appear so broad, judging from the probable errors given, that I can't be sure without more careful . . . hm-m-m." Glancing back at Nakamura: "Just where are we with relation to the star?"

"Approximately two million kilometers from the center of its mass. We are being drawn toward it, of course, since an orbit has not yet been established, but have enough radial velocity of our own to—"

"Never mind." The sophistication dropped from Maclaren like a tunic. He said with a boy's eagerness, "I would like to get as near the star as possible. How close do you think you can put us?"

Nakamura smiled. He had a feeling Maclaren could prove likable. "Too close isn't prudent. There would be meteors."

"Not around this one!" exclaimed Maclaren. "If physical theory is anything but mescaline dreams, a dead star is the clinker of a supernova. Any matter orbiting in its neighborhood became incandescent gas long ago."

"Atmosphere?" asked Nakamura dubiously. "Since we have nothing to see by, except starlight, we could hit its air."

"Hm-m-m. Yes. I suppose it would have some. But not very deep: too compressed to be deep. In fact, the radio photosphere, from which the previous watches estimated the star's diameter, must be nearly identical with the fringes of atmosphere."

"It would also take a great deal of reaction mass to pull us back out of its attraction, if we got too close," said Nakamura. He unclipped the specialized slide rule at his belt and made a few quick computations. "In fact, this vessel cannot escape from a distance much less than three-quarters million kilometers, if there is to be reasonable amount of mass left for maneuvering around afterward. And I am sure you wish to explore regions farther from the star, yes-s-s? However, I am willing to go that close."

Maclaren smiled. "Good enough. How long to arrive?"

"I estimate three hours, including time to establish an orbit." Nakamura looked around their faces. "If everyone is prepared to go on duty, it is best we get into the desired path at once."

"Not even a cup of tea first?" grumbled Sverdlov.

Nakamura nodded at Maclaren and Ryerson. "You gentlemen will please prepare tea and sandwiches, and take them to the engineer and myself in about ninety minutes."

"Now, wait!" protested Maclaren. "We've hardly arrived. I haven't even looked at my instruments. I have to set up—"

"In ninety minutes, if you will be so kind. Very well, let us assume our posts."

Nakamura turned from Maclaren's suddenly mutinous look and Sverdlov's broad grin. He entered the shaftway and pulled himself along it by the rungs. Through the transparent plastic he saw the observation deck fall behind. The boat deck was next, heavy storage levels followed, and then he was forward, into the main turret.

IT was a clear plastic bubble, unshuttered now when the sole outside illumination was a wintry blaze of stars.

Floating toward the controls, Nakamura grew aware of the silence. So quiet. So uncountably many stars. The constellations were noticeably distorted, some altogether foreign. He searched a crystal darkness for Capella, but the bulge of the ship hid it from him. No use looking for Sol without a telescope, here on the lonely edge of the known.

Fear of raw emptiness lay tightly coiled within him. He smothered it by routine: strapped himself before the console, checked the instruments one by one, spoke with Sverdlov down the length of the ship. His fingers chattered out a computation on a set of keys, he fed the tape to the robot, he felt a faint tug as the gyros woke up, swiveling the vessel into position for blast. Even now, at the end of acceleration to half lightspeed and deceleration to a few hundred kilometers per second, the *Cross* bore several tons of reaction-mass mercury. The total mass, including hull, equipment, and payload, was a bit over one kiloton. Accordingly, her massive gyroscopes needed half an hour to turn her completely around.

Waiting, he studied the viewscreens. Since he must back down on his goal, what they showed him was more important than what his eyes saw through the turret in the nose. He could not make out the black sun. *Well, what do you expect?* he asked himself angrily. *It must be occulating a few stars, but there are too many.* "Dr. Maclaren," he said into the intercom, "can you give me a radio directional on the target, as a check?"

"Aye, aye." A surly answer. Maclaren resented having to put his toys to work. He would rather have been taking spectra, reading ionoscopes, gulping gas and dust samples from outside into his analyzers, every centimeter of the way. Well, he would just have to get those data when they receded from the star again.

Nakamura's eyes strayed down the ship herself, as shown in the viewscreens. *Old,* he thought. *The very nation which built her has ceased to exist. But good work. A man's work outlives his hands. Though what remains of the little ivory figures my father carved to ornament our house? What chance did my brother have to create, before he shriveled in my arms? No!* He shut off the thought, like a surgeon clamping a vein, and refreshed his memory of the *Cygnus* class.

This hull was a sphere of reinforced self-sealing plastic, fifty meters across, its outside smoothness broken by hatches, ports, air locks, and the like. The various decks sliced it in parallel planes. Aft, diametrically opposite this turret, the hull opened on the fire chamber. And thence ran two thin metal skeletons, thirty meters apart, a hundred meters long, like radio masts or ancient oil derricks. They comprised two series of rings, a couple of centimeters in diameter, with auxiliary wiring and a spidery framework holding it all together—the ion accelerators, built into and supported by the gravitic transceiver web.

"A ten-second test blast, if you please, Engineer Sverdlov," said Nakamura.

The instruments showed him a certain unbalance in the distribution of mass within the hull. Yussuf bin Suleiman, who had just finished watch aboard the ship and gone back to Earth, was sloppy about . . . no, it was unjust to think so . . . say that he had his own style of piloting. Nakamura set the pumps to work. Mercury ran from the fuel deck to the trim tanks.

By then the ship was pointed correctly and it was time to start decelerating again. "Stand by for blast . . . Report . . . I shall want one-point-five-seven standard gees for—" Nakamura reeled it off almost automatically.

It rumbled in the ship. Weight came, like a sudden fist in the belly. Nakamura held his body relaxed in harness, only his eyes moved, now and then a finger touched a control. The secret of judo, of life, was to hold every part of the organism at ease except those precise tissues needed for the moment's task— Why was it so damnably difficult to put into practice?

MERCURY fed through pipes and pumps, past Sverdlov's control board, past the radiation wall, into the expansion chamber and through the ionizer and so as a spray past the sunlike heart of a thermonuclear plasma. Briefly, each atom endured a rage of mesons. It broke down, gave up its mass as pure energy, which at once became proton-antiproton pairs. Magnetic fields separated them as they were born: positive and negative particles fled down the linear accelerators. The plasma, converting the death of matter directly to electricity, charged each ring at a successively higher potential. When the particles emerged from the last ring, they were traveling at three-fourths the speed of light.

At such an exhaust velocity, no great mass had to be discharged. Nor was the twin stream visible; it was too efficient. Sensitive instruments might have detected a pale gamma-colored splotch, very far behind the ship, as a few opposite charges finally converged on each other, but that effect was of no importance.

The process was energy-eating. It had to be. Otherwise surplus heat would have vaporized the ship. The plasma furnished energy to spare. The process was a good deal more complex than a few words can describe, and yet less so than an engineer accustomed to more primitive branches of his art might imagine.

Nakamura gave himself up to the instruments. Their readings checked out with his running computation. The *Cross* was approaching the black star in a complex spiral curve, the resultant of several velocities and two accelerating vectors, which would become a nearly circular orbit seven hundred fifty thousand kilometers out.

He started to awareness of time when Ryerson came up the shaftway rungs. "Oh," he exclaimed.

"Tea, sir," said the boy shyly.

"Thank you. Ah . . . set it down there, please . . . the regulations forbid entering this turret during blast without inquiring of the—No, no. Please!" Nakamura waved a hand, laughing. "You did not know. There is no harm done."

He saw Ryerson, stooped under one and a half gravities, lift a heavy head to the foreign stars. The Milky Way formed a cold halo about his tangled hair. Nakamura asked gently, "This is your first time in extrasolar space, yes?"

"Y-yes, sir." Ryerson licked his lips. The blue eyes were somehow hazy, unable to focus closer than the nebulae.

"Do not—" Nakamura paused. He had been about to say, "Do not be afraid," but it might hurt. He felt after words. "Space is a good place to meditate," he said. "I use the wrong word, of course. 'Meditation,' in Zen, consists more of an attempt at identification with the universe than verbalized thinking. What I mean to say," he floundered, "is this: Some people feel themselves so helplessly small out here that they become frightened. Others, remembering that home is no more than a step away through the transmitter, become careless and arrogant, the cosmos merely a set of meaningless numbers to them. Both attitudes are wrong, and have killed men. But if you think of yourself as being a *part* of everything else—integral—the same forces in you which shaped the suns . . . do you see?"

"The heavens declare the glory of God," whispered Ryerson, "and the firmament showeth His handiwork . . . It is a terrible thing to fall into the hands of the living God."

He had not been listening, and Nakamura did not understand English. The pilot sighed. "I think you had best return to the observation deck," he said. "Dr. Maclaren may have need of you."

Ryerson nodded mutely and went back down the shaft.

I preach a good theory, Nakamura told himself. *Why can I not practice it? Because a stone fell from heaven onto Sarai, and suddenly father and mother and sister and house were not. Because Hideki died in my arms, after the universe had casually tortured him. Because I shall never see Kyoto again, where every morning was full of cool bells. Because I am a slave of myself.*

And yet, he thought, *sometimes I have achieved peace. And only in space.*

Now he saw the dead sun through a viewscreen, when his ship swung so that it transitted the Milky Way. It was a tiny blackness. The next time around, it had grown. He wondered if it was indeed blacker than the sky. Nonsense. It should reflect starlight, should it not? But what color was metallic hydrogen? What gases overlay the metal? Space, especially here, was not absolutely black: there was a certain thin but measurable nebular cloud around the star. So conceivably the star might be blacker than the sky.

"I must ask Maclaren," he murmured to himself. "He can measure it, very simply, and tell me. Meditation upon the concept of blacker than total blackness is not helpful, it seems." That brought him a wry humor, which untensed his muscles. He grew aware of weariness. It should not have been;

he had only been sitting here and pressing controls. He poured a cup of scalding tea and drank noisily and gratefully.

Down and down. Nakamura fell into an almost detached state. Now the star was close, not much smaller than the Moon seen from Earth. It grew rapidly, and crawled still more rapidly around the circle of the viewscreens. Now it was as big as Batu, at closest approach to Sarai. Now it was bigger. The rhythms entered Nakamura's blood. Dimly, he felt himself become one with the ship, the fields, the immense interplay of forces. And this was why he went again and yet again into space. He touched the manual controls, assisting the robots, correcting, revising, in a pattern of unformulated but bodily known harmonies, a dance, a dream, yielding, controlling, unselfness, Nirvana, peace and wholeness . . .

Fire!

The shock rammed Nakamura's spine against his skull. He felt his teeth clashed together. Blood from a bitten tongue welled in his mouth. Thunder roared between the walls.

He stared into the screens, clawing for comprehension. The ship was a million or so kilometers out. The black star was not quite one degree wide, snipped out of an unnamed alien constellation. The far end of the ion accelerator system was white hot. Even as Nakamura watched, the framework curled up, writhed like fingers in agony, and vaporized.

"What's going on?" Horror bawled from the engine room.

The thrust fell off and weight dropped sickeningly. Nakamura saw hell eat along the accelerators. He jerked his eyes around to the primary megameter. Its needle sank down a tale of numbers. The four outermost rings were already destroyed. Even as he watched, the next one shriveled.

It could not be felt, but he knew how the star's vast hand clamped on the ship and reeled her inward.

Metal whiffed into space. Underloaded, the nuclear system howled its anger. Echoes banged between shivering decks.

"Cut!" cried Nakamura. His hand slapped the pilot's master switch.

THE silence that fell, and the no-weight, were like death. Someone's voice gabbled from the observation deck. Automatically, Nakamura chopped that interference out of the intercom circuit. "Engineer Sverdlov," he called. "What happened? Do you know what is wrong?"

"No. No." A groan. But at least the man lived. "Somehow the . . . the ion streams . . . seem to have . . . gotten diverted. The focusing fields went awry. The blast struck the rings—but it couldn't happen!"

Nakamura hung onto his harness with all ten fingers. *I will not scream,* he shouted. *I will not scream.*

"The 'caster web seems to be gone, too," said a rusty machine using his throat. His brother's dead face swam among the stars, just outside the turret, and mouthed at him.

"Aye." Sverdlov must be hunched over his own viewscreens. After a while that tingled, he said harshly: "Not yet beyond repair. All ships carry a few replacement parts, in case of meteors or—We can repair the web and transmit ourselves out of here."

"How long to do that job? Quickly!"

"How should I know?" A dragon snarl. Then: "I'd have to go out and take a closer look. The damaged sections will have to be cut away. It'll probably be necessary to machine some fittings. With luck, we can do it in several hours."

Nakamura paused. He worked his hands together, strength opposing strength; he drew slow breaths, rolled his head to loosen the neck muscles, finally closed his eyes and contemplated peace for as long as needful. And a measure of peace came. The death of this little ego was not so terrible after all, provided said ego refrained from wishing to hold Baby-san in its arms just one more time.

Almost absently, he punched the keys of the general computer. It was no surprise to see his guess verified.

"Are you there?" called Sverdlov, as if across centuries. "Are you there, pilot?"

"Yes. I beg your pardon. Several hours to repair the web, did you say? By that time, drifting free, we will have crashed on the star."

"What? But—"

"Consider its acceleration of us. And we still have inward radial velocity of our own. I think I can put us into an orbit before the whatever-it-is force has quite destroyed the accelerators. Yes."

"But you'll burn them up! And the web! We'll damage the web beyond repair!"

"Perhaps something can be improvised, once we are in orbit. But if we continue simply falling, we are dead men."

"No!" Almost, Sverdlov shrieked. "Listen, maybe we can repair the web in time. Maybe we'll only need a couple of hours for the job. There's a chance. But caught in an orbit, with the web melted or vaporized . . . do you know how to build one from raw metal? I don't!"

"We have a gravitics specialist aboard. If anyone can fashion us a new transmitter, he can."

"And if he can't, we're trapped out here! To starve! Better to crash and be done!"

Nakamura's hands began to dance over the keyboard. He demanded data of the instruments, calculations of the computers, and nothing of the autopilot. For no machine could help steer a vessel whose thrust-engine was being unpredictably devoured. This would be a manual task.

"I am the captain," he said, as mildly as possible.

"Not any more!"

Nakamura slapped his master switch. "You have just been cut out of the control circuits," he said. "Please remain at your post." He opened the intercom to the observation deck. "Will the two honorable scientists be so kind as to stop the engineer from interfering with the pilot?"

VII.

FOR a moment, the rage in Chang Sverdlov was such that blackness flapped before his eyes.

When he regained himself, he found the viewscreens still painted with ruin. Starlight lay wan along the frail network of the transceiver web and the two sets of rings which it held together. At the far end the metal glowed red. A few globs of spattered stuff orbited like lunatic fireflies. Beyond the twisted burnt-off end of the system, light-years dropped away to the cold blue glitter of a thousand crowding stars. The dead sun was just discernible, a flattened darkness. It seemed to be swelling visibly. Whether that was a real effect or not, Sverdlov felt the dread of falling, the no-weight horrors, like a lump in his belly.

He hadn't been afraid of null-gee since he was a child. In his cadet days, he had invented more pranks involving free fall than any two other boys. But he had never been cut off from home in this fashion. Krasna had never been more than an interplanetary flight or an interstellar Jump away.

And that cookbook pilot would starve out here to save his worthless ship?

Sverdlov unbuckled his harness. He kicked himself across the little control room, twisted among the pipes and wheels and dials of the fuel-feed section like a swimming fish, and came to the tool rack. He chose a long wrench and arrowed for the shaftway. His fury had chilled into resolution: *I don't want to kill him, but he'll have to be made to see reason. And quickly, or we really will crash!*

He was rounding the transmitter chamber when deceleration resumed. He had been going up by the usual process, grab a rung ahead of you and whip your weightless body beyond. Suddenly two Terrestrial gravities snatched him.

He closed fingers about one of the bars. His left arm straightened, with a hundred and ninety kilos behind. The hand tore loose. He let go the wrench and caught with his right arm, jamming it between a rung and the shaft wall. The impact smashed across his biceps. Then his left hand clawed fast and he hung. He heard the wrench skid past the gyro housing, hit a straight dropoff, and clang on the after radiation shield.

Gasping, he found a lower rung with his feet and sagged for a minute. The right arm was numb, until the pain woke in it. He flexed the fingers. Nothing broken.

But he was supposed to be in harness. Nakamura's calculations might demand spurts of ten or fifteen gravities, if the accelerators could still put out that much. The fear of being smeared across a bulkhead jolted into Sverdlov. He scrambled over the rungs. It was nightmarishly like climbing through glue. After a thousand years he burst into the living quarters.

MACLAREN sat up in one of the bunks. "No further, please," he said.

The deceleration climbed a notch. His weight was iron on Sverdlov's shoulders. He started back into the shaft. "No!" cried Ryerson. But it was Maclaren who flung off bunk harness and climbed to the deck. The brown face gleamed wet, but Maclaren smiled and said: "Didn't you hear me?"

Sverdlov grunted and re-entered the shaft, both feet on a rung. *I can make it up to the bubble and get my hands on Nakamura's throat.* Maclaren stood for a gauging instant, as Sverdlov's foot crept toward the next rung. Finally the physicist added with a sneer in the tone: "When a technic says sit, you squat . . . colonial."

Sverdlov halted. "What was that?" he asked slowly.

"I can haul you out of there if I must, you backwoods pig," said Maclaren, "but I'd rather you came to me.

Sverdlov wondered, with an odd quick sadness, why he responded. Did an Earthling's yap make so much difference? He decided that Maclaren would probably make good on that promise to follow him up the shaft, and under this weight a fight on the rungs could kill them both. Therefore—Sverdlov's brain seemed as heavy as his bones. He climbed back and stood slumping on the observation deck. "Well?" he said.

Maclaren folded his arms. "Better get into a bunk," he advised.

Sverdlov lumbered toward him. In a shimmery wisp of tunic, the Earthling looked muscular enough, but he probably massed ten kilos less, and lacked several centimeters of the Krasnan's height and reach. A few swift blows would disable him, and it might still not be too late to stop Nakamura.

"Put up your fists," said Sverdlov hoarsely.

Maclaren unfolded his arms. A sleepy smile crossed his face. Sverdlov came in, swinging at the eagle beak. Maclaren's head moved aside. His hands came up, took Sverdlov's arm, and applied a cruel leverage. Sverdlov gasped, broke free by sheer strength, and threw a blow to the ribs. Maclaren stopped that fist with an edge-on chop at the wrist behind it; almost, Sverdlov thought he felt the bones crack. They stood toe to toe. Sverdlov drew back the other fist. Maclaren punched him in the groin. The Krasnan doubled over in a jag of anguish. Maclaren rabbit-punched him. Sverdlov went to one knee. Maclaren kicked him in the solar plexus. Sverdlov fell over and struck the floor with three gravities to help.

Through a wobbling, ringing darkness, he heard the Earthling: "Help me with this beef, Dave." And he felt himself dragged across the floor, somehow manhandled into a bunk and harnessed.

His mind returned. Pain stabbed and flickered through him. He struggled to sit up. "That was an Earthman way to fight," he pushed out through a swelling mouth.

"I don't enjoy fighting," said Maclaren from his own bunk, "so I got it over with as soon as possible."

"You—" the Krasnan lifted grotesquely heavy hands and fumbled with his harness. "I'm going to the control turret. If you try to stop me this time—"

"You're already too late, brother Sverdlov," said Maclaren coolly. "Whatever you were setting out to forestall has gone irrevocably far toward happening."

The words were a physical blow.

"It's . . . yes," said the engineer. "I'm too late." The shout burst from him: "We're all too late, now!"

"Ease back," said Maclaren. "Frankly, your behavior doesn't give me much confidence in your judgment about anything."

It rumbled through the ship. That shouldn't be, thought Sverdlov's training; even full blast ought to be nearly noiseless, and this was only fractional. Sweat prickled his skin. For the first time in a violent life, he totally realized that he could die.

"I'm sorry for what I called you," said Maclaren. "I had to stop you, but now I apologize."

Sverdlov made no answer. He stared up at a blank ceiling. Oddly, his first emotion, as rage ebbed, was an overwhelming sorrow. Now he would never see Krasna made free.

VIII.

SILENCE and no-weight were dreamlike. For a reason obscure to himself, Maclaren had dimmed the fluoros around the observation deck, so that twilight filled it and the scientific apparatus crouched in racks and on benches seemed to be a herd of long-necked monsters. Thus there was nothing to drown the steely brilliance of the stars, when you looked out an unshuttered port.

The star hurtled across his field of view. Her eccentric orbit took the *Cross* around it in thirty-seven minutes. Here, at closest approach, they were only half a million kilometers away. The thing had the visual diameter of three full Moons. It was curiously vague of outline: a central absolute blackness, fading toward deep gray near the edges where starlight caught an atmosphere more savagely compressed than Earth's ocean abyss. Through the telescope, there seemed to be changeable streaks and mottlings, bands, spots, a hint of color too faint for the eye to tell . . . as if the ghosts of burned-out fires still walked.

Quite oblate, Maclaren reminded himself. *That would have given us a hint, if we'd known. Or the radio spectrum; now I realize, when it's too late, that the lines really are triplets, and their broadening is Doppler shift.*

The silence was smothering.

Nakamura drifted in. He poised himself in the air and waited quietly.

"Well?" said Maclaren.

"Sverdlov is still outside, looking at the accelerators and web," said Nakamura. "He will not admit there is no hope."

"Neither will I," said Maclaren.

"Virtually the whole system is destroyed. Fifty meters of it have vanished. The rest is fused, twisted, short-circuited . . . a miracle it continued to give some feeble kind of blast, so I could at least find an orbit." Nakamura laughed. Maclaren thought that that high-pitched, apologetic giggle was going to be hard to live with, if one hadn't been raised among such symbols. "We carry a few spare parts, but not that many."

"Perhaps we can make some," said Maclaren.

"Perhaps," said Nakamura. "But of course the accelerators are of no importance in themselves, the reconstruction of the web is the only way to get home . . . What has the young man Ryerson to say about that?"

"Don't know. I sent him off to check the manifest and then look over the stuff the ship actually carries. He's been gone a long time, but—"

"I understand," said Nakamura. "It is not easy to face a death sentence when one is young."

Maclaren nodded absently and returned his gaze to the scribbled data sheets in one hand. After a moment, Nakamura cleared his throat and said awkwardly: "Ah . . . I beg your pardon . . . about the affair of Engineer Sverdlov—"

"Well?" Maclaren didn't glance up from the figures. He had a lot of composure of his own to win back.

The fact is, he thought through a hammer-beat in his temples, *I am the man afraid. Now that there is nothing I can do, only a cold waiting until word is given me whether I can live or must die . . . I find that Terangi Maclaren is a coward.*

Sickness was a doubled fist inside his gullet.

"I am not certain what, er, happened," stumbled Nakamura, "and I do not wish to know. If you will be so kind . . . I hope you were not unduly inconvenienced—"

"No. It's all right."

"If we could tacitly ignore it. As I think he has tried to do. Even the best men have a breaking point."

I always knew that there must one day be an end to white sails above green water, and to wine, and No masks, and a woman's laughter. I had not expected it yet.

"After all," said Nakamura, "we must work together now."

"Yes."

I had not expected it a light-century from the home of my fathers. My life was spent in having fun, and now I find that the black star has no interest at all in amusing me.

"Do you know yet what happened?" asked Nakamura. "I would not press you for an answer, but—"

"Oh, yes," said Maclaren. "I know."

BENEATH a scrapheap of songs and keels, loves and jokes and victories, which mattered no longer but would not leave him, Maclaren found his brain working with a startling dry clarity. "I'm not sure how much we can admit to the others," he said. "Because this could have been averted, if we'd proceeded with more caution."

"I wondered a little at the time." Nakamura laughed again. "But who would look for danger around a . . . a corpse?"

"Broadened spectrum lines mean a quickly rotating star," said Maclaren. "Since the ship was not approaching in the equatorial plane, we missed the full Doppler effect, but we might have stopped to think. And tripled lines mean a Zeeman splitting."

"Ah." Nakamura sucked in a hiss of air. "Magnetism?"

"The most powerful bloody magnetic field ever noticed

around any heavenly body," said Maclaren. "Judging from the readings I get here, the polar field is . . . oh, I can't say yet. Five, six, seven thousand gauss—somewhere on that order of magnitude. Fantastic! Sol's field is only fifty-three gauss. They don't ever go much above two thousand. Except here."

He rubbed his chin. "Blackett effect," he went on. The steadiness of his words was a faintly pleasing surprise to him. "Magnetic field is directly related to angular velocity. The reason no live sun has a field like this dead thing here is that it would have to rotate too fast. Couldn't take the strain; it would go whoomp and scatter pieces of star from hell to tiffin." An odd, perverse comfort in speaking lightly: a lie to oneself, persuading the subconscious mind that its companions were not doomed men and a black sun, but an amorous girl waiting for the next jest in a Citadel tavern. "As this star collapsed on itself, after burning out, it had to spin faster, d' you see? Conservation of angular momentum. It seems to have had an unusual amount to start with, of course, but the rotational speed is chiefly a result of its degenerate state. And that same superdensity allows it to twirl with such indecent haste. You might say the bursting strength is immensely greater."

"Yes," said Nakamura. "I see."

"I've been making some estimates," said Maclaren. "It didn't actually take a very strong field to wreck us. We could easily have been protected against it. Any ion-drive craft going close to a planet is—a counter-magnetic circuit with a feedback loop—elementary. But naturally, these big ships were not meant to land anywhere. They would certainly never approach a live sun this close, and the possibility of this black dwarf having such a vicious magnetism . . . well, no one ever thought of it."

He shrugged. "Figure it out yourself, Captain Nakamura. The old H, r, v formula. A proton traveling at three-fourths *c* down a hundred-meter tube is deflected one centimeter by a field of seven one-hundredths gauss. We entered such a field at a million kilometers out, more or less. A tenuous but extremely energetic stream of ionized gas hit the outermost accelerator ring. I make the temperature equivalent of that velocity to be something like three million million degrees Absolute, if I remember the value of the gas constant correctly.

The closer to the star we got, the stronger field we were in, so the farther up the ions struck.

"Of course," finished Maclaren in a tired voice, "all these quantities are just estimates, using simple algebra. Since we slanted across the magnetic field, you'd need a vectoral differential equation to describe exactly what happened. You might find occasion to change my figures by a factor of five or six. But I think I have the general idea."

"Yes-s-s," said Nakamura, "I think you do."

They hung side by side in dimness and looked out at the eye-hurting bright stars.

"Do you know," said Maclaren, "there is one sin which is punished with unfailing certainty, and must therefore be the deadliest sin in all time. Stupidity."

"I am not so sure." Nakamura's reply jarred him a little, by its sober literal-mindedness. "I have known many . . . well, shall I call them unintellectual people . . . who lived happy and useful lives."

"I wasn't referring to that kind of stupidity." Maclaren went through the motions of a chuckle. "I meant our own kind. Yours and mine. We bear the guilt, you know. We should have stopped and thought the situation over before rushing in. I did want to approach more slowly, measuring as we went, and you overruled me."

"I am ashamed," said Nakamura. He bent his face toward his hands.

"No, let me finish. I should have come here with a well-thought-out program in mind. I gave you no valid reasons *not* to establish a close-in orbit at once. My only grumble was that you wouldn't allow me time to take observations as we went toward the star. You were perfectly justified, on the basis of the information available to you—Oh, the devils take it! I bring this up only so you'll know what topics to avoid with our shipmates—who must also bear some of the blame for not thinking—because we can't afford quarrels." Maclaren felt his cheeks crease in a sort of grin. "I have no interest in the guilt question anyway. My problem is strictly pragmatic: I want out of here!"

Ryerson emerged from the living-quarter screen. Maclaren saw him first as a shadow. Then the young face came so near that he could see the eyes unnaturally bright and the lips shaking.

"What have you found, Dave?" The question ripped from him before he thought.

Ryerson looked away from them both. Thickly: "We can't do it. There aren't enough replacement parts to make a f-f-functioning . . . a web—we can't."

"I knew that," said Nakamura. "Of course. But we have instruments and machine tools. There is bar metal in the hold, which we can shape to our needs. The only problem is—"

"Is where to get four kilos of pure germanium!" Ryerson screamed it. The walls sneered at him with echoes. "Down on that star, maybe?"

IX.

SQUARE and inhuman in a spacesuit, Sverdlov led the way through the engineroom air lock. When Ryerson, following, stepped forth onto the ship's hull, there was a moment outside existence.

He snatched for his breath. Alien suns went streaming past his head. Otherwise he knew only blackness, touched by meaningless dull splashes. He clawed after anything real. The motion tore him loose and he went spinning outward toward the dead star. But he felt it just as a tide of nausea, his ears roared at him, the scrambled darks and gleams made a wheel with himself crucified at the hub. He was never sure if he screamed.

The lifeline jerked him to a halt. He rebounded, more slowly. Sverdlov's sardonic voice struck his earphones: "Don't be so jumpy next time, Earthling," and there was a sense of direction as the Krasnan began to reel him in.

Suddenly Ryerson made out a pattern. The circle of shadow before him was the hull. The metallic shimmers projecting from it . . . oh, yes, one of the auxiliary tank attachments. The mass-ratio needed to reach one-half c with an exhaust velocity of three-fourths c is 4.35—relativistic formulas apply rather than the simple Newtonian exponential—and this must be squared for deceleration. The *Cross* had left Sol with a tank of mercury on either side, feeding into the fuel deck.

Much later, the empty containers had been knocked down into parts of the aircraft now stowed inboard.

Ryerson pulled his mind back from the smugness of engineering data. Beyond the hull, and around it, behind him, for X billion light-years on all sides, lay the stars. The nearer ones flashed and glittered and stabbed his eyes, uncountably many. The outlines they scrawled were not those Ryerson remembered from Earth: even the recognizable constellations, like Sagittarius, were distorted, and he felt that as a somehow ghastly thing, as if it were his wife's face which had melted and run. The farther stars blent into the Milky Way, a single clotted swoop around the sky, the coldest color in all reality. And yet farther away, beyond a million light-years, you could see more suns—a few billion at a time, formed into the tiny blue-white coils of other galaxies.

Impact jarred Ryerson's feet. He stood erect, his bootsoles holding him by a weak stickiness to the plastic hull. There was just enough rotation to make the sky move slowly past his gaze. It created a dim sense of hanging head down; he thought of ghosts come back to the world like squeaking bats. His eyes sought Sverdlov's vague, armored shape. It was so solid and ugly a form that he could have wept his gratitude.

"All right," grunted the Krasnan. "Let's go."

THEY moved precariously around the curve of the ship. The long thin frame-sections lashed across their backs vibrated to their cautious footfalls. When they reached the lattice jutting from the stern, Sverdlov halted. "Show you a trick," he said. "Light doesn't diffuse in vacuum, makes it hard to see an object in the round, so—" He squeezed a small plastic bag with one gauntleted hand. His flashbeam snapped on, to glow through a fine mist in front of him. "It's a heavy organic liquid. Forms droplets which hang around for hours before dissipating. Now, what d' you think of the transceiver web?"

Ryerson stooped awkwardly, scrambled about peering for several minutes, and finally answered: "It bears out what you reported. I think all this can be repaired. But we'll have to take most of the parts inboard, perhaps melt them down—re-machine them, at least. And we'll need wholly new sections to replace what boiled away. Have we enough bar metal for that?"

"Guess so. Then what?"

"Then—" Ryerson felt sweat form beneath his armpits and break off in little globs. "You understand I am a graviticist, not a mattercasting engineer. A physicist would not be the best possible man to design a bridge; likewise, there's much I'll have to teach myself, to carry this out. But I can use the operating manual, and calculate a lot of quantities afresh, and . . . well . . . I think I could recreate a functioning web. The tuning will be strictly cut-and-try: you have to have exact resonance to get any effect at all, and the handbook assumes that such components as the distortion oscillator will have precise, standardized dimensions and crystal structure. Since they won't—we have not the facilities to control it, even if I could remember what the quantities are—well, once we've rebuilt what looks like a workable web, I'll have to try out different combinations of settings, perhaps for weeks, until . . . well, Sol or Centauri or . . . or any of the stations, even another spaceship . . . resonates—"

"Are you related to a Professor Broussard of Lomonosov Academy?" interrupted the other man.

"Why, no. What—"

"You lecture just like he used to. I am not interested in the theory and practice of mattercasting. I want to know, can we get home?"

Ryerson clenched a fist. He was glad that helmets and darkness hid their two faces. "Yes," he said. "If all goes well. And if we can find four kilos of germanium."

"What do you want that for?" Sverdlov asked.

"Do you see those thick junction points in the web? They are, uh, you might call them giant transistors. Half the lattice is gone: there, the germanium was simply whiffed away. I do know the crystallo-chemical structure involved. And we can get the other elements needed by cannibalizing, and there is an alloying unit aboard which could be adapted to manufacture the transistors themselves. But we don't have four spare kilos of germanium aboard."

Sverdlov's tone grew heavy with skepticism: "And that balloon head Maclaren means to find a planet? And mine the stuff?"

"I don't know—" Ryerson wet his lips. "I don't know what else we can do."

"But this star went supernova!"

"It was a big star. It would have had many planets. Some of the outermost ones . . . if they were large to start with . . . may have survived."

"Ha! And you'd hunt around on a lump of fused nickel-iron, without even a sun in the sky, for germanium ore?"

"We have an isotope separator. It could be adapted to . . . I haven't figured it out yet, but—For God's sake!" Ryerson found himself screaming. "What else can we do?"

"Shut up!" rapped Sverdlov. "When I want my earphones broken I'll use a hammer."

He stood in a swirl of golden fog, and the gray-rimmed black eye of the dead star marched behind him. Ryerson crouched back, hooked into the framework and waiting. At last Sverdlov said: "It's one long string of ifs. But a transistor doesn't do anything a vacuum tube can't." He barked a laugh. "And we've got all the vacuum we'll ever want. Why not design and make the equivalent electronic elements? Ought to be a lot easier than—repairing the accelerators, and scouring space for a planet."

"DESIGN them?" cried Ryerson "And test them, and redesign them, and—Do you realize that on half rations we have not quite six months' food supply?"

"I do," said Sverdlov. "I feel it in my belly right now." He muttered a few obscenities. "All right, then. I'll go along with the plan. Though if that clotbrain of a Nakamura hadn't—"

"He did the only thing possible! Did you *want* to crash us?"

"There are worse chances to take," said Sverdlov. "Now what have we got, but six months of beating our hearts out and then another month or two to die?" He made a harsh noise in the radiophone, as if wanting to spit. "I've met Sarai settlers before. They're worse than Earthlings for cowardice, and nearly as stupid."

"Now, wait—" began Ryerson. "Wait, let's not quarrel—"

"Afraid of what might happen?" jeered Sverdlov. "You don't know your friend Maclaren's dirty-fighting tricks, do you?"

The ship whirled through a darkness that grew noisy with Ryerson's uneven breathing. He raised his hands against the bulky robot shape confronting him. "Please," he stammered. "Now wait, wait, Engineer Sverdlov." Tears stung his eyes. "We're all in this together, you know."

"I wondered just when you'd be coming up with that cliché," snorted the Krasnan. "Having decided it would be oh, so amusing to tell your society friends, how you spent maybe a whole month in deep space, you got me yanked off the job I really want to do, and tossed me into a situation you'd never once stopped to think about, and wrecked us all—and now you tell me, 'We're all in this together!' " Suddenly he roared his words: "You mangy son of a muckeating cockroach, I'll get you back—not for your sake, nor for your wife's—for my own planet, d'you hear? They need me there!"

It grew very still. Ryerson felt how his heartbeat dropped down to normal, and then still further, until he could no longer hear his own pulse. His hands felt chilly and his face numb. A far and terrified part of him thought, *So this is how it feels, when the God of Hosts lays His hand upon a man,* but he stared past Sverdlov, into the relentless white blaze of the stars, and said in a flat voice:

"That will do. I've heard the story of the poor oppressed colonies before now. I think you yourself are proof that the Protectorate is better than you deserve. As for me, I never saw a milli of this supposed extortion from other planets: my father worked his way up from midshipman to captain, my brothers and I went through the Academy on merit, as citizens of the poorest and most overcrowded world in the universe. Do you imagine you know what competition is? Why, you blowhard clodhopper, you wouldn't last a week on Earth. As a matter of fact, I myself had grown tired of the struggle. If it weren't for this wretched expedition, my wife and I would have started for a new colony next week. Now you make me wonder if it's wise. Are all colonials like you—just barely brave enough to slander an old man when they're a safe hundred light-years away?"

Sverdlov did not move. The slow spin of the *Cross* brought the black star into Ryerson's view again. It seemed bigger, as the ship swooped toward periastron. He had a horrible sense of falling into it. *Thou, God, watchest me,* with the cold ashen eye of wrath. The silence was like a membrane stretched close to ripping.

Finally, very slow, the bass voice came. "Are you prepared to back up those words, Earthling?"

"Right after we finish here!" shouted Ryerson.

"Oh." A moment longer. Then: "Forget it. Maybe I did speak out of turn. I've never known an Earthman who wasn't . . . an enemy of some kind."

"Did you ever try to know them?"

"Forget it, I said. I'll get you home. I might even come around one day and say hello, on your new planet. Now let's get busy here. Our first job is to start the accelerators operating again."

The weakness which poured through David Ryerson was such that he wondered if he would have fallen under gravity. *Oh, Tamara,* he thought, *be with me now.* He remembered how they had camped on a California beach . . . had it all to themselves, no one lived in the deserts eastward . . . and the gulls had swarmed around begging bread until both of them were helpless with laughter. Now why should he suddenly remember that, out of all the times they had had?

X.

WHEN the mind gave up and the mathematics became a blur, there was work for Maclaren's hands. Sverdlov, and Ryerson under him, did the machine-tool jobs; Nakamura's small fingers showed such delicacy that he was set to drawing wire and polishing control-ring surfaces. Maclaren was left with the least skilled assignment, least urgent because he was always far ahead of the consumption of his product: melting, separating, and re-alloying the fused salvage from ion accelerators and transceiver web.

But it was tricky in null-gee. There could not be any significant spin on the ship or assembly, out on the lattice, it would have become too complicated for so small a gang of workers. Coriolis force would have created serious problems even for the inboard jobs. On the other hand, weightless melt had foul habits. Maclaren's left arm was still bandaged, the burn on his forehead still a crimson gouge.

It didn't seem to matter. When he looked in a mirror, he hardly recognized his face. There hadn't been much physical change yet, but the expression was a stranger's. And his life had narrowed to these past weeks, behind them lay only a dream. In moments when there was nothing else to do he might still play a quick chess game with Sverdlov, argue the merits of *No* versus Kabuki with Nakamura, or shock young Ryerson by a well-chosen dirty limerick. But thinking back, he saw how such times had become more and more sparse. He had quit trying to make iron rations palatable, when his turn in the galley came up; he had not sung a ballad for hundreds of the *Cross'* black-sun years. He shaved by the clock and hung onto fastidiousness of dress as pure ritual, the way Nakamura contemplated his paradoxes or Ryerson quoted his Bible or Sverdlov thumbed through his nude photographs of past mistresses. It was a way of telling yourself, *I am still alive.*

There came a moment when Maclaren asked what he was doing other than going through the motions of survival. That was a bad question.

"You see," he told his mirror twin, "it suggests a further inquiry: Why? And that's the problem we've been dodging all our mutual days."

He stowed his electric razor, adjusted his tunic, and pushed out of the tiny bathroom. The living section was deserted, as it had been most of the time. Not only were they all too busy to sit around, but it was too narrow.

Outside its wall, he moved through the comfort of his instruments. He admitted frankly that his project of learning as much as possible of the star was three-quarters selfish. It was not really very probable that exact knowledge of its atmospheric composition would be of any use to their escape. But it offered him a chance, for minutes at a time, to forget where he was. Of course, he did not admit the fact to anyone but himself. And he wondered a little what reticences the other men had.

THIS time he was not alone. Nakamura hovered at an observation port. The pilot's body was outlined with unwavering diamond stars. But as the dead sun swung by, Maclaren saw him grow tense and bring a hand toward his eyes, as if to cover them.

He drifted soundlessly behind Nakamura. "Boo," he said.

The other whirled around in air, gasping. As the thresh of arms and legs died away, Maclaren looked upon terror.

"I'm sorry!" he exclaimed. "I didn't think I'd startle you."

"I . . . it is nothing." Nakamura's brown gaze held some obscure beggary. "I should not have—It is nothing."

"Did you want anything of me?" Maclaren offered one of his last cigarettes. Nakamura accepted it blindly, without even saying thanks. *Something is very wrong with this lad,* thought Maclaren. Fear drained in through the glittering viewport. *And he's the only pilot we've got.*

"No. I had . . . I was resting a few moments. One cannot do precision work when . . . tired . . . yes-s-s." Nakamura's hunger-gaunted cheeks caved in with the violence of his sucking on the tobacco. A little crown of sweat-beads danced around his head.

"Oh, you're not bothering me." Maclaren crossed his legs and leaned back on the air. "As a matter of fact, I'm glad of your company. I need someone to talk with."

Nakamura laughed his meaningless laugh. "We should look to you for help, rather than you to us," he said. "You are the least changed of us all."

"Oh? I thought I was the most affected. Sverdlov hankers for his women and his alcohol and his politics. Ryerson wants back to his shiny new wife and his shiny new planet. You're the local rock of ages. But me—" Maclaren shrugged. "I've nothing to anchor me."

"You have grown quieter, yes." The cigarette in Nakamura's hand quivered a little, but his words came steadily now.

"I have begun to wonder about things." Maclaren scowled at the black sun. By treating it as a scientific problem, he had held at arm's length the obsession he had seen eating at Ryerson—who grew silent and large-eyed and reverted to the iron religion he had once been shaking off—and at Sverdlov, who waxed bitterly profane. So far, Maclaren had not begun thinking of the star as a half-alive malignancy. But it would be all too easy to start.

"One does, sooner or later." Nakamura's tone held no great

interest. He was still wrapped up in his private horror, and that was what Maclaren wanted to get him out of.

"But I don't wonder efficiently. I find myself going blank, when all I'm really doing is routine stuff and I could just as well be thinking at my problems."

"Thought is a technique, to be learned," said Nakamura, "just as the uses of the body—" He broke off. "I have no right to teach. I have failed my own masters."

"I'd say you were doing very well. I've envied you your faith. You have an answer."

"Zen does not offer any cut-and-dried answers to problems. In fact, it tries to avoid all theory. No human system can comprehend the infinite real universe."

"I know."

"And that is my failure," whispered Nakamura. "I look for an explanation. I do not want merely to be. No, that is not enough . . . out here, I find that I want to be justified."

Maclaren stared into the cruelty of heaven. "I'll tell you something," he said. "I'm scared spitless."

"What? But I thought—"

"Oh, I have enough flip retorts to camouflage it. But I'm as much afraid to die, I'm struggling as frantically and with as little dignity, as any trapped rat. And I'm slowly coming to see why, too. It's because I haven't got anything but my own life—my own minute meaningless life of much learning and no understanding, much doing and no accomplishing, many acquaintances and no friends—it shouldn't be worth the trouble of salvaging, should it? And yet I'm unable to see any more in the entire universe than just that: a lot of scurrying small accidents of organic chemistry, on a lot of flyspeck planets. If things made even a little sense, if I could see there was anything at all more important than this bunch of mucous membranes labeled Terangi Maclaren . . . why, then there'd be no reason to fear my own termination. The things that mattered would go on."

NAKAMURA smoked in silence for a while. Maclaren finished his own cigarette in quick nervous puffs, fought temptation, swore to himself and lit another.

"I didn't mean to turn you into a weeping post," he said. And he thought: *The hell I didn't. I fed you your psychological medicine right on schedule. Though perhaps I did make the dose larger than planned.*

"I am unworthy," said Nakamura. "But it is an honor."

He stared outward, side by side with the other man. "I try to reassure myself with the thought that there must be beings more highly developed than we," he said.

"Are you sure?" answered Maclaren, welcoming the chance to be impersonal. "We've never found any that were even comparable to us. In the brains department, at least. I'll admit the Van Mannen's abos are more beautiful, and the Old Thothians more reliable and sweet tempered."

"How much do we know of the galaxy?"

"Um-m-m . . . yes."

"I have lived in the hope of encountering a truly great race. Even if they are not like gods—they will have their own wise men. They will not look at the world just as we do. From each other, two such peoples could learn the unimaginable, just as the high epochs of Earth's history came when different peoples interflowed. Yes-s-s. But this would be so much more, because the difference is greater. Less conflict. What reason would there be for it? And more to offer, a billion years of separate experience as life forms."

"I can tell you this much," said Maclaren, "the Protectorate would not like it. Our present civilization couldn't survive such a transfusion of ideas."

"Is our civilization anything so great?" asked Nakamura with an unwonted scornfulness.

"No. I suppose not."

"We have a number of technical tricks. Doubtless we could learn more from such aliens as I am thinking of. But what we would really learn that mattered—for this era of human history lacks one—would be a philosophy."

"I thought you didn't believe in philosophies."

"I used a wrong word. I meant a *do*—a way. A way of . . . an attitude? That is what life is for, that is your 'Why'—it is not a mechanical cause-and-effect thing, it is the spirit in which we live."

Nakamura laughed again. "But hear the child correcting the master! I, who cannot even follow the known precepts of Zen, ask for help from the unknown! Were it offered me, I would doubtless crawl into the nearest worm-hole."

And suddenly the horror flared up again. He grabbed Maclaren's arm. It sent them both twisting around, so that their outraged senses of balance made the stars whirl in their skulls. Maclaren felt Nakamura's grip like ice on his bare skin.

"I am afraid!" choked the pilot. "Help me! I am afraid!"

They regained their floating positions. Nakamura let go and took a fresh cigarette with shaking fingers. The silence grew thick.

Maclaren said at last, not looking toward the Saraian: "Why not tell me the reason? It might relieve you a bit."

Nakamura drew a breath. "I have always been afraid of space," he said. "And yet called to it also. Can you understand?"

"Yes. I think I know."

"It has—" Nakamura giggled. "Unsettled me. All my life. First, as a child I was taken from my home on Earth, across space. And now, of course, I can never come back."

"I have some pull in the Citadel. A visa could be arranged."

"You are very kind. I am not sure whether it would help. Kyoto cannot be as I remember it. If it has not changed, surely I have, yes-s-s? But please let me continue. After a few years on Sarai, there was a meteor fall which killed all my family except my brother. A stone from space, do you see? We did not think of it that way, then. The monastery raised us. We got scholarships to an astronautical academy. We made a voyage together as cadets. Have you heard of the *Firdawzi* disaster?"

"No, I'm afraid not." Maclaren poured smoke from his mouth, as a veil against the cosmos.

"Capella is a GO star like Sol, but a giant. The *Firdawzi* had been long at the innermost planet of the system, a remote-controlled survey trip. The radiations caused a metal fatigue. No one suspected. On our cruise, the ship suddenly failed. The pilot barely got us into an orbit, after we had fallen a long way toward Capella. There we must wait until rescue came. Many died from the heat. My brother was one of them."

Stillness hummed.

"I see," said Maclaren at last.

"Since then I have been afraid of space. It rises into my

consciousness from time to time." Maclaren stole a glance at Nakamura. The little man was lotus-postured in midair, save that he stared at his hands and they twisted together. Wretchedness overrode his voice. "And yet I could not stop my work either. Because out in space I often seem to come closer to . . . oneness . . . that which we all seek, what you have called understanding. But here, caught in this orbit about this star, the oneness is gone and the fear has grown and grown until I am afraid I will have to scream."

"It might help," said Maclaren.

Nakamura looked up. He tried to smile. "What do you think?" he asked.

Maclaren blew a meditative cloud of smoke. Now he would have to pick his words with care—and no background or training in the giving of succor—or lose the only man who could pull this ship free. Or lose Nakamura: that aspect of it seemed, all at once, more important.

"I wonder," Maclaren murmured, "even in an absolutely free society, if any such thing could exist—I wonder if every man isn't afraid of his bride."

"What?" Nakamura's lids snapped apart in startlement.

"And needs her at the same time," said Maclaren. "I might even extend it beyond sex. Perhaps fear is a necessary part of anything that matters. Could Bach have loved his God so magnificently without being inwardly afraid of Him? I don't know."

He stubbed out his cigarette. "I suggest you meditate upon this," he said lightly. "And on the further fact, which may be a little too obvious for you to have seen, that this is not Capella."

Then he waited.

Nakamura made a gesture with his body. Only afterward, thinking about it, did Maclaren realize it was a free-fall prostration. "Thank you," he said.

"I should thank you," said Maclaren, quite honestly. "You gave me a leg up too, y' know."

Nakamura departed for the machine shop.

Maclaren hung at the viewport a while longer. The rasp of a pocket lighter brought his head around.

Chang Sverdlov entered from the living section. The cigar in his mouth was held at a somehow resentful angle.

"Well," said Maclaren. "How long were you listening?"

"Long enough," grunted the engineer.

He blew cheap, atrocious smoke until his pocked face was lost in it. "So," he asked, "aren't you going to get mad at me?"

"If it serves a purpose," said Maclaren.

"Uh!" Sverdlov fumed away for a minute longer. "Maybe I had that coming," he said.

"Quite probably. But how are the repairs progressing outside?"

"All right. Look here," Sverdlov blurted, "do me a favor, will you? If you can. Don't admit to Ryerson, or me, that you're human—that you're just as scared and confused as the rest of us. Don't admit it to Nakamura, even. You didn't, you know . . . so far . . . not really. We need a, a, a cocky dude of a born-and-bred technic—to get us through!"

He whirled back into the quarters. Maclaren heard him dive, almost fleeing, aft along the shaftway.

XI.

NAKAMURA noted in the log, which he had religiously maintained, the precise moment when the *Cross* blasted from the dead star. The others had not even tried to keep track of days. There was none out here. There was not even time, in any meaningful sense of the word—only existence, with an unreal impression of sunlight and leaves and women before existence began, like an inverted prenatal memory.

The initial minutes of blast were no more veritable. They took their posts and stared without any sense of victory at their instruments. Nakamura in the control turret, Maclaren on the observation deck feeding him data, Sverdlov and Ryerson watchful in the engine room, felt themselves merely doing another task in an infinite succession.

Sverdlov was the first who broke from his cold womb and knew himself alive. After an hour of poring over his dials and viewscreens, through eyes bulged by two gravities, he ran a hand across the bristles on his jaw. "Holy fecal matter," he whispered, "the canine-descended thing is hanging together."

And perhaps only Ryerson, who had worked outside with him for weeks of hours, could understand.

The lattice jutting from the sphere had a crude, unfinished look. And indeed little had been done toward restoring the transceiver web; time enough for that while they hunted a planet. Sverdlov had simply installed a framework to support his re-fashioned accelerator rings, antimagnetic shielding, circuits, and incidental wires, tubes, grids, capacitors, transformers . . . He had tested with a milliampere of ion current, cursed, readjusted, tested again, nodded, asked for a full amp, made obscene comments, readjusted, retested, and wondered if he could have done it without Ryerson. It was not so much that he needed the extra hands, but the boy had been impossibly patient. When Sverdlov could take no more electronic misbehavior, and went back into the ship and got a sledge and pounded at an iron bar for lack of human skulls to break, Ryerson had stayed outside trying a fresh hookup.

Once, when they were alone among galaxies, Sverdlov asked him about it. "Aren't you human, kid? Don't you ever want to throw a rheostat across the room?"

Ryerson's tone came gnatlike in his earphones, almost lost in an endless crackling of cosmic noise. "It doesn't do any good. My father taught me that much. We sailed a lot at home."

"So?"

"The sea never forgives you."

Sverdlov glanced at the other, couldn't find him in the tricky patching of highlight and blackness, and suddenly confronted Polaris. It was like being stabbed. How many men, he thought with a gasp, had followed the icy North Star to their weird?

"Of course," Ryerson admitted humbly, "it's not so easy to get along with people."

And the lattice grew. And finally it tested sound, and Sverdlov told Nakamura they could depart.

The engine which had accelerated the *Cross* to half light speed could not lift her straight away from this sun. Nor could her men have endured a couple of hundred gravities, even for a short time. She moved out at two gees, her gyros holding the blast toward the mass she was escaping, so that her elliptical orbit became a spiral. It would take hours to reach a point where the gravitational field had dropped so far that a hyperbolic path would be practicable.

Sverdlov crouched in his harness, glaring at screens and indicators. That cinder wasn't going to let them escape this easily! He had stared too long at its ashen face to imagine that.

There would be some new trick, and he would have to be ready. God, he was thirsty! The ship did have a water-regenerating unit, merely because astronautical regulations at the time she was built insisted on it. Odd, owing your life to some bureaucrat with two hundred years of dust on his own filing cabinets. But the regenerator was inadequate and hadn't been used in all that time. No need for it: waste material went into the matterbank, and was reborn as water or food or anything else, according to a signal sent from the Lunar station with every change of watch.

But there were no more signals coming to the *Cross.* Food, once eaten, was gone for good. Recycled water was little more than enough to maintain life. *Fire and thunder!* thought Sverdlov, *I can smell myself two kilometers away. I might not sell out the Fellowship for a bottle of beer, but the Protector had better not offer me a case.*

A soft *brroom-brroom-brroom* pervaded his awareness, the engine talked to itself. Too loud somehow. The instruments read O.K., but Sverdlov did not think an engine with a good destiny would make so much noise. He glanced back at the viewscreens. The black sun was scarcely visible. It couldn't be seen at all unless you knew just where to look. The haywired ugliness of the ion drive made a cage for stars. The faintest blue glow wavered down the rings. Shouldn't be, of course. Inefficiency. St. Elmo's fire danced near the after end of the assembly. "Engine room to pilot. How are we making out?"

"Satisfactory." Nakamura's voice sounded thin. It must be a strain, yes, he was doing a hundred things manually for which the ship lacked robots. But who could have anticipated—?

Sverdlov narrowed his eyes. "Take a look at the tail of this rig, Dave," he said. "The rear negatron ring. See anything?"

"Well—" The boy's eyes, dark-rimmed and bloodshot, went heavily after Sverdlov's pointing finger. "Electrostatic discharge, that blue light—"

"See anything else?" Sverdlov glanced uneasily at the megameters. He did not have a steady current going down the accelerators, it fluctuated continually by several per cent. But was the needle for the negatron side creeping ever so slowly downward?

"No. No, I can't."

"Should'a put a thermocouple in every ring. Might be a very weak deflection of ions, chewing at the end-most till all at once its focusing goes blooey and we're in trouble."

"But we tested every single—And the star's magnetic field is attenuating with every centimeter we advance."

"Vibration, my cub-shaped friend. It'd be easy to shake one of those jury-rigged magnetic coils just enough out of alignment to—*Hold it!*"

The terminal starboard coil glowed red. Blue electric fire squirted forth and ran up the lattice. The negative megameter dropped ten points and Sverdlov felt a little surge as the ship wallowed to one side from an unbalanced thrust.

"Engine room stopping blast!" he roared. His hand had already gone crashing onto the main lever.

The noise whined away to a mumble. He felt himself pitched off a cliff as high as eternity.

"What's the trouble?" barked Maclaren's voice.

Sverdlov relieved himself of a few unrepeatable remarks. "Something's gone sour out there. The last negatron accelerator began to glow and the current to drop. Didn't you feel us yaw?"

"Oh, Lord, have mercy," groaned Ryerson. He looked physically sick. "Not again."

"Ah, it needn't be so bad," said Sverdlov. "Me, I'm surprised the mucking thing held together this long. You can't do much with baling wire and spit, you know." Inwardly, he struggled with a wish to beat somebody's face.

"I presume we are in a stable orbit," said Nakamura. "But I would feel a good deal easier if the repair can be made soon. Do you want any help?"

"No. Dave and I can handle it. Stand by to give us a test blast."

Sverdlov and Ryerson got into their spacesuits. "I swear this smells fouler every day," said the Krasnan. "I didn't believe I could be such a filth generator." He slapped down his helmet and added into the radio: "So much for man the glorious star-conqueror."

"No," said Ryerson.

"What?"

"The stinks are only the body. That isn't important. What counts is the soul inside."

Sverdlov cocked his bullet head and stared at the other armored shape. "Do you actually believe that guff?"

"I'm sorry, I didn't mean to preach or—"

"Never mind. I don't feel like arguing either." Sverdlov laughed roughly. "I'll give you just one thing to mull over, though. If the body's such a valueless piece of pork, and we'll all meet each other in the sweet bye and bye, and so on, why're you busting every gut you own to get back to your wife?"

He heard an outraged breath in his earphones. For a moment he felt he had failed somehow. There was no room here for quarrels. *Ah, shaft it,* he told himself. *If an Earthling don't like to listen to a colonial, he can jing-bangle well stay out of space.*

They gathered tools and instruments in a silence that smoldered. When they left the air lock, they had the usual trouble in seeing. Then their pupils expanded and their minds switched over to the alien gestalt. A raw blaze leaped forth and struck them.

Feeling his way aft along the lattice, Sverdlov sensed his anger bleed away. The boy was right—it did no good to curse dead matter. Save your rage for those who needed it, tyrants and knaves and their sycophants. And you might even wonder—it was horrible to think—if they were worth it either. He stood with ten thousand bitter suns around him; but none was Sol or Tau Ceti. O Polaris, death's lodestar, are we as little as all that?

He reached the end of the framework, clipped his life line on, and squirted a light-diffusing fog at the ring. Not too close, he didn't want it to interfere with his ion stream, but it gave him three-dimensional illumination. He let his body float out behind while he pulled himself squinting-close to the accelerator.

"Hm-m-m, yes, it's been pitted," he said. "Naturally it would be the negatron side which went wrong. Protons do a lot less harm, striking terrene matter. Hand me that counter, will you?"

Ryerson, wordless and faceless, gave him the instrument. Sverdlov checked for radioactivity. "Not enough to matter," he decided. "We won't have to replace this ring, we stopped the process in time. By readjusting the magnetic coils we can compensate for the change in the electric focusing field caused by its gnawed-up shape. I hope."

Ryerson said nothing. *Good grief,* thought Sverdlov, *did I offend him that much?* Hitherto they had talked a little when working outside, not real conversation but a trivial remark now and then, a grunt for response . . . just enough to drown out the hissing of the stars.

"Hello, pilot. Give me a microamp. One second duration."

Sverdlov moved out of the way. Even a millionth of an ampere blast should be avoided, if it was an anti-proton current.

Electric sparks crawled like ivy over the bones of the accelerator. Sverdlov, studying the instruments he had planted along the ion path, nodded. "What's the potentiometer say, Dave?" he asked. "If it's saying anything fit to print, I mean."

"Standard," snapped Ryerson.

Maybe I should apologize, thought Sverdlov. And then, in a geyser: *Judas, no! If he's so thin-skinned as all that, he can rot before I do.*

The stars swarmed just out of reach. Sometimes changes in the eyeball made them seem to move. Like flies. A million burning flies. Sverdlov swatted, unthinkingly, and snarled to himself.

After a while it occurred to him that Ryerson's nerves must also be rubbed pretty thin. You shouldn't expect the kid to act absolutely sensibly. *I lost my own head at the very start of this affair,* thought Sverdlov. The memory thickened his temples with blood. He began unbolting the Number One magnetic coil as if it were an enemy he must destroy as savagely as possible.

"O.K., gimme another microamp one-second test."

"Try shifting Number Two a few centimeters forward," said Ryerson.

"You crazy?" snorted Sverdlov. *Yes, I suppose we're all a bit crazy by now.* "Look, if the deflected stream strikes here, you'll want to bend it down like so and—"

"Never mind." Ryerson could not be seen to move, in the bulk of his armor, but Sverdlov imagined him turning away with a contemptuous shrug. It took several minutes of tinkering for the Krasnan to realize that the Earthling had visualized the interplay of forces correctly.

He swallowed. "You were right," he emitted.

"Well, let's get it reassembled," said Ryerson coldly.

Very good, Earth snob, sir. Sverdlov attacked the coils for several more minutes. "Test blast." Not quite. Try another setting. "Test blast. Repeat." That seemed to be it. "Give me a milliamp this time . . . A full amp . . . hm-m-m." The current had flowed too short a time to heat the ring, but needles wavered wildly.

"We're still getting some deflection," said Sverdlov. "Matter of velocity distribution. A certain small percentage of the particles have abnormal velocities and—" He realized he was crouched under Ryerson's hidden eyes babbling the obvious. "I'll try sliding this one a wee bit more aside. Gimme that vernier wrench—So. One amp test blast, please."

There was no further response from the instruments. Ryerson let out a whistling sigh. "We seem to have done it," he said.

We? thought Sverdlov. *Well, you handed me a few tools!*

Aloud: "We won't know for sure till full thrust is applied."

"Of course." Ryerson spoke hesitantly. Sverdlov recognized the tone, it was trying to be warm. Ryerson was over his fit of temper.

Well, I'm not!

"There isn't anything to be done about that except to try it and see, is there?" went on the Earthling.

"And if we still get significant deflection, drag on our suits and crawl back here—maybe a dozen times? No!"

"Why, that was how we did it before."

"I'm getting awfully hungry," said Sverdlov. Suddenly it flared out of him. "I'm sick of it! I'm sick of being cooped up in my own stink, and yours, I'm sick of the same stupid faces and the same stupid remarks, yes, the same stars even! I've had enough! Get on back inside. I'll stay here and watch under acceleration. If anything goes wrong, I'll be right on the spot to fix it."

"But—"

Nakamura's voice crackled above the mutter of stars. "What are you thinking of, Engineer Sverdlov? Two gravities would pull you off the ship! And we're not maneuverable enough to rescue you."

"This life line is tested for two thousand kilos," said the Krasnan. "It's standard procedure to make direct high-acceleration checks on the blast."

"By automatic instruments."

"Which we haven't got. Do you *know* the system is fully adjusted? Are you so sure there isn't some small cumulative effect, so the thing will quit on you one day when you need it the most?"

Maclaren's tone joined in, dry and somehow remote: "This is a curious time to think about that."

"I am the engineer," said Sverdlov stiffly. "Read the ship's articles again."

"Well," said Nakamura. "Well, but—"

"It would save time," said Ryerson. "Maybe even a few days' worth of time, if the coils really are badly maladjusted."

"Thanks, Dave," said Sverdlov clumsily.

"Well," said Nakamura, "you have the authority, of course. But I ask you again—"

"All I ask of *you* is two gravities' worth of oof for a few seconds," interrupted Sverdlov. "When I'm satisfied this ring will function properly, so we won't have to be forever making stops like this, I'll come inside."

He hooked his legs about the framework and began resetting the instruments clamped onto it. "Get on back, Dave," he said.

"Why . . . I thought I would—"

"No need to."

"But there is! You can't read every dial simultaneously, and if there's work to be done you'll need help."

"I'll call you if I want you. Give me your tool belt." Sverdlov took it from reluctant hands and buckled it around himself. "There is a certain amount of hazard involved, Dave. If I should be unlucky, you're the closest approximation to an engineer the ship will have. She can't spare both of us."

"But why take any risk at all?"

"Because I'm sick of being here! Because I've got to fight back at that black coal or start howling! Now get inside!"

AS he watched the other blocky shape depart him, Sverdlov thought: *I am actually not being very rational, am I now? But who could expect it, a hundred light-years from the sun?*

As he made ready, he puzzled over what had driven him. There was the need to wrestle something tangible; and surely to balance on this skeleton of metal, under twice his normal weight, was a challenge. Beyond that, less important really, was the logic of it: the reasons he had given were sound enough as far as they went, and you could starve to death while proceeding at the pace of caution.

And below it all, he thought, was a dark wish he did not understand. Li-Tsung of Krasna would have told him to live at all costs, sacrifice all the others, to save himself for his planet and the Fellowship. But there were limits. You didn't have to accept Dave's Calvinism—though its unmerciful God seemed very near this dead star—to swallow the truth that some things were more important than survival. Than even the survival of a cause.

Maybe I'm trying to find out what those things are, he thought confusedly.

He crawled "up" till his feet were braced on a cross-member, with the terminal accelerator ring by his right ankle but the electroprober dial conveniently near his faceplate. His right hand gripped a vernier wrench, his left drew taut the life line. "Stand by for blast," he said into his radio. "Build up to two gees over a one-minute period, then hold it till I say cut."

Nothing happened for a while except the crawling of the constellations as gyros brought the ship around. Good boy, Seiichi! He'd get some escape distance out of even a test blast. "Stand by," it said in Sverdlov's earphones. And his weight came back to him, until he felt an exultant straining in the muscles of shoulder and arm and leg and belly; until his heart thudded loud enough to drown out the thin crackling talk of the stars.

The hull was above him now, a giant sphere upheld on twin derricks. Down the middle of each derrick guttered a ghostly blue light, and sparks writhed and fountained at junction points. The constellations shone chill through the electric discharge.

Inefficient, thought Sverdlov. *The result of reconstruction without adequate instruments. But it's pretty. Like festival fireworks.* He remembered a pyrotechnic display once, when he was small. His mother had taken him. They sat on a hired catamaran and watched wonder explode softly above the lake.

"Uh," grunted Sverdlov. He narrowed his eyes to peer at the detector dial. There certainly was a significant deflection yet, when whole grams of matter were being thrown out every second. It didn't heat up the ring very much, maybe not enough to notice; but negatrons plowed through terrene electron shells, into terrene nuclei, and atoms were destroyed. Presently there would be crystal deformation, fatigue, ultimate failure. He reported his findings and added with a sense of earned boasting: "I was right. This had to be done."

"I shall halt blast, then. Stand by."

Weightlessness came back. Sverdlov reached out delicately with his wrench, nipped a coil nut, and loosened the bolt. He shifted the coil itself backward. "I'll have this fixed in a minute. There! Now give me three gees for about thirty seconds, just to make sure."

"Three? Are you certain you—"

"I am. Fire!"

It came to Sverdlov that this was another way a man might serve his planet: just by being the right kind of man. Maybe a better way than planning the extinction of people who happened to live somewhere else. *Oh, come off it,* he told himself, *next thing you'll be teaching a Humane League kindergarten.*

The force on him climbed, and his muscles rejoiced in it.

At three gees there was no deflection against the ring . . . or was there? He peered closer. His right hand, weighted by the tool it still bore, slipped from the member on which it had been leaning. Sverdlov was thrown off balance. He flung both arms wide, instinctively trying not to fall. His right went between the field coils and into the negatron stream.

Fire sprouted.

Nakamura cut the drive. Sverdlov hung free, staring by starlight at his arm. The blast had sliced it across as cleanly as an industrial torch. Blood and water vapor rushed out and froze in a small cloud, pale among the nebulae.

There was no pain. Not yet. But his eardrums popped as

pressure fell. "Engine room!" he snapped. A part of him stood aside and marveled at his own mind. What a survival machine, when the need came! "Emergency! Drop total accelerator voltage to one thousand. Give me about ten amps down the tube. Quick!"

He felt no weight, such a blast didn't exert enough push on the hull to move it appreciably. He thrust his arm back into the ion stream. Pain did come now, but in his head, as the eardrums ruptured. One minute more and he would have the bends. The gas of antiprotons roared without noise around the stump of his wrist. Steel melted. Sverdlov prodded with a hacksaw gripped in his left hand, trying to seal the spacesuit arm shut.

He seemed far away from everything. Night ate at his brain. He asked himself once in wonderment: "Was I planning to do this to other men?"

When he thought the sleeve was sealed, he withdrew it. "Cut blast," he whispered. "Come and get me." His airtanks fed him oxygen, pressure climbed again inside the suit. It was good to float at the end of a life line, breathing. Until he began to strangle on his own blood. Then he gave up and accepted the gift of darkness.

XII.

NOW, about winter solstice, day was a pale glimmer, low in the south among steel-colored clouds. Tamara had been walking since the first light sneaked across the ocean, and already the sun was close to setting. She wondered if space itself could be blacker than this land. At least you saw the stars in space. On Skula you huddled indoors against the wind, and the sky was a blind whirl of snow.

A few dry flakes gusted as she came down off the moor to the beach. But they carried no warmth with them, there was not going to be a snowfall tonight. The wind streaked in from a thousand kilometers of Atlantic and icebergs. She felt the cold snap its teeth together around her; a hooded cloak was small protection. But she *would* not go back to the house. Not till day had drained from the world and it would be unsafe to remain outdoors.

She said to herself, drearily: "I would stay here even then, except it might harm the child, and the old man would come looking for me. David, help me, I don't know which would be worse!"

There was a twisted pleasure in being so honest with herself. By all the conventions, she should be thinking only of David's unborn baby, herself no more than its vessel. But it was not real to her . . . not yet . . . so far it was only sickness in the mornings and bad dreams at night. The reality was Magnus Ryerson, animallike hairiness and a hoarse grumble at her for not doing the housework his way and incomprehensible readings aloud—his island and his sea and his language lessons!

For a moment her hands clawed together. If she could so destroy Magnus Ryerson!

She fought for decorum. She was a lady. Not a technic, but still a professor's daughter; she could read and write, she had learned to dance and play the flute, pour tea and embroider a dress and converse with learned men so they were not too bored while waiting for her father . . . the arts of graciousness. Her father would call it contrasocial, to hate her husband's father. This was her family now.

But.

Her boots picked a way down the hillside, through snow and heather bushes, until she came out on a beach of stones. The sea came directly in here, smashing at heaped boulders with a violence that shivered through the ground. She saw how the combers exploded where they struck. Spindrift stung her skin. Beyond the rocks was only a gray waste of galloping white-bearded waves, and the wind keening down from the Pole. It rolled and boomed and whistled out there.

She remembered a living greenish blue of southern waters, how they murmured up to the foot of palm trees under infinitely tall skies.

She remembered David saying wryly: "My people were Northerners as far back as we can trace it—Picts, Norse, Scots, sailors and crofters on the Atlantic edge—that must be why so many of them have become spacemen in the last several generations. To get away!"

And then, touching her hair with his lips: "But I've found what all of them were really looking for."

It was hard to imagine that David's warmth and tenderness and laughter had arisen in this tomb of a country. She had always thought of the religion which so troubled him—he first came to know her through her father, professor and student had sat up many nights under Australian stars while David groped for a God not all iron and hellfire—as an alien stamp, as if the legendary Other Race Out There had once branded him. The obscurity of the sect had aided her: Christians were not uncommon even today, but she had vaguely imagined a Protestant was some kind of Moslem.

Now she saw that Skula's dwellers and Skula's God had come from Skula itself, with winter seas in their veins. David had not been struggling toward normality; he had been reshaping himself into something which—down underneath—Magnus Ryerson thought was not human. Suddenly, almost blindingly, Tamara remembered a few weeks ago, one night when the old man had set her a ballad to translate. "Our folk have sung it for many hundreds of years," he said—and how he had looked at her under his heavy brows.

He hath taken off cross and iron helm,
He hath bound his good horse to a limb,
He hath not spoken Jesu name
Since the Faerie Queen did first kiss him.

Tamara struck a fist into one palm. The wind caught her cloak and peeled it from her, so that it flapped at her shoulders like black wings. She pulled it back around her, shuddering.

The sun was a red sliver on the world's rim. Darkness would come in minutes, so thick you could freeze to death fumbling your way home. Tamara began to walk, quickly, hoping to find a decision. She had not come out today just because the house was unendurable. But her mind had been stiff, as if rusted. She still didn't know what to do.

Or rather, she thought, *I do know, but haven't saved up enough courage.*

WHEN she reached the house, the air was already so murky she could almost not make out whitewashed walls and steep snowstreaked roof. A few yellow gleams of light came through cracks in the shutters. She paused at the door. To go in —! But there was no choice. She twisted the knob and stepped through. The wind and the sea-growl came in with her.

"Close the door," said Magnus. "Close the door, you little fool."

She shut out all but a mumble and whine under the eaves, hung her cloak on a peg and faced around. Magnus Ryerson sat in his worn leather chair with a worn leather-bound book in his hands. As always, as always! How could you tell one day from the next in this den? The radiglobe was turned low, so that he was mostly shadow, with an icicle gleam of eyes and a dirty-white cataract of beard. A peat fire sputtered forlornly, trying to warm a tea kettle on the hob.

Ryerson put the book down on his lap, knocked out his archaic pipe—it had made the air foul in here—and asked roughly: "Where have you been all day, girl? I was about to go look for you. You could turn an ankle and die of exposure, alone on the ling."

"I didn't," said Tamara. She exchanged her boots for zori and moved toward the kitchen.

"Wait!" said Magnus. "Will you never learn? I want my high tea just at 1630 hours—Now. You must be more careful, lass. You're carrying the last of the Ryersons."

Tamara stopped. There was a downward slant to the ancient brick floor, she felt vaguely how her body braced itself. More nearly she felt how her chilled skin, which had begun to tingle as it warmed, grew numb again.

"Besides David," she said.

"If he is alive. Do you still believe it, after all these weeks?" Magnus began scraping out his pipe. He did not look at her.

"I don't believe he is dead," she answered.

"The Lunar crew couldn't establish grav-beam contact. Even if he is still alive, he'll die of old age before that ship reaches any star where men have an outpost. No, say rather he'll starve!"

"If he could repair whatever went wrong—"

The muffled surf drums outside rolled up to a crescendo. Magnus tightened his mouth. "That is one way to destroy yourself . . . hoping," he said. "You must accept the worst, because there is always more of the worst than the best in this universe."

She glanced at the black book he called a Bible, heavy on one of the crowded shelves. "Do your holy writings claim that?" she asked. Her voice came out as a stranger's croak.

"Aye. So does the second law of thermodynamics." Magnus knocked his pipe against the ashtray. It was an unexpectedly loud noise above the wind.

"And you . . . and you . . . won't even let me put up his picture," she whispered.

"It's in the album, with my other dead sons. I'll not have it on the wall for you to blubber at. Our part is to take what God sends us and still hold ourselves up on both feet."

"Do you know—" Tamara stared at him with a slowly rising sense of horror. "Do you know, I cannot remember just what he looked like?"

She had had some obscure hope of provoking his rage. But the shaggy-sweatered broad shoulders merely lifted, a little shrug. "Aye, that's common enough. You've the words, blond hair and blue eyes and so on, but they make not any real image. Well, you didn't know him so very long, after all."

You are telling me I am a foreigner, she thought. *An interloper who stole what didn't belong to me.*

"There's time to review a little English grammar before tea," said the old man. "You've been terrible with the irregular verbs."

He put his book on the table—she recognized the title, *Kipling's Poems,* whoever Kipling had been—and pointed at a shelf. "Fetch the text and sit down."

Something flared in the girl. She doubled her fists. "No."

"What?" The leather face turned in search of her.

"I am not going to study any more English."

"Not—" Magnus peered as if she were a specimen from another planet. "Don't you feel well?"

She bit off the words, one after another: "I have better ways to spend my time than learning a dead language."

"Dead?" cried the man. She felt his rage lift in the air between them. "The language of fifty million—"

"Fifty million ignorant provincials, on exhausted lands between bombed-out cities," she said. "You can't step outside the

British Isles or a few pockets on the North American coast and have it understood. You can't read a single modern author or scientist or . . . or anybody . . . in English—I say it's dead! A walking corpse!"

"Your own husband's language!" he bawled at her, half rising.

"Do you think he ever spoke it to anyone but you, once he'd . . . he'd escaped?" she flung back. "Did you believe . . . if David ever returns from that ship you made him go on . . . and we go to Rama—did you imagine we'd speak the language of a dying race? On a new world?"

SHE felt the tears as they whipped down her face, she gulped after breath amidst terror. The old man was so hairy, so huge. When he stood up, the single radiglobe and the wan firelight threw his shadow across her and choked a whole corner of the room with it. His head bristled against the ceiling.

"So now your husband's race is dying," he said like a gun. "Why did you marry him, if he was that effete?"

"He isn't!" she called out. The walls wobbled around her. "You are! Sitting here in your dreams of the past, when your people ruled Earth—a past we're well out of! David was going where . . . where the future is!"

"I see," Magnus Ryerson turned half away from her. He jammed both fists into his pockets, looked down at the floor and rumbled his words to someone else—not her.

"I know. You're like the others, brought up to hate the West because it was once your master. Your teacher. The white man owned this planet a few centuries ago. Our sins then will follow us for the next thousand years . . . till your people fail in their turn, and the ones you raised up take revenge for the help they got. Well, I'm not going to apologize for my ancestors. I'm proud of them. We were no more vicious than any other men, and we gave . . . even on the deathbed of our civilization, we gave you the stars."

His voice rose until it roared. "And we're not dead yet! Do you think this miserable Protectorate is a society? It isn't! It's not even a decent barbarism. It's a glorified garrison. It's one worshipping the *status quo* and afraid to look futureward. I went to space because my people once went to sea. I gave my sons to space, and you'll give yours to space, because that's where the next civilization will be! And you'll learn the history and the language of our people—your people—you'll learn what it *means* to be one of us!"

His words rang away into emptiness. For a while only the wind and a few tiny flames had voice. Down on the strand, the sea worried the island like a terrier with a rat.

Tamara said finally: "I already know what it means. It cost me David, but I know."

He faced her again, lowered his head and stared as if at an enemy.

"You murdered him," she said, not loudly. "You sent him to a dead sun to die. Because you—"

"You're overwrought," he broke in with tight-held anger. "I urged him to try just one space expedition. And this one was important. It could have meant a deal to science. He would have been proud afterward, whatever he did for a career, to say, 'I was on the *Cross.*' "

"So he should die for his pride?" she said. "It's as senseless a reason as the real one. But I'll tell you why you really made him go . . . and if you deny you forced him, I'll say you lie! You couldn't stand the idea that one child of yours had broken away—was not going to be wrenched into your image—had penetrated this obscene farce of space exploration, covering distance for its own sake, as if there were some virtue in a large number of kilometers. David was going to live as nature meant him to live, on a living soil, with untanked air to breathe and with mountains to walk on instead of a spinning coffin . . . and his children would too . . . we would have been happy! And that was what you couldn't stand to have happen!"

Magnus grinned without humor. "There's a lot of meaningless noise for a symbolics professor's daughter to make," he said. "To begin at the end, what proof have you we were meant to be happy?"

"What proof have you we were meant to jump across light-years?" she spat. "It's another way of running from yourself—no more. It's not even a practical thing. If the ships only looked for planets to colonize, I could understand. But . . . the *Cross* herself was aimed for three giants! She was diverted to a black clinker! And now David is dead . . . for what? Scientific curiosity? You're not a research scientist, neither was he, and you know it. Wealth? He wasn't being paid more than he could earn on Earth. Glory? Few enough people on Earth care about exploration; not many more on Rama; he, not at all. Adventure? You can have more adventure in an hour's walk through a forest than in a year on a spaceship. I say you murdered your son because you saw him becoming sane!"

"Now that's enough," growled Magnus. He took a step toward her. "I've heard enough out of you. In my own house. And I never did hold with this new-fangled notion of letting a woman yap—"

"Stand back!" she yelled. "I'm not *your* wife!"

He halted. The lines in his face grew suddenly blurred. He raised his artificial hand as if against a blow.

"You're my son's wife," he said, quite gently. "You're a Ryerson too . . . now."

"Not if this is what it means." She had found the resolution she sought. She went to the wall and took her cloak off its peg. "You'll lend me your aircar for a hop to Stornoway, I trust. I will send it back on auto-pilot and get transport for myself from there."

"But where are you going?" His voice was like a hurt child's.

"I don't know," she snapped. "To some place with a bearable climate. David's salary is payable to me till he's declared dead, and then there will be a pension. When I've waited long enough to be sure he won't come back, I'm going to Rama."

"But, lass . . . propriety—"

"Propriety be damned. I'd rather have David's child, alive."

She slipped her boots back on, took a flashlight from the cupboard, and went out the door. As she opened it, the wind came straight in and hit Magnus across the face.

XIII.

"In the land of Chinchanchou,
Where the winds blow tender
From a sea like purple wine
Foaming to defend her,
Lives a princess beautiful

(May the gods amend her!)
Little known for virtue, but
Of most female gender."

AS he came around the gyro housing and pulled himself forward to the observation deck, David Ryerson heard the guitar skitter through half a dozen chords and Maclaren's voice come bouncing in its wake. He sighed, pushed the lank yellow hair back out of his eyes, and braced himself.

Maclaren floated in the living section. It was almost an insult to see him somehow clean all over, in a white tunic, when each man was allowed a daily spongeful of water for such purposes. And half rations had only leaned the New Zealander down, put angles in his smooth brown countenance; he didn't have bones jutting up under a stretched skin like Ryerson, or a flushed complexion and recurring toothache like Nakamura. It wasn't fair!

"Oh, hullo, Dave." Maclaren continued tickling his strings, but quietly. "How does the web progress?"

"I'm done."

"Hm-m-m?"

"I just clinched the last bolt and spotwelded the last connection. There's not a thing left except to find that germanium, make the transistors, and adjust the units." Ryerson hooked an arm around a stanchion and drifted free, staring out of sunken eyes toward emptiness. "God help me," he murmured, "what am I going to do now?"

"Wait," said Maclaren. "We can't do much except wait." He regarded the younger man for a while. "Frankly, both Seiichi and I found excuses not to help you, did less out there than we might have, for just that reason. I've been afraid you would finish the job before we found our planet."

Ryerson started. Redness crept into his chalky face. "Why, of all the—" His anger collapsed. "I see. All right."

"These weeks since we escaped have been an unparalleled chance to practice my music," remarked Maclaren. "I've even been composing. Listen.

"In their golden-masted ships

Princes come a-wooing
Over darkling spindrift roads
Where the gales are brewing.
Lusty tales have drawn them thence,
Much to their undoing:
When they seek the lady's hand
She gives them *the—"*

"Will you stop that?" screamed Ryerson.

"As you like," said Maclaren mildly. He put the guitar back into its case. "I'd be glad to teach you," he offered.

"No."

"Care for a game of chess?"

"No."

"I wish to all the hells I'd been more of an intellectual," said Maclaren. "I never was, you know. I was a playboy, even in science. Now . . . I wish I'd brought a few hundred books with me. When I get back, I'm going to read them." His smile faded. "I think I might begin to understand them."

"When we get back?" Ryerson's thin frame doubled in midair as if for a leap. "If we get back, you mean!"

NAKAMURA entered. He had a sheaf of scribbled papers in one hand. His face was carefully blank. "I have completed the calculations on our latest data," he said.

Ryerson shuddered. "What have you found?" he cried.

"Negative."

"Lord God of Israel," groaned Ryerson. "Negative again."

"That pretty well covers this orbit, then," said Maclaren calmly. "I've got the elements of the next one computed—somewhere." He went out among the instruments.

A muscle in Ryerson's cheek began to jump of itself. He looked at Nakamura for a long time. "Isn't there anything else we can do?" he asked. "The telescopes, the—Do we just have to *sit?"*

"We are circling a dead sun," the pilot reminded him. "There is only feeble starlight to see by. A very powerful instrument might photograph a planet, but not the telescopes we have. Not at any distance greater than we could find them gravitationally. S-s-so."

"We could make a big telescope!" exclaimed Ryerson. "We have glass, and . . . and silver and—"

"I've thought of that." Maclaren's tones drifted back from the observation section. "You're welcome to amuse yourself with it, but we'd starve long before a suitable mirror could be ground with the equipment here."

"But—Maclaren, space is so big! We could hunt for a million years and never find a planet if we can't . . . can't see them!"

"We're not working quite at random." Maclaren reappeared with a punched tape. "Perhaps you've forgotten the principle on which we are searching. We position ourselves in an orbit about the star, follow it for a while, check our position repeatedly, and compute whether the path has been significantly perturbed. If it has been, that's due to a planet somewhere, and we can do a Leverrier to find that planet. If not—if we're too far away—we quarter to another arc of the same path and try again. Having exhausted a whole circumference thus, we move outward and try a bigger circle."

"Shut up!" rasped Ryerson. "I know it! I'm not a schoolboy. But we're *guessing!*"

"Not quite," said Maclaren. "You were occupied with the web when I worked out the secondary principle . . . yes, come to think of it, you never did ask me before. Let me explain. You see, by extrapolating from data on known stellar types, I know approximately what this star was like in its palmy days. From this, planetary formation theory gives me the scale of its one-time system. For instance, its planets must have been more or less in the equatorial plane; such quantities as mass, angular momentum, and magnetic field determine the Bode's Law constants; to the extent that all this is known, I can draw an orbital map.

"Well, then the star went supernova. Its closer planets were whiffed into gas. The outermost giants would have survived, though badly damaged. But the semimajor axes of their orbits were so tremendous—theoretically, planets could have formed as much as a light-year from this star—that even a small percentage of error in the data makes my result uncertain by Astronomical Units. Another factor: the explosion filled this space with gas. We're actually inside a nonluminous nebula. That would shorten the orbits of the remaining planets; in the course of millions of years they've spiraled far inward. In one way that helps us: we've an area to search which is not hopelessly huge. But on the other hand, just how long has it been since the accident? What's the density distribution of the nebula now, and what was it back then? I've taken some readings and made some estimates. All very crude, but—" Maclaren shrugged—"what else can we do? The successive orbits we have been trying are, more or less, those I have calculated for the surviving planets as of today. And, of course, intermediate radii to make sure that we will be measurably perturbed no matter where those planets actually are. It's just a matter of getting close enough to one of them."

"If our food lasts," groaned Ryerson. "And we have to eat while we finish the web, too. Don't forget that."

"We're going to have to reorganize our schedules," declared Maclaren thoughtfully. "Hitherto we've found things to keep us occupied. Now we must wait, and not go crazy waiting." He grinned. "I hereby declare the *Southern Cross* dirty limerick contest open and offer a prize of—"

"Yes," said Ryerson. "Great sport. Fun and games, with Chang Sverdlov's frozen corpse listening in!"

SILENCE clapped down. They heard the air mumble in the ventilators.

"What else can we do with our poor friend?" asked Nakamura softly. "Send him on a test rocket into the black sun? He deserved better of us. Yes-s-s? Let his own people bury him."

"Bury a copy of him!" shrieked Ryerson. "Of all the senseless—"

"Please," said Nakamura. He tried to smile. "After all . . . it is no trouble to us, and it will comfort his friends at home; maybe yes? After all, speaking in terms of atoms, we do not even wish to send ourselves back. Only copies." He laughed.

"Will you stop that giggling!"

"Please." Nakamura pushed himself away, lifting astonished hands. "Please, if I have offended you, I am so sorry."

"So sorry! So sorry! Get out of here! Get out, both of you! I've seen more of you than I can stand!"

Nakamura started to leave, still bobbing his head, smiling

and hissing in the shaftway. Maclaren launched himself between the other two. He snapped a hand onto either wrist.

"That will do!" They grew suddenly aware, it was shocking, how the eyes burned green in his dark face. His words fell like axes. "Dave, you're a baby, screaming for mother to come change you. Seiichi, you think it's enough to make polite noises at the rest of the world. If you ever want to see sunlight again, you'll both have to mend your ideas." He shook them a little. "Dave, you'll keep yourself clean. Seiichi, you'll dress for dinner and talk with us. Both of you will stop feeling sorry for yourselves and start working to survive. And the next step is to become civilized again. We haven't got the size, or the time, or the force to beat that star: nothing but manhood. Now go off and start practicing how to be men!"

They said nothing, only stared at him for a few moments and then departed in opposite directions. Maclaren found himself gazing stupidly at his guitar case. *I'd better put that away till it's requested,* he thought. *If ever. I didn't stop to think, my own habits might possibly be hard to live with.*

After a long time: *Seems I'm the captain now, in fact if not in name. But how did it happen? What have I done, what have I got?* Presently, with an inward twisting: *It must be I've less to lose. I can be more objective because I've no wife, no children, no cause, no God. It's easy for a hollow man to remain calm.*

He covered his eyes, as if to deny he floated among a million unpitying stars. But he couldn't hunch up that way for long. Someone might come back, and the captain mustn't be seen afraid.

Not afraid of death. Of life.

XIV.

SEEN from a view turret on the observation deck, the planet looked eerily like its parent star which had murdered it. Ryerson crouched in darkness, staring out to darkness. Against strewn constellations there lay a gigantic outline with wan streaks and edgings of gray. As he watched, Ryerson saw it march across the Milky Way and out of his sight. But it was the *Cross* which moved, he thought, circling her hope in fear.

I stand on Mount Nebo, he thought, *and down there is my Promised Land.*

Irrationally—but the months had made them all odd, silent introverts, Trappists because meaningful conversation was too rare and precious to spill without due heed—he reached into his breast pocket. He took forth Tamara's picture and held it close to him. Sometimes he woke up breathing the fragrance of her hair. *Have a look,* he told her. *We found it.* In a heathen adoration: *You are my luck, Tamara. You found it.*

As the black planet came back into sight, monstrously swallowing suns—it was only a thousand or so kilometers away—Ryerson turned his wife's image outward so she could see what they had gained.

"Are you there, Dave?"

Maclaren's voice came from around the cylinder of the living section. It had grown much lower in this time of search. Often you could scarcely hear Maclaren when he spoke. And the New Zealander, once in the best condition of them all, had lately gotten thinner than the other two, until his eyes stared from caves. But then, thought Ryerson, each man aboard had had to come to terms with himself, one way or another, and there had been a price. In his own case, he had paid with youth.

"Coming." Ryerson pulled himself around the deck, between the instruments. Maclaren was at his little desk, with a clipboard full of scrawled paper in one hand. Nakamura had just joined him. The Saraian had gone wholly behind a mask, more and more a polite unobtrusive robot. Ryerson wondered whether serenity now lay within the man, or the loneliest circle of hell, or both.

"I've got the data pretty well computed," said Maclaren.

Ryerson and Nakamura waited. There had been curiously little exultation when the planet finally revealed itself. *I,* thought Ryerson, *have become a plodder. Nothing is quite real out here—there is only a succession of motions, in my body and my brain—but I can celebrate no victory, because there is none, until the final and sole victory: Tamara.*

But I wonder why Terangi and Seiichi didn't cheer?

Maclaren ruffled through his papers. "It has a smaller mass and radius than Earth," he said, "but a considerably higher density suggesting it's mostly nickel-iron. No satellite, of course. And, even though the surface gravity is a bit more than Earth's, no atmosphere. Seems to be bare rock down there . . . or metal, I imagine. Solid, anyhow."

"How large was it once?" murmured Nakamura.

Maclaren shrugged. "That would be pure guesswork," he said. "I don't know which planet of the original system this is. One or two of the survivors may have crashed on the primary by now, you see. My personal guess, though, is that it was the 61 Cygni C type—more massive than Jupiter, though of less bulk because of core degeneracy. It had an extremely big orbit. Even so, the supernova boiled away all its hydrogen and probably some of the heavier elements, too. But that took time, and the planet still had this much mass left when the star decayed into a white dwarf. Of course, with the pressure of the outer layers removed, the core reverted to normal density, which must have been a pretty spectacular catastrophe in itself. Since then, the residual stellar gases have been making the planet spiral slowly inward, for hundreds of megayears. And now—"

"Now we found it," said Ryerson. "With three weeks' food supply to spare."

"And the germanium still to get," said Maclaren.

Nakamura drew a breath. His eyes went to the deck "beneath" his feet. Far aft was a storage compartment which had been left open to the bitterness of space; and a dead man, lashed to a stanchion.

"Had there been four of us," he said, "we would have consumed our supplies already and be starving. I am most humbly grateful to Engineer Sverdlov."

Maclaren's tone was dry. "He didn't die for that reason."

"No. But has he given us less merely because it was an accident?"

THEY floated a while in stillness. Then Maclaren shook himself and said: "We're wasting time. This ship was never intended to land on a planet. Since I've already informed you any world we found might very likely use vacuum for sky, and you didn't object, I assume the aircraft can make a landing."

Nakamura crossed his legs and rested impassively, hands

folded on his lap. "How familiar are you with the standard exploratory technique?" he inquired.

"Not very," confessed Maclaren. "I gather that aircraft are preferred for reasons of mass economy."

"And even more for maneuverability. A nuclear-powered vessel, using wings and turbojets, can rise high into an atmosphere, above the worst air resistance, without having to expend the reaction mass of a rocket. Likewise it can land more easily and safely in the first place. The aircraft which we carry, dismantled, are intended to leave their orbiting mother ship with a short rocket burst, slip into the atmosphere of a new planet, and descend. The return is more difficult, of course, but they get into the stratosphere before applying the non-ionic rocket drive. This in turn takes them into space proper, where their ion accelerators will work. Naturally, the cabins being sealed, any kind of atmosphere will serve them.

"Now, this is for exploration purposes. But these auxiliary craft are also capable of landing on rockets alone. When the time has come to establish a beam-relay station, some airless lifeless satellite is chosen, to avoid the necessity of quarantine. The craft shuttle back and forth, carrying the ship's dismantled transceiver. This is reassembled on the surface. Thereby the satellite's own mass becomes available to the matterbank, and any amount of material can be reconstructed according to the signals from the home station. The first things sent through are usually the parts for a much larger transceiver station, which can handle many tons of mass at a time."

"Well, good," said Maclaren. "That was more or less what I thought. Let's land and—oh, oh."

Ryerson felt a smile tugging his lips, though it was not a happy one. "You see?" he murmured.

Maclaren regarded him closely. "You don't seem too discouraged," he said. "There must be an answer."

Ryerson nodded. "I've already spoken with Seiichi about it, while you were busy determining the exact characteristics of the planet. It's not going to be fun, but—Well, let him tell you."

Maclaren said slowly: "I had hoped, it was at least possible, that any planet we found would have a surviving satellite, small enough to land the whole ship on, or lay alongside, if you want to consider it that way. It would have been the best thing for us. But I'm sure now that this lump has no companion of any kind. So we'll have to get our germanium down there."

"Which we could also have done, had we been fortunate enough to locate the planet sooner," Nakamura told him. "We can take aircraft down to the surface even now. But we would have to transship all the mining and separating equipment, establish a working space and an airdome—It is too much work for three men to do before our three weeks of supplies are eaten up, and then the actual mining would still remain."

Maclaren nodded. "I should have thought of this myself," he said. "I wonder how sane and sensible we are—how can we measure rationality, when we are all the human race we know for tens of light-years? Well. So I didn't think and you didn't talk. Nevertheless, I gather there's a way out of our dilemma."

"Yes," said the pilot. "A riskful way, but any other is certain death. We can take the ship down, and use her for our ready-made workshop and airdome."

"The *Cross*? But . . . well, of course the gravitation here is no problem to her, nor the magnetism now that the drive is shielded—but we can't make a tail landing. We'd crumple the web, and . . . hell's clanging bells, she can't land at all! She's not designed for it! Not maneuverable enough, why, it takes half an hour just to swing her clear around on gyros."

Nakamura said calmly, "I have made calculations for some time now, preparing for this eventuality. There was nothing we could do before knowing what we would actually find, but I do have some plans drawn up. We have six knocked-down auxiliary craft. Yes? It will not take long to assemble their non-ionic rocket drives, which are very simple devices, clamp these to the outside hull, and run their control systems through the ship's console. I think if we all work hard we can have it assembled, tested, and functioning in two or three days. Each pair of rockets should be so mounted as to form a couple which will rotate the ship around one of the three orthogonal space axes. No? Thus the spaceship will become most highly responsive to piloting. Furthermore, we shall cut up the aircraft hulls, as well as whatever else we may need and can spare for this purpose, such as interior fittings. From this, we shall construct a tripod enclosing and protecting the stern assembly. It will be clumsy and unbalanced, of course—but I trust my poor maneuverings can compensate for that—and it will be comparatively weak—but with the help of radar and our powerful ion-blast, the ship can be landed very gently."

"Hm-m-m." Maclaren rubbed his chin. His eyes flickered between the other two faces. "It shouldn't be hard to fix those rocket motors in place, as you say. But a tripod more than a hundred meters long, for a thing as massive as this ship—I don't know. If nothing else, how about the servos for it?"

"Please." Nakamura waved his words aside. "I realize we have not time to do this properly. My plan does not envision anything with self-adjusting legs. A simple, rigid structure must suffice. We can use the radar to select a nearly level landing place."

"All places are, down there," said Maclaren. "That iron was boiling once, and nothing has weathered it since. Of course, there are doubtless minor irregularities, which would topple us on our tripod—with a thousand tons of mass to hit the ground!"

Nakamura's eyes drooped. "It will be necessary for me to react quickly," he said. "That is the risk we take."

WHEN the ship was prepared, they met once on the observation deck, to put on their spacesuits. The hull might be cracked in landing. Maclaren and Ryerson would be down at the engine controls, Nakamura in the pilot's turret, strapped into acceleration harness with only their hands left free.

Nakamura's gaze sought Maclaren's. "We may not meet again," he said.

"Possible," said Maclaren.

The small, compact body held steady, but Nakamura's face thawed. He had suddenly, after all the time which was gone, taken on an expression; and it was gentle.

"Since this may be my last chance," he said, "I would like to thank you."

"Whatever for?"

"I am not afraid any more."

"Don't thank me," said Maclaren, embarrassed. "Something like that, a chap does for himself, y' know."

"You earned me the time for it, at least." Nakamura made a weightless bow. *"Sensei,* give me your blessing."

Maclaren said, with a degree of bewilderment: "Look here, everybody else has had more skill, contributed more, than I. I've told you a few things about the star and the planet, but you—Dave, at least—could have figured it out with slightly more difficulty. I'd never have known how to reconstruct a drive or a web, though; and I'd never be able to land this ship."

"I was not speaking of material survival," said Nakamura. A smile played over his mouth. "Still, do you remember how disorganized and noisy we were at first, and how we have grown so quiet since and work together so well? It is your doing. The highest interhuman art is to make it possible for others to use *their* arts." Then, seriously: "The next stage of achievement, though, lies within a man. You have taught me. Knowingly or not, Terangi-san, you have taught me. I would give much to be sure you will . . . have the chance . . . to teach yourself."

Ryerson appeared from the lockers. "Here they are," he said. "Tin suits all around."

Maclaren donned his armor and went aft. *I wonder how much Seiichi knows. Does he know that I've stopped making a fuss about things, that I didn't exult when we found this planet, not from stoicism but merely because I have been afraid to hope?*

I wouldn't even know what to hope for. All this struggle, just to get back to Earth and resume having fun? No, that's too grotesque.

"We should have issued the day's chow before going down," said Ryerson. "Might not be in any shape to eat it at the other end."

"Who's got an appetite under present circumstances?" said Maclaren. "So postponing dinner is one way of stretching out the rations a few more hours."

"Seventeen days' worth, now."

"We can keep going, foodless, for a while longer."

"We'll have to," said Ryerson. He wet his lips. "We won't mine our metal, and gasify it, and separate out the fractional per cent of germanium, and make those transistors, and tune the circuits, in any seventeen days."

Maclaren grimaced. "Starvation, or the canned willy we've been afflicted with. Frankly, I don't think there's much difference."

Hastily, he grinned at Ryerson, so the boy would know it for a jest. Grumbling was not allowed any more; they didn't dare. And the positive side of conversation, the dreaming aloud of "when we get home," had long since worn thin. Dinner-table conversation had been a ritual they needed for a while, but in a sense they had outgrown it. Now a man was driven into his own soul. *And that's what Seiichi meant,* thought Maclaren. *Only, I haven't found anything in myself. Or, no. I have. But I don't know what. It's too dark to see.*

He strapped himself in and began checking instruments.

"Pilot to engine room. Read off!"

"Engine room to pilot. Plus voltage clear. Minus voltage clear. Mercury flow standard—"

The ship came to life.

And she moved down. Her blast slowed her in orbit, she spiraled, a featureless planet of black steel called her to itself. The path was cautious. There must be allowance for rotation; there must not be too quick a change of velocity, lest the ponderous sphere go wobbling out of control. Again and again the auxiliary motors blasted, spinning her, guiding her. The ion-drive was not loud, but the rockets roared on the hull like hammers.

And down. And down.

Only afterward, reconstructing confused memories, did Maclaren know what had happened; and he was never altogether sure. The *Cross* backed onto an iron plain. Her tripod touched, on one foot, on two. The surface was not quite level. She began to topple. Nakamura lifted her with a skill that blended main drive and auxiliaries into one smooth surge—such skill as only an utterly relaxed man could achieve, responding to the immense shifting forces as a part thereof. He rose a few hundred meters, changed position relative to the ground, and tried again. The tripod struck on two points once more. The ship toppled again. The third leg went off a small bluff, no more than a congealed ripple in the iron. It hit ground hard enough to buckle.

Nakamura raised ship barely in time. For an instant he

poised in the sky on a single leg of flame, keeping his balance with snorts of rocket thrust. The bottom of the *Cross'* stern assembly was not many meters above ground.

Suddenly he killed the ion drive. Even as the ship fell, he spun her clear around on the rotator jets. The *Cross* struck nose first. The pilot's turret smashed, the bow caved in, automatic bulkheads slammed shut to save the air that whistled out. That was a great mass, and it struck hard. The sphere was crushed flat for meters aft of the bow. With her drive and her unharmed transceiver web aimed at the sky, the ship rested like Columbus' egg.

And the stars glittered down upon her.

Afterward Maclaren wondered: Nakamura might well have decided days beforehand that he would probably never be able to land any other way. Or he might have considered that his rations would last two men an extra week. Or perhaps, simply, he found his dark bride.

XV.

THE planet spun quickly about its axis, once in less than ten hours. There went never a day across its iron plains, but hunger and the stars counted time. There was no wind, no rain, no sea, but a man's radio hissed with the thin dry talk of the stars.

When he stood at the pit's edge and looked upward, Maclaren saw the sky sharp and black and of an absolute cold. It had a somehow three-dimensional effect; theory said all those crowding suns, blue-white or frosty gold or pale heartless red, were alike at optical infinity, but the mind sensed remoteness beyond remoteness, and whimpered. Nor was the ground underfoot a comfort, for it was almost as dark, starlit vision reached a few meters and was gulped down. A chopped-off Milky Way and a rising constellation—the one Maclaren had privately named Risus, the Sneer—told him that a horizon existed, but his animal instincts did not believe it.

He sighed, slapped a glare filter across his faceplate, and began cutting. The atomic hydrogen torch was lurid enough to look upon, but it jostled the stars out of his eyes. He cut rapidly, ten-kilo slabs which he kicked down into the pit so they wouldn't fuse tight again. The hole itself had originally been blasted, but the *Cross* didn't carry enough explosive for him to mine all his ore that way.

Ore, he reflected, was a joke. How would two men on foot prospect a sterilized world sealed into vacuum a hundred million years ago? And there would have been little point in it. This planet had boiled once, at least on the surface; and even the metallic core had been heated and churned, quite probably to melting, when crushed atoms expanded to normal dimensions. The entire globe must be nearly uniform, a one alloy lump. You took any piece, crushed it, gasified it, ionized it, put it through the electromagnetic isotope separator, and drew forth as much—or, rather, as minutely little—germanium as any other piece would have given you. From the known rate of extraction by such methods you could calculate when you would have four kilograms. The date lay weeks away.

Maclaren finished cutting, shut off his torch and hung it on its generator, and climbed into the bucket of the crane at the pit's edge. His flash-beam threw puddles of light on its walls as he was lowered. At the bottom he moved painfully about, loaded the bucket, and rode back to the surface. A small electric truck waited, he spilled the bucket into its box. And then it was to do again, and still again, until he had a full load.

Thank God and her dead designers, the *Cross* was well equipped for work on airless surfaces, she carried machines to dig and build and transport. But, of course, she had to. It was her main purpose, to establish a new transceiver station on a new moon; everything else could then come straight from the Solar System.

It had been her purpose.

It still was.

Maclaren climbed wearily onto the truck seat. He and his spacesuit had a fourth again their Earth-weight here. His headlights picked out a line of paint leading toward the ship. It had been necessary to blast the pit some distance away, for fear of what ground vibrations might do to the web or the isotope separator. But then a trail had to be blazed, for nature had given no landmarks for guide, this ground was as bare as a skull.

Existence was like lead in Maclaren's bones.

After a while he made out the *Cross,* a flattened sphere

crowned with a skeleton and the Orion nebula. It was no fun having everything upside down within her; a whole day had gone merely to reinstall the essential items. Well, Seiichi, you did what seemed best, and your broken body lies honored with Chang Sverdlov's, on the wide plains of iron.

Floodlights glared under the ship. Ryerson was just finishing the previous load, reducing stone to pebbles and thence to dust. Good timing. Maclaren halted his truck and climbed down. Ryerson turned toward him. The undiffused glow reached through his faceplate and picked a sunken, bearded face out of night, little more than nose and cheekbone and bristling jaw. In his unhuman armor, beneath that cavernous sky, he might have been a troll. *Or I might,* thought Maclaren. *Humanity is far from us. We have stopped bathing, shaving, dressing, cooking . . . pretending; we work till our brains go blank, and then work some more, and crawl up the ladder into the ship for a few hours' uneasy sleep, and are awakened by the clock, and fool our shriveled bellies with a liter of tea, and put a lump of food in our mouths and go out. For our time has grown thin.*

"Hello, Nibelung," said Ryerson.

Maclaren started. "Are you getting to be a telepath?"

"It's possible," said Ryerson. His voice had become a harsh whisper. His glance searched darkness. "Anything is possible here."

"After we put this load through," said Maclaren, evading the other thought, "we'd better move the slag out of the ship. That ninety-nine-plus per cent of material we don't use piles up fast."

Ryerson clumped heavily to the truck and began unloading. "And then out once more, cutting and loading and grinding and . . . merciful God, but I'm tired! Do you really imagine we can keep on doing heavy manual work like this, after the last food has been eaten?"

"We'll have to," said Maclaren. "And, of course, there is always—" He picked up a rock. Dizziness whirled through him. He dropped the stone and sank to his knees on the ground.

"Terangi!" Ryerson's voice seemed to come from some Delphic deep, through mists. "Terangi, what's wrong?"

"Nothing," mumbled Maclaren. He pushed at the other

man's groping arms. "Lea' me be . . . all right in a minute . . ." He relaxed against the stiffness of armor and let his weakness go through him in tides.

After a while, some strength returned. He looked up. Ryerson was just feeding the last rocks into the crusher. The machine ate them with a growl that Maclaren felt through the planet and his body. It vibrated his teeth together.

"I'm sorry, Dave," he said.

" 'S all right. You should go up and bunk for a while."

"Just a spell. Maybe we shouldn't have cut our rations as short as we have."

"You do seem to've been losing weight even faster than me," said Ryerson. "Maybe you ought to have an extra ration."

"Nah. It's metabolic inefficiency, brought on by well-spent years of wine, women, and off-key song."

Ryerson sat down beside him. "I'm a bit short of breath myself. Let's both take a break while the stuff goes through the crusher."

"Well," said Maclaren, "if your tailbone insulators can stand it, I suppose mine can."

THEY remained in silence for a while. The machine rumbled in their flesh and the stars muttered in their heads.

"How long do you think it will take to prepare the web?" asked Maclaren. "I mean, what's your latest estimate?"

"Hitherto I've underestimated the time for everything," said Ryerson. "Now, I just don't know. First we'll have to get our germanium. Then, to make the units . . . I don't know. Two weeks, three? And then, once all the circuits are functioning, they'll have to be tuned. Mostly by guesswork, since I don't really know the critical constants. That will take x time, depending on how lucky we are."

"We'll open the last can of food soon," said Maclaren. In itself it was a totally useless reminder, but it was leading up to something they had both avoided.

Ryerson continued to squirm: "They say tobacco helps kill appetite."

"It does," said Maclaren, "but I smoked the last butts months ago. Now I've even lost the addiction. Though of course I'll happily rebuild same the moment we strike Earth."

"When we come home—" Ryerson's voice drifted off like a murmur in sleep. "We haven't talked about our plans for a long time."

"It got to be too predictable, what every man would say."

"Yes. But is it now? I mean, do you still want to take that sailboat cruise around Earth, with . . . er . . . a female crew and a cargo of champagne?"

"I don't know," said Maclaren, faintly surprised to realize it. "I hadn't thought—Do you remember once in space, we talked about our respective sailing experiences, and you told me the sea is the most inhuman thing on our planet?"

"Hm-m-m—yes. Of course, my sea was the North Atlantic. You might have had different impressions."

"I did. Still, Dave, it has stuck in my mind, and I see now you are right. Any ocean is, is too—big, old, blind for us—too beautiful." He sought the million suns of the Milky Way. "Even this black ocean we're wrecked in."

"That's odd," said Ryerson. "I thought it was your influence making me think more and more of the sea as a . . . not a friend, I suppose. But hope and life and, oh, I don't know. I only know, I'd like to take that cruise with you."

"By all means," said Maclaren. "I didn't mean I'd become afraid of the water, just that I've looked a little deeper into it. Maybe into everything. Hard to tell, but I've had a feeling now and then, out here, of what Seiichi used to call insight."

"One does learn something in space," agreed Ryerson. "I began to, myself, once I'd decided that God hadn't cast me out here and God wasn't going to bring me back, it wasn't His part —Oh, about that cruise. I'd want to take my wife, but she'd understand about your, uh, companions."

"Surely," said Maclaren. "I'd expect that. You've told me so much about her, I feel like a family friend."

I feel as if I loved her.

"Come around and be avuncular when we've settled—Damn, I forgot the quarantine. Well, come see our home on Rama in thirty years!"

No, no, I am being foolish. The sky has crushed me back toward child. Because she has gallant eyes and hair like a dark flower, it does not mean she is the one possible woman to fulfill that need I have tried for most of my life to drown out. It is only that she is the first woman since my mother's death whom I realize is a human being.

And for that, Tamara, I have been slipping three-fourths of my ration back into the common share, so your man may innocently take half of that for his. It is little enough I can do, to repay what you who I never saw gave to me.

"Terangi! You are all right, aren't you?"

"Oh. Oh, yes, of course." Maclaren blinked at the other armored shape, shadowy beside him. "Sorry, old chap. My mind wandered off on some or other daisy-plucking expedition."

"IT'S an odd thing," said Ryerson. "I find myself thinking more and more frivolously. As this cruise of yours, for instance. I really mean to join you, if you're still willing, and we'll take that champagne along and stop at every sunny island and loaf about and have a hell of a good time. I wouldn't have expected this . . . what has happened . . . to change me in that direction. Would you?"

"Why, no," said Maclaren. "Uh, I thought actually you—"

"I know. Because God seemed to be scourging me, I believed the whole creation must lie under His wrath. And yet, well, I have been on the other side of Doomsday. Here, in nightmare land. And somehow, oh, I don't know, but the same God who kindled that nova saw equally fit to . . . to make wine for the wedding at Cana."

Maclaren wondered if the boy would regret so much self-revelation later. Perhaps not if it had been mutual. So he answered with care, "Oddly enough, or maybe not so oddly, my thinking has drifted in the other direction. I could never see any real reason to stay alive, except that it was more fun than being dead. Now I couldn't begin to list all the reasons. To raise kids into the world, and learn something about the universe, and not compromise with someone's version of justice, and—I'm afraid I'm not a convert or anything. I still see the same blind cosmos governed by the same blind laws. But suddenly it matters. It matters terribly, and means something. What, I haven't figured out yet. I probably never will. But I have a reason for living, or for dying if need be. Maybe that's the whole purpose of life: purpose itself. I can't say. But I expect to enjoy the world a lot more."

Ryerson said in a thoughtful tone: "I believe we've learned to take life seriously. Both of us."

The grinder chuted its last dust into the receptacle. The gasifier was inboard; and the cold, not far from absolute zero, was penetrating the suit insulators. Ryerson got up. Shadows lapped his feet. "Of course," he said, his voice suddenly cracked, "that doesn't help us a great deal if we starve to death out here."

Maclaren rose with him. The floodlamps ridged both their faces against the huge hollow dark. Maclaren caught Ryerson's eyes with his own. For a moment they struggled, not moving under the constellations, but sweat sprang out upon Ryerson's forehead.

"You realize," said Maclaren, "that we actually can eat for quite a while longer. I'd say, at a guess, two more months."

"No," whispered Ryerson. "No, I won't."

"You will," Maclaren told him.

He stood there another minute, to make certain of his victory, which he meant as a gift to Tamara. Then he turned on his heel and walked over to the machine. "Come on," he said, "let's get to work."

XVI.

MACLAREN woke up of himself. For a moment he did not remember where he was. He had been in some place of trees, where water flashed bright beneath a hill. Someone had been with him, but her name and face would not come back. There was a lingering warmth on his lips.

He blinked at the table fastened to the ceiling. He was lying on a mattress—

Yes. The *Southern Cross,* a chilly knowledge. But why had he wakened early? Sleep was the last hiding place left to him and Dave. They stood watch and watch at the web controls, and came back to their upside-down bunkroom and ate sleep. Life had shrunken to that.

Maclaren yawned and rolled over. The alarm clock caught his eye. Had the stupid thing stopped? He looked at the second hand for a while, decided that it was indeed moving. But then he had slept for holy shark-toothed sea gods, for thirteen hours!

He sat up with a gasp. Bloodlessness went through his head. He clung to his blankets and waited for strength to come back. How long a time had it been, while his tissues consumed themselves for lack of all other nourishment? He had stopped counting hours. But the ribs and joints stuck out on him so he sometimes listened for a rattle when he walked. Had it been a month? At least it was a time spent inboard, with little physical exertion; that fact alone kept him alive.

Slowly, like a sick creature, he climbed to his feet. If Dave hadn't called him, Dave might have passed out, or died, or proven to have been only a starving man's whim. *With a host of furious fancies*—Maclaren shambled across to the shaftway. The transceiver rooms were aft of the gyros, they had been meant to be "down" with respect to the observation deck whenever there was acceleration and now they were up above. Fortunately, the ship had been designed in the knowledge she would be in free fall most of her life. Maclaren gripped a rung with both hands. *I could use a little free fall right now,* he reflected through the dizziness. He put one foot on the next rung, used that leg and both hands to pull the next foot up beside it; now, repeat; once more; one for Father and one for Mother and one for Nurse and one for the cat and so it goes until here we are, shaking with exhaustion.

Ryerson sat at the control panel outside the receiving and transmitting chambers. It had been necessary to spotweld a chair, with attached ladder, to the wall and, of course, learn how to operate an upside-down control panel. The face that turned toward Maclaren was bleached and hairy and caved-in; but the voice seemed almost cheerful. "So you're awake."

"The alarm didn't call me," said Maclaren. He panted for air. "Why didn't you come rouse me?"

"Because I turned off the alarm in the first place."

"What?" Maclaren sat down on what had been the ceiling and stared upward.

"You'll fall apart if you don't get more rest," said Ryerson. "You've been in worse shape than me for weeks, even before the . . . the food gave out. I can sit here and twiddle knobs without having to break off every eight hours."

"Well, maybe." Maclaren felt too tired to argue.

"Any luck?" he asked after a while.

"Not yet. I'm trying a new sequence now. Don't worry, we're bound to hit resonance soon."

MACLAREN considered the problem for a while. Lately his mind seemed to have lost as much ability to hold things as his fingers. Painfully, he reconstructed the theory and practice of gravitic mattercasting. Everything followed with simple logic from the fact that it was possible at all.

The signals necessarily used a pulse code, with amplitude and duration as the variables; there were tricky ways to include a little more information through the number of pulses per millisecond, if you set an upper limit to the duration of each. It all took place so rapidly that engineers could speak in wave terms without too gross an approximation. Each transceiver identified itself by a "carrier" pattern, of which the actual mattercasting signal was a modulation. The process only took place if contact had been established, that is, if the transmitter was emitting the carrier pattern of a functioning receiver: the "resonance" or "awareness" effect which beat the inverse-square law, a development of Einstein's great truth that the entire cosmos is shaped by what momentarily happens to each of its material parts.

The 'caster itself, by the very act of scanning, generated the signals which recreated the object transmitted. But first the 'caster must be tuned in on the desired receiving station. The manual aboard ship gave the call pattern of every established transceiver: but, naturally, gave it in terms of the standardized and tested web originally built into the ship. Thus, to reach Sol, the book said, blend its pattern with that of Rashid's Star, the initial relay station in this particular case. Your signal will be automatically bucked on, through several worlds, till it reaches Earth's Moon. Here are the respective voltages, oscillator frequencies, et cetera, involved; add them up and use the resultant.

Ryerson's handmade web was not standardized. He could put a known pattern into it, electronically, but the gravitics would emit an unknown one, the call signal of a station not to be built for the next thousand years. He lacked instruments to measure the relationship, so he could not recalculate the appropriate settings. It was cut and try, with a literal infinity of choices and only a few jackleg estimates to rule out some of the possibilities.

Maclaren sighed. A long time had passed while he sat thinking. Or so his watch claimed. He hadn't noticed it go by, himself.

"You know something, Dave?" he said.

"Hm-m-m?" Ryerson turned a knob, slid a vernier one notch, and punched along a row of buttons.

"We are out on the far edge of no place. I forgot how far to the nearest station, but a devil of a long ways. This haywire rig of ours may not have the power to reach it."

"I knew that all the time," said Ryerson. He slapped the main switch. Needles wavered on dials, oscilloscope tracings glowed elfhill green, it whined in the air. "I think our apparatus is husky enough, though. Remember, this ship has left Sol farther behind than any other ever did. They knew she would —a straight-line course would just naturally outrun the three-dimensional expansion of our territory—so they built the transceiver with capacity to spare. Even in its present battered state, it might reach Sol directly, if conditions were just right."

"Think we will? That would be fun."

Ryerson shrugged. "I doubt it, frankly. Just on a statistical basis. There are so many other stations by now—*Hey!*"

Maclaren found himself on his feet, shaking. "What is it?" he got out. "What is it? For the love of heaven, Dave, what is it?"

Ryerson's mouth opened and closed, but no sounds emerged. He pointed with one bony arm. It shook.

Below him—it was meant to be above, like a star—a light glowed red.

"Contact," said Maclaren.

The word echoed through his skull as if spoken by a creator, across a universe still black and empty.

Ryerson began to weep, silently, his lips working. "Tamara," he said. "Tamara, I'm coming home."

Maclaren thought: *If Chang and Seiichi had been by me now, what a high and proud moment.*

"Go on, Terangi," chattered Ryerson. His hands shook so he could not touch the controls. "Go on through."

Maclaren did not really understand it. Not yet. It was too

swift a breaking. But the wariness of a race which had evolved among snakes and war spoke for him:

"Wait, Dave. Wait a minute. Just to be certain. Put a signal through. A teletype, I mean; we've no voice microphone, have we? You can do it right at that keyboard."

"What for?" screamed Ryerson. "What for? If you won't go through, I will!"

"Just wait, is all." Suddenly Maclaren was begging. All the craziness of months between stars that burned his eyes woke up; he felt in a dim way that man must live under conditions and walk in awe, but this is one of the prides in being a man. He raised powerless hands and cried—it was not much above a whisper—"There could be some distortion, you know. Accidents do happen, once in a great while, and this web was made by hand, half of it from memory—Send a message. Ask for a test transmission back to us. It won't take long and—My God, Dave, what kind of thing could you send home to Tamara if the signal was wrong?"

RYERSON'S chin quivered in its beard, but he punched the typer keys with hard angry strokes. Maclaren sat back down, breathing quickly and shallowly. So it was to become real after all. So he would again walk beneath the tall summer clouds of Earth.

No, he thought. *I never will. Terangi Maclaren died in an orbit around the black sun, and on the steel planet where it is always winter. The I that am may go home, but never the I that was.*

Ryerson bent over so he could look into the screen which gave him an image of the receiving chamber.

Maclaren waited. A long while passed.

"Nothing," said Ryerson. "They haven't sent a thing."

Maclaren could still not talk.

"A colonial station, of course," said Ryerson. "Probably one of the outpost jobs with two men for a staff . . . or, another spaceship. Yes, that's likeliest, we're in touch with an interstellar. Only one man on watch and—"

"And there should be a bell to call him, shouldn't there?" asked Maclaren, very slowly.

"You know how they get on the long haul," said Ryerson. He

smote his chair arm with a fist that was all knobs. "The man is sleeping too hard to hear a thing. Or—"

"Wait," said Maclaren. "We've waited long enough. We can afford a few more minutes, to make certain."

Ryerson blazed at him, as if he were an enemy. "Wait? Wait, by jumping hell! No!"

He set the control timer for transmission in five minutes and crept from his seat and down the ladder. Under the soiled tunic, he seemed all spidery arms and legs, and one yellow shock of hair.

Maclaren stood up again and stumbled toward him. "No," he croaked. "Listen, I realize how you feel, but I realize it's space lunacy too, and I forbid you, I forbid—"

Ryerson smiled. "How do you propose to stop me?" he asked.

"I . . . but can't you wait, wait and see and—"

"Look here," said Ryerson, "let's assume there is a freak in the signal. A test transmission comes through. At best, the standard object is merely distorted . . . at worse, it won't be recreated at all, and we'll get an explosion. The second case will destroy us. In the first case, we haven't time to do much more work. I doubt if I could climb around on the web outside any more. I know you could not, my friend! We've no choice but to go through. Now!"

"If it's a ship at the other end, and you cause an explosion," whispered Maclaren, "you've murdered one more man."

Drearily, and as if from far away, he recognized the hardness which congealed the other face. Hope had made David Ryerson young again. "It won't blow up," said the boy, and was wholly unable to imagine such a happening.

"Well . . . probably not . . . but there's still the chance of molecular distortion or—" Maclaren sighed. Almost experimentally, he pushed at Ryerson's chest. Nothing happened; he was so much more starved that he could not move the lank body before him.

"All right," said Maclaren. "You win. I'll go through."

Ryerson shook his head. "No, you don't," he answered. "I changed my mind." With a lilt of laughter: "I stand behind my own work, Terangi!"

"No, wait! Let me . . . I mean . . . think of your wife, at least . . . please—"

"I'll see you there," cried Ryerson. The blue glance which he threw over his shoulder was warm. He opened the transmitter room door, went through, it clashed shut upon him. Maclaren wrestled weakly with the knob. No use, it had an automatic lock.

Which of us is the fool? I will never be certain, whatever may come of this. The chances are all for him, of course . . . in human terms, reckoned from what we know . . . but could he not learn with me how big this universe is, and how full of darkness?

MACLAREN stumbled back toward the ladder to the chair. He would gain wrath, but a few more minutes, by climbing up and turning off the controls. And in those minutes, the strangely terrifying negligent operator at the other end might read the teletype message and send a test object. And then Ryerson would know. Both of them would know. Maclaren put his feet on the rungs. He had only two meters to climb. But his hands would not lift him. His legs began to shake. He was halfway to the panel when its main switch clicked down and the transmitting engine skirled.

He crept on up. *Now I know what it means to be old,* he thought.

His heart fluttered feebly and wildly as he got into the chair. For a while he could not see the vision screens, through the night that spumed in his head. Then his universe steadied a little. The transmitter room was quite empty. The red light still showed contact. So at least there had been no destruction wrought in the receiving place. Except maybe on Dave; it didn't take much molecular warping to kill a man. *But I am being timid in my weakness. I should not be afraid to die. Least of all to die. So let me also go on through and be done.*

He reached for the timer. His watch caught his eye. Half an hour since Dave left? Already? Had it taken half an hour for him to creep this far and think a few sentences? But surely Dave would have roused even the sleepiest operator. They should have sent a teletype to the *Cross:* "Come on, Terangi. Come on home with me." What was wrong?

Maclaren stared at the blank walls enclosing him. Here he could not see the stars, but he knew how they crowded the outside sky, and he had begun to understand, really understand what an illusion that was and how hideously lonely each of those suns dwelt.

One thing more I have learned, in this last moment, he thought. *I know what it is to need mercy.*

Decision came. He set the timer for ten minutes—his progress to the transmitter room would be very slow—and started down the ladder.

A bell buzzed.

His heart sprang. He crawled back, feeling dimly that there were tears on his own face now, and stared into the screen.

A being stood in the receiving chamber. It wore some kind of armor, so he could not make out the shape very well, but though it stood on two legs the shape was not a man's. Through a transparent bubble of a helmet, where the air within bore a yellowish tinge, Maclaren saw its face. Not fish, nor frog, nor mammal, it was so other a face that his mind would not wholly register it. Afterward he recalled only blurred features, there were tendrils and great red eyes.

Strangely, beyond reason, even in that first look he read compassion on the face.

The creature bore David Ryerson's body in its arms.

XVII.

WHERE Sundra Straits lay beneath rain—but sunlight came through to walk upon the water—the land fell steep. It was altogether green, in a million subtle hues, jungle and plantation and rice paddy, it burned with green leaves. White mists wreathed the peak of a volcano, and was it thunder across wind or did the mountain talk in sleep?

Terangi Maclaren set his aircar down on brown-and-silver water and taxied toward the Sumatra shore. Each day he regained flesh and strength, but the effort of dodging praus and pontoon houses and submarines still tired him. When his guide pointed: "There, tuan," he cut the engines and glided in with a sigh.

"Are you certain?" he asked, for there were many such huts of thatch and salvaged plastic along this coast. It was a wet world here, crowding brown folk who spent half their cheerful existences in the water, divers, deckhands, contracting their labor to the sea ranches but always returning home, poverty, illiteracy, and somehow more life and hope than the Citadel bore.

"Yes, tuan. Everyone knows of her. She is not like the rest, and she holds herself apart. It marks her out."

Maclaren decided the Malay was probably right. Tamara Suwito Ryerson could not have vanished completely into the anonymous proletariat of Earth. If she still planned to emigrate, she must at least have a mailing address with the Authority. Maclaren had come to Indonesia quickly enough, but there his search widened, for a hundred people used the same P.O. in New Djakarta and their homes lay outside the cosmos of house numbers and phone directories. He had needed time and money to find this dwelling.

He drove up onto the shore. "Stay here," he ordered his guide, and stepped out. The quick tropic rain poured over his tunic and his skin. It was the first rain he had felt since . . . how long? . . . it tasted of morning.

She came to the door and waited for him. He would have known her from the pictures, but not the grace with which she carried herself. She wore a plain sarong and blouse. The rain filled her crow's-wing hair with small drops and the light struck them and shattered.

"You are Technic Maclaren," she said. He could scarcely hear her voice, so low did it fall, but her eyes were steady on his. "Welcome."

"You have seen me on some newscast?" he inquired, banally, for lack of anything else.

"No. I have only heard. Old Prabang down in the village has a nonvisual set. But who else could you be? Please come in, sir."

Only later did he realize how she broke propriety. But then, she had declared herself free of Protectorate ways months ago. He found that out when he first tried to contact her at her father-in-law's. The hut, within, was clean, austerely furnished, but a vase of early mutation-roses stood by David's picture.

Maclaren went over to the cradle and looked down at the sleeping infant. "A son, isn't it?" he asked.

"Yes. He has his father's name."

Maclaren brushed the baby's cheek. He had never felt anything so soft. "Hello, Dave," he said.

Tamara squatted at a tiny brazier and blew up its glow. Maclaren sat down on the floor.

"I would have come sooner," he said, "but there was so much else, and they kept me in the hospital—"

"I understand. You are very kind."

"I . . . have his effects . . . just a few things. And I will arrange the funeral in any way you desire and—" His voice trailed off. The rain laughed on the thatch.

She dipped water from a jar into a tea kettle. "I gather, then," she said, "there was no letter that he wrote?"

"No. Somehow . . . I don't know. For some reason none of us wrote any such thing. Either we would all perish out there, and no one else would come for fifty or a hundred years, or we would get back. We never thought it might be like this, a single man." Maclaren sighed. "It's no use trying to foresee the future. It's too big."

She didn't answer him with her voice.

"But almost the last thing Dave said," he finished awkwardly, "was your name. He went in there thinking he would soon be home with you." Maclaren stared down at his knees. "He must have . . . have died quickly. Very quickly."

"I have not really understood what happened," she said, kneeling in the graceful Australian style to set out cups. Her tone was flattened by the effort of self-control. "I mean, the 'cast reports are always so superficial and confused, and the printed journals so technical. There isn't any middle ground any more. That was one reason we were going to leave Earth, you know. Why I still am going to, when our baby has grown just a little bit."

"I know how you feel," said Maclaren. "I feel that way myself."

She glanced up with a startled flirt of her head that was beautiful to see. "But you are a technic!" she exclaimed.

"I'm a human being too, my lady. But go on, ask me your question, whatever you were leading up to. I've a favor of my own to ask, but you first."

"No, what do you want? Please."

"Nothing very important. I've no claim on you, except the

fact that your husband was my friend. I'm thinking of what you might do for his sake. But it will wait. What did you wonder about?"

"Oh. Yes. I know you tuned in the aliens' transceiver and didn't realize it. But—" Her fists clenched together. She stared through the open door, into the rain and the light, and cried forth: "It was such a tiny chance! Such a meaningless accident that killed him!"

Maclaren paused until he had all his words chosen. Then he said, as gently as might be:

"IT wasn't so wildly improbable. All this time we've known that we couldn't be the only race reaching for the stars. It was absurd to think so; that would have been the senseless unlikelihood. Well, the *Cross* was farther out than men had ever gone before, and the alien spaceship was near the aliens' own limit of expansion. It was also bound for Alpha Crucis. Odd what a sense of kinship that gives me, my brother mariner, with chlorine in his lungs and silicon in his bones, steering by the same lodestar. Contact was certain eventually, as they and we came into range of each other's signals. Your David was the man who first closed the ring. We were trying call patterns we could not measure, running through combinations of variables. Statistically, we were as likely to strike one of their patterns as one of ours."

The water began to boil. She busied herself with the kettle. The long tresses falling past her face hid whether she was crying or not. Maclaren added for her, "Do you know, my lady, I think we must have called hundreds of other space-traveling races. We were out of their range, of course, but I'm sure we called them."

Her voice was muffled: "What did the aliens think of it?"

"I don't know. In ten years we may begin to talk to them. In a hundred years, perhaps we will understand them. And they us, I hope. Of course, the moment David . . . appeared . . . they realized what had happened. One of them came through to me. Can you imagine what courage that must have taken? How fine a people your man has given us to know? There was little they could do for me, except test the *Cross'* web and rule out all the call patterns which they use. I kept on trying, after that. In a week I finally raised a human. I went through to his receiver and that's all. Our technicians are now building a new relay station on the black star planet. But they'll leave the *Cross* as she is, and David Ryerson's name will be on her."

"I thought," she whispered, still hiding her face, "that you . . . I mean, that quarantine rules—"

"Oh, yes, the Protectorate tried to invoke them. Anything to delay what is going to happen. But it was useless. Nothing from the aliens' planet could possibly feed on Terrestrial life. That's been established already, by the joint scientific commission; we may not be able to get the idea behind each other's languages yet, but we can measure the same realities! And of course, the aliens know about us. Man just can't hide from the universe. So I was released." Maclaren accepted the cup she offered him and added wryly: "To be sure, I'm not exactly welcome at the Citadel any more."

She raised large eyes to him. He saw how they glimmered. "Why not?" she asked. "You must be a hero to—"

"To spacemen, scientists, some colonials, and a few Earthmen glad of an end to stagnation. Not that I deserve their gratitude. There are three dead men who really did all this. But at any rate, my lady, you can foresee what an upheaval is coming. We are suddenly confronted with—Well, see here, the aliens must be spread through at least as large a volume of space as man. And the two races don't use the same kind of planets. By pooling transceiver networks, we've doubled both our territories! No government can impose its will on as many worlds as that.

"But more. There are sciences, technologies, philosophies, religions, arts, insights they have which we never imagined. It cannot be otherwise. And we can offer them ours, of course. How long do you think this narrow little Protectorate and its narrow little minds can survive such an explosion of new thought?" Maclaren leaned forward. He felt it as an upsurge in himself. "My lady, if you want to live on a frontier world, and give your child a place where it's hard and dangerous and challenging—and everything will be possible for him, if he's big enough—stay on Earth. The next civilization will begin here on Earth herself."

Tamara set down her cup. She bent her face into her hands

and he saw, helpless, how she wept. "It may be," she said to him, "it may be, I don't know. But why did it have to be David who bought us free? Why did it have to be him? He didn't mean to. He wouldn't have, if he'd known. I'm not a sentimental fool, Maclaren-san, I know he only wanted to come back here. And he died! There's no meaning in it!"

XVIII.

THE North Atlantic rolled in from the west, gray and green and full of thunder. A wind blew white manes up on the waves. Low to the south gleamed the last autumnal daylight, and clouds massed iron-colored in the north, brewing sleet.

"There," pointed Tamara. "That is the place."

Maclaren slanted his aircar earthward. The sky whistled around him. So Dave had come from here. The island was a grim enough rock, harshly ridged. But Dave had spoken of gorse in summer and heather in fall and lichen of many hues.

The girl caught Maclaren's arm. "I'm afraid, Terangi," she whispered. "I wish you hadn't made me come."

"It's all we can do for David," he told her. "The last thing we'll ever be able to do for him."

"No." In the twilight, he saw how her head lifted. "There's never an end. Not really. His child and mine, waiting, and—At least *we* can put a little sense into life."

"I don't know whether we do or whether we find what was always there," he replied. "Nor do I care greatly. To me, the important thing is that the purpose—order, beauty, spirit, whatever you want to call it—does exist."

"Here on Earth, yes," she sighed. "A flower or a baby. But then three men die beyond the sun, and it so happens the race benefits a little from it, but I keep thinking about all those people who simply die out there. Or come back blind, crippled, broken like dry sticks, with no living soul the better for it. Why? I've asked it and asked it, and there isn't ever an answer, and finally I think that's because there isn't any why to it in the first place."

Maclaren set the car down on the beach. He was still on the same search, along a different road. He had not come here simply to offer David's father whatever he could: reconciliation, at least, and a chance to see David's child now and then in the years left him. Maclaren had some obscure feeling that an enlightenment might be found on Skula.

Truly enough, he thought, men went to space, as they had gone to sea, and space destroyed them, and still their sons came back. The lure of gain was only a partial answer; spacemen didn't get any richer than sailors had. Love of adventure . . . well, in part, in some men, and yet by and large the conquerors of distance had never been romantics, they were workaday folk who lived and died among sober realities. When you asked a man what took him out to the black star, he would say he had gone under orders, or that he was getting paid, or that he was curious about it, or any of a hundred reasons. Which might all be true. And yet was any of them the truth?

And why, Maclaren wondered, did man, the race, spend youth and blood and treasure and all high hopes upon the sea and the stars? Was it only the outcome of meaningless forces—economics, social pressure, maladjustment, myth, whatever you labeled it—a set of chance-created vectors with the sardonic resultant that man broke himself trying to satisfy needs which could have been more easily and sanely filled at home?

If I could get a better answer than that, thought Maclaren, *I could give it to Tamara. And to myself. And then we could bury our dead.*

He helped her out of the car and they walked up a path toward an ancient-looking cottage. Light spilled from its windows into a dusk heavy with surf. But they had not quite reached it when the door opened and a man's big form was outlined.

"Is that you, Technic Maclaren?" he called.

"Yes. Captain Magnus Ryerson?" Maclaren stepped ahead of Tamara and bowed. "I took the liberty, sir, of bringing a guest with me whom I did not mention when I called."

"I can guess," said the tall man. "It's all right, lass. Come in and welcome."

As she passed over the uneven floor to a chair, Tamara brushed Maclaren and took the opportunity to whisper: "How old he's grown, all at once!"

Magnus Ryerson shut the door again. His hands, ropy with veins, shook a little. He leaned heavily on a cane as he crossed the room and poked up the fire. "Be seated," he said to Maclaren. "When I knew you were coming, I ordered some whiskey from the mainland. I hope it's a good make. I drink not, you see, but be free to do so yourself."

Maclaren looked at the bottle. He didn't recognize the brand. "Thank you," he said, "that's a special favorite of mine."

"You've eaten?" asked the old man anxiously.

"Yes, thank you, sir." Maclaren accepted a glass. Ryerson limped over the floor to give Tamara one.

"Can you stay the night? I've some extra beds in the garret, from when the fisher lads would come by. They come no more, there's no reason for it now, but I've kept the beds."

Maclaren traded a look with Tamara. "We would be honored," he said.

Magnus Ryerson shuffled to the hob, took the tea kettle, poured himself a cup and raised it. "Your health." He sat down in a worn chair by the fire. His hands touched a leather-bound book lying on its arm.

THERE was silence for a while, except that they could all hear the waves boom down on the strand.

Maclaren said finally: "I . . . we, I mean . . . we came to —offer our sympathy. And if there was anything I could tell you . . . I was there, you know."

"Aye. You're kind." Ryerson groped after a pipe. "It is my understanding he conducted himself well."

"Yes. Of course he did."

"Then that's what matters. I'll think of a few questions later, if you give me time. But that was the only important one."

Maclaren looked around the room. Through its shadows he saw pilot's manuals on the shelves, stones and skins and gods brought from beyond the sky; he saw the Sirian binary like twin hells upon darkness, but they were very beautiful. He offered: "Your son was in your own tradition."

"Better, I hope," said the old man. "There would be little sense to existence, did boys have no chance to be more than their fathers."

Tamara stood up. "But that's what there isn't!" she cried all at once. "There's no sense! There's just dying and dying and dying. What for? So that we can walk on another planet, learn another fact? What have we gained? What have we really done? And why? What did we do that your god sends our men out there now?"

She clamped her hands together. They heard how the breath rasped in her. She said at last, "I'm sorry," and sat back down.

Magnus Ryerson looked up. And his eyes were not old. He let the surf snarl on the rocks of his home for a while. And then he answered her: "*'For that is our doom and our pride.'*"

"What?" She started. "Oh. In English. Terangi, he means—" She said it in Interhuman.

Maclaren sat quite still.

Ryerson opened his book. "They have forgotten Kipling now," he said. "One day they will remember. For no people live long, who offer their young men naught but fatness and security. Tamara, lass, let your son hear this one day. It is his song too, he is human."

The words were unknown to Maclaren, but he listened and thought he understood.

"We have fed our sea for a thousand years
And she calls us, still unfed,
Though there's never a wave of all her waves
But marks our English dead:
We have strawed our best to the weed's unrest,
To the shark and the sheering gull,
If blood be the price of admiralty,
Lord God, we ha' paid it in full!—"

When Ryerson had finished, Maclaren stood up, folded his hands and bowed. "*Sensei,*" he said, "give me your blessing."

"What?" The other man leaned back into shadows, and now he was again entirely old. You could scarcely hear him under the waves outside. "You've naught to thank me for, lad."

"No, you gave me much," said Maclaren. "You have told me why men go, and it isn't for nothing. It is because they are men."